Crawling Through Thorns

Crawling Through Thorns is the story of half a lifetime: an account of events that happened as a life unfolded. None of the characters that emerge through these pages are intended to be representative of those that inhabited the historical reality of my life, with the exception of world-renowned theologians who were my teachers in Berkeley.

This is a work of fiction – but a true story, nevertheless.

To list all of the people who helped me whilst writing *Crawling Through Thorns* would be impractical. Each person has been thanked personally, but I want to acknowledge two men; Roger Williams and Jupp Korsten. Without Roger's patience, under-standing and wisdom this novel would have been excessively long and, at times, incoherent. Diolch Roger. And Jupp, my first reader... and so much more. Danke, lieber Schatz.

John Sam Jones
Yr Hen Farcdy, Talsarnau
Spring 2008

Crawling Through Thorns

John Sam Jones

PARTHIAN

Parthian
The Old Surgery
Napier Street
Cardigan
SA43 1ED

www.parthianbooks.co.uk

First published in 2008
© John Sam Jones 2008
All Rights Reserved

ISBN 978-1-905762-36-1

Editor: Roger Williams

Cover design by Marc Jennings
Cover photo © Getty Images
Typeset by Lucy Llewellyn
Printed and bound by Dinefwr Press, Llandybïe, Wales

Published with the financial support of the Welsh
Books Council.

British Library Cataloguing in Publication Data

A cataloguing record for this book is available from
the British Library

Beth yw credu? Gwarchod tref
Nes dyfod derbyn.
Beth yw maddau? Cael ffordd trwy'r drain
At ochr hen elyn.

What is believing? Holding out
Until relief comes.
And forgiving? Crawling through thorns
To the side of an old foe.

Pa Beth yw Dyn? by Waldo Williams
Translated by Emyr Hymphreys

John Sam Jones has worked in education and public health for more than twenty years and is currently employed as the Schools Adviser for Personal and Social Education in Denbighshire. He lives with his civil partner in a farmhouse in the Rhinog Mountains. His books include *Fishboys of Vernazza*, *With Angels and Furies* and *Welsh Boys Too*, which was an Honour Book winner in the North American Library Association Stonewall Book Awards.

July

From: 'John Sam Jones' <johnsamjones@quickmail.com>
To: 'Everyone'
Subject: Don't go breaking my heart
Date: 16:44:23 Wednesday 16 July

On Monday I watched my heart on a screen... twice... in two different hospitals. It's a humbling experience. I was fully conscious both times; I'd chosen not to be sedated because I wanted to watch the show.

Suspected indigestion can turn out to be something far more sinister. For three weeks I swallowed the Rennies and drank bicarbonate of soda – and even thumped my chest, just below and to the right of my left nipple, thinking I might release the trapped wind. When I finally saw my GP, he listened to my tale with an expression suggesting disbelief – especially the bit about the eight-hour hike the previous Sunday up

i

Carnedd Llewellyn. The almost constant discomfort of indigestion had sullied my enjoyment of the gorgeous views across Eryri. Very calmly, he gave me a large dose of aspirin and sent me to hospital in an ambulance.

The heart has two arteries supplying it – the left and the right coronary arteries. Lying on my back in the X-ray lab at the hospital, I watched on the screens as the physician coaxed the catheter from its entry point in my femoral artery (in the groin – not much dignity there after the nurse had sloshed the whole area with bright red antiseptic!) up into the cardiac cataract. The frequent infusions of dye through the catheter showed up the entire arterial system of my heart – first the right, and all its branches, and then the left. And there was the blockage, as clear as day even to my untrained eye: the main branch of the left artery, the one that feeds the left ventricle; clogged-up to the extent that the dye went from pencil thickness to a hair's breadth. No wonder I was having lower chest pain... of a type no amount of bicarb was going to budge!

Then the setting shifted and I lived out a scene from a hospital soap. The physician explained that he only did cardiac catheterisation as a diagnostic procedure and announced that the blockage he'd seen on the screen was suitable for 'stenting', but I'd have to be transferred immediately to the Cardio-Thoracic Unit at Broadgreen Hospital, where they'd have the surgical back up to do a by-pass if anything went wrong. With flashing lights, whining sirens and a capped tube in my groin holding the artery open, I was transported through the tunnel to Liverpool.

Another 'cath-lab' (interesting that they're not called operating theatres), another physician, more red anti-septic sloshed about, and six huge screens less than a metre away from me to watch events unfold.

It took the doctor just fifteen minutes to inflate a little balloon at the blocked site and then insert a titanium stent to keep the affected branch open. I was so taken up by what I could see on the screens that I was almost able to forget that a team of theatre staff were on hand to perform a by-pass should the balloon cause a burst.

For 24 hours after being un-blocked and stented I was wired up to machines that measure just about everything that can be measured, and at hourly inter-vals a nurse would come and inspect the hole in my groin. All the readings from this array of machines must have pleased the vigilant carers; I was discharged after an hour-long counselling session, the gist of which was to keep taking the pills (six different drugs) and try to get back to normal as soon as possible.

I'm a late-forties non-smoker. I'm at the top end of my weight range, and have never been overweight. My cholesterol level is 4.3 (some dispute as to whether being under 5 or 6 is okay, but 4.3 is pretty good). I drink alcohol only moderately, and whilst I'm not athletic (I don't jog, play squash, swim lengths), I can hike 25 miles on a Saturday with relative ease. 'Five-a-day' has been a mantra in our home for years and I drink more than 2 litres of water a day.

But there's a strong family history of heart disease – and I guess I just got the bad genes!

I may never have another episode like this one... I may have one within months. What's pretty obvious is that I'm very lucky... both heart specialists I spoke with suggested that had I been overweight or a smoker, the nature of my blocked artery – in the branch that carries oxygen to the left ventricle – would almost certainly have caused a serious heart attack – or worse.

It's been an interesting few days... the awe I feel having witnessed this technology – watching my heart beating and seeing the obstruction released – will take some time to find its context in my life. I think it will take much longer to get my head around the everyday implications of having a heart condition.
John Sam

I pressed 'send' and within an hour there were a dozen responses. Over the next few days my in-box was clogged. Despite the drug-induced dislocation, I went slowly through the messages of encouragement. Richard from Parthian – who'd published my short stories, and must have recalled some of the conversations we'd had over cups of coffee – suggested that in the weeks of convalescence I could start work on a memoir. I thought he might be humouring me.

August
Bank Holiday Friday

From the castle he looked out across the town's rooftops to the hollow where the abandoned Victorian asylum looked both ominous and forlorn. In the few weeks since his heart had faltered he'd gathered memories around him that seemed to offer comfort against the distress that now pervaded his days. The detour to Denbigh was part of this harvesting. The madhouse leaked its stories through the lead-stripped roof. Even these bleak remembrances of drugs, locked wards and electric shocks were a consolation.

He sipped the Vermentino that Russell had chosen for them to drink with the grilled tuna steaks. The dry, spicy crispness tingled on his tongue and he was grateful for such a simple pleasure. In the polished mahogany tabletop he saw his own reflection; the hair was greyer now and the face more drawn. The dying summer sun's last rays glinted on the wide blade of the fish knife and he allowed the dancing light to distract him. He tried to ignore the Lloyd-Webber show song that Elaine Paige was crooning from the top-of-the-range Bang & Olufsen. It wasn't his idea of music to dine by. Fingering the ornately moulded handle of the serving fork he thought it might be heavy enough to be silver. He couldn't see a hallmark, but it probably was silver; everything about Russell's home screamed 'wealthy' and not just the sheer size of the house and its location on a bluff above Barmouth Bay. It had been called Awel-y-Môr when John was a boy, but that was too much of a mouthful for Russell, who called it The Laurels. There were Persian carpets on the restored parquetry and the walls were hung with John Elwyn, Claudia Williams and Kyffin. The soft furnishings were satin, velvet and silk, and in the guest bedroom's en-suite the sunken bath had gold taps, and the heated blue floor-tiles warmed cold toes. Russell had finally come into his mother's old money and spent it lavishly. The house was filled with beautiful things and John particularly coveted the B&O hi-fi and a couple of the Kyffins, but Russell lacked the *joie de vivre* to pull it all together and make it a home.

Russell wheeled their food through from the kitchen on a gold handled trolley with a squeaky wheel. 'So when did you stop calling yourself Siôn Idris and become plain John Jones?' he quizzed, with barely a trace of the Canadian accent John had found so appealing all those years ago.

'After I left Aberystwyth, I suppose.' He hunched his shoulders as if he needed to protect himself from some of the memories. 'I went to Aber straight from Barmouth and somehow… I don't know; it was as if both places had kept me… small and closed-in.'

'You were willing enough to push the boundaries when I knew you,' Russell cut in with a hint of accusation. He wiggled his little finger: 'And you were never small!'

'And you're still a bit one-tracked,' John fired back, thinking that Russ hadn't matured much, and wondering if he'd been too eager to accept his invitation.

'You know what they say about a dirty mind, John,' he quipped, laughing his throaty smoker's chortle. 'It's a pleasure for ever.'

John watched the sun through the open French window as it dropped behind the Lleyn peninsula. Elaine, duetting with Barbara Dickson, sang about some man they thought they knew so well. Embarrassed by his host, John wondered if he'd stay for the whole of the bank holiday weekend.

Russell Talbert set the platter of grilled tuna, the bowl of mixed salad and the basket of herb and onion bread on the table. He sensed John's discomfort and wondered if it was a symptom of his recent illness. 'You and Klaus have had a rough couple of months then,' he ventured, holding up the bottle of Stone Pine 2001 in an offertory gesture.

'That's a bit of an understatement,' John said, holding out his glass. 'When you're forty-seven you don't expect to get clogged arteries, especially when you're as fit as I am... well, as fit as I thought I was, I mean.'

'But they didn't have to —' Russell ran a finger down his chest to suggest a surgeon's incision.

'No. Angioplasty with stenting; maybe you've seen it on television? They inflate a balloon inside the blocked bit of artery and then keep it open with a little titanium tube.'

'So you're fine now?' he asked uncertainly.

'As long as I keep taking the tablets,' John said with a hint of irony. 'I'm knackered a lot of the time because of the beta-blockers. That's why I didn't want to go to Germany with

Klaus. And I'm still going to the cardiac rehab clinic, and they don't like you to miss any of the sessions.'

'My invitation was opportune then,' he said, his smile warmly generous.

You're so full of contradictions, John thought as he acknowledged the timeliness of it all. 'It was strange to bump into you at Theatr Clwyd like that,' he said.

'Meeting you and Klaus made my evening. You're so lucky; he's a lovely man. How long have you been together?'

'I think it's eighteen years, come December.'

'God, you should be proud of yourselves. The most I ever managed was about five.' Russell's slate-blue eyes seemed to dull from the effort all of the men in his life had cost him. Elaine was being Evita on the balcony of the Casa Rosada. There was an uneasy silence as they helped themselves. Russell didn't like silences. 'So, you're not back at work then?'

'No. Maybe a couple of days a week after the rehab programme finishes, but I can't see me going back full time until after Christmas. And maybe, even then —' John's thoughts drifted momentarily.

'Something this serious makes you start to re-evaluate —' Russell tapped his chest, but he broke off when he saw the anxious, lost look in John's eyes. 'Is the tuna alright?' he asked after a few seconds.

'Hmm? The tuna? Yes, it's very good.'

And in John's smile, Russell saw the boy he'd fallen for all those years ago.

Russell had just finished saying how much he liked living in Barmouth.

'I'm sure it's different if you come to live here from away,'

4

John said, before scooping up the last spoonful of summer pudding from the cut crystal dessert bowl. He'd passed up on the whipped cream and was feeling a bit smug that he'd resisted. 'I hated living here.'

'Did you ever tell me that you'd grown up here?' Russell asked. 'When you mentioned it on the phone the other day it came as quite a surprise.'

'As I remember it, Russell, we didn't spend that much time talking during those few weeks together in Aberystwyth, it was just one long lusty tumble.' And after a moment's reflection, John was laughing. 'You were called Russ back then and you had a curly perm!'

Russell shook his balding head, trying to obliterate the memory. 'My God, what were we like? A curly perm?'

'And those twenty-four inch bell-bottoms and cheesecloth tie and dyes,' John teased, liking the Armani silk shirt his host was wearing.

'But we were *together* for more than just a few weeks,' Russell said, looking serious. 'Weren't we?'

'No. Six weeks, two months at most,' John asserted. 'I think I was fitted in between Simon Whatney and that Douggie-what's-his-name who sang with the Elizabethan Madrigals.'

'Simon Whatney,' Russell said with a singsong in his voice and a breaking smile. 'I wonder what became of him?'

'Probably best not to go there; drag up too many ghosts and you're sure to have sleepless nights.'

Russell sniggered, and after a momentary pause he changed direction. 'Have you still got family here?'

'Nope. We buried my mother about four years ago and my dad went a couple of years before her.'

Russell's quiet smile conveyed condolence. 'And you didn't

5

want to keep the house for holidays or for renting out?'

'We thought about it. My brother's been doing a bit of family tree research and on my dad's side we've lived either in Barmouth itself, or along the Mawddach between here and Dolgellau, for about 250 years. That's how we both carry Idris as a second name.'

Russell looked puzzled, as though he'd missed a connection.

'Cader Idris,' John said. 'Don't tell me you've lived in Barmouth for three years and haven't climbed Cader yet?'

Russell grinned sheepishly and shook his head. 'Can you see me in climbing boots?'

'Well, I don't think we can do it this time around,' John said, stroking his chest as if it were the back of a cat. 'But you can see, can't you, that we're a family that's lived in the shadow of the "giant's seat" in more ways than one. Dad carried the name, and his dad was just plain Idris Jones.'

'God, that's just amazing for someone from migrant stock like me. Don't you and your brother feel like you've broken something important?'

John shrugged and shook his head. 'Keeping the place to rent to tourists seemed like more hassle than it was worth and neither of us wanted to come back here to live. Bill's a surgeon in Liverpool and his kids are Scousers through and through. And for me, Barmouth was... well, let's just say that when I was young it choked the life out of me.'

After clearing the things from the table and filling the dishwasher, Russell suggested a walk along the prom. John declined. The fatigue from the beta-blockers had already kicked in and he was fighting off the attacks of exhaustion. Russell said he'd go on his own, just for half an hour to walk off his

6

dinner. John watched him descend the path that cut through the gorse bushes to a small oak wood where he'd often played as a child. When he disappeared beneath the oak leaf canopy, John turned from the French window.

Flicking through the CDs on the rack next to the player – Bassey, Garland, Midler, Minnelli, Streisand and film music – he yearned to hear some Wagner on the Bang & Olufsen. With no neighbours to worry about he could turn it right up. He sank into the leather sofa with a long sigh. In the still, pink dusk he watched the stars emerge over Barmouth Bay. The whisperings of the reawakened asylum memories began to murmur. Earlier, driving across Wales, when those distant voices had unnerved him, Sibelius' second symphony had calmed the turbulence. Now, when he needed 'Wotan's Farewell' or the 'Song to the Evening Star', all he had were the torch songs of Russell's gay icons.

Barmouth
Through the 60s and 70s

Annie Jones washed up in the evenings during the holiday season at a guesthouse on the promenade. Bobby-Nansi, the man who owned Wavecrest – a tall, blue granite Victorian with sandstone bay windows to three floors – was a particular man, his net curtains always whiter than the others in the terrace. He was one of only a few hoteliers that did an evening meal, but he was expensive. That summer he charged twenty-four-and-six per head, all-in, when others in the row were charging twenty-two shillings.

Before Annie Jones married, everyone called her Annie-Singer. The old treadle machine was still in the hall under the stairs and some of the old women still brought her their sewing. Soon after marrying Idris Jones in 1926 she became Annie-Idris-Bloc, because her husband, a carpenter, was known as Idris-Bloc. Little John Idris called her Nana because she was the grandmother that didn't speak Welsh. She did a bit of bed and breakfast herself, just the one room to pay the rates, but she couldn't be bothered with offering an evening meal, unless it was for the two girls who came from Manchester during the last week of July and the first week of August every year, and even then Annie could still get to Bobby-Nansi's by seven. Bobby-Nansi always called her Mrs Jones because she was a good few years older than him, and in return she called him Mr Pugh because he was employing her.

On a Saturday morning in the season, between nine and ten, Annie would call into Wavecrest to collect her wages from Mr Pugh. He was good like that; she never had to ask for her pay, it was always ready for her in an envelope. Then she'd sit at a corner table in the Mona Café with a milky coffee and decide how much she could afford to put into her Post Office book. Sometimes, because he liked the Mona's iced buns, John Idris went with her. It was on such a morning that he asked his nana why everyone called Mr Pugh Bobby-Nansi.

'It's like Griff-the-bread,' she said. 'He's really Mr Griffith. And there's Glyn-y-glo, but he's Mr Williams in the coal yard.'

'So why isn't Mr Pugh called Bobby-bed-and-breakfast?' John asked, with sticky icing around his mouth.

'Well, it's —' Annie couldn't tell the child it was because Mr Pugh was so lady-like. 'It's because he looked after his mam when she was old and her name was Nansi. But you boys must never call him that,' she continued, pointing with a gnarled finger. 'His name is Mr Pugh and he's a very kind man.'

*   *   *

One Saturday at the end of that holiday season, when Wavecrest had closed its doors on the last of the visitors, Bobby

Pugh went on a bender. When the *Cors y Gedol* Hotel closed its public bar at half past two, Bobby was invited through to the residents' lounge. He had another few gins, but when he got too loud he was turned out. In the cool autumn air he was suddenly very drunk and he almost knocked John Idris off the pavement outside the tobacconist's shop on Beach Road. John Idris remembered how Nana had said that Mr Pugh was a very kind man, so when he fell against the lamppost, John shot into Ozzie's sweet shop to tell 'Mr Ozzie' that Mr Pugh had fallen over. When they both came out onto the pavement, one of the Jenkins boys, the biggest thug of them all, was kicking Mr Pugh and calling him nancy-boy. Mr Ozzie got the fright of his life when Jenkins grabbed him by the lapels of his jacket and shouted at him to mind his own business.

*   *   *

On the Sunday afternoons of their childhood, John Idris and his brother William Idris were packed off to Sunday school at Calfaria, their shoes polished, their Sunday best neatly ironed, brushed off, and smelling faintly of naphtha. Hardly anyone in the council houses had a car so everyone took the bus or walked, but there were no buses on a Sunday. They'd call out their goodbyes to Dad, who always went to the bath while Mam was getting them ready. After Mam had warned them perhaps three or four times not to talk to strangers or loiter on the way, they'd set off on a walk that took them thirty or forty minutes, depending on their route and whether they stopped to play; scuffing their shoes kicking an old tin around – or just exploring.

They'd walk along the cinder lane that edged the football pitch and then pass through the dingy alley behind the old slaughterhouse. That brought them to the allotments where Jack-Haleliwia grew runner beans. Sometimes he'd give some to their mam, wrapped in yellowing pages of *The Cambrian News*. They'd have them for tea with lots of pepper and a knob of Stork margarine, and rashers of bacon, crisp and a bit salty; they were the best runner beans the boys had ever tasted. Sometimes Jack-Haleliwia exposed himself to the boys and he'd give them sweets to keep his secret; usually Everton mints in twisted paper wrappers or fruit gums from a box battered by weeks in his jacket pocket. From the allotments they'd hike on up the hill to the war memorial. In front of the pink marble obelisk, Billy, because he was older, would toss the thruppenny-bit Mam had given him for the *casgliad* plate and they'd let chance take them on the bottom road towards the gas works or up the 100 steps.

John counted those steps every Sunday that the thruppence landed on 'heads' and there were never more than eighty-six, but then, Barmouth was like that in those days, lots of things weren't quite as they seemed. Mr Baker was their butcher and one of the bread shops was called Lamb's. Mr Mathias Williams, who was the Sunday school superintendent and worked in the council offices collecting the rents, was called Matty-the-milk by everyone, and Mrs Harp played the organ in the Catholic church. Then there was Miss Morris, who taught the infants; she lived in a flat at number three Gibraltar View, but the only view over their back wall was the tannery yard.

At the top of the eighty-six steps you could look out over the rooftops to the Memorial Park and the bowling green. If you stood on the wall at the top of the steps you could see the sea, and sometimes you'd catch a glimpse of Dolly-Dieppe through the back bedroom window of Park House, wrestling naked with her French husband... but they didn't wrestle as well as Billy-Two-Rivers on the television.

John Idris always crossed his fingers that the thruppenny-bit wouldn't land on 'tails'. The two rust streaked gasometers rose and fell like a metal giant's belly after a roast lamb dinner and a large helping of gooseberry tart with rice pudding. Their shifting bulk frightened him and made him feel very small. On a Sunday afternoon the road past the gas works was always strewn with chip papers from the night before, and lumpy puddles of sick. Every now and then they'd count the seagulls that feasted on the leftovers but this game usually left him with a bellyache. Only when they'd passed the back bar of the Royal Hotel, and the greasy chippy in the Arches, did the road become less foul. Once in a while the boys managed to creep past the chemical factory gates without disturbing the guard dogs, but usually they jumped up at the high wire fence, yowling and snarling. Their heightened aggravation had nothing to do with the fact that Billy threw stones at them.

Calfaria stood in solid, Victorian redbrick pride between Gaynor Morgan's Ladies' Wear and the Gwalia Café, set back off the street behind wrought iron railings and two well-clipped yew trees that served as a backdrop to many a wedding party. The perms-and-pearls brigade gathered in the bay window of the Gwalia on Saturday mornings to drink frothy coffee and eat Lamb's cream-horns and Welsh cakes. On Sundays, these same ladies would parade their lavish hats from Gaynor's, and between the rude oak benches, cushioned on ruby velvet worn smooth with the years, they'd preen their feathers and fox tails as Enoch Lloyd got into a *hwyl* in the pulpit over hell's fire and damnation.

John Idris was in Miss Gruffudd's Sunday school class. From October to April, Miss Gruffudd wore a fur coat that she didn't take off during the lesson. She had a wrinkled face that she tried to smooth out with too much powder puff and she moved her false teeth around her mouth when she wasn't speaking, and sometimes when she was. She and her coat smelled of lavender, unless she sat too close to the three bar electric fire; then Miss Gruffudd's fur would start to pong, a mixture of scorched toast and the tannery yard. When she noticed the unpleasant whiff she'd '*twt-twt*' and, muttering about the faulty wiring, she'd turn off the fire. Then the children would button up their coats as the damp coldness penetrated the arc in which they sat.

Miss Gruffudd's mission was to ensure that her class – her *plant bach* she called them – knew their Bible stories. John Idris had liked the story of the ten plagues that were sent to afflict the Egyptians because Pharaoh's heart was hardened. He wasn't sure what a hardened heart was, but those Egyptians were naughty not to let the Hebrews go. The plague of frogs was funny, but the boils weren't so nice, and all those babies dying was very frightening. John decided that he'd better not let his heart get hard, or be a naughty boy.

Miss Gruffudd taught her class the *Rhodd Mam*, the children's catechism of the Calvinistic Methodists, as well as, if not better than, they could recite their times tables after one term with Mr Roberts in Standard One. But there was always a lot of giggling amongst her *plant bach*. Welsh has got some difficult sounds for people with loose false teeth.

'*Anrhydedda dy dad a'th fam*,' she said, introducing the fifth commandment one gloomy Sunday afternoon.

Pronouncing the letter *rh* in the second syllable of *anrhydedda*, which means to honour, isn't easy at the best of times and the trill of her tongue displaced her top set. All the children burst into fits of laughter.

13

'You'll all be punished if you carry on being so naughty,' she shouted over the sniggering. 'Remember those plagues!'

* * *

During the Easter holidays a new climbing frame was erected on the primary school yard. It became the focus of play throughout that summer term. Sometimes it was a wild-west fort, from which they'd fight off Cochise and his Apache raiders, or Dr Who's Tardis, that took them to the strange worlds of the Zarbi, the Rills, and to where the Daleks threatened to 'exterminate them' in their nasally electronic voices.

It was Dewi Hughes that John first noticed scrambling up one of the vertical bars in a funny sort of way. Five feet off the ground, Dewi was clinging to the pole, his legs pushing up as if he was climbing, though he just hung there with a grin on his face. When John laughed at him and mocked his climbing style, Dewi slid down and ran off to scorch ladybirds with his pocket magnifying glass. Over the next couple of weeks he saw Dewi clinging to the pole more than once and wondered whether he was a bit simple, beaming that stupid smirk.

Then it happened to John. His pinkle, rubbing against the pole, got hard, and a tingly, whooshing feeling took his breath away. Because he didn't have words to describe what had happened, and because Mam and Dad had warned him and Billy many a time not to touch their pinkles when they got hard, he wondered if it was something bad, and kept it secret. Then he thought about Miss Gruffudd's descriptions of the boils, the locusts and the dead babies, and for more than a week at playtime he joined in the games of football and rounders, avoiding the climbing frame – just in case. But there

14

were no signs of any plagues. From the football field, John saw that Dewi Hughes clung to the pole most days, and there was no great catastrophe. After half term, John asked Dewi if he had the same tingly whoosh and their common experience became a bond that made them best friends.

In the first days of the summer holidays, when they weren't playing on the beach or swimming by the deckchair stand where 'uncle' Kelly Roberts, the deckchair-man, watched out for them, they built a den up in the old quarry. There they smoked Cadets from the cigarette machine by the station and looked at the *Playboy* magazines Dewi had found behind the workbench in his father's workshop. With no pole to cling to, they discovered that touching themselves could bring on the tingly whoosh. John was a bit envious because Dewi already had a few curly hairs; Dewi was jealous because John's was bigger. After the first few times they started to play with one another and John liked that more than playing with himself.

Then, one Friday morning towards the end of July, the *Prince of Wales* hit the wooden piles of the toll bridge at Penmaenpool. The pleasure boat from Barmouth sank and lives were lost. The headline in the *Liverpool Daily Post* the following morning read 'Five-shillings-a-head holiday cruise ends in disaster as boat capsizes in Welsh estuary – Eleven drown'. John Idris sat in his dad's lap and they read the report together; four of the eleven were children – a boy and three girls. His dad gave him a long cuddle, kissing his head through his salt-and-sun-bleached hair, but John could only think about all of the dead babies from the Bible story in Miss Gruffudd's Sunday school class and knew that his heart must be hardening because of the games he and Dewi played. He didn't play with Dewi again. He tried not to touch his pinkle when it got hard, which seemed to happen a lot.

In the park next to the allotments there was a high slide. At the top of the steps was a small, enclosed platform from which the slide itself sloped steeply to the ground some fifteen feet below. With room for three or four children, the platform often served as a den, its wooden slats heavily carved with love-hearts and initials, its floor strewn with cigarette butts. It was here that John met Gregory Goodwin one afternoon late in the summer.

Gregory was older by a few years, but still not old enough, or bold enough, to smoke in public, so he'd sit in the den and roll his own with papers and tobacco that he'd stolen from his granddad's 'baccy drawer'. Sometimes, when he could see from his vantage point high above the park that there was no one around, he'd play with himself.

'Bet you I can shoot my spunk through that gap,' Greg said to John after they'd smoked a ciggy, pointing with the fingers of his left hand at the space above a kicked-in, splintered slat. His right hand was moving, deep in his pocket.

John Idris knew, from the dirty drawings he'd seen on the back of the cubicle doors in the public toilets on the quayside, that something was supposed to shoot out, but his own testicles had yet to receive their hormonal messengers. 'Bet you can't,' he said, considering the gap and wanting to see it happen so that he'd know what to expect.

After that first time, because Greg had curly ginger hair and freckles, John called him Carrot. They met at the top of the slide a few more times, and when the weather turned colder and wetter, they crawled through a loose panel of corrugated iron into the old barn behind the spectator's stand next to the football pitch to shelter.

He was with Carrot in the dusty gloom of the barn when he shot for the first time. Well, it was more of a dribble really, and because it was unexpected it spattered onto Carrot's school blazer. Carrot swore and tried to rub it off with a snotty handkerchief but only succeeded in rubbing it into the navy-blue woollen felt fabric.

'I'll tell my mam that one of the Jenkins boys gobbed on me,' Gregory said, eyeing the stain as he pushed his way out of the barn.

*　　*　　*

Friday 21 October 1966, Mr Davies wrote on the blackboard in English to denote the beginning of an English lesson after the mid-morning playtime. John Idris liked Mr Davies, his class teacher since moving up to Standard Five, the last year at primary school, but concentrating on English grammar wasn't easy with only three-quarters of an hour to go before Auntie Gwen's chocolate sponge pudding with chocolate custard. Auntie Gwen, who worked with his mam in the school canteen, always made chocolate pudding on a Friday.

The sponge pudding was sweet and sticky and the custard was thick. Mr Parry, the headmaster, rapped a spoon against a glass. He looked very serious. The rich chocolate cake coated John's teeth and clung to the roof of his mouth. Mr Parry asked everyone to be quiet for a minute to respect the children who'd been killed in an accident in South Wales. He said a prayer in Welsh and English for the people of Aberfan and the children of Pantglas School. John ran his tongue over his front teeth to dislodge the pudding. He wondered if Greg had got into trouble for the stain on his blazer.

Billy sat with his dad on the settee and John Idris cuddled up to his mam in the big armchair to watch the six o'clock news, her warm softness reassuring him. After the bulletin, Dad heaped more coal on the fire and they sat together for a long time. Billy wanted to know why the slag tips had got so big. John wanted to know why God had sent another plague like the one that had killed all the babies in the Bible.

'God loves children,' Mam said. 'He didn't want these little children to die. It was a terrible accident, *cyw*.'

He wanted to believe his mam, but Miss Gruffudd was a teacher so she had to know better... and what he'd been doing with Carrot was so naughty. Aberfan was his punishment. He knew it.

He didn't go near the old barn again. Within months the Goodwins moved away. He got stiffies very often, but he didn't touch himself when it was hard in case another disaster happened.

*   *   *

By the time John Idris Jones was old enough to go to the secondary school in Harlech diesel locomotives had finally replaced the steam trains. There was an early September storm and a high tide on his first morning; for a few hundred yards on each side of the halt in Llanaber the waves splashed over the train. Older boys pushed and jostled the new kids towards the opened windows. The woollen felt of his new school blazer remained sodden throughout that first day.

Despite the soggy start, John loved his new school. His new English teacher, Miss Roberts, was an enthusiastic young woman who challenged her class to find new words every day and read everything they could get their hands on. The man who taught him history made him tingle – and once, as he leaned over to check John's work, John got one of those embarrassing stiffies that just seemed to happen when you were eleven. And there was a huge library, with an encyclopaedia that had pictures of men's and women's bits, and thick dictionaries with words like *cunt, fuck, masturbate* and *homosexual*.

There were newspapers, magazines and what Miss Roberts called 'journals' in the school library too: *The Times, The Guardian, New Society, Christian* and *The British Weekly*. John didn't read them every day, but he read them often enough to know that 'homosexual' was never used much as an adjective. It was a noun, and it always appeared alongside other nouns like thief, criminal, blackmailer, alcoholic, murderer, pervert and even unstable psychotic. In one of the little blue exercise books they'd been given for vocabulary he wrote out some of the sentences that contained these words.

Sometimes Mam would bring a heap of magazines from 'the girls' in the canteen and he'd find references to homosexuals in problem pages. The agony aunts always recommended a visit to the doctor... and psychiatric treatment.

*   *   *

John was surprised one Sunday when Dad told him and Billy they were both old enough to decide for themselves whether they wanted to go to chapel. They hadn't been going every Sunday morning because even Mam seemed to have lost interest. There had been a succession of washed-out clergymen filling in since Enoch Lloyd had retired. All that *hwyl* and hellfire was laughable and their incoherent ramblings had jaded

John's sense of the religious, stifling any desire to explore his own spirituality. The last few times he'd been, he'd shown more interest in the lavish hats and fur coats. His dad had raised an eyebrow when John had declared he was going to be a fashion designer and taken to sketching evening dresses and chapel hats with flower power motifs in psychedelic designs.

*   *   *

The first time they called John a *bum-boy* he hadn't really understood what they'd meant; then it was *shirt-lifter*, which had really baffled him. *Effing queer* was much more straightforward, even though he couldn't understand why they were calling him that. But then, as the months passed, he came to recognise that what he'd secretly known about himself was becoming obvious to others. It was unspeakable.

By the time the name-calling had become a daily event, the name-callers had grown bored and dissatisfied by his apparent indifference to their taunts so they began to push him around. In the changing rooms, before and after games, they flicked their towels at him. One day they even forced his head into the toilet bowl while two of the boys pissed on it and another pulled the chain. Everyone was laughing when the games teacher came to see what all the commotion was about; he laughed too. John had thought many times about telling his mam, but how could he talk about the unspeakable?

He couldn't remember when he'd actually started to believe he was a bad person; perhaps it had been during those months when none of his *friends* would let themselves be seen with him. He'd spent lots of time on his own then and all the bad names they'd called him seemed to get inside him.

20

In the summer of 1970 John Denver was on the radio all the time, 'Leaving, On A Jet Plane'. On the beach, John met one of the fairground boys who sometimes took the money for the bumper cars. Their talk became dirty and when they each noticed the other's stiffy, poking out their skimpy trunks, they went into the toilets on the quay. It wasn't like anything he'd done with Dewi or Carrot. He could remember how dirty he felt afterwards, recalling the smell of the greasy-haired youth's sweat and the taste of the white scum under his foreskin. The rancidly pissy stench of the squalid public toilet seemed to cling to the air and taint his every breath for what seemed like weeks. After that it wasn't just the bad names that made him feel wicked. He was gripped by guilt and wanted a jet plane to take him away from it all.

There were many boys and even some men after that first time. Despite all the promises he'd made to himself, never to do it again, and the desperate prayers to have such feelings taken away, he let himself be tempted again and again. First the eyes would catch the gaze of another and linger; they were always holidaymakers, playing such games with the likes of Bobby-Nansi was unthinkable and he didn't know anyone else who might have wanted to play. After stares that seemed to loiter there'd be quiet smiles and perhaps the nod of a head, then one or the other would lead the way into the toilets – on the prom, by the cinema, on the quay – where they'd stand for longer than was possible if it had been just for a pee. When each was confident of the other's intention, a kind of knowing that John came to understand and which became more certain with experience, a place would be negotiated; a tent or a beach hut, even the rocks and caves at the bottom of Llanaber cliffs. Caravans were best of all because the curtains could be drawn and the door locked. Failing these options, and if they were both desperate enough, it would be in one of the cubicles against walls smeared with lurid messages and cartoon phalluses.

Sometimes, when he let himself remember, the shame was suffocating. Then he'd try to rationalise his behaviour and see what there was to be grateful for in such dangerous liaisons. Sex education at Ysgol Ardudwy, its curriculum barely discussed by the embarrassed, middle-aged, respectable chapelgoers on the governing board, had failed to acknowledge the real world of sexually transmitted infections and unplanned pregnancies; the legacy of the swinging 60s. It was these men and boys, in holiday shorts and suntan cream, who'd taught him about sex. Some had even shown tenderness.

Others had been brutish, especially in the days of his inexperience, taking what they wanted by threat or by force. Not that he'd ever been beaten up; he'd never had to lie about a swollen lip or a black eye. Even those who'd said *yes* to his *nos* hadn't been violent in that sense; they'd just held him down more firmly than was comfortable and pushed harder. John Idris soon learned that clenching the muscle as tight as he could only made it hurt more, so his *no* was usually interpreted as a *yes* as he relaxed to save himself the pain. After learning about using loads of spit, with the boy from Wolverhampton – the one he'd seen every day for a fortnight because they'd liked each other – it became easier and more convenient to say *yes* even though he never liked *that*.

Then, when he was sixteen, just days after Bobby-Nansi had been found hanging in Wavecrest's stairwell at the end of a rope tied to the top landing newel post, a fat American tourist offered him a crisp five-pound note to do just what he'd done with so many others for nothing more than a guilty conscience, and he could afford to buy Elton John's latest, with 'Rocket Man' and 'Crocodile Rock'. And with some of the money he got from Nana for getting nine O-levels he went to the Pavilion cinema to see *Love Story*. Like Ali MacGraw's Jenny Cavilleri, he fell in love with Ryan O'Neal too.

*   *   *

'I want to do zoology, botany and history of art,' he told the head-teacher and the sixth form tutor in his post-results interview.

'But the sixth form has just got too small, John. You know that we've only been offering biology as an A-level for the last couple of years,' the head said.

'And the timetable isn't flexible enough to mix arts and sciences,' the sixth form tutor put in. 'What about chemistry and maths with biology?'

John wondered if his dad or his mam would have helped him stand his ground, but they'd been too busy to come to school during an August weekday, and in all the discussions they'd had at home they'd kept saying that his teachers were better qualified to advise him. 'We haven't got an O-level between us,' Mam had said. 'Why don't you talk to Billy?' And Billy, too occupied with being a lifeguard on the beach patrol and ogling girls in bikinis during his last long summer holiday from the Medical School in Liverpool, said that he thought John would be better off doing maths, chemistry and biology.

Falling in love with the new maths teacher didn't make pure and applied mathematics any less incomprehensible, and although he could do chemistry, he disliked it. But Mrs Edwards was lovely and *Biology – A Functional Approach* by M. B. V. Roberts became his bible. When he felt like screaming 'I hate

23

fucking chemistry and I can't get my head around simple harmonic motion and differential equations', he'd sit with Bethan and Judith in the prep room at the back of the biology lab and they'd put the world right over cups of instant coffee. Mrs Edwards turned a blind eye to their secret stash and sometimes she'd even have a coffee with them. She was interested in their thoughts beyond their studies. They discussed the terrorist attack at the Munich Olympics and considered the implications of the Americans' final withdrawal from Vietnam. She wanted to know if they'd seen *Cabaret* or *Jesus Christ Superstar*, or read *Jonathan Livingston Seagull*.

John slogged through his two years in the sixth form. He saw the achievement of good grades as his ticket to freedom – and for as long as he was studying, filling his mind with facts and formulae, theories and statistics, there was no room to brood on the nouns that qualified the noun he couldn't bring himself to own as a badge of identity, or feel bad about all those men and boys. For weeks at a time he didn't even think about sex; occasional fantasies about the maths teacher lost their allure and eventually failed to arouse him.

That summer after the A-level exams – while Terry Jacks sang about the joy and fun of seasons in the sun and Richard Nixon was finally forced to resign – John worked long hours, everyday, in the chip shop on the quay. It was easier that way; it kept all the inner truths hidden and he began to believe that he wasn't attracted to men after all; it really had just been a phase like one of the agony aunts in his mam's magazine had suggested.

He got an 'A' in biology and a distinction in the biology special paper; Mrs Edwards gave him a hug and kissed him on the cheek. A C-grade in chemistry was as much as he'd hoped for and better than he'd expected. An O-level pass in maths was a less cruel way of saying that he'd failed. A few days after the exam results a rejection slip from Liverpool University was pushed through the letterbox.

August
Bank Holiday Friday Night

John was disorientated when he woke up, but seeing Russell, slouched in an easy chair reading a thick Ian Rankin, he regained his equilibrium. 'How was your walk?' he asked, startling Russell from his adventure with Rebus and Edinburgh's low life.

'There was a lot of cruising by the cottage at the end of the prom,' he quipped.

John shifted beneath the light, soft blanket. 'Thanks for this.'

'It's turned really chilly so I thought it was best to throw something over you. If you hadn't woken up when I got to the end of my chapter I was going to leave you here.'

'Do you still —' John cut himself off. Fingering the label on the blanket that confirmed it was cashmere, he concluded that he had no right to ask. 'What's the beach at Dyffryn like, it's gone naturist hasn't it?' John said to disguise his hesitation.

'Lots of cruising there too. And no, I don't, not in the toilets or on the beach. There's some talk about police harassment...

and besides, after I was diagnosed I went off sex.'

'I didn't know,' John offered, but he'd guessed as much. That gaunt look had been a real give-away after Ranley and Tom. He hoped there was a suggestion of empathy in his voice; he didn't want to offer any platitudes.

'No. Why should you have known?'

Sensing a defensiveness in Russell's words, John shifted his gaze and took in the large Kyffin on the opposite wall. Then he wondered what the local police were up to. 'Harassment is just not on you know... they're supposed to be working to nationally agreed guidelines,' he said to bridge the unease that had crept between them.

'Someone needs to tell North Wales Police then,' Russell said.

'Perhaps it's just local maverick coppers,' John said. 'I worked with a group at police headquarters in Colwyn Bay on the new guidelines.'

'You did?'

'We thrashed out the policy on sex in public places about two years ago, when I was the Chair of the liaison group.'

'You got political then?' Russell quipped, inviting a conversation.

'Yes... but that'll have to wait, Russell. I'm knackered.'

'D'you want some hot chocolate, or a whiskey. I think there's a bottle of malt —'

'No, I'm ready for bed.'

Russell watched the reflection of the moon over the bay from his bedroom window. He chastised himself for not being bold enough to ask John to sleep with him. The fear and stark loneliness of AIDS was always worse at night and it had been a long time since he'd known the comfort of a warm body to cuddle.

Late August

Driving up the Mawddach estuary, the yellow of the gorse and the purple of the heather were almost too vivid in the bright sunshine of the tranquil, late summer's morning. Curious breezes whispered across the wide expanse of unbroken water, exciting ripples where the sunlight skipped. John felt the sadness of Russell Talbert's situation break through the morning's beauty.

Despite his early misgivings, John conceded that Russell had been a generous and gracious host, and even good company. That Russell had bad taste – despite an eye for beautiful things – wasn't something John could hold against him. But in twenty-odd years there had been too many sick men in his life and he wasn't sure there was room for another. When Russell had asked him to come and stay again, with Klaus, John had smiled and said that his lover had always liked coming to Barmouth to hike and swim. That had, he supposed, been an implicit consent to further visits.

Through the course of the weekend, John had come to realise that Russell was trawling his history; he'd need people. He had enough money, of course, to pay for professional carers when his body finally tired of the combination therapies. But sometime in the future, when the dementia and the diarrhoea would start to overwhelm him, Russell wanted people around him he could trust. John wondered if there was enough history between them, and whether he had enough heart to go through another lingering death. He wondered about the Kyffins too, and whether he could be bought. He pushed the callow thought from his mind and jabbed at the CD button. To the scraping sawing of a violin on Rufus Wainwright's 'Agnus Dei' he tried to concentrate on the road ahead, but Ranley, a boy from Liverpool, all those years ago, seemed insistent that they share the journey. Ranley pulled John back.

Through pigeon shit and grime, Felix Rossi's statue of Minerva, the goddess of wisdom, cast her gaze over the city from the Town Hall's dome. Despite her watchfulness, Liverpool had slipped into an unwise, wanton indifference about itself. Derelict buildings scarred the cityscape, giving new meaning to 'adventure playground' for Scouse kids. In the vandalised shells of Georgian terraces and sixties maisonettes, with empty lager cans and used condoms strewn about, and dumped sofas, clapped-out washing machines – even discarded syringes and bloodied needles – arson was just another game to play. Generations of soot, smoke and exhaust fumes sullied the three graces of Liver, Docks Board and Cunard on the waterfront, and inside many a civic building the cancerous blight of the Labour Militants was eating away at what remained of the city's infrastructure. Decades of decline had brought down a once great commercial hub, made rich from the trade in sugar and cotton – and slaves. In the litter-strewn streets, ill-famed for rocking flagstones that fractured wrists and ankles, shoppers looked weighed down by more than just their Kwik-Save carrier bags. John wondered about the garish net curtains, flounced across the streaky windows of Walton's two-up-two-down Victorian terraces and Everton's tower blocks; were the brash pinks, dazzling lime greens and brassy blues, *de-rigueur* in the mid-eighties, the only splashes of colour in Liverpudlian lives?

Minerva could have peed into the gloomy alley where Scarlett's Bar was protected from drunken Scallys out on a bender and a bit of queer bashing by steel doors and two hefty bouncers. Industrial concrete steps beyond the steely, pumped-up muscle Marys led down from street level. There, a chemically pungent smell of lavender air-freshener stung at the back of the nose, but that was better than the stench from the toilets that backed up with the highest tides on the Mersey. Poster-sized images were carelessly taped onto the flaking plaster walls of the stairway that dropped to a dimly lit, ruby-curtained doorway: Rhett Butler, the Tara plantation and Scarlett O'Hara herself.

The bar was small; twenty punters made a crowd. Through an ever-present fug of cigarette smoke in the low-ceilinged basement, Christmas tree lights around a huge picture of Vivien Leigh and Clark Gable, dancing at the Atlanta ball, flashed all year round. In an alcove, no more than eight feet square, a mirrored globe hung above a 'dance floor'; it cast diamonds of silvery light that chased along the walls before getting lost in the silky folds of nicotine-stained ceiling drapes.

'What's wrong with you, queen?'

John looked up from his glass of lime and lemonade and acknowledged Andy Radley with a nod. Because of the play of his names everyone called him Ranley.

'You've got a face on you like a hen's hole,' Ranley accused, standing with his hands on hips that swayed provocatively to Sade's 'Smooth Operator' in a classically mincing pose. The tight yellow T-shirt, which did nothing for his puny build, had darker, damp patches in the armpits. John noticed that the scars on his face were less angry now, and he remembered how an embittered, drug-crazed ex-lover had glassed Ranley in Paco's. In the chaos of the casualty department at the Royal Liverpool Hospital the junior doctor had panicked when Ranley told him he was positive for HTLV-III, the virus all the newspapers had taken to calling the AIDS virus. Because splashes of Ranley's blood had spattered across his own face, John had revisited the dilemma of whether to test or not. With no effective treatment, and no cure in sight, there still didn't seem much point.

'I've just lost my job,' John said.

'Join the ranks of Maggie's millions,' Ranley quipped. 'What's green and gets you drunk?'

'I've heard that one before,' John jibed, with almost a smile. 'Won't be long now till I draw my first Giro.'

'D'you want another one to drown your sorrows?' Ranley asked, gesturing towards John's glass. 'Double vodka and lime?'

'You can get me a Coke, if you like.'

'You're still on the wagon then?'

'That's what Hep-B does to you, Ranley. I've been a good boy for two years.'

Ranley turned his own face into a hen's hole. 'Oh purr-lease!' Then he fetched the drinks.

31

'So, what did you do to get yourself the sack?' Ranley asked on his return.

'I didn't get the sack. I'm on a two-year contract and they're just not going to renew.'

'That's what happens with short term funding, innit?'

'It's a bit more involved than that,' John said, wondering if he wanted to go over it all with Ranley, or just let it drop.

'You're a hospital social worker at the Royal, aren't you?'

'No. A chaplain.'

Ranley's flirty brown eyes opened with surprise.

'It's a Welsh-speaking ministry. I go to visit people who come over from Wales for heart bypasses and hip replacements... y'know, and cancer patients at Clatterbridge. I even go and see those that get banged up in Walton nick.'

'You work for God?' Ranley said, expressing astonishment and derision.

John shrugged, and took a long draft from his glass of cola.

'Fuck!' Ranley exclaimed, scratching his sweaty armpit. 'We've worked together for more than a year setting up the Mersey AIDS Support Group and I never knew you were one of the fucking enemy. I wouldn't piss on the church if it was on fire.'

'I know the feeling,' John said. The meeting in Aberystwyth, earlier that day, with his boss from the Home Mission Board, flashed before his eyes.

'What happened? Some bitchy ex with an axe to grind went and outed you, hmm?'

'Not exactly.'

Ranley heard the quality of dismissal in John's voice.

'Okay, so you don't want to talk about it,' Ranley said. 'Least now you'll have plenty of time to train more phone-liners and work on that buddy training course you've been promising at the steering group meetings. And if that funding comes through from the health authority maybe you could be the co-ordinator.'

'Don't hold your breath, Ranley. Some of us from the finance sub-group had a meeting with the bods at the regional health authority last week. They want to see the AIDS Support Group and Body Positive come together before they'll consider funding us.'

'Didn't I tell you that BP should have voted me in as their chairman?' Ranley protested with a few sharp jabs of his fingers against his chest. 'For as long as that Nick and his mates run the show they'll want to keep Liverpool Body Positive like a members-only club.'

'Not so loud,' John whispered with a conspiratorial nudge. 'He just walked in.'

'Oh God… if he sees me talking to you all cosy like this he'll think we're plotting a coup or something.'

'A takeover? That's a really sound idea, Ranley,' John said.

Tina Turner's velvet voice sung from the sound system.

'Come and be my *Private Dancer*,' Ranley said. 'He'll go'n sit with someone else if we're on the dance floor.'

Andy Radley wasted away with staggering briskness during the late autumn of 1987. The staff on the Infectious Diseases Unit at Fazakerley Hospital, a clutch of his friends and two buddies from MASG worked tirelessly to care for him as wave after wave of infection raked his system and a tumult of tumours devoured choice titbits from his brain. Then the young consultant explained that there wasn't much more they could do, except keep him comfortable.

In one of the lucid times that pushed out the delirium,

Ranley decided that he wanted to die at home. His mother, a bony woman whose brittle skin was stretched so obstinately across her scrawny cheeks it looked like it might tear if she ever dared to smile, chain-smoked her way through her reasons for not being able to care for him. John, still MASG's buddy coordinator, worked out a rota that complemented the care offered by the community health and social services. They kept Ranley comfortable and clean – and even cheerful – in his cramped bedsit for twelve lingering weeks. Physically little more than a skeleton, he died in the arms of his MASG buddy, surrounded by posters of Diana Ross.

On a gorgeous spring day at the end of May, John conducted Andrew Radley's memorial service.

'My old Queen says she'd like a private funeral,' Ranley had said when John asked if he'd thought about what he wanted. 'My Ma thinks lots of my mates are too over-the-top and they'll turn it into a show; y'know, a reason to get all dressed up, and she won't cope with all the trannies competing with her for who can look the dowdiest. So I've thought about it... and she can have her private little funeral... then I want you to do me the loudest, most bad-taste memorial service.'

'We can work on it together,' John said. 'But you need to know that I don't do bad-taste very well.'

Ranley's Memorial Bash included a tape of Bette Midler singing 'The Rose' and Diana Ross singing 'Reflections', 'Reach Out And Touch' and 'Chain Reaction'. Some readings from Tagore's *Book of Comfort* betrayed a more thoughtful Andrew who'd have been unknown to his mates from Paco's, Sadie's and Scarlett's. As John scattered his ashes into the Mersey from the railings of the prom at Otterspool, Diana Ross posed her questions: *Do you know where you're going to? Do you like the things that life is showing you?*

The *Clause* passed into law and became Section 28 of the Local Government Act (1988) later that day; local authorities could no longer 'intentionally promote homosexuality' or 'promote the teaching in any maintained school of the acceptability of homosexuality as a pretended family relationship.' John considered the implications for the funding of gay and lesbian support groups and the ramifications of the state viewing the relationships he formed as 'pretend' relationships. Listening again to Ranley's Diana Ross tape on the car's cassette player, he played the 'Theme From Mahogany', over and over. He really didn't like what life was showing him.

A traffic jam and the police control around a car accident outside Bala brought John back to the present and he drove home to Rufus Wainwright's *Want Two*. After the long bank holiday weekend the house was stuffy so he opened all the downstairs windows before unpacking his bag and checking the answering machine with its manically blinking light. There were three messages; two were from Klaus's bridge partner – something about an up-coming competition, and the other was from Elen Morgan's daughter: 'Mam's in Bronglais Hospital and things aren't looking very good. I just thought that I should let you know... and if you do decide that you'd like to come to Aberystwyth to see her, perhaps you could give me a ring... visiting is family only now, and I'd need to let them know you were coming.'

Mulling over the kitchen calendar, where he and Klaus scribbled up their comings and goings (and where they sometimes had to pencil-in time to be with one another), John noted the appointment for a blood test, the cardiac rehab session and the lunch in Liverpool with his brother Bill. After considering the possibilities, he rang Elen Morgan's daughter. He was apprehensive, tapping the numbers into the phone; her message had been sandwiched between the bridge calls and in the days since it had been left Elen's condition may have deteriorated. Beca's hello was cheerful.

'She's been a bit better since Sunday,' Beca explained. 'Last night they had her sitting in the chair for an hour. I combed her hair and she looked quite tidy... but.... Well, she's eighty-six and there's not much of her.'

'I could come down to Aberystwyth on Thursday.'

'Oh John, she'd love to see you. She thinks the world of you; you're the son she never had, you know that... and she's been so worried about you, with your heart and all.'

Aberystwyth
1974

Miss Davies with the squinting eye told him, at the end of every lesson, that to play the piano as well as he might he'd have to practise with considerably more diligence. John hadn't even become an adequate pianist. Perhaps, if he'd spent more time exploring the keyboard, and less time exploring the forbidden parts of his body on the rainy afternoons of his adolescence, he'd have done better.

He played 'The Entertainer' by Scott Joplin. Despite being whistled by everyone who'd seen *The Sting* over the last months, he sensed that it was out of place and time. He could almost hear the generations of Calvinistic Methodist ghosts, who'd worshipped in the United Theological College chapel for a century or more, grunting their disapproval from the vacant pews. He consciously drowned their grumbles by playing louder.

Aberystwyth was his second university choice. He'd never seriously thought that he wouldn't follow Billy to Liverpool; a real city with cinemas, theatres, nightlife and enough people in which to get lost when he might have wanted to be a stranger, but re-sitting maths had been too humiliating to contemplate, and he knew he couldn't have coped with Barmouth, or his mam and dad, for another year.

All the students living in the college called it Theol Coll. Most were university boys who'd accepted late offers from Aber and not found a place to live in the halls of residence. Of the few that studied theology – they were known as 'theologs' or 'Jesus-freaky-theologs' (JFTs), the distinction based on the degree of their fundamentalism and evangelical zeal – barely a dozen were actually candidates for the ordained ministry. A sign of the times, John thought. Who needed God in the 1970s?

Theol Coll was a small, independent college that had seen better days. Funded by the Presbyterian Church, and strapped for cash, it was shabby both outside and in. The rooms were stark, with lino on the floors and mismatched furniture ready for the junk shop – with the possible exception of an odd piece that might have found its way to an antique dealer. But the college chapel was opulent, with its purple velvet curtains, plush carpeted aisle and a grand piano. Afternoon light from the large bay windows, opening onto the sweep of the bay, dappled on the oak wall panelling, burnished to a warm lustre from years of careful polishing. John played another Joplin rag.

The heavy door swung open. Paul Wynne, a second-year Jesus-freaky-theolog, blew into the chapel like an autumn storm, a grimace on his face, and his hands, lost under tresses of long, fair hair, covering his ears from the din. Of all the JFTs, Paul was the one John had made a point of avoiding. From a distance he seemed pleasant enough, but the badges he wore pinned to his sweaters and jackets, with slogans like *Jesus*

Saves – but not with the Woolwich and *Jesus Loves You – but it's not free love*, were enough to put anyone off. Religion was the last thing John was looking for in Aberystwyth.

'It must be ages since you've had any real practice,' Paul ventured. 'Don't you know how to use the pedals?'

John mumbled an excuse and apologised for playing 'trendy' music in the chapel. Paul smiled and pushed alongside him on the long piano stool. After squeezing his fists and clacking his finger joints, Paul paused over the keyboard for some seconds, almost frozen. Then his hands began to move swiftly and fluidly over the keys. John recognised the piece as a 'classic', but couldn't name it.

Paul Wynne knew he was good. His style was flamboyant, his hands rising high above the keys, Liberace fashion. John moved from the piano stool to make way for this exuberance. Watching him play, John allowed himself to see Paul Wynne for the first time, beyond the silly badges and the Jesus freak label. The skin of his round face was clear and tanned, his long hair shining golden in the sun that streamed through the window. A small scar, just below his full, Mick Jagger lips, added some interest and his eyes danced, blue and green, like a candle flame sprinkled with salt. He presented a confusing mixture of sobriety and slightly camp sexuality. John's mind filled with erotic thoughts, which startled him after so many months of certainty that he'd passed through that phase. The short-lived fantasy of Paul's fingers playing over his body reawakened old anxieties. Then the music stopped, and Paul offered an unexpected observation in Welsh.

'I saw you in Peniel this morning.'

'Yes,' John said with a dismissive shrug, but realising too that the comment indicated Paul had noticed him amidst the many other faces.

'Did you like the service? Rhys Morgan's a good preacher, don't you think?'

'It was... fine. Yes.' John said, becoming flustered. He hadn't listened to the sermon and he didn't want to be drawn into a religious discussion with a JFT. 'I was brought up to go to chapel, but I try not to make a habit of it. I think I was just feeling a bit homesick... and there's not much else to do in Aber on a Sunday morning.'

'That's when most people sleep off their hangovers,' Paul quipped.

John smiled, liking his lack of stuffiness.

'But there must be some spiritual spark that needs to be ignited if going to chapel was even on your list of options?' Paul said with more gravity.

John wondered about telling the suddenly inquisitive little JFT to fuck off but the unexpectedness and the power of the sexual attraction he felt towards Paul unbalanced him and he allowed himself to be drawn into a conversation he didn't want to have. 'Why d'you wear all of those stupid badges?' he asked, with accusation more caustic than he'd intended.

Paul made an inquiring gesture that seemed to invite John to answer his own question.

'So you're the New Messiah,' John jibed.

'I'm famous for my badges,' Paul said with a chuckle that allayed John's goading. 'They're just a bit of fun really; but sometimes, when people read them... well, they either think I'm a bit of a nut, or they ask about them... just like you're asking me about them, and that gives me all sorts of opportunities to evangelise.'

John realised that he'd been caught, fair and square, in Paul's little game and, though he was irritated by his own

40

gullibility, he found himself succumbing to desire. He felt his cock twitch and wondered if his erection was obvious through his tight jeans. He went through the motions of blowing his nose, stuffed the handkerchief back into his pocket and left his hand caressing his hard-on to conceal the bulge. He barely took in the detail of their conversation. Paul was smiling, and saying something about how God's salvation had made him a new person. But then, with a glance at his watch and a silent whistle, Paul got to his feet. 'Time flies! I'll see you around. I'm in room six up on D floor.' He touched John's shoulder as he took his leave. 'Call in sometime. D6, okay?'

And then he was gone.

In the chapel's stillness John was suddenly aware of the waves crashing onto the rocks towards Castle Point and a flood of memory washed over him. As if his mind was compartmentalised behind closed doors, door after door now flew open. The nouns in the newspapers that had left him secure in the knowledge that he was unnatural and anti-social streamed through his consciousness. That touch to his shoulder brought back so many touches from boys and men that had quenched a desire and fuelled so much shame and guilt. And because the touch was Paul's... and because of that morning's service in Peniel... and because he was sitting alone in the chapel, he thought about it all in religious terms and he knew that he was sinful.

In the toilet, next to the laundry room in the basement, he unzipped himself.

Too suddenly he was drowning in a sickening sense of his own filthiness.

*   *   *

Michael, John's room mate, liked their room. He'd arrived the day before John and made his choices, taking the bed nearest the radiators and the desk in the bay window with the sea view, leaving John the bed by the rattling side-window and the desk in a gloomy corner.

Michael liked his own company. A bookish lad, excited by the academic challenge before him, he'd even spent the summer months after his A-levels reading the set texts for each of his first year courses. He planned to study for between six and eight hours every day, and the desk with the sea view was the perfect place to do that. Despite his high grades, and Edinburgh's eagerness to take him, he'd come to Aberystwyth – his second choice – because it was closer to home. Every other weekend Michael intended to take the train back to Shrewsbury so that his mother could do all his laundry. In three years' time he'd get a first and then do a PhD.

John disliked Michael from the moment he stepped into room C2. It was already Michael's room... his bed, his desk, his space. But more than this, John saw in him a pampered mother's boy, a younger version of Bobby-Nansi.

*   *   *

After that Sunday afternoon in the chapel, John noticed Paul more often. With just one sitting in the dining hall at meal times, one library – intended for the Theologs but used by some university boys – a TV room, and a large stairwell where students congregated on the landings to chat, there was an easy intimacy that encouraged friendship. Paul would always acknowledge John when they saw one another... and John liked the attention.

'D'you want some tea?' Paul asked at the end of a news bulletin dominated by a report from Belfast, where republican prisoners had set fire to the Maze prison and the resulting deployment of British troops had sparked riots on the city's streets.

'Yes,' John said, already questioning his motives. He'd never paid much attention to current affairs, but for more than a week, knowing Paul would be watching, he hadn't missed the nine o'clock news.

In the small student kitchen on B floor, Paul made a pot of tea and talked about the situation in Northern Ireland. He seemed to be able to speak with knowledge, even authority, about almost anything. John liked this about him, perhaps because he didn't know what he thought about a whole range of issues, from painting out English road signs to Watergate and IRA bombings. In Paul he saw maturity and confidence that he felt he lacked in himself.

'You're settling in all right then?' Paul asked, a bit unexpectedly.

'Yes... I haven't knuckled down to my studies yet, and Michael and I don't get on too well —'

'That's why you work in the library sometimes.'

'It's quiet there, and the view's nice,' John said. *And because I get to look at you*, he thought.

'That's why I like it too,' Paul said before downing his tea. 'And I like to think that if I sit amongst all those academic tomes long enough I'll absorb some of all that learning by osmosis.'

John laughed.

'Let me rinse your mug,' Paul said, reaching forward. His hand touched John's as the mug was exchanged. 'You still haven't called in... D6, remember?'

'Okay,' John said.

In the toilet next to the laundry room, when the sinful feelings came, John wondered if Paul's confidence in life really did come from faith in a loving God. He wanted to believe in such a God... not the one who bestowed harsh judgement.

*   *   *

Thursday was a heavy day for first year biologists, with three fifty-minute lectures in the morning and a four-hour practical in the zoology laboratory after lunch. Being alert to the complexity of protozoan mouthparts at nine o'clock in the morning wasn't easy, but the turmoil that stewed in John's mind since he'd met Paul made concentration even more difficult. A hot and sexy, desirable man who wore *Jesus Saves* badges on his chest was bewildering.

At the end of the lecture, Wendy, one of the gang John had started to hang out with, broke through his reverie. 'Are you coming to the Union for a coffee?'

'No, I've got some things to do,' he blurted, his brusqueness making her frown as she moved off to join the shove for a position in the scrum at the campus coffee bar.

Sitting on a bench near a newly planted azalea bed, slim evidence of the landscaping that the university authorities had promised would accompany the ambitious building programme on the new hillside campus, John took in the town, squeezed between Cardigan Bay, Penglais Hill and the heavy, low sky. The sea was like a canvas of blotched paints, the blues dark, with greens and greys all running together.

He thought about Paul. Perhaps if he talked openly and honestly with him some clarity might come and he'd be able to refocus on his studies. But it wouldn't be easy. He'd never told

44

anyone that he was... a pervert. Queer, cocksucker and poof weren't easy words to own. 'Homosexual' remained unspeakable. Could he tell Paul that he was *one*? None of it ran off John's tongue without difficulty, and there were no Welsh words, or none that he knew.

The biochemistry lecture on amino acids might just as well have been a lesson in the complexities of some foreign language grammar. Between the peptide linkages that strung alanine, valine and lysine into polypeptides, the words he might use to describe his situation to Paul corrupted the chemistry.

Only the certainty of a red mark against his name in the lab register persuaded him to attend a futile afternoon of bug watching. The protozoa he peered at through the microscope failed to engage him and the afternoon seemed to drag. By four o'clock he'd had enough and he tidied together the few sketches which bore little resemblance to the creatures that had been the focus of the class's scientific voyeurism. John left the laboratory without glancing in the direction of the tutor or any of the demonstration staff, fearing that if he caught someone's eye a comment would be made about his early departure.

A wind blew in off the sea, carrying a light drizzle. Seeing the blackening sky out over the bay, he ran to his car, thinking that winter wasn't far away. Sitting in the loose-springed driver's seat of the rusting old Vauxhall Viva, shivering from the chill, he began to second-guess himself. Michael would be 'in residence' as always, and he was the last person John wanted to be with. Still uncertain of his intentions, he started the car. The engine ignited first time, surprising him; Aberystwyth's salty dampness didn't seem to suit the ageing confusion of pipes and wires under the bonnet.

He drove aimlessly around town for about twenty minutes

and then parked on the prom in front of the King's Hall. Elton John's 'Bennie And The Jets' erupted from the basement amusement arcade, but the cheery pings of the pinball machines failed to seduce him. Pulling up the hood of his parka against the damp wind, John walked towards Constitution Hill. The Cliff Railway was already closed for the winter. At the end of the prom he kicked the railing on the low wall; kicking the bar was a student tradition in Aberystwyth – an excuse for a study-break. The grey sea churned as the gusty wind strengthened. For a while he watched the waves crash into the cliffs. And then the rain blew in and he got soaked.

Driving through the torrent, just a short distance back to Theol Coll, he decided to leave the car by the pier. He hoped that the stormy sea wouldn't throw up any pebbles during the night that might hole the rust-scarred bodywork. The loose spring in the driver's seat twanged as he got out, and the pelting rain made a dull thudding noise on the sodden canvas of his jacket. An angry roar of thunder vented overhead as he reached Theol Coll.

The rain hammered on the glass roof, six floors above, sending echoes around the yawning stairwell. John lingered at his mailbox, but without any letters to distract him he dithered about bearing his soul to Paul. The speech he'd rehearsed, contaminated by amino acids and infected with protozoa, seemed stilted. He took the stairs two steps at a time, hoping there might be a film showing at the Coliseum to divert him.

On the first landing, one of the theologs was ringing the bell for the evening service. His broad smile beckoned John into the chapel. Instantly regretting his impulsiveness, John moved to the pew at the back and hoped he'd go unnoticed, but he dropped his bag and the contents spilled to the floor. Everyone turned around to see the cause of the commotion and he felt the embarrassment rise through him like the chill of a draught. The stares had been fleeting, but they seemed to see through to his core. He sat with his head bowed, more out of shame than any prayerful aspect, but some words came... 'Help me... please. Take these feelings away. Come into this mess of a life and make me normal.'

When the words dried up, John raised his head and watched the praying worshippers. In his mind's eye he saw the smelly public toilets where he'd groped other men, sucked cocks thrust through glory holes and been anonymously fucked in the cubicles. His stomach knotted and he felt sick. Then the sweetest music pierced this attack of self-loathing. Looking over to the piano, John saw Paul and felt the stab of sexual attraction. He pleaded with God to take these feelings away, but the knots in his stomach tightened. Knowing he'd throw up, he scuttled from the chapel.

In the cool, tiled sterility of the bathroom, he bathed his face in cold water and washed the foul taste from his mouth. He pulled the chain with some relief that a little of the filth was being washed away, but the reprieve was short-lived. Perhaps, if he could tell Paul his vile secret, everything would be alright.

On the landings, clutches of chatting students leaned against the banister edging the stairwell, a sure sign that chapel was over. John drew smiles and cheerful banter as he passed by, but he didn't pause to join in the talking. On D floor, he took the gloomy passage off the main landing that led to three small rooms at the back of the building. D6 seemed the most remote. A sliver of yellow shone from under the door.

He hesitated, and doubting that he'd find any words to

describe his experiences over the last weeks, he turned back to the stairs. At the banister, staring into the well, Mrs Edwards-biology smiled in his mind's eye. One of her pet sayings was 'He who hesitates is lost.' John took a couple of deep breaths to calm himself and went back to Paul's room, giving two sharp taps on the door.

Paul was writing at his desk. The room was cool, despite the glow from a two bar electric fire. The single light bulb, hanging from the ceiling beneath a cracked glass shade, cast a poor light. Paul looked up from his notes. 'I need just one minute more, or I'll lose this thread completely,' he said, nodding towards the bed. 'Sit down.'

The scratch of his fountain pen irritated the long silence, which John began to find uncomfortable.

'Are you okay?' Paul asked eventually, still writing. 'There's nothing wrong, is there?'

'Can't a friend just drop in... socially? You've invited me twice.'

Paul clicked the top back onto his pen and pushed it into the breast pocket of his brown corduroy jacket. Then, shifting in his chair so that their knees almost touched, he rested his elbow on the desk and stroked his lightly stubbled chin. 'I saw you leaving chapel in a bit of a rush.'

They caught one another's gaze, but John turned away, pretending to admire the print of Dali's Last Supper, which hung over the end of the bed.

'Ever since we met... in the chapel,' Paul ventured. 'D'you remember?'

John turned to look at him and quietly cursed the kindling of sexual arousal.

'Since the beginning really,' Paul said, 'I've had this feeling about you... that there's more to John Idris Jones than meets the eye.' He paused, and tried to read the pained expression that scored John's face. 'There is something wrong, isn't there?' He touched John's knee in a gesture of reassurance.

John stiffened. *God! He knows... but how?* And a wave of panic swept him up... and there were no words to describe himself... just the sense of how dirty he was. And his eyes brimmed with tears.

'Hush... it's okay,' Paul offered, moving to his side on the bed and taking John's hand in his own. 'If you want to tell me about it... just take your time.'

John heard Paul's assurances, and felt comforted... but the closeness of Paul's body and the intimacy of his touch were confusing. 'It's so hard to say,' John said, sniffing back the tears.

Paul squeezed John's hand and folded his arm around him in a further gesture of encouragement. John found solace in the warmth and pressure of his touch... until it triggered a wave of sexual excitement. He clung to Paul and a reluctant plea squeezed itself from somewhere deep inside him. 'You'll still be my friend if I tell you... well, something... terrible about myself.'

Paul hugged him, but because he wasn't sure enough of what to say there was a long silence.

Perplexed by the responses of his body, John pushed him away. 'I'm a homosexual,' he said quietly. Through the corner of his eye, he could see Dali's Jesus looking down on them. *God, he's staring at me too.* He tried to focus on the glowing elements of the electric fire and concentrate on what he wanted to say. 'I don't want to be this way, Paul.'

Still unsure of himself, Paul hoped that his face would convey compassion. John sensed that Paul was staring at him, just like the staring Jesus. *He's going to reject me.* And then the disciples from Dali's painting joined Jesus and Paul in their gloating, their eyes breaking through his flesh, tearing into his body. *The punishment for my sinfulness.* He covered his face in his hands and strained his muscles hard to keep the intruders' stares out. *Why me?*

Paul spoke softly in a mixture of Welsh and English, which didn't seem odd.

'I'm glad you've shared this with me,' he said, laying his hand tentatively on John's shoulder, trusting that his words and touch would reassure. 'I know it's difficult for you... but thanks for being so honest.'

The gentleness of this response released John's locked-up emotions in uncontrolled break down and Paul held him for a long time.

As John became calmer, Jesus and his disciples retreated, taking up their places allotted by Dali at the table, and he was alone again with Paul. 'I thought Jesus was supposed to be forgiving,' John accused, wiping the tears from his face. 'Don't you think Dali has given him condemning eyes?'

'D'you want me to take the picture down?'

'No. Taking it down won't help. He'll still be there, staring.'

And silence fell between them again.

Paul sensed John's vulnerability. From his pastoral care classes he understood that he needed to offer effective listening. When the time felt right, he took John's hand again. 'Can I ask you something about what you've told me?'

'Yes... but —'

'I know it's not easy,' Paul said. He fingered the scar at his lip. 'Are you sure you're a homosexual? You're still young. What? Eighteen or nineteen?'

'Eighteen, last May.'

'That's still young to be certain about something like this. Most of us pass through a phase, and in some boys it just lasts a bit longer. In another twelve or eighteen months a lot can happen. You *will* pass through this... you'll see.'

There was silence again. John shook his head and wanted to laugh at Paul's attempt to explain his situation away. *This isn't a phase, Paul. There have been too many men already.*

'So, you don't think these feelings and attractions are just a natural part of your growing up?' Paul offered, trying to read John's body language.

'No.'

'But how can you be so sure?' Paul bit his lip. 'Is this about masturbation?'

'Well —' John didn't know what to say to such a direct question.

'God knows, there are so many myths about it, especially among us Welsh Calvinists!' Paul was smiling as he said this. 'Wanking *is* normal, John. I wank... it's fun.'

'It's not just about wanking, Paul.'

'So what then, John? Has someone made advances to you?'

Which part of the story should I tell you, Paul? The games with Dewi and Carrot... or when I started cottaging?

'Or... have you had sex with another man and it's upset you... or he's hurt you... is that it?' Paul asked.

D'you want to know what Rahab and I have got in common? Oh yes, I know my Bible... Miss Gruffudd in her fur coat was a good teacher. Shall I tell you about the time the American tourist paid me for a blowjob? It was such an easy way to earn extra pocket money... on my knees in the public toilets on the quayside where the visitors watched the lobster fishermen unloading their catch.

Paul remained patient, aware that whatever memories John was reliving were an open wound.

Too frightened to tell Paul about the company of men whose semen he'd tasted, he remained silent. And when the silence became a burden he lied. 'I've had sex with another man just once... and now, when I wank, I only think about him.'

'And when you say you had sex with this man, how far did you go? Was it just mutual masturbation, or —'

'Yes, we did that... and a few other things.'

'If you told me what happened it might help.'

John's mouth was dry. His erection ached. He wasn't sure how much to say, or how explicit to be, and he wasn't sure how Paul was hearing what he was saying. 'Do you really want me to carry on with this?'

'Yes, tell me what you did together —' He paused, his brow furrowed in self-reflection. 'I just think it would help you to get it all off your chest.'

So John spun a web of lies about his sex life, even boasting that he'd had sex with a girl. Paul listened carefully, offering quiet acceptance as the fable unfolded. John's brazen dishonesty and the sexual feelings aroused by Paul's willingness to be so intimate left him feeling squalid.

It was late when he finally left D6. In the toilet, next to the laundry room in the basement, he imagined loving Paul.

*　　*　　*

The wake-up bell jarred him to some degree of consciousness. Michael, standing at the washbasin brushing his teeth, farted twice. Through the window, John watched the mist swirl between the pier's piles and the promenade's railings. He recalled Paul's closeness, and the sexual feelings it had stirred, and he remembered the lies he'd told... and the familiar feelings of remorse returned. He dressed without washing. *With so much filth on the inside, what's the point?*

The dining hall wasn't busy enough for him to go unnoticed. He played his fork through the scrambled eggs on his plate and forced himself not to look over in Paul's direction. Then Paul's laughter rose above the breakfast table banter and John glanced at him. Paul smiled. John heard fragments from their conversation the night before: 'Invite Jesus into your heart, John. Repent... ask for forgiveness.' *But I contaminate you and everything that you stand for.*

And John fled.

At the top of Penglais he took one of the lanes that led to an isolated bay just north of Aberystwyth and then followed the signs to Borth and Ynyslas beach. Kicking pebbles across the sand, the autumn sun warm on his face, he realised that he couldn't flee the wretched feelings inside him. Later, walking in the slacks between the sand dunes, he thought about the impact Paul was having on his life; when John felt shame for what he was and what he'd done, he wanted to hide himself away from Paul... but most of the time he wanted to be with him.

Along the shore of the Dyfi, the sand hard-rippled after the ebbing tide, his thoughts followed him. *Homosexuality? Has God made me this way – just to condemn me?* 'What do I have to do for it... this forgiveness?' he yelled into the stillness around him.

The sun caught the windows of a cluster of houses on the other side of the river. Distracted by the dazzle, the beauty of the estuary struck him. Aberdyfi, white-washed and shimmering across the water, clung to the hill side through the rusting trees, calm and quiet now that the tourist season had ended. But the tranquillity around him wasn't infectious and he was caught again in the turbulence of his thoughts. Feeling exposed, a wave of anxiety washed over him. He ran back to his car and drove along the lanes that edged the expanse of Borth bog.

After only a few miles he stopped by a stream running from a tunnel of oaks. The trees weren't skeletal, but breaths of breeze off the sea helped to strip them, bearing their tangled branches to another winter. The stillness and the stream's mumbled babble calmed him. 'What must I do to repent?' he whispered to the trees. A waft of wind rustled their leaves. 'What do I owe you, God?' he asked the gurgling water. 'What do I have to pay to have all this guilt and dirt taken away?'

He knelt on the bank, where the chatter of the stream eased his sense of isolation, and prayed, a gush of words and phrases, some in Welsh and some in English. 'Our Father, who art in heaven, hallowed be thy name... you know what I've done.' And God was watching him suck cocks. 'I can't hide from you any more.' His knees felt damp from the grass. 'Help me to...' he searched for words. 'Help me to know who you are... and what you want from me.' The stream gurgled, distracting him, and his knees felt wet. 'Forgive us our trespasses as we forgive those who trespass against us... forgive me – for all those cocks... all those men.' Dali's Jesus stared at him again. 'I didn't ask to be *one*,' he pleaded with the gawping Jesus. 'I'm really not any of those things they say about people like me in the papers; I'm not! I don't want to be *one*.' And Paul came to him, his touch comforting. 'Paul says that I have to ask for forgiveness,' John told Jesus. 'But I don't know what that means... Fuck! I don't know what any of this means.'

*   *   *

Paul looked up from a fusty Hebrew textbook. 'How was your day?' he asked, reading the grimness in John's face. 'Let me give you a hug.'

'No... don't touch me.'

Paul rifled through the clutter on his desk. 'I saw this in Galloway's and thought you might like it,' he said, offering a postcard. 'There's a bit here that might be helpful.'

John was hesitant.

'"...You are a child of the universe, no less than the trees and the stars,"' Paul read, pointing with his finger. '"You have a right to be here. And whether or not it is clear to you, the universe is unfolding as it should...".'

'That sounds high-and-mighty,' John said, taking the card and scanning the text with difficulty because of the Gothic script. The title, *Desiderata*, meant nothing to him.

'I'd like to know what's going on in that head of yours,' Paul said.

Dali's Jesus was staring again. *God, I'm so fucked-up. I need you, Paul – but...* 'I want to be with you,' John said.

'So, let's have a walk and then go'n get something to eat,' Paul quipped.

'You don't get any of this, do you?'

Paul bit his lip and sighed. It was hard for him to think that he might be out of his depth, and harder still to realise that John's story was rekindling his own uncertainties. 'I can't be with you like *that*,' he said.

'I'm sorry... I didn't mean to offend you.' *Fuck... I can't keep fouling your life like this.* 'I'd better go.' *But I don't want to be on my own.*

55

'I'll knock on your door when it's time for supper,' Paul said as John was leaving.

*   *   *

The refectory was packed. The clammy smell of fried fish and a fog of cigarette smoke closed over them. Paul smiled, and flirted, with the bottle-blonde grandmother serving chips; she piled his plate high. John took a tired looking omelette and some limp salad. They shared a long table with a group of students enjoying their after supper smoke. John pushed the food around his plate. Paul ate with gusto, and though he sensed John's discomfort he was too unsure of himself to talk.

'I'm sorry,' John blurted, shoving his plate across the table. 'I have to go.'

Outside, the first pearls of rain blew in off the sea. He wanted to run away. *But there's nowhere to run to, and nowhere to hide because the demons are already inside me.* He sat on the pavement, the rain cold on his face.

Paul didn't hurry, but leaving the refectory, he caught sight of his friend, a dark shape on the pavement some yards away. 'I'm going for a walk,' Paul said. 'I don't think this rain will last long, and besides, I've been doing Isaiah in Hebrew all day and it's time I had a bit of fresh air.'

They walked for a while in silence. Paul was mildly irritated that he wasn't alone; he'd have welcomed the solitude to think about his response to John's erratic behaviour. Standing on Trefechan Bridge looking back at the lights of the town and the hillside campus beyond, Paul decided to try reasoning with him. 'I don't really understand why you're still feeling like this when you're with me,' he said. 'You've been so open about yourself, and I've told you, time and again, that I accept you and don't judge you.'

Here's my chance to tell you I've been lying.

'Is there something else?' Paul asked, looking concerned. 'Something you haven't told me?'

'There's no more to tell,' John said, his face contorted.

'So... what do I have to do?' Paul pleaded, with an edge of impatience. 'You don't have to feel ashamed with me... you don't. Lots of men have homosexual experiences; it's a part of learning about who we are, and finding out what's right for us.' He pushed his hand through his soggy hair and took a couple of deep breaths to dispel his irritation and then put his arm over John's shoulder. 'Look... being a homosexual isn't a fault, it's just something that happens. And like you said, you've had sex with a girl and enjoyed it. That means you've got a chance... so forget about the men. Find yourself a girlfriend and move on.'

John pressed himself into Paul's body, delighting in their closeness. *It's you I want, not a girlfriend.*

Another squally shower blew across the harbour and they took refuge in a pissy bus shelter. Paul started to talk about his studies and his sense of *call*. John tried to be interested – and understand – but the more Paul talked about his vocation, the more impossible it seemed that John's love for this man could be realised. When Paul talked about 'Jesus Christ as a paradigm for our lives', John lost the thread... and imagined they were making love together.

When the rain stopped they walked again. The pubs along the prom heaved with students doing what they were famous for doing at the weekend – getting drunk on Allbright Bitter.

'Do you fancy a pint?' John asked, not even sure if Paul was a drinker.

57

'I'm too cold to drink beer,' Paul quipped. 'What about a cup of tea?'

*　　*　　*

'The waterproofing on this jacket is rubbish,' Paul said as John poured their teas. 'Let's go up to my room; I need to put some dry clothes on.'

Because of the clean laundry, heaped on the chair, D6 seemed cluttered.

'Your hair's wet,' Paul said, handing John a clean towel from the top of the pile.

John towel-dried his hair and when he emerged from the towel's softness Paul had hung up his jacket and was patting his shoulders with his hands. 'I'm wet through,' Paul said. Tugging the yellow polo neck over his head, he inadvertently pulled his T-shirt from inside his jeans. John noticed the hairs down from Paul's navel, poking through the gap above his belt, and he felt his cock stiffen. Free of the sweater, Paul tucked his T-shirt back into his jeans and his nipples stood out hard against the white cotton.

'You're so sexy,' John said, startled by his boldness.

'Try not to confuse sex and love,' Paul whispered gently, taking John in his arms. 'Love is God's greatest gift... and His love can take all that self-hatred away.'

'I don't know, Paul,' John said.

'Just know that God loves you... and that I love you,' he offered, his lips almost touching John's cheek.

'I don't know what that means,' John said, pulling away. 'I'm sexually attracted to you... and aroused by you. I know that much. Every time I see you I get this —' He touched his

58

hard cock through his jeans. 'When I'm not with you, I want to be with you… and when I'm with you, I get a hard-on. But I don't want it to feel dirty, Paul. I want us to be together, and I want it to be beautiful.'

Paul bit his tongue hard to stop the responses of his own body to their intimacy. 'Why don't you release all that sexual tension,' he ventured after a moment's doubt. 'We can't talk when you're so —'

'Okay, I'll come back in a few minutes,' John said, almost relieved.

'You don't have to go if you don't want to,' Paul said, his words faltering with caution. 'It's me who's turning you on, so… it might help you if I try to focus the images you have while you're wanking… maybe on the girl you had sex with? You could fantasise about her.'

'No.' John shook his head and moved to the door. 'I couldn't, not with you watching. I'll come back.'

'Okay… please yourself; I just thought it might help.'

Reaching for the door handle John felt a stab of disappointment. 'Well, I suppose it might…'

'You can use my bed if you want to,' Paul said.

This isn't real, John thought, kicking off his shoes. *It's just not real*. He lay on the bed and began to touch himself.

'Picture her in your mind,' Paul began, his voice mellow. 'She's beautiful, and she wants you. Her skin is soft, and warm… and she's got full, heavy breasts. She's wearing a musky perfume that's teasing your senses. She touches you… there… and as she opens each button of your shirt, her fingers trace little patterns on your chest… all the way down. She's unbuckling your belt now, and pulling down the zip… releasing that tension. And her touch is really exciting you.'

59

I love it when you talk like this, Paul – it's really sexy. And here you are, lying with me on your bed and I'm running my hands through your hair. Kissing you. Tasting you.

'She's pulling your jeans down, and little movements of her hands brush your legs. With her finger she traces the shape of your balls... and now she's touching you through your pants... before slipping her hand inside. You've peeled her blouse away and her breasts, the nipples hard and pointed with excitement, brush against your chest. You kiss her neck... her lips —'

Your muscles feel hard through your T-shirt. Your hands caress... and press... and rub. Your tongue traces shapes across my chest. You stroke my cheek. You move your hand down my belly and tease my cock with your finger.

'She's pulling your shirt off, and now she's nibbling your nipples and they get hard between her lips. You're both naked now, your bodies moving together.'

And slowly I take off your clothes and your body is hard against mine.

'She's wet, and ready to take you.'

Your tongue is hard and wet, teasing and provoking... and you taste me.

'Her cunt slides against your cock. She teases you. Your finger, wet from her juices, excites her. And now she wants you inside her... deeper and deeper... but gently... so gently.'

And you're heavy on me now, your cock hard between my thighs... your kisses soft.

'And now she wants you to thrust deeper into her... but slowly, slowly... ever so slowly.'

You're wet and hot, and you've pushed into me, your breath heavy, your kisses so urgent. We climb, hard and fast, until you almost reach – then slowly, slowly... so slowly, until we reach.

And you kiss me... and you're grateful for what we've shared.
And we lie together, exhausted and content.

When the spasms of his orgasm subsided, John watched Paul observing him from the chair. Paul's breathing was shallow, his cheeks were flushed and the bulge in his jeans was obvious. John felt a trickle of semen spill over from the pool in his navel and the viscous rivulet tickled as it flowed down the flat of his stomach.

Paul tossed a box of tissues onto the bed. 'When you've cleaned up, and got dressed, we can talk,' he offered. And sounding embarrassed he said, 'Excuse me... I need to pee.'

John was pulling on his jeans when Paul returned.

'I don't know what to say,' John said, buckling his belt. 'Feels like it ought to be something serious and meaningful.'

'I don't want you to say anything that's not what you want to say.'

'Okay.'

They both looked awkwardly at one another. John reached for his sweater. Paul scooped up the soiled tissues from the bed and put them in the waste bin.

'I love you,' John said.

Paul bit his lip, and sighed. It wasn't what he wanted to hear.

John wrung his hands at Paul's reproach. 'Alright... I'm sorry... I'm really grateful that you're doing so much to help me – and I admire you.'

Paul shrugged and searched the air for words.

'You're so certain about what you believe – about God and things. That's how I want to be, but sometimes I feel I'll only find God through you.'

'Perhaps that's why you like the closeness between us,' Paul said.

'Yes... but then for me it gets all sexual.'

'That closeness can always be there because we're brothers in Jesus Christ,' Paul said, retreating to the safety of evangelical platitudes. 'I want you to listen carefully to what I'm going to say, because I want you to hear what's in my heart.' He took John's hands in his own. 'I'm not rejecting you, but because of who I am, and because of my faith, I can't be sexual with you in the way that you'd like us to be. There's a part of me that's sad about that. But I'm going to kiss you, and my kiss will be as much as I can offer you to seal the friendship between us.'

And the touch of Paul's lips re-ignited John's fire.

'Now it's late, John,' he said, pointing to the alarm clock on the bedside table. 'You'd better go.'

*   *   *

Back in room C2, John lay on his bed in the darkness and only slowly emerged from the bewilderment caused by Paul's kiss. *He's as queer as I am... but he loves God more than he can love me.* And the walls seemed to close in on him, and the blankets weighed heavily and pressed him down. He dressed quickly.

On the landing, an eerie light shone through the glass roof over the stairwell. He leaned over the banister. The stairs descended into blackness and he imagined falling into the void. Seconds later he was out on the street. A cold, salty wind, blowing up from the bay, bathed his face and he felt the terror of falling begin to ease.

At the horribly expensive 24-hour petrol station near the new cinema, he filled the tank. It was almost two-thirty. A little more than a couple of hours later, beyond Caernarfon, he picked up the road signs for Paul's village. The street lighting was poor, and swirling fish and chip wrappings haunted the shadowy streets. John drove around the village, but kept coming back to the same small square, where many a shop front was boarded up and a derelict chapel stood forlorn, its windows broken, a weathered For Sale sign hanging askew. He didn't know where Paul lived, and any notion that he might feel closer to Paul by walking the streets of his village seemed suddenly futile. He turned back for Aberystwyth. It was after eight when he drove down Penglais Hill.

A huddle of university boys in plus fours, woollen knee socks and baggy sweaters stood by the dining hall door, waiting for the breakfast bell. 'I hope you left her looking better than you look yourself this morning,' one lad joshed. 'Phantom fucker,' another jibed. A cheer went up for the phantom fucker.

John forced a smile and waved with bravado, but on the stairs, with pulses of tiredness crashing over him, he started to cry. In his hurry to put distance between himself and the barracking, he bumped into Paul on the first landing.

'Been to kick the bar already?' Paul asked.

John pushed past him without a word.

Despite the traffic of his thoughts he drifted into an exhausted sleep, until the lunch bell roused him. Still dressed in the previous day's clothes, he sniffed his armpits; sweet enough, he thought. He hadn't eaten much in two days and the smell of a thick Theol Coll Saturday soup, drifting up through the stairwell, made him think about his hunger.

On the stairs, Stewart, one of the zoology crowd, asked if he'd go to the football game on Penparcau fields, and the piss-up that followed. John declined the invitation, but walked with him into the dining hall. They sat at a table with two other university boys, Josh and Hugh.

'We're going to see *Blazing Saddles* later on,' Josh said. 'D'you two want to come?'

'I'm a reserve for the game this afternoon,' Stewart said. 'And then we're going to get bevvied.'

'What about you, John?' Josh asked.

'No thanks. I've got a date with my laundry, and then I need to get some sleep.'

'You're okay, are you?' Hugh asked.

John's grunt could have been interpreted in many ways.

'Only you've seemed a bit distant in the last few days, and you look fucking knackered.' Hugh meant well.

'That's because he is *fucking* knackered... isn't that right, John?' Stewart said with a playful nudge. 'Rumour has it that John's getting more than his fair share,' he told Josh and Hugh with an exaggerated wink.

'Why don't you all just mind your own fucking business,' John spat, slamming a chunk of bread into his soup, sending splashes across the table.

'Hey John, we're just teasing,' Stewart called after him as he stormed out.

On the prom, John leaned against the railings and watched the waves crash onto the rocks at Castle Point. He hated the fact that his life had become the focus of too many people's attentions, and an urge to escape surged through him. But something felt like it tore inside him. He watched a wave smash into the high promenade wall and knew that his life only had any meaning through Paul Wynne. *But what am I pulling Paul into?*

In The Angel, opposite the old market hall, he downed three

whiskies in quick succession. He'd never been much of a drinker and he didn't much like the taste of whisky, but from the messed-up lives of people in films, he knew that it was what people drank when they wanted to escape. His mouth burned from the taste of neat Scotch. When 'time' was called, he bought a bottle of cheap sherry over the bar and sat in Castle Gardens. After only a few slugs from the bottle he felt sick, but he forced himself to guzzle it down.

He vomited over some gravestones in St Michael's cemetery. Two prim ladies with purple perms under headscarves were laying flowers.

'You alright, *bach*?' the one in the red scarf asked.

'He's drunk,' the one in the blue scarf sniggered. 'See the bottle he's got?'

'There's disgusting behaviour,' the one in the red scarf protested loudly.

He wanted to die, and he remembered the bottle of aspirin in the cupboard of the washstand in C2. In Laura Place, stumbling against the churchyard wall, he vomited again. He threw the half empty bottle of sherry over his shoulder and heard it smash against a headstone. The purple rinsed ladies came out of the cemetery. 'You should be ashamed of yourself,' the one in the blue scarf called from across the street.

Down one of Theol Coll's warren of corridors he heard the muffled announcement of the football results from someone's radio. The air in room C2 smelled stale. On his knees, John fumbled through the things in the washstand cupboard looking for the pill bottle. *Only six left? Michael, that ponsy fucking bastard, with his headaches!* He slumped to the floor, and the enormity of what he'd been contemplating frightened him so much that he cried.

Some time later, the smell of vomit, splashed on his jeans and shoes, startled him to some degree of self-awareness. He stripped, heaped the stinking clothes into a plastic bag, and wrapped in a towel, he went to the bathroom to soak away the filth and rid himself of his own stench. When his head began to clear, and he realised that he wasn't drunk, the awful reality of his desire to die cut a deep wound of stinging panic. He needed Paul.

John unfolded the events of the last hours.

'And d'you really believe that death is any kind of answer to your troubles, John?' Paul asked, his face betraying anxiety and confusion.

John's eyes glazed over.

'Think about what killing yourself would do to your family... and your friends. And what about me? I'd spend the rest of my life feeling that I'd failed you.'

John shrugged.

Paul took a few deep breaths to compose himself. 'So... you don't think you're drunk then?' he quizzed.

'No.'

'Are you dizzy?' Paul asked, looking unconvinced.

'No.'

'Any blurred or double vision?'

'I'm not drunk, Paul,' John pressed.

He took John's hands, cupped them in his own, and stroked the skin at John's wrists gently with his thumbs. It was a long time before either of them spoke again.

'You're sure you want to die?' Paul asked with palpable heaviness.

'Yes,' John said, looking directly into his eyes. 'Yes. Being a homosexual isn't okay in 1974, and it won't be okay in 1984 or 1994. It'll never be acceptable... and I can't live like this, trying to hide all the time. It would be better for me, and for everyone else —'

Paul still held John's hands. A chasm of silence opened up between them. 'Perhaps you're right,' Paul ventured into the abyss, letting John's hands drop. 'One homosexual less to foul God's creation.'

Taking his dressing gown from the hook behind the door, Paul removed the cord; then he locked the door. With a look of grave concentration, he tied two knots, a couple of inches apart, in the centre of the cord. 'So, perhaps I should kill you,' he said.

John's stare conveyed confusion. Paul stroked John's cheek, and then placed the cord around his neck. 'Let me just get these two knots in the right position; there, one on each side of the windpipe. I saw this in a film; it's a really quick way to kill someone.'

The cord tightened and the knots came together. John sensed Paul's closeness; his breath on his cheek... his lips, kissing him. 'I love you,' Paul whispered through his kisses.

John, astounded by Paul's words, heard his own heart pounding, loud against the quiet of the room. And he heard the sound of his own choking.

'Aren't you afraid that this won't be an end to anything, John?' Paul asked.

Through the din of his heart's pounding... through the pain, the panic and the fear, John's cock went stiff. He choked for Paul to stop and the cord fell to the floor.

Paul's arms folded around John's limp body and he whispered, '"You're a child of the universe, no less than the trees and the stars. You have a right to be here".' Then Paul kissed him. 'You have a right to be here,' he repeated, between kisses, lifting him onto the bed and holding him until his tears subsided. 'It's alright,' he said when John seemed calm.

'No,' John whimpered. 'I'm frightened... and confused. Everything about you turns me on.'

Paul wondered if John could feel just how aroused he'd also become by their intimacy, and he wanted to explain the pledge he'd made to Jesus, but the words wouldn't come. They held one another for a long time. In John's head, the whisperings of a silent voice spoke words that left him wanting more than Paul was willing to give. *Unless I try harder.*

John eased his hand from beneath Paul's thigh and began to touch himself. Paul made no gesture of discomfort. Freeing his other hand, he unbuckled his belt, unfastened his jeans, and wriggled free of them. Paul ran his fingers through John's hair. John touched himself again. Paul pulled himself closer into John's warmth.

'Take your clothes off,' John whispered. 'Please, let me love you.'

'I can't,' Paul said. 'I made a promise.'

'But you want to.'

'Yes... but —'

John took Paul's hand and closed it around him. Without flinching, Paul stroked and fondled. John was taken aback by the vigour of his grip and he felt for Paul's cock, swollen inside his jeans.

'No,' Paul whispered, pulling away, but still working his hand. 'You know that I can't. Just lie back and enjoy what I can give you.'

Paul took a tissue and wiped John's semen from his hand. 'I'm sorry,' he said, looking away. 'That shouldn't have happened.'

He sighed heavily, aware that Dali's Jesus was looking at him. 'I thought it would help you,' he said, searching for words. 'Maybe... it helped to save your life; perhaps that's justification enough. But it shouldn't have happened. I'm sorry.'

So now I've pulled you into all of my shit.

*   *   *

Sunday morning brought rain from a sky heavy with fury. John sensed it was God's way of showing disapproval. An hour would pass before the breakfast bell. For a while he lay in bed and watched the inky cloud islands pass the window. His head felt thick from too little sleep. *What did I make Paul do?*

Suddenly weary of the voices of indictment that had slashed at him through the night, he thought about chapel; he'd agreed to go with Paul. He sloped to the bathroom. There he soaped and sponged himself for a long time to remove the filth, cleansing and purifying, so that he'd be worthy. Back in C2, he searched the drawers for clean underwear and found a fresh shirt hanging at the back of the wardrobe. He had to rub a stain off his only tie; everything had to be clean, to compensate. Buttoning up his waistcoat, he wondered if the fine woollen fabric and elegant cut of his new suit would fool anyone into thinking he was decent.

Most of the theologs were away early, travelling to fill a pulpit, and few of the university boys bothered to get up for breakfast. Just one table was set. Paul sat with Euros, another theolog. John acknowledged them both, and seated himself next to Paul. Through the large bay windows, banks of leaden clouds lurched and rumbled and rain lashed against the glass, muting their conversation. A flash of lightning lit up the comparative

69

gloom. *God's pretty angry with us, Paul*. A rumble of thunder confirmed it.

'Are you coming with us to Peniel, Euros?' John asked.

'No,' he said with a gleaming, crooked smile. 'Alfred Place this morning; I'm up for a bit of hellfire and damnation with the evangelicals.'

They all laughed.

'But I'm preaching this afternoon and I still haven't finished my sermon, so I'm out of here in five minutes.'

After he'd left them, John and Paul continued their breakfast in silence.

John drove through the drenched, deserted streets. Paul sat, stiff and silent beside him, the tension between them tangible. Turning into Queen's Road, John felt his insides tighten. 'I'm not sure about this...' he began.

'God's reaching out to you, John,' Paul offered. 'And there's nothing you can do that'll put you outside His love.'

He parked as close as he could to the chapel. Already the faithful were gathering. Umbrellas blew inside out and Sunday dignity gave way to a dash through the downpour.

John stood for the hymns and bowed for the prayers. He tried to look thoughtful during the sermon, and suitably devout, but streams of self-injuring thoughts strafed his mind until the final 'Amen' was spoken.

'Sit for a while longer,' Paul said, gripping John's arm as he stood up to leave. 'We'll go through to the vestry when the crowd's gone. I want you to meet Rhys and Elen Morgan. They're lovely... and there's a good chance we'll get supper after tonight's service.'

John wanted to protest, but he didn't want to make a scene

and have people look at him, so he sat and waited. Paul spoke to lots of people. At one point he went up the aisle to a woman dressed in black; he cupped his hand around her elbow and their talking looked solemn. The organist practised a new piece and one of the elders took down the board displaying the hymn numbers. After much shuffling, he replaced the board with that evening's selection. A woman in a showy, Sunday-best hat picked at the ornate flower arrangement. And then Paul was back at his side. 'Come on through to the back.'

Rhys Morgan shook John's hand.

That's the hand I wank with.

'I've seen you here a few times,' Rhys said with a kindly smile. 'I hope that means you've found a welcome here, and you'll keep coming back to us.' He was hard to age, John thought. The thick, greying hair suggested late fifties, but the clerical collar looked too big and the skin around his neck was pallid and wrinkled. 'And you're from Barmouth? Wasn't Enoch Lloyd your minister?'

'Enoch Lloyd? He's been retired a good few years,' John said, taken by the blueness of the minister's eyes, which were bright and alive – and younger than the rest of him.

'Now, there was a preacher who got into a *hwyl*,' Rhys said with fondness. 'But his theology was a bit thin.'

John laughed benignly, but made no comment; he wasn't sure how solid a man's theology needed to be.

'And this is Elen, my wife,' Rhys said, introducing the woman in a tweed suit who'd walked across the vestry to join them.

'I'm John Idris Jones,' he said, shaking her hand.

With that, Rhys Morgan was approached by one of the elders, who clearly wanted some serious talk. He excused himself.

'And what do I call you?' Elen Morgan asked, her eyes dancing. 'John Idris or John?' She looked younger than her husband, slight and still slim, her auburn hair embroidered with silver threads. The autumn colours of her tweed were warm, but her smile was warmer, her face friendly and open.

'The Idris is there to distinguish me from all the other John Joneses,' he said, instantly easy with her. 'It's usually John to my face, and John Idris if you're talking about me.'

'And how have you settled in Aberystwyth, John?'

'It's better than I expected.'

'Oh?' she offered, immediately interested in him because he hadn't given the standard reply to the standard question put to all freshers.

'I wanted to go to Liverpool, but I messed up.'

'Well,' she said, her eyes glinting. 'The unexpected can sometimes send us off on a road we never imagined we'd travel, but it doesn't mean that the journey's any less worthwhile.'

John sensed she was speaking from the experience of excursions along many unforeseen byways. 'I'd rather be in Aberystwyth than anywhere else just now,' he said.

Paul came to them, all smiles.

'So you two know one another,' Elen Morgan said. 'Why don't you both come and have supper with us after the service tonight?'

'That would be great, Mrs Morgan,' Paul said, giving John a secretive wink that said 'what did I tell you?'

The sun tried its best to push through the clouds as they drove back to Theol Coll.

*   *   *

72

Since his arrival in Aber, John hadn't re-established the routine of Sunday afternoon study. He wasn't enthusiastic about any of his courses; botany and zoology lectures largely covered familiar ground, topics that he'd done at A-level, and the lab work was tedious, intended, he suspected, to bring students from diverse backgrounds up to scratch. Indeed, he'd felt little pressure to put in the hours, and despite skipping a few lectures, he didn't feel he'd fallen behind. But he yearned for a regular work schedule that might rekindle his academic curiosity, and he wondered, too, whether steeping himself in academia might help to close all those hidden doors so recently thrown open by his infatuation with Paul. He reached for the expensive biochemistry textbook, bought in a flush of anticipation and excitement during the first days of term, but then, reflecting on the dull and uninspiring lectures, he put the book back on the shelf. He'd forgo another Sunday and catch up on lost sleep.

Michael's return with suitcases full of clean laundry woke him up. It was just after two-thirty and he'd only been in bed about an hour. They exchanged few words, and John decided not to say anything about the aspirins. He dressed quickly, and though he wasn't clear about his intentions, he left C2 and skipped down the stairs. For a while he scanned the notice boards on the walls around the stairwell. Amidst the jumble of announcements, one drew his attention: *The Church and the Permissive Society: Join the Sunday Library Group for this timely discussion on sexual morality, this Sunday at 3.00 p.m. in Theol Coll Library. Tea and biscuits free.* In small print at the foot of the notice he read, *The Sunday Library Group is a fortnightly open meeting run by the Theol Coll Evangelical Alliance.*

Without too much consideration, he walked into the library.

Two Jesus freaks were shifting the study tables to the book-lined walls. 'Is this where the discussion is happening?' John asked.

'Yes, but you're a bit early. Would you mind helping with the chairs?'

Adam, who solicited his help, was older than most of the students studying for the ministry. He'd worked for years as a gas fitter before 'being saved'. Simon, the other student, was a second year physicist who'd 'found the Lord Jesus Christ and invited him into my heart'. Before they'd finished putting twenty chairs into a circle, others began to arrive and by three o'clock all the chairs were taken. Looking around the group, John realised that they weren't all from Theol Coll, and Simon, who sat next to him, said that the discussions of the Sunday Library Group were always announced at the Evangelical Church in Alfred Place.

Adam, who seemed to be in charge, welcomed 'the visiting brethren' to the meeting and invoked everyone to prayer. 'Lord Jesus,' he began, his eyes closed, his hands reaching out in front of him with palms wide open as if he expected someone to give him something. 'We *just* want to thank you for bringing us safely to this important meeting this afternoon... and we *just* ask that you guide our thoughts, Lord Jesus. *Just* guide us to your truth, Lord, through your holy word. We *just* ask that you will reveal to us, through your holy scriptures, the right place for sexual relations in our lives. And Lord Jesus, we *just* pray that all those people who are indulging in free love will repent of their sin and turn to you for forgiveness. Lord Jesus, we praise you; we *just* praise you and thank you for coming into our hearts. Lord Jesus, we praise you... Lord Jesus, we praise you...' And others joined in, repeating over and over 'Lord Jesus, we praise you' until Adam said a final 'Amen.'

After a few minutes' silence, when all of the people in the circle except John kept their heads bowed, Adam, holding a Bible in each hand, spoke again. 'I'm going to read a selection of texts from these holy scriptures, which will help us focus our minds for this discussion about sexual morality in today's permissive society. I'll be reading from first Corinthians, from Hebrews and Romans, and from one Timothy. As you'll hear, each reading underlines God's law about sexual relations between men and women within marriage. So, I'm starting to read from first Corinthians, chapter six, beginning at verse nine.'

And he read from the 'thou' and 'thy' version of King James: 'Know ye not that the unrighteous shall not inherit the kingdom of God? Be not deceived: neither fornicators, nor idolaters, nor adulterers, nor effeminate, nor abusers of themselves with mankind, nor thieves, nor...'

The list went on, but John stopped listening. He thought about the 'effeminate' and the 'abusers of themselves with mankind' and wondered who they might be in less archaic language.

Adam's voice broke into his thoughts. 'I'll read the same text from a more modern translation,' he said, opening his copy of the New English Bible. 'Starting at verse nine again. "Surely you know that the unjust will never come into the possession of the Kingdom of God. Make no mistake: no fornicator or idolater, none who are guilty either of adultery or of homosexual perversion, no thieves..."'

John's thoughts lingered uncomfortably on what he'd heard. *So I can't 'possess the kingdom of God'!*

Adam read other texts, his voice weaving with John's thoughts. From Hebrews, there was something about marriage being honourable, and that all people should keep to their marriage bonds. Adam coupled it with a verse from Corinthians: 'the head of every man is Christ and the head of the woman is the man'. From Romans, there was a judgement against 'shameful passions', and a reference to 'men, in their turn, giving up natural relations with women' and 'men who burned with lust for other men'. John knew that feeling all too well. The text went on about men who 'behave indecently with males, and are paid in their own persons the fitting wage of such perversion'.

Discussion wasn't slow to kindle. A boy, whose face was acne scarred, talked about the contraceptive pill being misused by unmarried women. He wanted its availability limited to married couples. Then a fat girl protested that the recent Abortion Act allowed the killing of babies. Another girl, who looked sallow and sad, said that being able to choose the pill, and having such easy access to abortion, made women promiscuous. Simon wanted to talk about legislation, passed in the sixties, that had contributed to the permissiveness of their times; he was especially scornful of the act that decriminalised homosexual acts. 'It comes to something when the law of the land sends out a message that sexual perversion is acceptable,' Simon said in an anguished voice. 'But God's law isn't so wishy-washy.'

Adam kept interrupting the succession of contributions, always seeking to remind the group that as Christians, it was their duty to love the sinner, but condemn their sin. No one really entered into real debate; lots of statements were made, which seemed superficially consistent with the biblical texts, but none were challenged, and certainly no one questioned the content of the texts themselves. John knew, from the few sermons that had engaged him, that the historical context of a

Bible passage, and sometimes even the translation from Hebrew and Greek, could have a bearing on its contemporary understanding.

John's mind began to race with two jostling ideas; being a homosexual, as much as he rejected it for himself, didn't feel like something he'd ever chosen. It was 'deeper inside' than a choice. And yet, the Sunday Library Group was certain that God saw homosexuals, along with adulterers, as a perversion of His purpose. *But people can choose not to commit adultery... they only became adulterers by their action. I can't choose not to be a homosexual... even if I could choose to be celibate, I'd still be one.* He was judged, and condemned, not on the basis of his behaviour and actions, but on the basis of who he was.

John had no words to describe the 'deeper inside' of himself, and the Sunday Library Group's position, that the only moral sexual behaviour was heterosexual sex within marriage, wasn't a stance he felt he could counter alone. His silence, seemingly the wisest option, felt like a betrayal of himself.

They drank tea and ate biscuits. The sad, sallow girl who'd gone on about abortions and the pill stood next to him. 'You didn't say anything,' she said, in a tone that was more judgemental than a simple observation deserved to be.

'I didn't feel I had anything constructive to add,' John said.

For a moment she looked perplexed. 'When were you saved?' she asked.

From similar conversations he'd heard around Theol Coll, he knew she was expecting a date and a time. He thought about telling her to 'fuck off' but she looked too fragile for such language.

'Please excuse me,' he offered. 'I need to go. I have some work to do.'

It was almost five o'clock. In half an hour, he'd meet Paul and they'd go to the evening service at Peniel. Part of him looked forward to supper with the Morgans; Elen Morgan had seemed so genial. But another part of his brain told him he'd soil their lives too. To escape the collision of thoughts he walked out onto the pier and watched a boy play a pinball machine. Elton John sang out from the jukebox... *'Don't let the sun go down on me.'* But night was already falling.

*   *   *

'About last night,' Paul said, as they pulled away from the curb. 'I don't want you to feel bad about it. I think I said something about being sorry... and that it shouldn't have happened.'

They were both pensive.

'I've been thinking about it all day. It was unkind of me to say that I did it because I felt I should – to help you. But —' He bit his lip and pushed back his hair.

'You don't have to —' John put into his disquiet.

'I do,' Paul interrupted. 'I did what I did. I wanted to share with you like that, so I shouldn't have made it seem as though I was so reluctant. I wanted to, but... the thing is —'

'Are you saying you want us to be lovers?' John asked.

'You're not stupid, John. It must be pretty clear that I fancy you rotten. But it's not right for me.'

He reached out and touched John's thigh. 'But then, when I thought you were going to kill yourself —'

'Fucking hell,' John spat. 'Sounds like we're both totally screwed up.'

'I did what I believed was the right thing to do, and I take responsibility for that, even if it turns out to be a mistake.'

In the silence that fell between them, Paul sensed the relief from being able to say what he'd needed to say. John was just more bewildered.

On a Sunday evening the students sat on Peniel's balcony. John thought it daft that this tradition was upheld; there were no more than twenty of them up there, where 300 could have sat, and the floor of the Victorian barn-of-a-chapel was half empty. The organist played something familiar. John used the music to calm himself after Paul's confession. Breathing deeply with the rhythm of the melody, he asked God for help, and in the asking, he realised that he had to reject the vengeful God of the Sunday Library Group if he was going to have any hope of coming through the crisis that was upon him.

Rhys Morgan gave the call to worship, wrenching John from his thoughts. Seeing the white lace cloth covering the vessels on the table at the foot of the pulpit, John realised that the service would include Holy Communion. The muscles in his belly tied themselves in knots and he broke into a sweat. Some of Adam's readings came back to him: 'The unjust will never come into the possession of the Kingdom of God, make no mistake, none who are guilty either of adultery or of homosexual perversion.'

No... no.

The congregation began to sing the first hymn. With such a scant scattering up in the balcony he felt exposed. Pulling himself together, he joined in the standing and sitting, the hymn singing and the bowing of heads, but throughout the service Adam kept reminding him of his 'homosexual perversion'.

Rhys Morgan finished his sermon and began the communion liturgy. 'The Bread which we break, is it not the communion of

79

the Body of Christ? We who are many are one Bread, one Body, for we are all partakers of the one Bread.'

John knew that he wouldn't be able to take the bread. Eating it would make him a part of them... one bread, one body. Adam's readings flooded back, and he knew he had no right to be there. He was a perversion of God's purpose, and had no right to be alive. When the elder tendered the neatly cubed bread on a silver platter John rejected the offer. Paul, sensing the conflict, placed an arm around his shoulder.

The service ended.

A sweep of polished oak stairs led from the balcony and opened into a narrow porch. Because of the rain, a small crowd had gathered to chat and await their rides. Paul was well known in the Peniel community and many people acknowledged him. John was introduced to a mathematics professor, a surgeon from the hospital and the headteacher of a local school. So many of the congregation seemed to be significant people in the local community.

'You must come to dinner one evening with Paul,' said the wife of the professor of Welsh history.

Amongst Aberystwyth's elite, John's sense of depravity deepened.

Elen Morgan emerged from the sea of faces. 'You're alright, are you?' she asked, taking John by the arm and leading him away from the departing congregation. 'You look a bit flushed.'

'I'm fine, Mrs Morgan,' he heard himself say, though he wasn't at all. 'I just feel a bit hot, but I'm okay.'

'Well... if you're sure,' she said, her gaze questioning.

'I was —' but he changed his mind. 'I lost Paul in the crowd and I was wondering whether to go home, or knock on your door, or —'

'Well, you can't go without your supper,' she said, pointing the way. 'I think Paul's already gone in with Rhys.'

In the next minutes, John's mood swung. He liked her.

'If we go in quietly, we'll probably find them discussing the sermon,' Elen Morgan said as she shook her umbrella by the back door of the manse, a grand Victorian villa siding onto the chapel.

In the hall they could hear voices. Paul was making an abstract theological point, which seemed to flow from the main thesis of Rhys Morgan's sermon.

'That all sounds very deep,' she said after a moment's eavesdropping. 'When they get together they seem to find the most theoretical theological points to debate. Do you like to discuss theology, John?'

'Well… I've never really given theological things much thought, and I certainly don't feel I've got much of a contribution to make when trained theologians are at it.'

'But we've all got our own insights on things, however humble… even if we can't express them in theological language.' She seemed to be giving him permission to relax, and not feel cowed by the scholarly talk.

'Perhaps you're right,' he said, his smile boyish. 'But I'd need to spend a bit more time reflecting on things spiritual, instead of things scientific —

'You're a scientist then; I was about to ask. Physics?'

'No. Biological sciences.'

'How fascinating,' she said, her eyes gleaming. 'You can join them in the lounge,' she offered with the gesture of her hand. 'Or perhaps you'll come through to the kitchen with me?'

'I don't mind working for my supper.'

In his broad smile she thought she detected a glimpse of a

81

freer spirit beneath his sombre, even grave exterior. 'Come on then,' she said, with a girlish toss of her head. 'If you come here often enough you'll soon realise that there isn't much ceremony here.'

They turned into a cosy room, glowing with homeliness, where an old oak table was already set for supper. The willow-plated Welsh dresser was a jumble of old envelopes and family photographs, the odd pile of books and lots of post-cards. Two armchairs, one each side of the hearth, looked deeply comfortable with crocheted cushions. Elen Morgan put her hymnbook down on the dresser and reached for the apron that hung over the back of one of the dining chairs. 'We tend not to use the dining room, it's too big, and so expensive to keep warm,' she said, surveying the table. 'This is a lovely old house, but it's so impractical in this day and age.' She reached four linen napkins from a drawer in the dresser and placed them on the table. 'Now then, let's think about supper. Come into the kitchen with me and I'll hand you things to put on the table.'

'It's very kind of you to invite us,' John said, following her through to the adjoining room. 'One of the things I've missed since coming away is being in a home. Theol Coll's a bit like what I imagine a boarding school to be... and I'm sharing a room, which isn't easy.'

'The first few weeks away from home are hard for most people,' she said, rising from the fridge with a plate of cold cuts and a bowl of coleslaw. 'It's a great adventure, and you have the excitement of meeting new people and making new friends, but everyone finds it hard.'

He took the salad and cold meats from her and carried them to the table. When he walked back into the kitchen she caught his gaze and held his eye.

'But you are alright, John, aren't you?'

He heard himself say 'yes' for a second time in answer to her concern, and this time he wondered how much he might be able to tell her. 'Tell me,' he said, recalling her earlier question, and wanting to change the course of their talking. 'Do you like discussing theology?'

'Well, I suppose it goes with the territory,' she quipped. 'But I'm not your typical minister's wife.'

'No,' John ventured with a grin. 'I noticed you weren't wearing a hat.'

She laughed. 'That was just one of many battles, John *bach*. I speak my mind and sometimes, some people don't think that's appropriate. I do like talking theology, and because I have a brain I sometimes say things that members of the congregation find shocking... well, shocking for a minister's wife I mean!'

'And what about the kind of thing that Paul and Mr Morgan were just discussing?'

'Oh, I do find some of the really abstract arguments a bit difficult. I suppose that's because I find them hard to relate to my experience of God in everyday life. I like to think that I'm very down-to-earth.'

'That makes me feel a bit better. I was anxious I might be completely out of my depth tonight.'

'I can assure you the ability to debate theological arguments isn't a qualification for supper,' she said, laughing – but not mocking him. 'And I certainly hope it's not a qualification for getting into heaven, otherwise I might be in trouble.' She laughed again, and winked at him. 'Theological debate is alright in its place, but I don't think God is too concerned about how clever and erudite we make our arguments. What's most important, if we're open enough to it, is that God finds us where we are.'

'You really believe that, do you?' he asked, recalling the ruthless God of the Sunday Library Group.

'Why? Do you find that difficult?' she said, wondering if John was more conservative than she'd supposed, and whether she'd spoken unwisely.

'It's not that I find it difficult... it's just a way of thinking about God that I've never considered.' He rubbed his chin self-consciously, and tried to weigh up what he could say.

'Have I said something that seems blasphemous to you?' Elen Morgan asked.

'No, not at all. I'm just not really sure what I think. Some of the students at Theol Coll are a bit... rigid. Their God seems to like people who've been saved at a certain time of day on a particular day of the week.' He wondered whether to tell her about the meeting in the library, but wasn't sure enough of her yet. 'I don't really see their kind of God "finding me where I am".'

'Have you been feeling pressured by some of the evangelicals?'

'Well, they do come over as being so certain about everything, and the world they live in doesn't seem to have any shades of grey; it's either this way or that way,' he said, flicking fingers on each hand in turn.

'Well, you've touched a raw nerve there,' she said, with a look of concentrated concern. 'This fundamentalist element seems to be getting stronger within the denomination. Many of our young people, coming through for the ministry, are of that ilk; it's a real worry. We've seen it in a number of candidates in the last years, and... well, they only ever come to Peniel once or twice; Rhys isn't *scriptural* enough for them! It's disturbing that they're so literal in their interpretations, and so selective in the bits of the Bible they choose to throw at you – chapter and verse.'

She paused to pour boiling water into the teapot.

'And they're so certain about everything,' she said, almost spitting out the word *certain*. 'I'm in my fifties, John, and if my life experience has brought me any certainty, then it's the knowledge that there are very few certainties.'

'So Mr Morgan isn't —' John didn't know how to finish his question.

'Rhys isn't what, *bach*, a fundamentalist?'

'Well —' John shrugged, uncertain of religious language.

'He's not likely to ask you if you've been *saved* or *if you've invited Jesus Christ into your heart*. Is that what's been happening to you at Theol Coll?'

'No, I haven't been pressured exactly, but I am puzzled.'

'Well, John, Rhys and I are here if you ever feel you want to talk.'

'Yes. Thank you.'

She smiled, and then, taking the teapot through, she looked over the table. 'Now, what else do we need here? I think that's everything. Will you go'n ask Paul and Rhys to come to the table please?'

They ate a generous supper and talked a lot; mostly about things John wasn't sure he knew very much about, which wasn't rudeness on the Morgans' part but his own lack of experience. The dinner table talk in Barmouth had rarely gone beyond what they'd done that day, the spiralling price of food and local news – never gossip – which his mam had heard from the other women she worked with in the school canteen.

Paul seemed to have something to say about all the topics they touched on, but it was Rhys Morgan's contributions that John liked; considered, well reasoned and clearly stated, but not dogmatic in any way.

It was past ten when John offered to wash up. Paul looked astonished when Elen Morgan accepted the offer and showed them both into the kitchen. It was almost eleven when they left.

'Are you alright,' Paul asked as they drove off.

'Yes, I had a really good evening. I like them, and Mrs Morgan is special.'

'I was thinking about earlier on; the communion service. You were upset.'

'Let's not talk about that. It's stopped raining. What about a quick walk; we could kick the bar?'

'It's late. Let's go back to Theol Coll.'

John turned onto the prom. The pier, illuminated with multi-coloured lights, marked their destination at the end of the bay's long sweep. At a distance, Theol Coll, basking in the glow of the pier's garish lights, looked less dingy, but as they approached, the shabbiness shone through. John sensed the sluice gates opening inside him.

'I need you to hold me,' John whispered as they reached C floor.

Paul's embrace couldn't fend off the onslaught by Adam and the Sunday Library Group. Their arguments were so scholarly, and spoken in such eloquent theological language. John tried to join in the debate; Elen Morgan's words, 'God finds us where we are,' were ridiculed and torn to shreds by texts, quoted chapter and verse. John pleaded with them to hear what was 'deeper inside' – and they recognised him as a homosexual. Adam took the cord of Paul's dressing gown and tied two new knots in it. He wound the cord around John's neck and then the members of the Sunday Library

Group made up two teams. In their game of tug-of-war, John was left hanging.

*   *   *

Paul hadn't slept much, and for more than an hour he'd needed to pee. Watching as the fingers of the clock approached six, he flipped the switch so the alarm wouldn't sound. John was asleep, and looked peaceful, despite tossing and turning for most of the night. It seemed a shame to rouse him now, but he switched on the light. 'You'd better get downstairs before this place starts to wake up,' he whispered after nudging John gently with his elbow.

'My head's stuffed with cotton wool,' John said after a few disorientated moments, his eyes, sunk in pools of blue-black ink, blinking against the light.

'Go and stand under a cold shower for ten minutes, that'll get you going.'

John pulled himself from Paul's bed and dressed. 'I'll see you later,' he said, self-consciously kissing Paul before letting himself out.

First thing in the morning, for long minutes, only cold water flowed from the hot taps in Theol Coll. John's skin goose-pimpled, but the fuzziness in his head began to clear, allowing fragments from the previous night to prick like shards. To keep the memories at bay, he concentrated on the day before him; at ten o'clock, his tutorial group would join another for an introductory seminar on the electron microscope, and after lunch he had a three-hour practical session in the botany lab.

Dressing in an old Aran sweater and a pair of faded denims, John wondered again if he ought to make time to do some laundry. Michael emerged from beneath his blankets; for a second, John thought what a lucky bastard Mike was that his mam still washed and ironed his clothes.

'How was your weekend, Michael?' John asked.

'It was good, thanks.' Michael stretched and yawned, got himself out of bed, and then pushed his hand into his pyjama-bottoms and scratched himself. 'What's this I'm hearing about you then?' he asked, smiling.

'About me?' John quizzed coyly. 'What have you heard?'

'That you're shagging some piece.'

'It's all lies, Michael,' John said with a wink, hoping that his roommate would let it drop. He didn't want anything to spoil the good mood that seemed to have settled over him in the freezing shower.

'So who is she?' Michael persisted, now scratching the thatch of hair in his armpit.

'You're like a terrier with a rabbit between its teeth,' John joshed, hoping he'd shut him.

'Everyone's talking about you, coming in before breakfast on Saturday morning looking —'

'God! Topic of conversation then, am I?' John spat. 'Fuck you.'

Out on the landing, John breathed deeply to reclaim his good mood. In the huddle outside the dining room, Stewart pushed alongside him. 'Are we with your group for the microscopy seminar today?'

'At ten o'clock?' John asked.

'That's the one. Maybe we could work together if they pair us off?'

'That's fine with me.'

They sat together at the table in the bay window. Stewart

poured milk on his cornflakes and wondered whether to say anything about Saturday lunchtime – when John had stormed out. Then, thinking John looked knackered he asked, 'Are you okay?'

'Why's everyone so concerned about my welfare?' It came out pricklier than John had intended.

'You do look pretty shagged-out, John,' he said, instantly regretting his choice of words.

'I'm okay, Stew... really.'

'Tell me to piss off if you like, but —'

'I've had some sleepless nights... that's all,' John interrupted. He took a few deep breaths and tried to keep his temper. 'I haven't settled as well as I thought I might... and sharing with Michael isn't easy.'

'I can imagine,' Stewart said with a grimace. 'If it helps, you're not the only one who's finding it hard to settle.'

Stewart ate his cornflakes and John scraped butter onto a piece of toast.

'The JFTs haven't been getting to you then?' Stewart asked.

John felt the flush of blood to his face. 'Fuck off, Stewart!'

John drove out of Aberystwyth over Trefechan Bridge and followed the coast south. The road edged high cliffs, and there seemed to be no access to any beaches where he might find some solitude. After falling to sea level, instead of cliffs and rocks, there were sandy strands beyond sheep grazed fields. He took a right turn into a lane and hoped it would lead to the shore. After only a few minutes the lane became a track, before opening to a small hollow and ending abruptly. Through squat clumps of sea lavender and purslane, a well-trodden path led through the dunes.

One end of the beach was rocky. For a while, he sat and watched the patterns of the tentacles of a couple of anemones in a rock pool... and then he was only aware of the cries of seabirds, and the sound of the waves as they rose and folded onto the beach.

Some time later, the wind picked up and drove the dry, sugary sand from above the seaweed strewn tide line into the air. It blew into his face, like pin pricks against his cheeks. He was cold and lonely.

He walked down the beach, the wind hard against him. The waves were wilder now, whipped by the approaching storm. He noticed a dead cormorant, oily and tangled in seaweed. *What does it feel like to drown? What must it be like to gasp for air, and to have the gasp quenched with brine? What's it like to feel your lungs fill with water – and to die?*

At the water's edge, already wet from the blown spume of the crashing waves, he thought how much better the world would be without him. With water up to his knees, he willed himself to fall between the folds of the waves.

Another cormorant. A wave threw it onto the beach. Its head was recognisable, but its wings and feet were hidden in a thick tar ball. On the sand it was unable to move, but it squawked. It was the squawking that distracted John, pulling him back. Its beak reached up in a defensive motion. John watched the head make jerking movements at the end of its long neck, fascinated, and horrified at the same time. The stare from its vivid green eyes was pleading and he felt an obligation that was beyond question to do something to save its life.

When he approached, the agile neck and dipping head sought to warn him off. He thought for a few moments, about a strategy that would enable him to carry the bird in such a way that he was protected from its large, pointed beak and ensure that he didn't get black, sticky tar all over him. He remembered the old blanket that his mother had suggested he carry in the boot of the car 'in case you break down one night in that old banger'. He ran up the beach and followed the short path back to where he'd parked. The boot was in chaos, but under his biochemistry lab notebook and white coat, he found the blanket.

After securing the bird he slung the load over his shoulder; it was heavier than he'd expected. Walking up the beach, he felt its head and neck pushing against his back and hoped that its head wouldn't find its way out of the blanket. Clearing some space in the boot, he wondered where the nearest RSPB might be. He drove back to Aberystwyth and sought advice at the police station.

The afternoon sun was already falling over the end of the pier. Simon and Garfunkel were singing from the jukebox of the amusement arcade in the basement of the King's Hall – *'Hello darkness, my old friend.'* Leaning against the prom railing watching the heavy waves crash onto the pebble beach, he wished he could escape the echoes of the voices from the Sunday Library Group that had become a chorus in his head. Even Saint Paul had a complete solo section with a repeated stanza: *'the unjust will never come into the possession of the Kingdom of God… make no mistake… none who are guilty of homosexual perversion.'*

Paul broke through the mantra. In his mind's eye, John saw him smile and heard him whisper reassuringly, 'Remember this… I'll always be with you in spirit… I'll always be with you.'

And he wanted Paul to make everything alright.

*　　*　　*

John told Paul about the allure of the waves, and how the oily cormorant had enticed him away. They lay together for a long time. John's first tentative kiss was returned, and the touches Paul offered as comfort became the caresses of a lover. There was a brutal urgency in their fumblings; tugging at each other's clothes. John gorged himself on Paul's flavours, the saliva sweet with apple, the salty musk of sweat, a warm sea of semen, vital and alive. Their first sex was sudden – even savage. Stillness followed, and John sensed a peace that was rare. *He's a part of me now. He's inside me... giving me life.*

Sitting with his back against the headboard, Paul's head resting against his thigh, John pored over his lover's nakedness and surveyed the contours that his tongue had explored. He noticed the neat appendix scar, the line of hairs down from his navel, the skin of his shrunken cock, darker than the skin of his flat belly. 'You're beautiful,' he whispered.

'What did you do to me?' Paul said sleepily, through the veil of hair that had fallen across his face.

'Just a few of the tricks I picked up on the way.'

'Show me some more,' Paul said, pulling John to him.

They lay awake. Paul asked God to forgive him. John wrestled with Paul's question: 'What did you do to me?' *Didn't I trick you into loving me?*

*   *   *

The last weeks of term were a kind of bedlam. They were together whenever they could be – mostly in bed. When they were apart, Paul prayed a lot and John became all of those strangers he feared. The IRA continued their bombings; in

Birmingham's Mulberry Bush, and The Tavern in the Town, their bombs killed seventeen and injured more than 100 people. In the wider world, Ford and Brezhnev reached broad agreement on limiting strategic nuclear weapons, Greece decided to abolish its monarchy, and Ian Smith agreed an immediate ceasefire with the black nationalists in Rhodesia. Helen Morgan, the first Miss Wales to become Miss World, had to abdicate her throne amid rumours that she was an unmarried mother, and much speculation that she'd be named in a divorce case. The exams came. There were Christmas decorations in the shops... and carol services.

Once, on a weekday afternoon, John went to the Morgans' house. Elen offered him tea and cake, and he swallowed back what he wanted to tell her... because he'd promised Paul it was their secret.

On the last day of term, after they'd climbed to the peak of pleasure, Paul said that it had to end.

Early September

On his way into Liverpool to meet his brother Billy, John reflected on Russell Talbert's need to trawl his history for people who might care for him. 'Thank God I've got Klaus,' John thought. At a corner table in Keith's Wine Bar on Lark Lane, a good twenty minutes too early, John sipped iced water and remembered a lunch with Klaus when they were twenty years younger.

Klaus Hensel was an almost bald twenty-something, who worked as a language assistant at a school in Woolton. What little hair he had was cut on a number-one by the old-fashioned barber on Lark Lane who still used a cut-throat razor to shave the nape, and then puffed the shaved bits with clouds of talc. Klaus lived in a bleak bedsit off Sefton Park, on a street of partly derelict Victorian villas. The bathroom he shared with five others stank like the stairway down to Scarlett's on the days of a high tide. He'd taken to swimming every day at the university pool, just so that he could have a hot shower in a relatively clean space. His body was lean and toned from all those lengths. A luxurious beard made up for what he'd lost on top, and through this undergrowth his often-rosy cheeks puffed. His eyes were considerate; a certain look from Klaus Hensel made you feel that he'd care for you. Idiomatic, and often incorrect, use of English was endearing, and within minutes of being introduced to new people he called them 'luv' in a fondly mocking, heavily accented attempt at Scouse.

The first time they met, in Scarlett's Bar, John found him physically attractive. Klaus was with a group of language assistants that evening, two chic French women and a swarthy Catalan from Barcelona, so their introduction had been fleeting. John got the sense that Klaus and the Catalan boy had something going on, and though they caught one another's gaze more than once, John had left the bar alone and hadn't given a passing thought to the handsome German.

About a week later, after an unsuccessful struggle with a sermon on a text that invited the affliction of the comforted when comfort of those afflicted by the ravages of age was called for, John took a walk around Sefton Park. The fresh air and the spring flowers failed to inspire him, so he turned into Keith's Wine Bar and found himself standing in the queue at the counter next to Klaus.

Over lunch they shared bits of their stories. Later in the afternoon, after coffee and cake, John asked about the Catalan.

'Ramon is very good looking and very nice, but he doesn't want to make sex with me. He has a boyfriend in Barcelona.'

As Keith's began to fill up with the early evening crowd, John and Klaus drank some wine. They both began to recognise the signs that they were falling in love.

'Are you John Jones?' a Scally waiter asked, breaking into John's thoughts.

'Yes.'

'There's been a pile-up on the M62 so your brother can't leave the hospital. He said he'd phone you later.'

'Thanks,' John said, thinking it was time he got a mobile phone. 'I'll just have some soup and bread then, please.'

*   *   *

On Thursday John drove to Aberystwyth to see Elen Morgan. The new student village, immediately on the right, always surprised him; little boxes on a hillside, cluttering the woodland and pasture of his memory. The university had more than doubled in size since his day and with all the new buildings it had lost its familiarity. Even the hospital had a new wing, thanks to Tony Blair's health policies and the Welsh Assembly Government's need for prestige projects. The new glass and steel reception area disorientated him.

A nurse with a ring through her eyebrow showed him to the side room. The south facing window's curtains were drawn to block the sun's glare. Against the sunlight filtering through the yellow and cream print, three large stains showed brown. Elen was sleeping, her head of wispy white hair barely making an impression on the pillow. She looked frailer and more gaunt than the last time he'd seen her, just three months before. The single pale green sheet, almost smooth and tucked neatly under her chin, had a large monogram proclaiming the NHS Trust's name and logo just next to where her bony thigh protruded – as though she were in an addressed envelope, ready for despatch. John sat in the only chair, between the bed and the window. The curtain billowed gently in the faintest breath of a breeze. He wasn't afraid of silences, or of approaching death. He remembered some of the times he'd sat at bedsides, when it had been his job to comfort and pray, and reflect on the hope offered by new treatments, or simply just be there so that the journey was less lonely.

'Oh John... it's you, *bach*,' she said in a voice that was stronger than he'd expected.

'I didn't mean to wake you, Elen.'

He kissed her cheek. Her skin was like tissue paper.

'I wasn't really asleep... but I drift now and again.' She eased her arm from beneath the loose sheet. 'Hold my hand, *bach*,' she said.

John edged his hand under hers so that her fingers rested in his palm. They looked too gnarled and fragile to hold. She drifted for a few minutes.

'You haven't come all the way just to see me,' she said, part question, part accusation.

'You know how much I like coming back to Aber.'

'You're so thoughtful.' Her rheumy eyes seemed to clear. 'And you've been so faithful to me over all these years... and to Rhys when he was alive.'

'A kindness passed on,' John said, remembering.

Elen smiled. She remembered too.

'Is Klaus with you?'

'No, he's visiting his parents and his nephews and nieces.'

She sighed and pressed her fingers into his palm.

'I didn't think it would be like this.'

'How should it be different, Elen?'

'Less difficult,' she said, closing her eyes.

She was away for longer, perhaps ten minutes.

'Read me a psalm, John *bach*,' she said, her eyes still closed.

97

'I thought you knew them all by heart, Elen,' John teased.

'I do... in Welsh, but read me one in English. I like thirty-four.'

Her well-thumbed Bible was on the locker next to a bottle of barley water. As he read the psalm she drifted off again, but he kept reading, and when he'd read the last verse he began to recite the same psalm, from memory, in Welsh. She joined in the last few verses and when they came to the end she took his hand between her twisted fingers.

'Do you remember the day they came for you... to the manse, all those years ago?'

'Yes, I do.'

'You looked into my eyes, and you pleaded with me... but I let them take you because —' Tears dripped onto her sunken cheeks. 'I have never asked you to forgive me for letting them take you, for letting you down so badly.'

John, surprised by the stinging hurt in her failing voice, and the realisation of her burden, felt his eyes moisten. His vision blurred, and he sucked back the tears. 'Oh, Elen... you didn't let me down —' he said, but stopped himself, understanding that platitudes wouldn't satisfy her.

'I've carried it all these years, John, like a bleeding sore inside me... and I want you to know that I'm sorry.'

And she squeezed his hand with surprising strength.

'I didn't know that this had been hurting you for so long,' John said. 'Please, let the wound heal now; you've crawled enough through the thorns.'

'Thank you,' she said, and smiled. 'Fancy you, remembering Waldo.'

She drifted away, and when she hadn't woken up after half an hour John kissed her cheek.

'Goodbye, Elen,' he whispered, his tears flowing freely.

Finding Beca's new house wasn't difficult. After crossing the Dyfi by the centuries-old stone bridge outside Machynlleth, John took the lane signposted for the Centre of Alternative Technology and, continuing past the Centre, he followed the twisting track up the Dulas valley. He caught only glimpses of the river through the pink-capped teasels that seemed to guard the banks like a military cordon.

'It's a beautiful spot,' John said after they'd hugged one another.

'Hefin's grandparents lived here in the valley and when he was small he'd come here in the holidays.'

Those eyes: Beca was her father's daughter.

'How is Hefin?'

'Oh, he's fine you know,' she said with an impatient backward swipe of her hand. 'He's in Cardiff today, meeting some people from the Assembly.'

'So he still finds plenty to do then.'

'He doesn't stop, John. I think he's busier now than before he retired. But... well, just look at this place; the builders have been gone nearly eighteen months and I don't think he's spent more than a day in the garden.'

'But you wouldn't want somewhere like this to look too manicured, Beca,' John offered, taking in the wilderness. 'It's been such a good summer for willowherb and loosestrife.'

'I can find you a sickle if you'd like to have a go at those thistles,' she said.

They moved into the kitchen through sliding patio doors, wide open against the afternoon heat. Their carpenter, using Welsh oak, had done a fine job of the kitchen cabinets, and the purple slate slabs on the floor, from Blaenau Ffestiniog – since the Dulas valley's state quarries had been closed for forty years and more, gave a sense of tradition and authenticity to what was, John thought, an otherwise fairly bland, modern house. They sat at an old oak table. The view down the valley would add tens of thousands to the value of the property if they ever decided to move on. John recognised the table, and was cast back to the manse.

'How did you find Mam then?' Beca asked as she poured out their teas.

'She's still very strong, and when she's actually with you she's all there.'

'She's rallied a bit, since the weekend,' she said, passing his tea. 'Help yourself, won't you... the fruitcake is from the wholefood café in Mach, and I knocked up the sponge this morning.'

For a few minutes, over their tea, John asked about her boys and Beca enquired about his health, and about Klaus.

'I probably shouldn't talk about arrangements, with Mam still —'

'It's not inappropriate, Beca,' John put into her hesitation.

'Well, we'd like you and Klaus to sit with the family, and if you'd be willing, we'd like you to say something, or read something. You can decide.'

'Thank you, Beca,' he said, and drank back his tears with his tea.

'You're still teaching at the university in Bangor, are you?' she asked, changing direction because thoughts of her mother's death had made her anxious and John's tears were embarrassing her.

'I teach a six-week module on sex and sexuality issues at the School of Nursing every spring,' John said, sniffing. 'But it's oversubscribed and the university would like to have me teach on a half-time secondment from the Public Health Department, but I don't think it's going to happen.'

'So, is there a lot of pressure on you to get back to work, after your —' She laid her hand on her breast.

'No, they've been very good.'

'Some more cake?'

Twisting with the road as it snaked north over the mountain pass at Tal-y-llyn, he reflected on his time with Elen in the hospital and his hour with Beca over tea. Old memories churned over... and he decided to talk with the psychologist at the rehab clinic about all this remembering.

Night

Driving hard through a dank mizzle that swathed the mountain pass at Tal-y-llyn, he imagined holding the steering wheel rigid against the sharp curves and flying off the precipice. Without Paul, there wasn't much left to live for. Then, beyond Dolgellau, speeding along the Mawddach on the recently opened stretch of pristine road, he toyed with the idea of driving into one of the new retaining walls that stopped the shale falling from the gouged hillside.

On the steep descent into town he searched for a mask his mam would recognise. Barmouth's harbour, swollen by the tide, glistened momentarily in a shaft of winter sunlight that pierced the grey sky. On the quayside, the Last Inn was doing steady lunchtime business, and through the steamed-up window of 'Griff's Plaice', Beti-siop-chips did her salt-and-vinegar shake. Along the prom, kids were playing football on the 'black patch' and the bandstand on the seaward side of the old parade ground had been partly dismantled after damage from a winter storm. He found a mask that seemed to fit.

'You look as if you could do with a good night's sleep, *cyw*,' Olwen Jones said after she'd hugged her son. 'I suppose you've had late night parties and goodness knows what.'

His mam's concern seemed petty, annoying even, but she clucked on.

'You could do with putting on a few pounds too; don't they feed you in that Theological College? *Duw*, you pay them enough for your keep!'

He followed her into the kitchen. She sliced a baked gammon.

'Stir the white sauce for me, *cyw*. I bet you've missed Mam's cooking, haven't you?'

He stirred the measured half pint of milk into the powdered sauce mix and lit the gas under the saucepan.

'We'll soon feed you up. There's plenty in for Christmas. I bet you'd like one of Mam's puddings, wouldn't you; a roly-poly or a spotted dick?'

Over the years he'd found ways of coping; they'd only had a couple of rows. He hated being called her *cyw*; he was nobody's 'chick'. She didn't seem to change. Perhaps, with all the turmoil inside him, he'd play by her rules and see how things went.

'A roly-poly with the damson jam you made in September would be great.'

Mam beamed a knowing smile.

Dad came in from some cash-in-hand wallpapering job. Dai Jones muttered his 'hello' and proceeded to wash his hands and face at the kitchen sink. He always washed in the kitchen. John wasn't ashamed of his family, but he disliked the fact that his dad was so locked into being working class. To be fair, Dai had always encouraged his boys to get a good education, and do

103

something in life that didn't involve getting their hands dirty and being out in all weather. But then, Dai would keep reminding them not to forget where they'd come from. That was fine. John didn't want to forget. But education, and different experiences away from Barmouth, seemed to put that intangible something Dai wanted them to hold onto beyond their grasp.

John said very little as they ate.

'Ifan-Bontddu was telling me that Jack-Haleliwia's had a stroke and things aren't looking very good for him,' Dai said.

'Well, there's a shame, and just before Christmas too,' Olwen clucked.

'Ifan was saying that Jack's allotment's all grown over,' Dai said. 'Perhaps I should go for it? What d'you think Ol? Old Jack had some good soil there.'

'D'you remember old Jack-Haleliwia, John?' Olwen asked. 'He used to give us new potatoes and runner beans.'

John grunted, remembering Jack... and his Everton mints.

'If you think you've got time for an allotment as well as everything else,' Olwen said. 'It would be nice to have some home grown veg; the stuff they've got in George Mason's is so poor.'

'Did you see in the paper that some peanut farmer from Georgia has announced that he's running for the presidency?' John said, just to provoke a response.

Dai looked at his son over his glasses as if to say 'What's that got to do with anything?' and Olwen looked at their plates and said she'd cut some more gammon.

Olwen made no comment, over her toast and the *News of the World*, when he said he was going to the service at Calfaria on Sunday morning.

'Must be the influence of that Theological College rubbing off,' Dai mumbled, looking over his copy of *The People*.

Everything was frosty. In the Memorial Park, the shrubs and trees were like ice sculptures against the blue winter sky. John climbed the 100 steps through the fog of his breath. Approaching the chapel he felt the trickle of filth begin to flow through his veins, but it didn't deter him from seeking the closeness to Paul he believed going to the service would bring.

The congregation was much diminished. Miss Gruffudd still rolled her false teeth, but her fur coat looked like it had a dose of mange on the left elbow. Her tired, wrinkled face beamed with pleasure on seeing John Idris 'back in the fold'. He felt cast back to his childhood, and through the eyes of little John Idris in Miss Gruffudd's Sunday school class, Paul seemed unreachable.

After the service, feeling foul and floundering, John walked around the quay to delay his return. Cader Idris, its summit snowy, looked dignified against the steel blue sky. A lone boatman rowed across the still harbour to a large cabin cruiser anchored in the main channel of the estuary. The calm beauty of the morning did nothing to ease the lurch of the thought mill, and he wondered about a life without Paul's love and reassurance. He ached for the safety of his embrace, but the finality of Paul's last words came back.

He struggled with the Sunday roast beef dinner, but his mam's *cyw* had to show that he could enjoy extra large portions of everything. Billy phoned during the damson jam roly-poly and custard. Because he still had more than a week to do with his surgical firm at the Royal Liverpool, he wouldn't be home until Christmas Eve. Olwen was disappointed. When Dai talked to him, John overheard his dad say that he'd put 'a few quid' in the post, without so much as a 'not again Billy'. He wondered why his dad didn't give Bill more of a hard time.

Late in the afternoon, during some grand forties musical on the television, Judith, one of the girls from school, rang.

'Thought you might like to come, tomorrow night; the Cors-y-Gedol, about half-seven,' she said with excitement. 'There's a lot of catching up to do. Neil's coming, and Bethan said she'd meet us in the Last at about nine. I'm going to phone Mike and Sandra too.'

'Maybe... I'm not sure Jude.'

'Oh, come on! I want to tell you all about Cardiff and medical school.'

'Yes... but... I just don't think I want to go out for a piss-up.'

'Who said anything about a piss-up? We're just going to have a few drinks and share stories.'

'Okay, so maybe I'll come.'

'Oh... don't bother, John, not if it seems like too much trouble! What's wrong with you anyway?

'There's nothing wrong; I just —'

Judith hung up the phone.

The next days were difficult. He kept out of his parents' way, staying in bed until after they'd both gone to work – though the thought looms saw to it that he didn't sleep very much. Olwen had a busy week, what with the school Christmas dinner and all the catering for the staff party, so John had the house pretty much to himself during the day. He sat for hours in the bay window of his bedroom and watched the sea. In the evenings, when Dai and Olwen settled in front of the coal fire in the back room to watch the television, smoking cigarette after cigarette, he shut himself away in the front sitting room with Dai's new stereo system.

Amongst his dad's records, mostly jazz and fifties popular music, he found half a dozen classical LPs. They seemed to be part of a mail order collection that built up over time. He played them all, but he especially liked Brahms' first symphony and Beethoven's fifth piano concerto, *The Emperor*, which he played over and over. Often, through the course of an evening, he'd re-live the times he'd spent with Paul, and when that became too painful he tried to lose himself in the music. Sometimes, Adam's crew came back to haunt him; then he'd turn up the stereo to drown their choruses of accusation. Once, trying to blast the Sunday Library Group's allegations from his head with *The Emperor* at full volume, he was found, crying, by Olwen.

'What's the matter, *cyw*?'

'It's — This music... it's so beautiful.'

'Well, you are a soft bugger,' she said, wondering in what other ways Aberystwyth had changed him. 'Turn it down, or we'll have them next-door banging on the wall.'

In the days before Christmas, the determination of Paul's decision to end their relationship as lovers took on a stark reality, piercing a wound that left John in physical pain. Without Paul to hold him when the bad feelings came, he found himself sinking into a bottomless pit of tangled thoughts.

*　　*　　*

On Christmas Eve there was a buzz of excitement in the house; Billy's homecomings always generated much expectation. Olwen Jones had decided to visit her 'old ladies' – three widows on whom she looked in from time to time.

She'd made them a few mince pies, and bought each one a box of Turkish delight. Then she'd meet Jane in the Milk Bar for a sandwich before doing her last minute bits and pieces. Dai Jones was working until lunchtime and then nipping into the Last for a drink with some of the boys, just because it was Christmas; he wasn't much of a drinker. John was sure he wouldn't be missed for a few hours.

The salty air of the coastal strip stopped the flurries of snow settling on the road north out of Barmouth. The hills immediately to his right were already dusted, and the bleak Rhinogs were swathed in a blanket of blizzard. Beyond Harlech, where the road pushed inland, snow fell steadily and the countryside looked strangely unfamiliar under its virginal veil; the whiteness of it all hurt his retinas. Outside Porthmadog he got stuck behind a gritter, and though this gave him the confidence to continue, the tailback made slow progress. It was only as the traffic faltered that he considered the possibility that Paul might not be at home. It frightened him to think that he might be unable to re-connect with his lifeline.

If he couldn't see Paul he'd kill himself. He mulled over the different ways of doing it. The weather conspired with him; a tragic car crash, skidding on the icy road, a head-on collision — No, he didn't want anyone else to be hurt; he'd drive the car into a wall then. He thought about the people who might attend his funeral, and how some would be agreeing with one another, over his coffin, that the world was better off without homosexuals like him. Adam and the Sunday Library Group intruded on the funeral proceedings with a triumphant burst of the Hallelujah Chorus.

Driving into the village square, with its boarded up shop fronts and derelict chapel, the snow stopped falling. Someone had put a nail in the For Sale sign, but it was still a bit askew. This time he knew to look out for Park Road. Paul didn't seem surprised to see him.

'You'd better come in.'

He was wearing jeans that were so tight they looked uncomfortable at the crotch. John noticed the curves, and remembered the pleasure he'd taken from Paul's body. He wanted to kiss him, but those words on that last day of term came back and John was unsure how to be with him.

'We can go into the front sitting room,' he said. 'I've just lit the fire.'

It was a small room with barely enough space for the over-stuffed sofa. John sank into its feather softness and Paul sat on a footstool, next to the fireplace. He rubbed the scar just below his lip and John sensed his friend's apprehension.

'How have you been then?' Paul asked.

'Fine,' John said, his face telling a different story.

'There's no point beating about the bush,' Paul said with a heavy sigh. 'Being home has given me some distance... and given me time to reflect on our relationship in Aber. It's much clearer now, and there are some things I need to say.'

John shrugged.

'You're probably not going to like it, but I need you to hear me out.'

John frowned. Paul fingered the scar again.

'Our relationship in Aber; it wasn't very... healthy, was it?'

John remembered how good their sex had been and sensed the stirrings.

'And I don't mean because it wasn't right for me. You got really dependent, and that wasn't good for either of us. You kept seeking me out, and then there was all that attention seeking

109

behaviour; how you were going to commit suicide because you felt so bad about yourself and that bizarre stuff about how I was breathing life into you. It got really weird, John.'

'But I love you,' he said, even as it dawned upon him that Paul's hard words had a ring of truth.

'And I love you too, but I'm out of my depth.' Paul pushed his fingers through his hair, sweeping it back from his face, and sighed. 'I tried to offer you reassurance, but when I look back now, I see that I made some wrong choices. You were crying out for help, but what you needed was not something I could give you.'

'So, what then?' John said, looking into the chasm of life without him.

'I think you're ill,' he said, almost coldly, into the void. 'I think you need to see a doctor.'

John remembered the letters in his mam's magazines and shook his head; the way Paul had said 'doctor' implied that he meant a psychiatrist. 'Why are you doing this to me?' he asked.

'Because I love you,' Paul said, and fingered the scar again. 'You need specialist help, John.'

John clasped his hands over his ears, not wanting to hear anymore.

'It's not shameful, John, being... ill like this; it's not your fault. Please, if you love me, you'll listen to what I'm saying.'

There was a cold common sense to his words that brought only a wintry bleakness that settled over John like the swathe of snow on the bowling greens of the park through Paul's sitting room window.

'Promise me you'll go'n see your GP, John. Just see what he's got to say; he'll be able to recommend someone. Do it for me... please.'

'Yes,' John said, because there was nothing more to say. He got up to leave, the brokenness inside him hurting terribly.

'You don't want some tea before you go? A mince pie, or a piece of Christmas cake?'

The gritters had kept the roads clear. His driving was automatic. Passing through Porthmadog and Harlech, streams of self-destructive thoughts became a torrent that overflowed. But he couldn't drive into a wall, despite Adam's mantra and the Sunday Library Group's chants, urging him on.

*   *   *

Outside Barmouth, where the road was high above the beach, a small lane climbed even higher to a large Victorian villa, Awel-y-Môr. It stood in its own grounds, the drive climbing through banks of cherry laurels. John knew the house, and the family that lived there; he'd played often as a child with Meurig, the family doctor's son. Driving beneath the laurels, he remembered times when he and Meurig were in Robin Hood's band of merry men, ambushing travellers. He'd missed Meurig a lot after he went off to boarding school in Colwyn Bay. It was Richard Roberts who answered the door.

'John Idris... Happy Christmas. Meurig expecting you, is he? I'll give him a call.'

'No —' For an instant, John's uncertainty intensified. He'd always called Meurig's dad Doctor-Richard; most of the town's kids did. But he wasn't a kid any longer. 'No, Dr Roberts, I haven't come to see Meurig. It's you I want to see, if you've got a few minutes.'

'Well, yes. Come in out of the snow,' he offered, looking

quizzically at John over the rims of his glasses. 'We can go in here,' he said, gesturing to the nearest door.

'I'm sorry... I should have made an appointment, not just called like this.'

'It must be important then. I'm glad you felt you could drop in.' He closed the door of the lounge behind them and gestured towards the sofa. 'So, what can I do for you?'

Words stuck in John's throat.

Richard Roberts coughed. 'If it's confidentiality that you're worried about, you're an adult now; whatever you talk to me about will be in confidence,' he said, wondering if John had got some girl pregnant, or if he'd picked up a venereal disease.

Still, John choked on his words.

'It's something about your life at university? You look tired. Are you finding it hard to cope, is that what's bothering you?'

'I'm sorry, I'm wasting your time,' John managed, and got up to go.

'I won't stop you leaving, if that's what you want.' He looked over his glasses again. 'You seem a bit anxious. Why don't you give it another try?'

John sat down again. He bit his lip and closed his eyes. He breathed in deeply, and sighed. 'I'm a homosexual. I hate myself... and I want to die.'

'I'm sorry,' Richard Roberts said. He coughed again to mask that he was taken aback. 'That's a nuisance for you.' He leaned towards John, cupping his chin in both hands and rubbing at the day's stubble. 'We're not a very understanding society about something like this,' he offered, feeling a wave of empathy for Dai and Olwen Jones, and trying to ignore the wrenching feeling in his gut. 'I'm sure it's a struggle, keeping something like this a secret.'

'I've been trying to deny it for a long time, but —'

'It's caught up with you.'

John had the sense that Doctor-Richard almost understood.

'Has something happened that's made you dwell on this more now, in the last weeks?'

John was surprised by his tenderness, and his sympathy, and he offered a much-abridged version of what had happened over the last months in Aberystwyth.

'And now you want to die?' Dr Richard asked, looking again over the rims of his glasses.

'Yes.'

'You've thought about killing yourself?'

John sighed and nodded his response.

'Just thoughts, John, or have you actually tried to harm yourself?'

'I've come close to... well, more than just thinking about it. But Paul was always there to support me.' The mention of his name sharpened the shards of brokenness inside him.

'He's your *special* friend, is he?' Richard Roberts asked.

John couldn't believe how gentle he was.

'Paul helped me a lot when I was down.'

'And he's a homosexual, is he?' Richard Roberts knew the law, and he needed to ascertain whether John, who wasn't yet twenty-one, had been groomed and then abused by an older man.

'No, he isn't!' It came out with too much force and John sensed that Richard Roberts knew he was lying. 'No, Paul's training to be a minister.'

'Well, it's good that there was someone there to help you... but now you're feeling alone with this, is that right?'

'I didn't know who else to talk to, Doctor-Richard,' John said, sucking back tears, a local kid again.

113

'I do understand. You must be feeling very frightened, and very desperate. I'm glad you came to see me.' He rubbed his stubbled chin and smiled, hoping to reassure John. 'On the basis of what you've told me, I would normally make an appointment for you to see a specialist within twenty-four hours, at the hospital in Denbigh... but the fact that it's Christmas Eve limits our options.'

'The loony bin,' John said.

'Yes... they treat people who are mentally ill in Denbigh, but they also care for people who are depressed and who've had breakdowns. I don't think you are mentally ill, John Idris, but these suicidal thoughts suggest that you've got a touch of depression, so I think you need to see a specialist.'

'You want me to see a psychiatrist, that's what you mean?'

'Yes... a specialist in depression.'

'Alright,' John said, trusting that the man who'd delivered him into the world in Barmouth's maternity home wouldn't do anything against his best interests.

'So... I'm going to phone Dr Arwel Thomas. I know him from our days in medical school, and I've got his home phone number somewhere; he's very nice, and he's very good.' He paused and offered John a questioning look.

'I understand,' John said.

'I'll be frank with you, John. I don't know what Dr Thomas' holiday arrangements are. I hope that he'll be able to see you on Monday or Tuesday; now that's a week away, so I'm going to give you some medicine that will help you over the next days.'

'But that's a long time... it's been very bad.'

'I'd rather that you didn't go to the hospital in Denbigh as an emergency admission, John. It's better, in the long run, if you go voluntarily to an out-patient's clinic.'

John understood what Richard Roberts was telling him, but he had no inkling of the implications.

'I'll give you a prescription for some tablets that will help to calm you. I want you to start taking them tonight. This isn't a pill for homosexuals, so the pharmacist won't know that you are —'

'I understand.'

'Good boy. Now, let's think about how you're going to manage for the next days. Has Billy come home yet?'

'This afternoon.'

'Do you think you can talk to him, like you've been talking to me?'

'I don't know,' John said and sighed. 'I feel like I'm letting everybody down.'

'Try not to think that way, John,' Richard Roberts said. It came out with less conviction than he'd hoped, and he began to interpret the uncomfortable tightness in his stomach. If Meurig had come home and told him he was a homo, he knew the ignominy of it would be humiliating. 'Most of us have times in our lives when we need a bit of help, and you've shown a lot of courage by coming here this afternoon,' he said, his voice carrying more authority. 'But if you can, try to talk with Billy.'

'I'll try,' John said, knowing that he wouldn't.

'There's something else, before you go.' There was an edge to the doctor's tone that made John pay attention. 'When we were talking, earlier, you said that when you're driving you feel an urge, sometimes, to drive into a wall. That is what you said, isn't it, John Idris?'

'Yes, Doctor-Richard.'

'So, I want you to drive straight home now, and then I want you to promise me that you won't drive again.'

John faltered.

'I need that promise, John Idris.'

'Alright.' It was the second time that day he'd been asked to make a promise.

Richard Roberts came to sit next to him on the sofa and put an arm around his shoulder. 'You are going to be all right,' he said with as much conviction as he could summon. 'Take the medication, and try to talk to Billy... and remember that you've promised not to drive.' He smiled his reassurance and wondered what was really going on in John's head. 'And I'll make you a promise too. If you want to come back here to see me at any time over Christmas, you must come... and I do mean any time.'

'Thank you,' John said.

'There's a morning surgery the day after Boxing Day. Come and see me then; we can have another chat.'

*   *   *

John dropped off his prescription at Parry's and said he'd call back in an hour to collect it. Without much enthusiasm, he did the necessary Christmas shopping; some lily of the valley talc for Nana and a tin of Erinmore Mixture for Taid. He got Mam a pair of slippers, a couple of tapes for Billy and a book of Giles' cartoons for Dad. In all of the shops there was a sense of well being and good will as people wished one another a Happy Christmas. Members of the local Round Table sang Christmas carols on the square. In the fading afternoon light, with the street lamps catching the falling snow in their glow, everything seemed set for that rare, perfect White Christmas.

All of the rooms at the front of the house lit up and John concluded that Billy had arrived. Parking the car, he sorted through the masks and found the one that beamed *happy-go-lucky, life-and-soul-of-the-party*. Over dinner, Billy entertained them with gruesome details from Saturday nights in casualty, and frightening stories about over-worked doctors falling asleep on duty.

After clearing the dinner things and washing up, Mam recruited her 'kitchen staff' and allotted them jobs. Billy and John peeled the vegetables. John told Billy how much he liked being in Aberystwyth.

'Let's cut the crap,' Billy said. 'Mam says you've been acting strange; spending lots of time on your own. She said you were crying.'

John wondered about opening up to him, but the 'happy mask' seemed to be working and he was sure the tranquillisers would soon kick in. He just wanted to put all his troubles on hold and go with whatever Christmas brought. 'Mam said that?' he said, feigning surprised bewilderment. 'I've been listening to a lot of music that's all. Dad's collecting classical LPs. I've really got into Beethoven.'

'Well, as long as you're okay. But you know what Mam's like; she thinks you're doing drugs.'

'Fuck, are you serious?' John asked, genuinely surprised this time.

'I hadn't been home ten minutes and she was quizzing me about the affects of marijuana and LSD for God's sake. Tell me you're not a fucking acid-head.'

'I'm not, Billy; honest.'

John changed the subject, and asked about the films his brother had seen in the big city.

Lots of people passed through their house in the next days.

117

Nana and Taid came for Christmas Day. Neighbours, carrying greetings and small gifts, were offered drinks and mince pies, and Olwen's canteen gang came for a few gins. John was sociable, and his 'happy mask' served him well; he even had second helpings of his mam's Christmas pudding and brandy sauce, it was so good. But at night, when the mask slipped, he felt the rawness inside him from his break-up with Paul, and when the sluice gates opened, he felt bad about himself. Adam and the Sunday Library Group maintained their whispered onslaught and convinced him that the only good homosexual was a dead one. In the long hours of sleepless-ness, he convinced himself that seeing the psychiatrist offered him one last hope.

*   *   *

Arwel Thomas peered through the fuzz of a hangover, feeling sick to the stomach. His head throbbed. When he finally focussed his eyes, he saw the bottle of Glenfiddich a colleague from the hospital had given him. Next to the bottle was an open Bible. Feeling every stiff muscle in his body, from being slouched in the chair too long, he lifted the bottle and held it to the fading winter sunlight spilling through a gap in the curtains. There was no more than an inch of whisky left. He felt both surprised and ashamed that he'd drunk so much, and he cursed Luned. Then he cursed himself for being so pig-headed; it would have been better if he'd gone to his sister's for a couple of days. Spending Christmas Day with his misery and a bottle of Scotch hadn't been a good idea. He got to his feet, felt dizzy, and staggered to the kitchen where he vomited in the sink. Then, for a long time, he let water from the cold tap flow over his head. He dried himself with a stained tea towel and took in the kitchen's chaos; days' worth of used cereal bowls, mugs and plates cluttered the table, and empty tins of baked beans, sardines and Heinz soups jumbled over the worktop and draining board.

She hasn't come back then.

In the bath, soaking away the aches and the smell of his sweat, Arwel cried. He remembered again how Luned had screamed that she'd had enough of his bullying. She wouldn't continue to let him dictate what she could and couldn't do, and she didn't care any more what St Paul said about how the relationships between men and women ought to be. Then she'd left. That had been on Sunday, after he'd made her go with him to chapel... and wear a hat.

Wrapped in a towel, he wandered around their bedroom, bewildered. Luned's clothes were ripped and torn, scattered about the room; he couldn't remember doing it. He buried himself beneath the blankets and tried to block out the evidence of his rage – and the reality that she'd left him.

The telephone on the bedside table rang. It took him some time to place Richard Roberts, but he gathered himself quickly and became the consultant psychiatrist that his old medical school classmate wanted to talk to.

'And you think he's a serious risk to himself?' Arwel asked, after Richard had outlined his young patient's situation.

'It's my judgement that he needs to see you as soon as possible.'

'I haven't got a clinic until the New Year; week beginning Monday the sixth,' he said. 'But I could see him before then —'

'Monday or Tuesday would be best, if you can do that,

Arwel; I know it's the holidays —'

'Tuesday after lunch then, say half-past-two,' he said without much consideration.

'New Year's eve?' Richard quizzed. 'You're sure that's okay?'

'It's fine... no social commitments this year.'

After he'd hung up the phone, Arwel Thomas went straight to his study and wrote *2:30pm John Idris Jones* in his diary on the last page of the year.

*   *   *

'So, how have you been?' Richard Roberts asked after John sat down.

'It's bad, Doctor-Richard,' John said. 'Especially at night. I keep hearing voices telling me to kill myself.'

'You're hearing voices now,' the doctor said gravely. 'You didn't tell me you were hearing voices.'

'Well, I hear things that people have said, and bits from the Bible, condemning me.'

'Did you talk to Billy?'

'No, I couldn't. He's gone back already.'

'The specialist I told you about, Dr Arwel Thomas, he can see you at the hospital in Denbigh on Tuesday afternoon.'

'That's good,' John said, feeling some fleeting relief.

'You're going to have to say something to your mam and dad. You promised me you wouldn't drive, so your dad will have to take you.'

John looked agitated.

'Have you thought about what you'll say to them?'

'No. There's no other way, is there?'

'I could talk to them, but you'd have to give me your permission.'

'No. I think that's for me to do.'

He told Mam and Dad that evening. It wasn't a rehearsed speech and it was thin on detail.

'I'm confused about lots of things in my life at the moment and Doctor-Richard thinks it would help me if I saw a specialist.'

'I knew there was something wrong, *cyw*,' Olwen said. 'Didn't I tell you Dai?'

'Why didn't you say something to us?' Dai asked, his tone accusing.

'Because it's difficult, Dad,' John said, knowing he was upsetting them, but not wanting to upset them even more by telling them he was a pervert.

Later, washing up the dishes with John, Mam let out a long sigh. 'Do you feel we've let you down, John Idris?'

Olwen remembered too many times when she'd decided it was best not to pry into the closed spaces in her son's life; why he wasn't chasing girls like Billy and all the other boys his own age... why she'd never found a well thumbed copy of Playboy under his mattress like the women she worked with in the canteen had done with their teenage boys... why he'd been so evasive, over the years, when she'd casually asked him what he'd been up to. John was too mixed up to read her question, and hear what she wanted him to say. She left the kitchen and sat with Dai in front of the television. They smoked cigarette after cigarette.

'I'm going to phone Richard Roberts and find out what this is all about,' Dai said.

'He's over eighteen, Dai,' Olwen protested. 'Doctor-Richard won't be able to tell you.'

The next days were difficult for them. Olwen and Dai wanted to show John that they cared for him, but with so much that had gone unspoken over the years, they barely knew where to begin. John wanted the days to pass; the appointment with Dr Arwel Thomas had become his last hope.

*   *   *

John had never been to Denbigh. It had turned milder and the snow had cleared so Dai Jones decided to take the shorter route, up to Ffestiniog, on through Pentrefoelas, and then across the Denbigh moors. They journeyed in silence through countryside that was rugged and beautiful. Snowdonia's snow-capped summits were like peaked meringues, glistening pinkish in the pale winter sun. To *ooh* and *aah* like tourists didn't seem appropriate. Dropping down from the moors, the Vale of Clwyd opened up before them, a patchwork of fields and villages against the spine of the Clwydian range. Moel Famau looked bedraggled in its torn shroud of melting grey snow. Denbigh castle stood high and ruined over the ancient town.

'Jesus Christ! Is that the place I'm taking you to?' Dai exclaimed, seeing the Victorian asylum up close for the first time as they drove down Castle Hill.

In the watery winter sunshine, the jaundiced stonework of the Jacobean-style monstrosity seemed to shimmer, which made it look like a mirage that didn't belong in the idyllic landscape. Seeing the high railings and the barred windows, John began to wonder about the truths of all the stories he'd grown up with about Denbigh's madhouse as a depository for deviants, the shamelessly wayward and the simple-minded.

The familiar and reassuring smell of disinfectant confirmed

that the North Wales Hospital was really not so different from any other hospital. After talking on the phone, the matronly woman behind the reception desk gave them directions to Dr Thomas' office. 'If he's not ready for you, his secretary will show you where you can wait,' she said, her manner friendly.

The woman who met them was more business-like.

'I'm sorry, but Dr Thomas has been delayed,' she said. The string of pearls on her huge bust rose and fell with the laboured breathing of a heavy smoker. 'Doctor doesn't usually see patients in his office so there isn't a waiting room, but perhaps you'd like to sit over there.'

She pointed to a small bay window, and the two office chairs she'd wheeled from an adjoining office where the staff were still on leave. They sat and watched the lawns through the window turn white.

'The weather forecast got it wrong again,' Dai said. 'I hope this doesn't take too long.'

'The gritters will be out,' John said.

After some minutes, the secretary returned holding a tray at arm's length because of her bust.

'I know you've come a long way, so I've brought you some coffee,' she said. 'Sorry about the mugs... and there's an ashtray too, in case you want a smoke. Sugar?'

Dai lit up an Embassy and drew heavily to calm himself. As they drank their sweet, watery coffee, a bent, dishevelled woman came along the corridor towards them. Her hands were held unnaturally at her waist in front of her, as though they were fastened to the belt of her shift; her thin fingers writhed like a siege of spiders.

'Have you got a penny?' she asked in Welsh, standing too close to Dai and shifting from one foot to the other. 'Mami's sent me to buy matches, so I have to have a penny.'

Dai went through the change in his pocket and gave her a two-pence piece.

'And a smoke,' she pleaded.

He offered her the open packet so that she could take a cigarette but she swiped the pack from his hand.

'Mami's a bitch,' she said, thrusting her prizes into a pocket. Then the spiders writhed again.

Dai looked uncertainly at John.

'I'll hit the bitch if she starts on me again. I'll hit the bitch,' and she began to howl.

'Maggie *fach*, what are you doing all the way over here?' came a voice from along the corridor in Welsh. A man in his mid-forties, slightly balding and thin as a rake, walked briskly towards them. 'Miss Lloyd,' he called out. The woman with the string of pearls poked her head around the door. 'Miss Lloyd, will you ring the ward and ask someone to come over and get Maggie?'

'Right away, Dr Thomas,' she said and disappeared into the office.

Arwel Thomas turned to John and his father.

'Mr Jones? John Idris Jones from Barmouth?'

'Yes,' John said, standing up.

'I'm sorry I was held up,' he said, turning back on himself. 'Come this way.'

John followed him into a nearby office as the howling woman skipped off along the corridor. Finishing his cigarette, Dai was taken aback by the woman's madness and the doctor's bad manners.

'Tell me what's brought you here,' Arwel Thomas ordered in English as they sat down.

John was uneasy with the psychiatrist's directness, but was relieved that he wasn't going to conduct the interview in Welsh. He noticed the doctor's creased shirtfront and the stain on his tie.

'Well?' Dr Thomas said, jabbing the end of a pen onto his desk.

'I've been thinking a lot about suicide.'

'Is there any reason why you feel you want to kill yourself?'

'I'm a homosexual.' John surprised himself; it was getting easier to say.

'Are your family chapel?' the doctor asked, in Welsh this time.

John wondered whether he'd heard correctly.

'Chapel? Yes, but we don't go very often.'

'And you're friendly with a boy who's training for the ministry.'

'Yes, he's been helping me sort myself out, but I'm not really sure what I believe.'

'But you do believe,' the doctor said.

John wasn't sure whether he was being asked if he believed, or being told that he did.

'Yes, but —' He wrung his hands and wished that they could start again; the doctor hadn't even introduced himself.

'But?' Arwel Thomas quizzed, in English again.

'Well, it's an abomination; to be a homosexual. I'm a perversion of God's purpose and it's hard to believe in a God who's so condemning.'

'What would getting better mean for you, John Idris?' He smiled, and John began to see some humanity.

'I'd like not to feel so ashamed, and not to feel suicidal.'

'Anything else?' he asked, more gently this time, his face softening.

125

'I wish I wasn't a homo... I want to be normal.'

Arwel Thomas' face broke into a kindly smile.

'I can help you, John Idris. I can make you better, but you must really want to become normal.'

'I do... I do,' John nodded.

'And you'd have to agree to come into the hospital for a short stay.'

John wrung his hands again, and shook his head slowly.

'John Idris, listen to me,' the psychiatrist said. 'We've got effective medicines now, anti-depressants and tranquillisers, that can bring you out of this depression very quickly... and if you really don't want to be a homosexual, there's a treatment that can help you, but you must really want that... and you will have to become an inpatient.'

John yielded. It was an offer of help, the only one, and it gave him hope. 'Alright,' he said.

'I know it's frightening John, but if you trust me —' He paused for a moment and looked into the depths of John's tired eyes. 'Would you like us to pray together?' he asked tentatively, in Welsh.

John realised that he'd already put all of his hopes in this man. 'Yes,' he murmured.

After inviting John to kneel beside him, Arwel Thomas prayed aloud and asked for God's guidance through John's course of treatment. They said The Lord's Prayer together. Then the psychiatrist got to his feet. 'Is it your father who's come with you?' he asked, brushing off fluff from the carpet that clung to the leg of his trousers.

John nodded his reply.

'I'd like to talk to him for a few minutes. Perhaps you'd ask him to come in. You can wait outside.'

John stood in the bay window and watched the snow falling until his father returned.

'Dr Thomas has made arrangements for you to stay in the male reception ward,' Dai said, looking shocked. 'It's not in this place, thank God! It's back up the road a few hundred yards. You won't be locked in, or anything like that, it's just like a normal hospital. God, I need a cigarette!'

'He said he could help me, Dad.'

'Let's hope that he can —' Dai looked pale and strained. 'Why did you let things get so bad, John? Why didn't you say something to us... sooner? Perhaps it wouldn't have come to this.'

'I'm sorry, Dad.'

'Your mam's going to be knocked for six.'

Dai Jones hadn't meant to add to his son's distress, he just wasn't very good at seeing events through other people's eyes. He craved the rush of nicotine and cadged a cigarette from the psychiatrist's buxom secretary.

*　　*　　*

'Look, it's not locked,' Dai said, pushing open the door to the long bungalow that was Gwynfryn, the male reception ward.

'Perhaps you'd better go, Dad, this snow looks set in for the night.'

'No, I'll see you settled. Mam will want to know you're alright.'

A male nurse met them in the corridor.

'Hello. I'm Chris Fisher. You're John Idris Jones, right?'

'Yes... this is my father.'

'Okay, Mr Jones, why don't you leave John with us now,' the nurse said, as if John were a parcel being exchanged. 'The weather's turned nasty and I know you've got a long way to go.

John and I have got a lot of paperwork to fill out, and he'll probably find it easier to settle if —'

'Oh, right then,' Dai said. He looked at his son and began to choke up. 'Right then —' he said again, and turned to leave.

In the car he cried, which was difficult for him. Men of his generation didn't cry. Damn that mad woman for stealing his cigarettes!

Chris Fisher put an arm around John's shoulder and walked him to the charge nurse's office.

'John's a bit upset,' Chris said.

Gareth Davies, the nurse in charge, was a thickset forty-year-old who still played rugby and had a crooked nose to show for it. He'd worked at the hospital for twenty-two years.

'You just take a few minutes to collect yourself, John,' he said.

'I'm alright,' John sniffed. 'Seeing my Dad go was —' He gulped back his tears. 'It feels like I'm being cut off from my family.'

'You're not on a section, John,' Gareth said. 'You're here as a voluntary patient, and we're here to help you.'

John wiped his eyes and forced a smile.

'Chris is going to take you through the admissions procedure... okay?' Gareth stood up to leave. 'You haven't got an overnight bag with you?'

'No, I didn't think I'd be staying.'

'I'll see what I can sort out for you... and leave some stuff on your bed,' he said as he left the office.

'We want to know everything about you; it's like This Is Your Life,' Chris quipped, pointing at a wodge of forms on the desk. He was fat and round-faced, with a bushy Mexican bandit moustache. After more than half an hour doing paperwork, John felt easy with him.

'Okay,' Chris said, closing the file. 'What about getting your bearings before tea?'

Gwynfryn was a T-shaped building. Along the top, the main corridor, there were wards, toilets and bathrooms. The dispensary and the charge nurse's office were also on this top corridor to the right of the T's stem, and the television lounge, quiet room, dining room and something mysteriously called the O.T. department were to the left. On both sides of the stem there were treatment and consulting rooms. The entrance to the ward was at the stem's base.

'And this is your bed,' Chris said. They were in the largest ward of sixteen beds and John's was on the right, nearest the door. 'Gareth's put some things here for you.'

John took in the frayed towel, the stained dressing gown, the green-striped pyjama top and the blue-striped trousers. 'Thanks,' he said.

'Why don't we go'n sit in the quiet room,' Chris said.

'All of the patients I've seen are so old,' John offered. 'Aren't there any people more my age here?'

'Those that could go home for Christmas have gone.'

'So just the really sick ones stayed?'

'The alcoholics... they didn't have anywhere to go or they stayed because that was the safest way to stay dry.'

Wondering about the waste of NHS resources on alcoholics, John asked, 'How long have you worked here?'

'I'm a second year student nurse; before that I was in medical school, but I failed too many exams so they kicked me out.'

'I'm sorry —'

'No need to be. I hated it. I never wanted to be a doctor, but my parents nagged and bullied. I'm much happier doing this.'

Their talk was interrupted by a shout that echoed down the corridors: 'Tea up. Come and get it.'

'Come on then, I'll introduce you to the troops,' Chris said.

They walked into the dining room.

'Look what Chris brought in from the snow,' someone slurred.

All but three of the places set at a single, long table were taken. Most of the men were old and unkempt.

'That's enough, Jan,' Chris said. 'This is John. He's just been admitted, so I want you to make him feel welcome.'

'Come and sit by me then,' Jan slurred again.

He was blonde, and in his thirties. A Nordic type, John thought, and very good-looking. Despite the chaos of his life, John could still open doors in his compartmentalised inner world and be turned on by a handsome man.

'I didn't mean to embarrass you,' Jan said in a loud, drunken whisper.

John smiled.

'I'm Jan. It's with a J... but you don't pronounce it. My mother's from Sweden see.'

'I'm John, with a J —'

'Don't be a fucking comedian,' Jan threatened, swaying in his seat.

John sucked in his breath sharply, but Jan's menacing gesture was muted by Chris Fisher's smile. 'Chicken pie and chips,' he said, offering the plate. 'That's all they've sent up from the kitchen.'

Jan scoffed it down. John picked at his plate; he wasn't hungry.

'I'm in here to be dried out,' Jan said between mouthfuls,

without a trace of indignation.

John waited for what he thought would be the inevitable question: 'What are you in for?' but it didn't come. 'How do they dry you out then?' he asked.

'Antabuse! Fucking antabuse,' Jan said shaking his head.

From the way Jan had mouthed the word, John got the impression that he was supposed to know what it meant.

'Okay...' he said. Then the room fell silent.

John helped to clear the plates after everyone had left and as he wiped down the table he heard his name being called from somewhere down the corridor.

'The doctor wants to see you,' Chris Fisher said, walking to meet him.

John looked anxious.

'It's just a physical, John,' Chris said. 'Part of the admission process... nothing to worry about. The drunks aren't bothering you, are they?'

'No, they're fine. I worked the pub queue in a late night chippy during the school holidays.'

'Ah... seen it all then, have you?' he said, laughing.

'I wouldn't go that far,' John said.

'I'm just teasing,' he offered, with a gentle squeeze at John's elbow. 'We're down here, on the left. Dr Arachchi is on duty, and I'll be staying in with you. One of the RMNs will be with us... maybe David? I'm not sure who's in this evening.'

'What's an RMN?'

'Sorry, we've got lots of acronyms around here; a registered mental nurse. That's what I'm training to be.' They walked almost to the entrance. 'Here we go. Room two.'

Inside the small consulting room, Chris introduced John to the doctor and nurse.

'Sit down here please, John Idris Jones. My name is Dr Jatunga Arachchi.' The short, slender Asian man spoke English that was precise and clipped.

'And I'm David Jones,' said another burly, rugby-player type.

'You are one of Dr Arwel Thomas' patients, is that right, John Idris?' Dr Arachchi asked.

'Yes,' John said after a moment's hesitation. He'd had very little experience of Asian people, next to none really – just the deckhands on the school cruise ship *Nevasa*; they'd done all the dirty work and cleaned up after people were seasick.

'I am one of the doctors in Dr Thomas' team. I will be seeing you regularly.'

John's ear wasn't attuned to Dr Arachchi's cadence, or to his accent, and he was slow to understand what he'd said.

'I have to carry out a physical examination of your body, John Idris. Will you strip to your underpants and lie on the couch please.'

His hands were cold. They probed and pressed and palpitated. He checked reflexes and pulses. He pulled down the waistband of John's pants, squeezed each of his testicles gently and then pulled back his foreskin. Then, washing his hands, he turned to David Jones.

'Can you take the boy's blood pressure please? I can never hear a bloody thing when I listen.'

After writing a couple of sentences in John's file, and noting the blood pressure reading that David had called out, Dr Arachchi asked John to get dressed.

'You seem quite fit,' he said when John was seated. 'But you look very tired. Do you sleep at night?'

'No, and even when I do drop off I usually wake up very early and then I can't go back to sleep.'

'At what time will you wake up in the night if you have been to sleep, John Idris?' Dr Arachchi asked.

'I don't know… three, maybe four o'clock.'

He wrote in the file again.

'Tell me why you have come here, John Idris,' he said, sitting back in his chair.

'Because Dr Thomas said he could help me,' John said, feeling anxious.

'Yes, yes, John Idris, but why do you need Dr Thomas' help? What trouble has brought you here?'

John didn't want to answer the question. Chris Fisher had been so friendly and helpful; he was afraid that if he said he was a homosexual, Chris might treat him differently. And David Jones looked so tough; John remembered the rugby boys who'd pushed his head down the toilet and pissed on him all those years ago.

'Do you understand my question, John Idris?' Dr Arachchi pressed. 'What is the nature of the problem that has brought you to see Dr Thomas?'

John wrung his hands and found himself giving in to the irritation that being called by both his names was causing.

'My name is John… right? Just John!'

Dr Arachchi nodded his head slowly and acknowledged John's assertion.

'It is very important that you tell me… John, if you can, why you have come here.'

'Because I want to die,' John spat.

'If you can, John, will you tell me why you want to die?'

'Because —' He looked at his shoes. He didn't want to see Chris and David's responses. 'Because I'm filthy and disgusting.'

'And why do you believe this to be true about yourself?'

'Because —'

'Because of what?' the doctor insisted.

'Because... homosexuals don't deserve to live.'

'You are a homosexual, and because of this you feel you want to harm yourself?' the doctor concluded.

'Yes,' John said, still looking at his shoes.

'Thank you, John Idris. That will be enough for today.'

Out in the corridor, John turned to Chris Fisher and dared to look into his face. He saw a look of concern.

'Are you okay, John?'

'I really didn't want to tell him, not in front of you. You've been so kind; I was afraid you'd be less friendly towards me.'

Chris raised his hands, questioning. 'I don't follow —'

'About being a homo,' John mouthed quietly, so no one would overhear.

'I already knew that,' Chris said. 'It's in your file.'

'Oh God, I didn't think it would be written down.'

Chris put an arm around him and they walked down the corridor. 'We're here to help you, John, not to judge you.'

'I just didn't think you'd write something like that down.'

'Don't worry about it; your medical notes are confidential. Come on, let's see what's on the telly.'

Jan was staring into the oblivion that lay somewhere between himself and the television screen, more drunk than before. After Chris left them, Jan seemed to become more aware.

'D'you want a swig?' he asked, grasping the bottle of vodka from inside his jacket in a fist at the end of an elastic arm.

'No thanks, Jan,' John said.

Over the next half hour, John felt a different kind of odium seep through him. Watching Jan, who was so good-looking, drinking himself into unconsciousness, John wondered about the waste of it all. In Jan, he could see a life being thrown away... and he could see himself in Jan. The calling of his name pulled him back.

'I'm John Jones,' he said to the man who approached him in the corridor.

'Hello, John. I'm Martin, one of the night staff.' He was slim, thirtyish and was wearing too much *Brut*. 'Mr Evans, the night charge nurse, wants to meet you. He always likes to get to know the newcomers. He likes to lay down the law.'

Uncertain whether Martin was being ironic, John followed him into the office and was introduced to a sharp-featured man in his sixties with a head of thick silver hair. Mr Evans had pinched cheeks and a pair of bi-focals on the end of a hooked nose.

'Sit yourself down while I read you the riot act.'

John heard the humour in his voice, but saw the seriousness in his eyes. 'Aye, aye sir,' he quipped and gave a mock military salute.

'That's what I like to see, Martin,' Mr Evans said, looking at John. 'A new recruit who recognises authority straight away.'

They all laughed.

'I'll do anything for my patients, if it's for their own good, but I won't stand any nonsense. As long as you understand that, we'll get along fine.'

'Yes, Mr Evans,' John said more seriously.

'Good. I'm glad we understand one other,' he offered, reaching for John's file. 'So, what's a bright kid like you doing in a place like this then?'

'It's all in the file,' John said, recalling what Chris had told him in the corridor; everything written down, a damning testament that would stalk him throughout his life.

'I don't usually have problems reading,' Mr Evans said, a spike in his tone. 'But I'd like to hear what you've got to say.'

'I'd probably kill myself if I wasn't here.'

'That's a pretty serious situation for someone who's only eighteen to be in,' he said, shaking his head slowly as he scanned the notes in the file. 'And why do you want to kill yourself.'

'Because I'm a homo, and that's the most disgusting thing a man can be.'

'Really?' Mr Evans quizzed. 'And what do you think about that, Martin?'

'You see some pretty despicable people in this job, even if they are sick,' Martin said.

Unsure of what Martin was inferring, John became anxious; did Martin think that he was despicable? Mr Evans interrupted his thoughts.

'It says here that you're not sleeping very well.'

'So you can read then,' John jibed, believing Martin had taken against him.

Mr Evans put his hand up, as if he was stopping traffic. 'Just take a deep breath, John. Don't lose it with me because I guarantee you'll come off worse than I will.'

John nodded, 'I'm sorry.'

'What about night sedation then? Will you take some pills to help you sleep?'

'I suppose so,' John said, shrugging his shoulders.

'If you come to the dispensary at quarter-past-nine we'll give you some Mogadon; then you'll have sweet dreams,' Mr Evans said, with a wink.

John got up to leave.

136

'Your father phoned to say that he got home alright. He's coming tomorrow, with your things, if the roads are clear.' Mr Evans extended his hand to John. 'Come on, it's better that we're friends.'

John stood before a door marked O.T. DEPARTMENT in bold letters. Turning the handle and finding the door unlocked, he pushed it open. Facing him, through four large windows, Denbigh's lights twinkled in the distance and flakes of snow, caught in the glow of the streetlamps, parachuted gracefully to the ground. Switching on the lights, the harsh fluorescents revealed a room neatly arranged with chairs around a dozen tables. The floor was strewn with cigarette ends, bits of cotton thread and slivers of fabric. Against one wall there was a grand piano, its ebony veneer scratched and stained. A small plaque, screwed to the piano's casing, read 'Donated to the Occupational Therapy Department by a grateful ex-patient – June 1966.' So that's what O.T. stood for. He wasn't much wiser.

John switched off the lights and sat in darkness, watching the snow. With so many stories from his childhood about the asylum it was hard to reconcile that he was now one of its patients; that he was *ill*. His thoughts lingered a while on his predicament, but when he failed to make any sense of what was happening to him he moved to the piano and played. His melody severed the silence. In the scar that tore through the still night the Sunday Library Group started to chant.

'You play well,' Martin said after switching on the lights.

'Not really,' John said, momentarily blinded by the glare.

'Why were you sitting in the dark?'

'So that no one can see how miserable I am.'

Martin sat next to him on the piano stool and put an arm

over his shoulder. John, already convinced that the nurse had taken against him, was surprised by this tender gesture.

'Come on, get a grip. You're going to be fine,' Martin said.

'So, what do you think?' John said sharply, shrugging off his arm.

'About what?' he asked, looking confused.

'In the office earlier; Mr Evans asked what you thought, remember?'

'About you being a homo? It doesn't matter what I think, does it?'

'In the mess that I'm in, what people think matters a lot.'

Martin fingered a few notes on the piano, sniffed, and ran his hands through his curly hair.

'What other people think shouldn't matter, John,' he said, scratching his head behind his ear. The thought of what two men might do together revolted him. 'It's what you think about yourself that's important; finding your own peace with who you are.'

'That's crap,' John erupted, slamming his hand onto the piano keys. 'How can you like yourself if people around you think you're disgusting... and they make fun of you and judge you?'

'None of us have judged you, John,' Martin said quietly.

'That's because you're paid to be nice to me, but it's what you all think, isn't it.' He hammered his fists into the keyboard and bit his lip hard because he didn't want to cry in front of Martin.

'I only came in to tell you that we'll be dishing out the medicines in a few minutes,' Martin said, getting up to leave. 'You're down for Mogadon, right?'

John nodded. He needed something to help escape from all these voices in his head.

After swallowing the two sleeping pills, John sought out the companionship of the television. The TV room was smoky, and the two men huddled close to the radiator were too drunk to care about what they were watching. Jan lay across one of the sofas, too far gone to be bothered about who saw the empty vodka bottle. John stood at the door for a moment, finding it hard to accept that he'd ended up in the madhouse with a drunkship of alcoholics on New Year's Eve.

In the quiet room, desperate to distract himself, he looked through a haphazard collection of books strewn across a shelf. Most were dog-eared Mills and Boon romances that held no promise of diversion. A pile of LPs lay beside a battered record player. In amongst the *Doris Day Collection*, some Perry Como and a Dorothy Squires double album, there was a recording of Mozart's Clarinet Concerto. A deep gouge in the vinyl ruined most of the first movement, but the second was beautiful and he played it over and over. The lone clarinet spoke of loneliness and despair, but the orchestra turned the same melody into something more noble and courageous; by the last chords of the movement he felt uplifted.

Feeling calmer, he turned into the charge nurse's office to say goodnight.

'Come and sit by the fire for a few minutes, John,' Mr Evans said with a smile. 'I think we might be able to squeeze one more cup from the pot, don't you, Martin?'

Martin poured him some tea.

'How are you feeling now?' Mr Evans asked.

'I don't know; none of it's making much sense.'

'After a day or two it won't seem so bad,' he said. 'Once you see that we can help, you'll forget the bad things you've heard about this place.'

For a few moments they drank their tea to the crackle of the logs Martin had put on the fire.

'You're going to have a busy day tomorrow,' Mr Evans said. 'Perhaps you'd better go to bed.'

'But it's New Year's Day.'

'And the machinery of this old hospital grinds on and on,' Martin quipped.

'Dr Arachchi wants you for an hour or so in the morning,' Mr Evans explained. 'He needs to build up your case history and explain a bit about the treatment.'

John sniffed at the cotton pyjamas Gareth Davies had left on his bed earlier. They smelled musty, so he slipped into bed in his underpants. The ward was filled with night noises; snores and sighs, and the occasional twang of bedsprings. One of the night-lights on the wall illuminated a clock, whose second finger jerked around the numbered dial towards 1975.

'You haven't slept much,' Martin whispered. The clock's twitching fingers showed ten-past-three. 'And you've been crying a lot.' He touched John's hand in a gesture of comfort. 'I can give you another Mogadon, if you like?'

'I'm so frightened.'

Martin held him for a long time.

*   *   *

'Wake up,' Chris Fisher said, shaking John's arm. 'Come on, it's breakfast time.'

John's head felt thick, but light at the same time. It was a strange sensation.

140

'We've left you 'til last, but you must get up now. The night staff are supposed to make the beds; it's not our job,' he said, smoothing out the sheet on the next bed. 'You've got ten minutes to get washed and dressed if you don't want to miss breakfast.'

John steadied himself more than once on the way to the bathroom. A cold shower did little to clear his head. Drying off, he had the peculiar sensation that all his actions were in slow motion, but that everything around him was at normal speed. He fiddled with his shirt buttons and ended up with two spare ones at the neck.

'Hey, steady on,' Chris said, coming up behind him in the corridor. 'That must have been some New Year's party.'

'It must be the sleeping pills,' John said.

'Let's get some porridge and some coffee down you.'

Helping to clear the breakfast things, John felt as if his head was floating somewhere above the rest of him – unconnected. If he moved his head too quickly, he felt dizzy. He dropped a cup and saucer and Chris suggested that he sit quietly for a while, until the doctor called for him.

He played the piano, a much-simplified piece by Chopin that he'd learned for an exam. A fuzzy drowsiness seeped through him and his playing was discordant. He repeated a section, just a few bars, that he'd never had problems with before, but he couldn't get it right. Chris found him crying.

'Dr Arachchi's ready for you.'

He sniffed back his tears of frustrated confusion and followed the nurse.

'We have a lot to do this morning, John Idris,' Dr Arachchi said. 'I will have to ask you many questions, to build up a comprehensive case history so that we can decide what is the best course of treatment for you.' He smiled. 'Do you understand, John Idris?'

'You don't have to keep calling me by both of my names,' John said, feeling irritated. 'Just call me John.'

Dr Arachchi wrote a sentence in the open file on the desk. 'Alright John. Can we start now?'

John nodded. The motion made him dizzy.

'First of all I have to ask you some very simple questions because I need to be sure you can concentrate and understand me.'

John's smile suggested scorn for the doctor's approach.

'Will you tell me please exactly where you are right now?'

'In your consulting room,' John offered with a snigger.

'Very good,' Dr Arachchi said. 'And can you tell me where this consulting room is?'

'In a hospital,' he said, not really believing the game they were playing.

'Very good again. And where is the hospital?'

'Denbigh in North Wales. This is Gwynfryn, the male reception ward.'

'Good... and who is the present monarch?'

John laughed, dismissively. 'The queen... Elizabeth the second,' he spat, shaking his head so that the doctor began to move across his field of vision.

'What about the Prime Minister, John?' Jatunga Arachchi asked, smiling broadly.

'Shit! I'm not sure. It's Heath or Wilson.'

And they all laughed.

'Alright John Idris, just one more little test. I want you to count backwards from 100, but take seven away each time.'

'I was never that good at sums, but —' He held onto the sides of the chair to stop the motion in his head. '100... 93... 87, no 86 I mean... 79... 72... 65... 58... 51... 40... 40... something. Fuck! This is stupid.'

'That is enough then,' Dr Arachchi said. He wrote a paragraph in John's file. Chris smiled and mouthed that he'd done alright.

Satisfied that his patient would be able to understand, and answer, his questions sensibly, Jatunga Arachchi began a searching interrogation, beginning with John's childhood. His delving left him with a picture of secure early years; a careful mother, who showed her children tenderness and love, and set them clear boundaries, and a father who worked hard to provide for them and found time to play with, and read to his boys after he came home from work. There had been walks in the countryside, learning the names of trees and plants; swimming at the beach and exploration of rock pools; holidays on a relative's farm, feeding chickens, cutting thistles with a sickle, and herding cows.

'Did either of your parents ever hit you?'

'No.'

'Were you ever interfered with, in a sexual way?'

'By my parents?' John exclaimed. He stared indignantly at the doctor, shaking his head

'And not by any other adult?'

'No.'

The doctor seemed especially interested that John had played more with girls than with boys, and that he'd played with dolls and liked dressing up.

'Would you like to have been a girl?'

'No.'

'Were your parents disappointed that you were a boy? Did they want a daughter?'

'I don't think so, but you'd really have to ask them about that.'

He wanted to know if John loved his parents, and to which of them he was closest.

'So, would you say that your father is weak and distant?' Dr Arachchi asked, after John had said that he was devoted to his mam.

John remembered all of the good times he and Billy had had with their dad. Of course, those times had been snatched between his real job, and all the odd jobbing he'd done, but Dai Jones wasn't weak, and any distance was of John's making, especially in the last few years.

They talked for a long time about sex, and John's sexual development; when he'd started to masturbate, and what images had accompanied the act. John remembered the climbing frame in his primary school, and the 'nice' feeling in his willy, sliding down the poles. Then there had been the games he'd played with Dewi and Carrot. He'd always thought about boys!

'And when did you start feeling ashamed?'

He remembered the ferryboat disaster and Aberfan, and that first time in the public toilet with the boy from the fairground.

'Dr Thomas has already told me that you have talked about the religious issues being a homosexual has raised for you,' Dr Arachchi said. 'I am not a Christian, so I do not think I want to talk about those aspects, but if you would like to talk to Dr Thomas again I can arrange it.'

'No, that's not necessary.'

'And what you want is to be a heterosexual; to be normal, is that right?'

'Yes,' John said.

Jatunga Arachchi wrote in John's file, and underlined one section that he'd written.

'Tell me about the voices you hear, John,' he said, after putting the cap back on his pen.

'I don't hear voices.'

'But you told your GP that you hear voices.'

John tried to remember what he'd said to Doctor-Richard.

'Well, do you hear voices, John Idris?' Dr Arachchi pressed.

'Only things that people have said, that seem to go around and around. But I don't hear *voices*.'

'Do they tell you to hurt yourself?'

He thought about Adam and the Sunday Library Group's choruses.

'They're not *voices*, Dr Arachchi,' John said. 'I'm not nuts like that. It's just bits of the Bible; verses that judge and condemn homosexuals... and bits of conversation that come back to me. I don't hear *voices* like mad people.'

But I do hear voices. I hear Adam's voice as clear as day. Does that mean I am mad? Does it?

The doctor wrote in the file for a long time. John looked at Chris Fisher, who smiled to reassure him.

'Dr Thomas and I have talked together about your case and I would like to explain what we think we can do to help you.' Dr Arachchi was sitting back in his chair, his legs crossed, his hands clasped over his knee. 'I want you to stop me, John, if there is anything that you do not understand... because I will ask you, at the end, to sign a form that says you agree with this treatment regime.'

'That's fine,' he said.

'The medications we propose are very straightforward; a combination of tranquillisers and antidepressants. We will start you off on them today.'

John nodded his understanding and acceptance.

'The tranquilliser is called Valium. It is quite a common medicine and it is very effective. After two or three days you should feel more relaxed.'

'Okay,' John muttered.

'It does have one or two side-effects; drowsiness, light-headedness... occasionally people feel a bit confused until they get used to it. But it is a very good medicine and we think you will benefit from it.'

John caught Chris' eye. Chris nodded, confirming the doctor's confidence in the drug.

'The second medicine is a bit more complicated. It is an antidepressant called Nardil. It is a very, very good medicine, but it has some drawbacks. You will have to be very careful with your diet. You have studied biochemistry at the university, is that right?'

'Yes.'

Dr Arachchi spent the next ten minutes explaining how monoamine-oxidase inhibitors worked to lift patients out of depression.

'So you will not be able to eat things like cheese, pickled herrings, broad beans... and a few more things. We will find you a treatment card that explains everything.'

'Well, if you think it's going to work for me,' John said with a gesture that indicated his agreement.

'Nardil can give you headache and make you feel drowsy, and sometimes patients get a dry mouth and complain that they feel weak,' he concluded.

'I trust that you and Dr Thomas only want what's good for me,' John said.

'Now I want to explain the treatment Dr Thomas and I have discussed to cure you of this homosexuality.' He leaned forward in his chair. 'You are sure that this is what you want, are you? To be cured of it?'

'Yes, I'm sure.'

'Dr Thomas is recommending Aversion Therapy. It's a behaviour modification technique based on one of the basic principles of behaviourism; the stimulus-response mechanism. When a pleasant experience is regularly associated with a particular, pleasing stimulus the behaviour is said to be positively reinforced.'

John thought Dr Arachchi sounded as if he was quoting from a textbook, but he understood what was being explained to him.

'In the same way, an unfavourable experience, linked with an unpleasant stimulus, causes negative reinforcement or deconditioning. You have heard of the work Pavlov did with dogs I suppose?'

'Yes, I know that he fed dogs just after ringing a bell, and taught them to associate the bell with feeding. Then, every time the bell rang the dogs would salivate.'

'Exactly; that was positive reinforcement,' the doctor said, pleased that John was grasping the concept. 'The same principles can be applied to the treatment for homosexuality. With Aversion Therapy we will help you recondition yourself by the positive reinforcement of heterosexuality and the negative reinforcement of homosexuality. Dr Thomas has assured me that it is a very effective treatment when the patient is highly motivated.'

'But can you do that just by ringing bells?' John asked.

'No, John Idris,' Dr Arachchi laughed. 'We will use electric shocks to negatively reinforce the homosexuality.'

John's look betrayed his disbelief.

'I did explain to you that the patient needs to be highly motivated if this treatment is to work successfully,' Dr Arachchi said.

John thought about Adam's utterances, and how dirty he'd been feeling. He thought about Mam and Dad, and how the shame of it all would be hard for them. He thought about wanting to die.

'Perhaps it does sound a little bit frightening, John Idris, but you know, medicine does not always taste very nice even though it does you good.'

John put his signature to the consent form.

'We will start the Aversion Therapy in the morning,' Dr Arachchi said, and dismissed his patient.

*   *   *

They sat quietly watching their son. The charge nurse had said they should let him sleep a while longer, but Olwen Jones willed him to wake up; they'd come a long way and she wasn't leaving until she knew he was settled.

'Not so bad, is it?' Dai whispered.

'It's clean enough,' she said. She'd already looked for dust and fluff under the bed. She squeezed John's hand discreetly, hoping to rouse him.

'And the nurses all seem nice enough,' Dai said, unsure whether he was trying to reassure Olwen or comfort his own unease.

'Can I get you some tea?' Chris Fisher asked, looking in on them.

'Yes please,' Olwen said. Not that she wanted a drink; she could do without getting caught short on the drive back over those moors, but at least she'd get to see if the cups and saucers were clean.

In the small kitchen, where the staff made their drinks and took short breaks, Gareth Davies was taking his first breather of the day.

'Sorry to disturb you boss,' Chris said. 'I'm just going to make John Idris's parents a cuppa.'

'Make sure the cups are clean,' the charge nurse quipped. 'She's already been running her finger along the windowsills.'

Making the tea, Chris thought again about John's session with Dr Arachchi that morning. 'Can I ask you something, off the record?'

'What?' Gareth asked, tossing aside the travel brochure someone had left lying around and dispelling his Majorcan beach daydream.

'This Aversion Therapy; it's a bit iffy don't you think?'

'What's iffy about it?'

'I thought it had been discredited.'

'John's very motivated to change, Chris.'

'When I was a medic I read some articles from the late sixties that say it's not really effective.'

'He doesn't want to he a homo,' Gareth said firmly. 'You can't blame the poor little bugger for signing up for it, can you?' He thought about his sons and looked into some vague, not too distant future. 'I wouldn't want either of my boys to be raving queers.'

'But it's so fucking primitive, Gareth; expecting people to respond like Pavlov's bloody dogs.'

'Christopher,' the charge nurse said, sounding like an annoyed father, 'You're a second year student nurse. If you want to qualify, and have a career at this hospital, you'd

149

better not challenge the likes of Arwel Thomas.'

Chris sighed heavily and sucked at his moustache. He wasn't sure what else he'd expected Gareth to say, but at least he'd voiced his concern.

'You'd better take those teas before they get cold.'

'Yes... okay boss.'

John was still asleep.

'I'd better wake him,' Chris said. 'We don't really want him to sleep all afternoon or he'll be up half the night.'

For a few moments John was completely disorientated.

'Oh... John Idris... *fy nghyw bach*... how are you?' Olwen coddled.

'Thanks for coming,' he said, slowly pulling himself up to hug her before letting his head fall back on the pillow. 'You'll have to give me a minute; they gave me something to help me sleep last night and it seems to have had a really delayed action. I was out for the count.'

'That's all right, *cyw*.'

'I'll just go and wash my face to wake myself up a bit.'

His dad helped him up. They hugged, and Dai Jones supported his son as he walked to the bathroom. John put his head under the cold tap.

'That's better,' he said more cheerily, rubbing his hair dry. 'Why don't you go back to Mam? I need a pee; I'll be out in a minute.'

'We've got your suitcase,' Olwen said, when John joined them again. 'I hope we've brought the right things.'

'Thanks. I'm sorry for all this trouble...' he began. He saw the redness around her eyes, betraying earlier tears. 'I'm sorry. I feel like I've let you both down.'

'You haven't let us down *cyw*. It's us. We've let you down.'

'No you didn't. You did your best for me and Billy.'

'Well, our best wasn't good enough then, was it?' she said brusquely.

John felt the pain of her sense of failure.

'It's not your fault, Mam, or yours, Dad.'

An uncomfortable silence settled around them.

'There were some books by your bed,' Dai said. 'I thought you might have been reading them so I put them in the case. And I made you a cassette; that Beethoven you were listening to.'

'Thanks, Dad —' But he was crying before he could say any more. He swallowed back the tears. 'I'm alright. All this'll pass. I will get better.'

Olwen held his hand until he regained some control. Dai, with an edge of impatience, broke the silence.

'Of course you'll get better, and we want to help you, but your mam and me... we don't know what's happening to you, so we don't know what to do.'

John unclasped his hand from his mam's and played uncomfortably with his fingers. He wanted to say something that they'd find helpful, but he didn't know what.

'Listen, John Idris,' Olwen said, trying to be more conciliatory. 'All you've told us is that you're confused about everything. I talked to Richard Roberts, but he said he couldn't tell us anything because you're an adult now, and that rude psychiatrist wouldn't tell your dad anything yesterday. We're completely in the dark. What can we do to help you, *cyw*?'

John hid his face in his hands and shook his head.

'I can't,' he said after a long time. 'I'm sorry, I don't know what to say.'

'Look at me, John Idris,' Olwen pleaded. 'There's nothing you can say that'll make your dad and me love you any less than we do.'

151

'I'm all mixed up,' John said, his strained features breaking through his fingers. 'I'm just so confused about everything.'

'So what do you want us to do?' Olwen asked, feeling helpless.

'Just carry on loving me, whatever happens.'

'But we do, John Idris... and we always will, *cyw*.'

And it was Olwen's turn to cry.

John showed them around so that they could see that it really was just like a normal hospital. They sat for a few minutes in the quiet room, poised on the edge of an ocean of silence.

'We had to say something to Nana and Taid. They're upset, especially because —'

'Because it's the loony bin in Denbigh,' John said into his dad's fumbling.

'Don't say that,' Olwen insisted.

John wondered how much longer they would stay.

'We had to tell them something,' Olwen offered up like an admission of guilt. 'We said you'd been studying too much and that you needed some rest. They send you their love, and want to know when they can come to see you.'

'God! It'll be all over town in a day or two, won't it?' John said. 'I hope people won't be... I mean, this place! I hope people will be okay about it.'

'Well, we'll see, won't we?' Dai said dismissively. 'What do we say if Nana and Taid want to come and see you?'

'Not yet, Dad; put them off. Maybe in a week or two, but not yet.'

'Billy had quite a shock too,' Olwen said. 'He'll try and come over, but he couldn't say when.'

They plunged into the silence.

This is too difficult for all of us. Why don't you go home?

'I've put writing paper and envelopes in the case for you,' Olwen gasped like a swimmer coming to the surface. 'Dad's put stamps in, and some ten pence pieces for the phone too; you'll have to let us know if there's anything else —'

'Thanks Mam.'

'And I've put you a few mince pies and a piece of Christmas cake, just in case they don't give you enough to eat.'

They dived into the silences more often and stayed submerged for longer with each dive.

'Well love, we'd better go,' Dai said.

'Yes, before it gets too late,' Olwen said, fighting to hold back her tears.

'Before the roads start to freeze,' John said.

They hugged and said good-bye. After he'd waved them down the drive John lay on his bed and wept; he wanted desperately to believe that they would still love him if they ever found out he was a homosexual.

Jan came and sat at his bedside.

'Were those your folks with you earlier?'

'I feel so guilty that I'm putting them through this,' John said, wiping the tears from his face. 'My mam looks as if she's aged ten years overnight.'

'Come on, don't go blaming yourself. Mothers always worry. You've had a breakdown. It's nothing to be ashamed of.'

'Who told you I've had *a breakdown*?'

'One of the nurses,' Jan said, hunching his shoulders as though who'd told him was of no significance. 'I asked somebody, Martin I think. Whoever it was said you've had a nervous breakdown.'

153

Is he going to ask me why?

'You're a student, aren't you? Working too hard I suppose?'

'Yes, something like that,' John quipped.

'Well, come on! Don't just lie there feeling sorry for yourself and getting upset over your father and mother; let's go and watch the telly or play cards. Can't have you breaking your heart like this, can we?'

When you're sober you're so nice, Jan.

'I'd like to play cards... I think I even saw a Scrabble game somewhere, if you'd like to play? But can we leave it for an hour or so? I need to unpack my case and sort myself out. Is that okay, Jan?'

'Yeah, sure. I'll be watching telly then,' he said as he left the ward.

'Jan!' John called after him.

'What?' he said from the corridor.

'Thank you.'

'Catch you later,' he said, his face a broad smile at the door.

Unpacking his suitcase, John thought about what Jan had said: *a nervous breakdown*. He'd heard the term before but he'd never really understood what it meant. In his mind's eye, he imagined tangled axons and blocked synapses.

'Nervous breakdown,' he mouthed quietly. 'I've had a nervous breakdown.' He liked the ambiguity of it. It could mean anything and he didn't have to give too much away. He felt relieved that he had an answer to give other patients when they asked him why he was there.

With everything from his suitcase stowed in his locker, he set about writing a letter to the Morgans in Aberystwyth. He wasn't clear of his motives for writing. The first letter – saying that he

154

regretted not opening up to Elen that afternoon she'd offered him tea and cakes – he tore into pieces. The one he sealed in an envelope and dropped in the patients' letterbox was brief – a nervous breakdown and the possibility that he might not return to Aberystwyth. He thanked them for their kindness and generosity.

He looked for Jan. One of the nurses said he'd gone out for a walk, which probably meant that he'd gone to buy alcohol. John played the piano for a while, and thought about Dr Arachchi and the electric shock therapy. It scared him and he wondered if there might be some other way, but then he began to drown in a more profound fear; the consequence of not trusting Arwel Thomas and Jatunga Arachchi, and the treatment they were offering, terrified him more than the treatment itself. He fumbled his way through a nocturne by Chopin, and as he played, he decided not to doubt or question the appropriateness of the treatment. If he didn't trust them, there was nothing left.

'Come and get it,' someone shouted.

He met Jan in the corridor and said that he'd looked for him; the glaze over his blank eyes told of another bout of drinking. They sat together in the dining room and Jan rambled in his drink.

'I bought her a little frilly dress; it was really pretty. But the fucking bitch put it in the dustbin. I fucking hate her. I'd like to wring her fucking neck.'

John didn't know what to say. He ate in silence, and Jan blathered on.

'You know, she won't let me see the baby. She got a fucking court order to keep me away. I'll fucking kill her. She put the little frilly dress in the fucking bin, and —' He belched and rubbed his belly. 'Can you fucking believe that? She threw the fucking dress in the fucking bin —'

'Is she your wife?'

'She's a fucking bitch, that's what she is. She kicked me out because I knock her around a bit. What the fuck does she know? And I sent the baby a Christmas present and she put it in the fucking bin.'

'What's the baby's name?' John asked tentatively.

'Amanda,' he said, tears welling up in his eyes.

In the following moments Jan began to swear loudly and with a swipe of his arm his plate flew to the floor, splattering food across the tiles. Leaving the dining room, he kicked over some chairs. Anxious that he'd been the cause of Jan's distress, John followed him down the corridor to the quiet room.

'I didn't mean to upset you,' John ventured from a safe distance, afraid that Jan might hit out at him.

Jan drew heavily on a cigarette held between nicotine stained fingers. 'You didn't,' he snapped, his hands shaking. 'Everything's just such a fucking mess and I'm not drunk enough.'

'We could play cards, or something.'

'Go and finish your tea, Johnny boy,' he said dismissively.

'D'you want to be on your own?' John offered.

'Who the fuck knows what I want?'

Then Jan kicked out at the sofa and John heard wood splinter.

'I need a fucking drink,' he said, making for the door.

John listened to the Mozart Clarinet Concerto. The sofa sagged uncomfortably after Jan's kicking, so he lay on the floor and let the music wash over him. The play of the melodies between the clarinet and the orchestra freed his mind.

'Medicines,' Martin called from the door. John followed him to the dispensary.

156

'You won't like the taste of this so you'd better knock it back in one,' Mr Evans said, handing him a plastic beaker.

'What is it?'

'It's very good for sending you to sleep.'

John sniffed the liquid in the beaker.

'God, it stinks.'

'It's a chloral hydrate mixture.'

'Is it going to make me feel light-headed like those pills I had last night?'

'Mistchloral can cause a bit of drowsiness, but you might feel a bit strange for a day or two anyway because you've started on the Valium and the Nardil today.' He pointed at the beaker in John's hand. 'Down in one, there's a good lad.'

'It's disgusting,' John said after slugging it back. 'I think you're trying to poison me.'

'No,' Mr Evans laughed. 'We're just anxious that you get back into a good sleeping habit. We don't want you lying awake half the night like last night.'

He lay in bed thinking about electric shocks and suicide... and Amanda's pretty dress in the dustbin. The night noises attacked each time he drifted into a drowsy stupor – snores and grunts, the twang of bedsprings. Then Adam's lament and the Sunday Library Group's choruses would pull him back into the despair of the night. Martin and Mr Evans were huddled around the fire when he went into the office sometime after two.

'I'm sorry to disturb you but that stuff you gave me doesn't seem to have worked. Is there anything else —'

'Back to bed, now! Move it!' Mr Evans cut him off.

'I just need something —'

'Now means now, John! You get yourself back into that bed,

or I'm going to get annoyed with you. You've had all the night sedation we can give you, so – back to bed. Move!'

John didn't understand why Mr Evans wasn't being sympathetic. He thrust two outstretched fingers towards him. 'Fuck off, Mr fucking Evans.' He ran from the office, back into the cage where no one cared for him.

After some time Martin came and sat on his bed.

'I can get you a couple of Mogadon if —'

'You can stick your fucking pills,' John spat, throwing off the nurse's hand. 'Better still, tell that bastard Evans to stick them. If his arse is as big as his mouth they'll go a long way.'

'Hey, steady on. I know he upset you, but being abusive isn't going to help.'

'He's a fucking bastard. I only asked for something to help me sleep. It's awful here, hearing all the snoring and all the chaos inside my head. I'm so frightened about what's happening to me.'

Martin stayed with John until the sobbing stopped and the panic felt less acute.

'I'll get you a couple of Mogadon,' he said, 'You should be able to sleep then.'

*   *   *

John's mouth tasted bitter and his eyes felt heavy behind the crusted lids. It took him some time to recognise the nurse who'd held him for so long; he felt the same floating sensation as before but now his vision was out of focus.

'Good morning,' Martin said. 'D'you have sweet dreams?'

Confused, he wondered whether it was still night time. Was it only minutes before that Martin had been holding him – and that he'd lost it with Mr Evans?

'I shouldn't have told him to fuck off, should I?'

'No, that wasn't very clever,' Martin agreed. 'Come on, shift your arse.'

'Will you tell him I'm sorry?'

'It's not for me to do your apologising for you,' he said, puffing up the pillows of the next bed.

John got to his feet and the whole world began to move, up... down... around... and then he was on the floor and Martin was standing over him.

'Did you bang your head?'

'No... but I'm all floaty.'

Martin helped him up and put him to sit in a chair. 'Stay there for a minute while I make your bed, then I'll help you to the wash room.'

John drifted into unconsciousness and only came to when Martin and David Jones virtually carried him through to one of the shower rooms. David stripped him and sat him on a stool in the shower stall. The cold water eventually brought him to some level of alertness.

'I think I'm awake now. Any chance of some hot water... it's bloody freezing in here?'

'Will you be alright or do you want me to stay with you?' David asked.

'Let me see if I can stand up.' He wasn't dizzy, but his head wasn't connected to the rest of him. 'I'm okay now... thanks.'

Soaping himself under the hot shower he thought about David; such a burly rugby player type. A door opened in his mind that led away from all the bewilderment and he began to touch himself.

'All these drugs haven't confused you, have they?' he whispered to his erection.

Dr Arachchi was waiting when David showed John into the consulting room at ten o'clock.

'Good morning, John Idris. How are you this morning?'

'I'm a bit lightheaded, but otherwise I'm fine.'

'Good, please sit down.'

Jatunga Arachchi smiled his gleaming white smile at David Jones. 'You are staying in with us, are you David?'

'Yes, and Chris Fisher will be along too. He's just gone to fetch the envelope from Dr Thomas' office.'

Jatunga Arachchi turned to John.

'While we are waiting, do you have any questions about this Aversion Therapy?'

John sighed deeply. He remembered playing the Chopin nocturne – how he'd made the choice not to doubt.

'You explained everything really well yesterday, but —'

'Yes?' Dr Arachchi encouraged.

'Well, these electric shocks. It's all a bit frightening really.'

'Have you changed your mind?' Dr Arachchi asked carefully.

'No...' John said, perhaps too quickly. 'But is it going to hurt? Will the shocks be really high?'

'Enough to give you a good jolt,' Dr Arachchi said, mimicking the jerk of an electric shock. 'It has to produce a sufficiently unpleasant stimulus for the negative reinforcement to be effective; that is the only way we can cure you.' He picked up a black box, about the size of a children's shoebox, from the desk in front of him. It had a calibrated dial on one side and some switches. Some coloured wires protruded from another side and there was a long lead with a plug. He thrust it towards David Jones. 'Do you know how this machine works?'

David took the box, and placing it on his knees, he separated the wires. 'It's quite straightforward, Dr Arachchi,' he said. 'It

160

plugs into the mains and the dial here can be set at anything from 25 to 150. Once it's set up it's just a case of attaching the electrodes and pushing the switch.'

There was a knock on the door and Chris Fisher came in with a large, brown package under his arm.

'The envelope,' Dr Arachchi said with a dazzling flash of white enamel.

'Dr Thomas' secretary said that there's a letter inside,' Chris said, handing it to the doctor.

'Please get undressed now, John Idris,' Jatunga Arachchi said as he emptied the contents of the parcel onto the desk. From amongst the half dozen magazines, he picked up a smaller envelope and read the enclosed letter.

John could see the cover page of two magazines. One was called *Big Boys* and carried the image of a burly, bare-chested man whose hands clasped his crotch. The other had a picture of a group of surfers on a beach under the title *California Dream Boys*. He stood in his underpants, self-conscious and embarrassed.

'Pants off too,' David said. 'We need to be able to see your responses.'

Naked, John stood before Dr Arachchi and the two nurses, his own hands clasped like the man in the photograph on the cover page of *Big Boys*.

'All right, David,' the doctor said, folding the letter and putting it back in the envelope. 'We need to set the dial at seventy-five. You will look after the machine please... I am not very good with technical things.'

'Seventy-five,' David said, as he fiddled with the dial and separated the wires. 'Did somebody remember the Elastoplast?'

Chris Fisher reached into his pocket for the reel of adhesive dressing. He cut two pieces about an inch and a half long and as David held the electrodes against John's left wrist Chris smoothed the tape over them.

'Okay,' David said. 'Everything's set here.'

Dr Arachchi smiled, and offered John the magazine called *Big Boys*.

'Please take it. I want you to go through the pages and find a man that you like. One that is appealing to you... one that you find sexy.'

The doctor's precise English jarred with the message his words conveyed and John scowled.

'I know it is not an easy thing... at the beginning like this... but just try to imagine that we are not here,' the doctor said, his head making twitching nods that were meant as encouragement. 'Find a man that really turns you on and fantasise about him. I want you to let yourself go. I want you to get hot... get sexually aroused and excited about the men in the magazine.'

John turned the pages and realised why the magazine was called *Big Boys*. He'd never seen this kind of pornography. The bodies of the men were tanned and muscular. Some were hairy, and most were naked, but one wore an unbuttoned police tunic and another was in grimy builder's overalls. John supposed it was an American magazine because all the cocks were circumcised.

'Let yourself get carried away, John,' Dr Arachchi encouraged. 'Men like this do excite you... hmm? Would you like to be with him... that one there, and feel his hands all over you?'

John turned the pages, feeling ashamed that his body was beginning to respond so visibly, but the images were sexy, and if he'd been alone he'd have enjoyed them. David Jones, Chris Fisher and Jatunga Arachchi were staring at him... and at his semi-erection as if it was a laboratory animal about to perform a trick. He couldn't ignore them, and in the circumstances he felt that what he was being asked to do was just too ridiculous. He closed the magazine and let it slip from his hand onto the doctor's desk.

'I'm sorry. It's a very nice magazine, but with the three of you watching me it's difficult to —' He clasped his hands over his swelling cock. 'It's very embarrassing for me.'

'You must try, John,' the doctor said sternly. 'This therapy can only work with your co-operation. Try! Look at the magazine again. Find the one that really excites you. Try again.'

The man in cowboy chaps, his naked bottom pushed towards the camera, was beautiful. John looked at him for a long time and began to imagine the feel of the leather. The man's sweaty body glistened in the sunshine and John caught the hint of his musk as he brushed his cheek against his thigh. He felt the excitement rise inside him as he kissed the cowboy's nipple... and in a fraction of a second the electric orgasm surged through his body jarring him rigid and leaving him limp.

Dr Arachchi handed him *Monica's Big Surprise*.

'Open it. Look at those tits... they are lovely, no? Look at that picture there: her legs are wide open, inviting you in. Does she excite you? Would you like to fuck her? Look at those juicy lips. It would be so wonderful to feel yourself pushing inside her. Much better than a hairy, shitty arse hole! Think of fucking her.'

John turned the pages and listened to Dr Arachchi's encouragement... and he began to feel disgusted by him. After a while the doctor took the magazine away and handed him another.

The pictures in *Robbie and Dale Take a Shower* were explicit and showed the boys having oral sex. John paused over one of the images and felt his flaccid penis begin to engorge... and David flipped the switch. Then Monica cupped her large breasts towards him and Dr Arachchi whispered sweet nothings about what she and John might do together. The *California Dream Boys* lived up to the title of the magazine; from its pages they smiled, all blond hair and white teeth, sun tanned and well hung. And the electric orgasm came again.

And so it went on, magazine after magazine, photograph after photograph.

Naked men with lithe bodies, their skin gleaming... electric shock.

Women... beautiful women... and Jatunga's pillow talk.

Muscular thighs and body hair... moist lips and big cocks... electric shock.

Large breasts and peaked nipples... such beautiful women.

Cocks: long cocks... erections... cocks being pummelled and cocks being sucked... electric orgasm.

Open legs and moist vagina lips... beautiful women... and Jatunga's foreplay.

Puckered ass cracks... finger-joshing... tongue rimming... shocking electric orgasm.

Jatunga's whisperings about what John could do with a beautiful woman.

Two men kissing... loving...fucking... another shock.

And the electrodes on his wrist felt hot.

What sort of therapy is this? What sort of treatment?

'Do you think you could fuck a woman if you had the chance, John?' Dr Arachchi asked. 'Could you? Or is the thought repulsive to you?'

'I've never said that women are repulsive to me. I've *never* said that.'

'So you could give a girl a good fuck if you had the opportunity?'

It seemed to John that they'd all become fourteen-year-olds

164

behind the bike shed at school, four boys together talking dirty.

'I suppose I could... yes,' John said.

Sweet-talking Jatunga became Dr Arachchi again. 'You have done very well today, John,' he said. 'I think we will stop on that really positive note. You can get dressed now. We can carry on tomorrow.'

David pulled off the Elastoplast and removed the electrodes.

'Are you okay, John?' Chris asked once they were out in the corridor.

'Yes, I'm fine.' But he wasn't fine at all.

'Come on then, I'll take you down to the O.T. room; everything's finally getting back to routine after the holidays.'

'So, what goes on there?' John asked.

'I'll introduce you to Big Meirwen, but don't you go telling her I called her that.'

Meirwen was in her mid-fifties. She had red hair from a bottle, make-up that was overdone and a bust bigger than Diana Dors. She ran the O.T. department, and as the senior occupational therapist she was responsible for seeing that the patients at Gwynfryn – the men, and the women from the next-door bungalow – had 'therapy' five days a week.

'All right then, *cariad*,' she said in a mixture of Welsh and English after Chris had introduced them. 'You can make one of these nice tea trays, if you like? You have to weave all this edging here. Or perhaps you'd like to make a Basil Brush? Like on the telly, you know? All the furry material comes ready cut, so all you have to do is sew it together and stuff it. They're lovely and cuddly, once they're made up; look at this one.'

She handed him the stuffed fox – a sad cousin of the puppet TV star.

165

'I think I'd rather go and read —'

'No... no, *cariad*,' Meirwen said, pushing him towards a table and pulling out a chair. 'O.T. is a very important part of helping you to get better. Basil Brush then, is it?'

'I'd rather not thank you. I'd be much happier —'

'Well, *cariad*, happy or not, you'll sit here until it's time for dinner and then you'll sit here all afternoon, so you might as well do something to pass the time.' Meirwen pushed him into a seat. 'You tell me when you're ready to start.'

John sat obediently. The radio blared out the round-up of the last year's hits; 1974 had been a good year. For a short time he strummed out the beat of the radio music on the table with his fingers and defied Meirwen's glower. But slowly the music faded and the activity around him died away as he got lost somewhere inside himself.

Chris tired to persuade him to come and eat some dinner. John had some awareness of Chris's presence; he could hear his voice and understand what he was saying, but the lost place inside himself felt like a safer place to be until the madness stopped. If he came out for dinner he might not find his way back in again.

Chris was alone with Gareth, the charge nurse. Gareth had put a Do Not Disturb sign up and closed the office door.

'It's fucking barbaric,' Chris said through clenched teeth.

'What's the matter, Christopher?'

'I sat through it, Gareth, and what we're doing to John is more like fucking torture.'

'Just calm down, Chris. A lot of the sights we see here are upsetting.'

'But if you follow the logic they could stick the electrodes on my wrist and turn me into a homo! We'd think that was really fucking iffy, wouldn't we?'

'And you say that John's just completely withdrawn since this morning's session?' Gareth said, avoiding Chris's inference.

'I think he understood when I talked to him.'

Gareth squeezed his right ear lobe between his finger and thumb and pulled it in a circular motion. It was a quirk Chris had noticed more than once when the boss was stressed.

'Have another go, Chris,' he said, his earlobe an angry red. 'See if you can get him talking.'

John was sitting in the quiet room listening to the clarinet piece.

'This is where you're hiding out then is it?' Chris said.

'I like this music.'

Chris sighed with relief that John had come back to them. 'What was going on with you in O.T. just before dinner?'

'I was just being quiet.'

'Can you remember that I came to talk to you?'

'Yes.'

'But you just didn't want to talk to me, is that it?'

'No... not exactly.' John wasn't sure he could explain the safe, still place he'd found inside himself, or describe what had happened after everyone had left the O.T. room for dinner. If he'd first thought of a nervous breakdown as tangled axons and blocked synapses, he'd now changed his mind; the neural pathway that had allowed him into the safe stillness of his 'deeper inside' was neither tangled nor blocked and he'd realised that he could come and go as he pleased.

And most of the time it pleased John not to be a patient at Gwynfryn.

*   *   *

167

On Monday morning, before the orgy with Jatunga and the boys and girls in the magazines, Chris Fisher handed John an envelope with an Aberystwyth postmark. In the quiet room, he sliced open the envelope with a care that almost amounted to reverence. Two letters fell out, one on mauve Basildon Bond, the other on a white sheet of A4 paper with a formal letterhead.

Elen Morgan had written in English, her handwriting brisk but clear and easily legible.

The Manse, Friday.

Dear John Idris

Your letter came as a bit of a shock today – although you had talked of strain when you called here not so very long ago. I had made a mental note of what you said, but had not realised that it was a matter of <u>immediate</u> importance. This now grieves me and I feel I should have offered more than tea and cakes. However, that is past. Please, please in the future, will you realise that Rhys and I are only too ready to 'bear burdens' – and we regard it as a great privilege and joy if there is <u>anything</u> we can do to be of some use to you. When you have been here the whole tone of the conversation has always been lively and full of laughter and I'm sorry if this means we have been insensitive or that it has made it more difficult for you. Life is laughter <u>and</u> stress – we know that well.

God bless – our prayerful thoughts are with you. We'd be delighted if you can keep in touch. We look forward to good news.

Very sincerely,
Elen Morgan

Through his tears he remembered her warm smile and her kindness, and how she'd said that she believed God found people where they are.

Even in this madness, Elen?

When he stopped crying he unfolded Rhys's typed letter, written in Welsh.

03/01/1975

Annwyl John

Cawsom cryn fraw y bore yma... *We had quite a shock when your letter arrived this morning. Your news saddened and pained us. Neither of us had realised that you were living under such a burden; had we done so, we would have encouraged you to share it with us.*

Thank you for putting your trust in us sufficiently to write. We will keep you in our thoughts and pray that you will recover fully in the course of time.

Life brings difficult times to everyone and it is always worth remembering those well-known and comforting words from Deuteronomy: 'The eternal God is your dwelling place, and underneath are the everlasting arms.' God is a place of refuge and God's 'everlasting arms' are always there to support us – through prayer we can lay all our burdens in God's arms. If you can find a copy of our hymnbook, hymn 491 may be helpful.

Keep trusting in God.

Get well soon and come back to us when you're ready.

Sincerely,
Rhys Morgan

Touched by their concern, and encouraged by the unembarrassed simplicity of their faith, John cried until his eyes were stinging. Then he eased the folded letters carefully back into the envelope and pushed it thoughtfully into the breast pocket of his shirt, under his pullover, so that he could carry their kindness with him. Mozart's clarinet brought him some peace until David fetched him for his session of Aversion Therapy.

Dr Arachchi changed his tactics. No more of Monica, with big breasts, or Sonja with a juicy cunt. All the pictures were of men, brawny and naked, and all the action was hard-core. With no women to offer respite, the electric shocks were more relentless. When Chris eventually yanked the Elastoplast from John's wrist and removed the electrodes, two red burn marks bore witness to David's diligence on the switch.

Big Meirwen smiled; 'You're here all afternoon so you might as well get on with it,' she said, placing a heap of furry material on the table in front of him. He sat next to a woman in her forties with sunken eyes and lipstick that was too red. She kept an eye on the line of his sewing, but sometimes she lost interest; she'd start to wail, and take off her blouse to reveal sagging breasts that weren't like the ones in Jatunga's magazines. Then John's needlework went a bit skew-whiff. Some time later, someone on the radio was singing 'If My Friends Could See Me Now'... He started to sing along and soon most of the furry fox stitchers joined in the singsong, tapping their feet to the rhythm and laughing. And then it fell quiet again and they continued to sew.

After the evening meal he sought out Jan for a game of cards, but Jan lay on his stomach across his bed embracing a bucket that was already filling up with vomit.

'I'm sorry you're not well,' John offered.

'It's the fucking Antabuse,' Jan groaned. 'They gave it to me this morning and then offered me whatever I wanted to drink, so I've had a skinful courtesy of the NHS.' He threw up again into the bucket. 'I think I'm going to die.'

'Probably,' John said. 'But not today, Jan. Shall I empty your bucket?'

As he carried the stinking load from the ward Jan puked all over himself.

'I'll call one of the nurses to come and clean you up,' John said.

*   *   *

Between Mozart's clarinet in the quiet room and the still centre of his 'deeper inside', John found some sanctuary from the madness all around him. He read the Morgans' letters many times; he nearly always cried, but after the tears different thoughts would come. 'God finds us where we are' he remembered Elen saying that first time they'd talked, and Rhys, in his letter, was saying that God was always there to embrace people in trouble with those 'everlasting arms'. Was this true for homosexuals too? Was the Morgans' God different to Adam's? Bigger somehow? The Sunday Library Group's God was so busy small-mindedly judging people and then condemning them. Was Rhys and Elen's God really any different, with arms wide enough even to embrace homos?

He let himself think about the possibility.

'Hello God, I'm John.'

'Hello John. I'm pleased to meet you.'

'Are you?'

'Yes.'

'But I'm a homosexual.'

'Yes, I know.'

'Elen Morgan says that you find people where they are.'

'She sounds like a wise woman. What do you think she means?'

'Don't really know, but I know what I'd like it to mean.'

'Well?'

'That you'll find me acceptable.'

'You're a part of what I've created, and I've given you free will.'

'What does that mean?'

'That's for you to work out! Why not let these old arms of mine hold you for a while and you just think about it?'

But it was the love-ins with Jatunga Arachchi, which Arwel Thomas had prayerfully arranged, that kept coming back to his mind's eye. Arwel Thomas's God wanted fundamental change, and now every pornographic image and electric orgasm had begun to feel like an assault against his 'deeper inside', just like Adam's litany and the Sunday Library Group's choruses. These gods seemed to want such different things. *The arms of the Morgans' God aren't wide enough to embrace the likes of me, a disgusting homosexual, are they?* He fingered the burn marks on his wrist. *Here's the evidence of how depraved I am. I need all these shocks to purge me of this thing.* Adam and the Sunday Library Group revved up the volume. *Their God's already taken sides – and I'm on the wrong side.*

He heard Chopin's Nocturne in some nook of memory and remembered his choice not to doubt the two doctors. He fingered the envelope with the Morgans' letters – for the time being he'd keep it close to him and perhaps, when he wasn't so mad, their words might make more sense.

*   *   *

Dr Arachchi presented two new magazines on Tuesday, *Bad Boys Games* and *Loaded – Ready to Shoot*. John wondered if the homosexual pornographers and the Aversion Therapists had struck a deal, and whether there was a special waiver from customs on mail orders that claimed to be 'for medicinal use only'. The electric shocks came regularly, accompanied by a litany of lurid sex talk aimed at turning John against his homosexual self. He clung to his faith in the doctors and their therapy, for what other hope did he have? In the dispensary, after the bad boys had played their games and the loaded shock box had been shot more times than John could count, Chris rubbed some ointment into the new pair of rubies in his bracelet.

On Wednesday there was a female quartet; Lucy and Brigitte joined Monica and Sonja. There were no electric shocks that day. No men, just fulsome breasts and parted legs with moist pink vaginas, and encouraging boys' dirty talk from Jatunga.

You're really getting off on this, aren't you boys?

*   *   *

He sat at the table in the O.T. room, his sewing untouched.

'You've got a visitor,' Chris Fisher called from the door. 'I've shown her into the quiet room.'

John pulled himself back from the calm of the 'deeper inside' and hurried along the corridor, his box of tricks open

173

so he'd be able to find the right mask as soon as he recognised his visitor. He pushed open the door of the quiet room and Bethan beamed her toothy smile. He donned the *I'm still your friend from school* mask, and for an instant he was cast back to the prep room at the back of the biology lab where they'd sat for hours drinking instant coffee with Judith. He felt a pang of guilt; wasn't it Bethan who'd come to his mind when Paul had asked if he'd ever had sex with a woman?

'Look at you?' he said, seeing not a schoolgirl but a sophisticated young woman.

Bethan had spent the autumn of a year off from education with her cousins in Canada. During her A-level year she hadn't been sure enough that she wanted to go to university, and because her father was loaded she'd been afforded the luxury of a year travelling.

'The new me,' she said, giving a twirl to show off the outfit she'd bought at an expensive boutique in Vancouver.

'It's gorgeous, Beth' he said and gave her a hug. 'And your hair is so much shorter.'

'It's easier this way,' she said, combing with her fingers. 'I'm off on an overland expedition in a couple of weeks. I'll be living out of a rucksack for three months.'

'God, really?' he gushed. 'Where to?'

'Cairo to Cape Town,' she sang with excitement.

'Wish I could come.'

An embarrassed silence gripped them both in painful realisation.

'Your mother told me about the breakdown,' she eased into their disquiet.

'A nervous breakdown,' he said, hoping she'd see the

174

confusion of tangled axons and not probe too much; Bethan had got an 'A' in biology too and she knew about axons and synapses.

'Doesn't sound like the John Idris I knew and loved at school,' she said, squeezing his hand in hers.

'Lots of the skeletons behind closed doors got rattled, Beth.'

'D'you want to talk?'

'No... but thanks.'

So she talked about Vancouver and Lake Louise and how, once the snow had come, the cars had to be plugged in to keep them from freezing... and then they walked in the winter sunshine around the landscaped gardens. Standing by her father's Rover they hugged and she kissed him on the cheek.

'Take care, love, and hurry home,' she said through the open car window as she drove away.

Dr Arachchi, his face a broad grin, met him in the corridor. 'Will you step into my room please, John Idris?'

'Not another session with the shock box —'

'No... I want to talk about your friend.'

Sitting opposite Dr Arachchi, John noticed the ruffled net curtain at the window.

'She is very pretty,' he said.

'Bethan... she's a friend from school.'

'Just a friend you say?'

John searched the doctor's quizzical expression and tried to read the inference of the enquiry.

'She held your hand when you were walking.'

'We're friends, that's all.'

Dr Arachchi leaned forward in his chair, his elbows on his knees and his chin supported by the thumbs of otherwise clenched fists. John recognised the matey Jatunga from their morning sessions with the girlie magazines.

'She embraced you before she drove off, and she kissed you,' Jatunga teased. 'You both looked very intimate together.'

'We were always close.'

'Does she have a boyfriend?'

'She was going out with a boy for about a year.' He knew that Bethan and Simon had broken up. Hadn't they talked about him in the prep room? John had been a regular agony aunt for Beth and Judith. He'd shared their angst about going on the pill and going all the way. Beth had even been indiscreet about poor Simon's premature ejaculations.

'Do you fancy her?' Jatunga asked.

'Like you want me to fancy Monica and Lucy you mean?'

'Well,' Jatunga smiled. 'Do you think you could fuck her?'

John felt his belly muscles knot. He fingered the ruby bracelet on his wrist. *If I stop trusting you I'm dead, but it doesn't mean I have to like you.* 'I don't know whether Bethan would fancy me like that.'

'But if she did fancy you, do you think you could screw her?'

She's one of the few friends I've got. Why would I want to throw that away by making a pass at her?

'The whole idea of having sex with a girl disgusts you?' Jatunga insinuated into John's introspection.

'I've told you before... I've never said that!'

'So you could fuck her if the opportunity was there?'

'I don't know... I suppose... but she's going abroad for three months in a week or two.'

'Why not put it to the test then?' Jatunga said, his eyes sparkling. 'You can go home for the weekend.' He smiled. 'Create the opportunity. Buy her a nice dinner with a few drinks to loosen you both up.' He winked and leaned forward to grasp John's shoulder in a matey gesture. 'I want you to come back on Sunday and tell me that you have tasted the sweet honey pot.'

You're giving me a sex prescription?

'Once you have tasted the honey pot you will never be interested in a hairy shitty arse again.'

'I'll have a go,' John said limply.

'That is not good enough, John Idris. Tell me you will go home and fuck her.'

'I'll go home and fuck her,' John said with robotic conviction.

Olwen sounded delighted on the telephone. That he was coming home for a weekend, so soon, had to be a sign that he was getting better.

Later, while playing the piano, a scheme came together in his head. He would go home for the weekend, but he wouldn't contact Beth; he'd listen to Brahms and Beethoven, and if the weather was fine he might walk along the beach, and on his return he'd herald Jatunga's inspired suggestion as a great success. They might stop giving him electric shocks then! Later still, listening to the night noises, he realised that his planned deception amounted to a decision not to trust Dr Arachchi and Dr Thomas. He tried to block the thoughts that crowded in on him about the likely consequences.

Thursday's ninety-minute excursion to the beach with the *California Dream Boys* confirmed Jatunga Arachchi's abhorrence of sexual contact between men. The shocks came every couple of minutes and the pillow talk was crude and hostile. John tried to find his way into the 'deeper inside' during the session, but the

177

surges of electricity must have confused those internal pathways. The ruby bracelet became heavier.

After an hour with Sonja and Brigitte on Friday morning, and a running commentary that left John in no doubt how he might give Bethan pleasure, Jatunga shook his hand and winked. 'Do not let me down now,' he said.

*   *   *

They spoke little on the journey back to Barmouth. On the car radio, a programme of American hits from 1974 played quietly; Dai Jones liked to have the radio on, but didn't really like to listen to it. John hummed to John Denver's 'Annie's Song' and Neil Diamond's 'Longfellow Serenade'. When Paul Simon sang 'Still Crazy After All These Years' he sang along, which made Dai uncomfortable.

It was shortly after three when they drove into town.

'I'll just call into Miss Lewis's to get some fags,' Dai said.

John turned up the radio and watched his dad's slow progress towards the tobacconist's; Dai knew everyone in town and there was always something to say. He saw Bethan, carrying bags of shopping, walking on the opposite pavement. Hoping that she wouldn't notice him, he turned to watch the people drink their teas through the steamed-up windows of the Milk Bar. Beth tapped on the passenger window. He smiled, and feigned delight at seeing her. She said they should go for a drink; being back in Barmouth was so boring after the excitement of Canada.

'The Last Inn at eight then,' she said before skipping along the pavement.

He had a fight with Olwen about going out that evening.

'You just want to wrap me up in cotton wool,' he yelled, frustrated by his mam's clucking, and stormed from the house.

Walking along the prom towards the quay he quickly calmed himself. It was a crisp, clear night. Pwllheli's lights danced on the horizon across Cardigan Bay and the Great Bear dived into the sea near Enlli. Bethan, already on her first Bacardi and Coke, was chatting to Nick the barman, when John pushed through the crowded bar.

'What d'you want?' she asked after they'd hugged.

'I'd better stick with bitter-lemon, I'm already on a cocktail of drugs.'

'It's so smoky in here,' she said to Nick as she paid for the drinks. 'Is upstairs open?'

They sat on a comfortably worn leather sofa before a crackling fire in the small upstairs lounge and Beth's intuition told her to talk. She didn't pry into John's troubled mind but carried him away with her stories of horse rides in the Rockies, skinny-dipping in clear Canadian lakes, preparations for the trek across Africa and love affairs after Simon. She drank lots of Bacardi – without much Coke. John didn't mind buying them – she'd come to the hospital after all. The sofa sagged a bit in the middle and had a tendency to coax and oblige a degree of closeness. John's arm was around her shoulder; Bethan's hand was on his thigh. Neither had appreciated their intimacy.

Dr Arachchi's 'sweet nothings' whispered into his consciousness. Bethan had snuggled into him and her head was resting on his chest. Her hair smelled of sweet herbs; he couldn't identify the thyme and rosemary of her hair conditioner because he didn't know those smells, but it was a fresh clean smell that teased his senses. Jatunga Arachchi whispered some more. John wanted to trust him again. He wanted to live.

179

'You smell lovely,' John said, easing his fingers through her hair.

'It's just my usual one,' she said.

Jatunga whispered his encouragements.

'I was just thinking,' he said.

'What?'

'Just that I was always a bit slow, at school.'

'You weren't slow! Brightest of the bunch you were!'

'No... with girls I mean.'

'But you had loads of girlfriends. There was me for starters, and Jude. And Jen and Liz. And you knocked around with Cath for a while.'

'Yes, but I never had a girlfriend. I was just "one of the girls" wasn't I?'

'We all trusted you,' Bethan said. 'There was never a hidden agenda with you.'

Jatunga egged him on.

'I always fancied you, you know.'

'You didn't!' she challenged, starting to giggle.

'I did... I do... but then, with the likes of gorgeous Simon, what chance did I ever have? I was dead jealous.'

'I never knew... I'm sorry,' she said, giving John a comforting squeeze.

Jatunga's whisperings focussed his mind.

'There's nothing to be sorry about. I never stopped fancying you.'

His left hand brushed her thigh before resting on her knee.

He felt her body stiffen. She untied herself from their intimacy and pulled herself up to the edge of the sofa. Her forehead wrinkled and she tried to focus on the horse brass that hung beside the fireplace.

'Is this why you've kept buying me all these Bacardis? To get me drunk?'

John listened for Jatunga's advice on how to deal with this turn of events but he was too busy looking at the women in the magazines.

Bethan stood up and steadied herself: 'You're a shit, John Idris Jones! I always thought you were better than this.'

Jatunga was drunk on the images and in no position to offer John counsel.

'You've no need to walk me home,' she said, buttoning up her coat. 'I'll get Nick to call me a taxi.'

The 'I'm sorry' that John wanted to offer was drowned in the wave of shame that washed over him.

Neither Brahms nor Beethoven could soothe the agitation of his disappointment in himself through that Sunday morning. He thought about phoning Beth to apologise, but the phone was in the hallway and he'd be overheard from any part of the house. And anyway, perhaps she wouldn't remember after all those Bacardis.

Dai said that it would be soon enough to leave for Denbigh after they'd eaten the leg of lamb Olwen had taken from the freezer the day before. The roast filled the kitchen with the smell of Sunday dinner. After his pronouncement, he dived into the pages of *The People*. John peeled and pared. Olwen made pastry for the apple tart and because the silence in the kitchen was oppressing her she clucked, asking her *cyw* at least four times if he'd taken his pills.

The vegetables prepared, John fled. He walked along the beach towards Llanaber, picking at shells and kicking at driftwood, constructing his speech for Dr Arachchi. Fucking

Bethan had been fantastic. His deception would be convincing. For a while he watched the shadows of the clouds make twenty shades of blue on the still surface of the sea.

Playing the piano in the O.T. room, John felt a peculiar sense of security fold over him.

'Hello, I'm Pete Watson.'

John heard the throaty voice and looked up from the piano. Under a thicket of khaki curls he saw a smiling face and the greenest eyes.

'I came in yesterday,' Pete said. 'What's your name?'

John introduced himself. Instantly attracted by this Art Garfunkel look-alike, he found himself in one of the rooms where sex with men was fun.

'Christ! They're all so old here; I'm glad to see someone more my own age.'

Shaking hands, John searched Pete's face for any sign that the attraction he felt might be mutual. 'You get used to them,' John said. 'When they're drunk enough they're quite harmless really.'

'So, how long have you been in?' Pete asked.

'Two weeks come Tuesday.'

'God, I hope I'm not in that long.'

They caught each other's eye, their look lingering longer than either found comfortable. John thought he saw a glimmer of interest.

'What you in for?' Pete quizzed.

'I've had a nervous breakdown, what about you?'

'I need to get off Phensedyl.'

John's eyebrows expressed his question.

'It's cough mixture,' he said in an abrupt, matter-of-fact way.

'I've been addicted to it for a couple of months... well, maybe a year or so. I go through bottles of the stuff so I'm here to go cold turkey.'

John thought he detected a trace of vulnerability in Pete's eyes as he spoke, a little-boy-lost impishness that excited him.

'D'you play chess?' Pete asked.

'Yes, but not well.'

They found a chessboard and an almost complete set of pieces in one of the drawers of a cabinet in the quiet room, along with a box of Cluedo.

'So Mrs Peacock is a white bishop and Colonel Mustard is the black horse,' Pete said after they'd set up the board.

They played for a couple of hours. John lost every game, but his mind hadn't been on the board.

After Martin had dispensed the night sedation Pete was keen to play some more chess.

'No thanks, I think I'll take a bath and go to bed,' John said.

There was one bathroom that was relatively private, with just a bathtub, a shower cubicle and a washbasin. None of the doors locked, but John flipped the sign on the door to 'occupied' and ran himself a bath. After only a couple of minutes of soaking in the sudsy warmth, Pete came in without knocking, just a towel around his waist.

'I thought I'd take a shower,' he said, yanking the towel away and stepping into the cubicle.

He left the curtain open. John watched as Pete touched himself and soon his own erection poked through the foam.

'Do you want it?' Pete said, thrusting his hips suggestively.

'Yes...' John said, rising from the bath and pushing into the shower beside him. They held one another – touching, kissing, stroking.

Then Jatunga's whisperings began and David threw the switch.

'I'll soap my ass so you can fuck me,' Pete said.

Jatunga was licking out a honey pot and saying how much nicer it was than a hairy shitty arse.

'No,' John yelled, loud enough to be heard above the whoosh of the shower before slumping against the tiled wall of the cubicle and sliding down its length.

'Okay, suck me off then,' Pete said, so taken up by the excitement of the moment that he didn't appreciate John's distress.

John lay like a crumpled washcloth on the floor of the shower stall. He fingered the ruby bracelet and sobbed with no control over his feelings.

When Pete realised John's anguish he went to fetch Martin.

*　　*　　*

'Have you brought me good news?' Dr Arachchi asked.

'Yes,' John said, with the broadest smile he could find in his box of tricks.

'Tell me about it,' the doctor said.

'It was wonderful, just like you said it would be.'

John tried to judge Jatunga Arachchi's response. He didn't want to sound so over-the-top that his story would seem spurious. But the doctor's smile could have sold toothpaste to a nation.

'Thank you for all of your encouragement,' John offered.

And the Sri Lankan's smile could have sold toothpaste to the world.

'So you fucked her,' Jatunga said like a fourteen-year-old poring over a wank mag.

'Twice,' John said, hoping that would seem natural. Once could have been a fluke. Twice showed that they'd both enjoyed it. 'And I tasted the honey pot.'

Jatunga's chest swelled with the pride of achievement.

'So, you have finished with men?'

'Definitely, Dr Arachchi. You've helped me find something so much better than a hairy shitty arse. I can't thank you enough.'

John wondered fleetingly whether he'd put enough conviction into the bit about the hairy shitty arse.

Jatunga Arachchi sat back in his chair and rocked gently on its back legs. 'I am very pleased with you. Congratulations.' Then he looked at Chris and David: 'John has done well, yes?'

David smiled, but Chris's face remained expressionless. John got the sense that Chris didn't believe a word of his story.

'Well done, John Idris,' Dr Arachchi said again. 'And what about the Aversion Therapy? How many more sessions do you think you will need?'

This wasn't a question John had worked out an answer for; he'd just assumed that the shocks would stop. Should he say that he didn't need any more treatments or would that seem premature? But then... if he suggested they continue would that make them suspect the whole of his story?

'I don't know,' John said. 'Do you think I need any more? I fucked her, isn't that enough?'

'Perhaps we will keep up the negative reinforcement for a few more days and reassess your situation on Wednesday or Thursday.'

John smiled; he had to show that he still trusted them. He stood and unbuckled his belt.

'Wire him up please,' the doctor said to David when John stood naked before them.

Chris smoothed the Elastoplast over the electrodes on John's wrist.

'I will see Dr Thomas this afternoon, John Idris,' Dr Arachchi said, handing John the magazine called *Big Boys*. 'Perhaps we will be able to discharge you before the weekend.'

David seemed more aggressive on the switch and John was rewarded with two bright new rubies in his bracelet.

Pete wasn't at lunch. John had wanted to apologise, and explain about what happened in the shower.

'He's discharged himself, the silly little fucker,' Jan said.

John played the piano for a while, but the melody couldn't calm the unease that settled over him. He didn't do much sewing, preferring the calm of the 'deeper inside'.

Sometime in the late afternoon Chris sat with John in the quiet room.

'Are you feeling okay about being discharged on Friday?'

'It's been agreed then?' John asked, more surprised than excited.

'It would appear that you convinced the doctors; they're pleased with their success.'

But you're not persuaded by any of it, are you Chris?

'So, what'll you do John?'

'Go back to university, of course. If I get back there on Sunday I'll only have missed two weeks of the new term.'

'I like your optimism, but... have you thought about taking a break? Maybe you could defer your place at uni and start again next September?'

'And do what?'

'Travel a bit, or maybe just have some time out?' He shrugged, and wondered just how frank he could be.

'I haven't got the money to go travelling,' John said thinking about Bethan's rich father.

'What about just taking some time to get yourself sorted then?' Chris offered. What he'd wanted to say was 'what about taking some time to learn to like yourself?' but he lacked the confidence to confront John with the sham of his performance that morning.

'But I'd have nowhere to go, Chris. I can't go home.' There was an edge of fluster in his voice. 'It's too intense there. They just want to cosset me... especially my mam; she's so overprotective now. All weekend she just kept asking me if I'd taken my pills. God, I'd be smothered.'

'When you see Dr Thomas perhaps you'd better talk about whether he thinks it's wise for you to go straight back to Aberystwyth.'

Walking away, Chris was disappointed in himself for not being more candid.

Jan was throwing up in a bucket. Pete was gone. Looking for envelopes and a note pad in the shambles of his locker drawer, John found the books his dad had packed in his suitcase. The letter to the Morgans, telling them he was coming back to Aber, could wait. He picked up Dylan Thomas' *Collected Poems 1934 – 1953*. Paul's postcard, the one with *Desiderata* in Gothic script, was marking a page. Fingering the card, Paul's presence flooded back and he recognised again how he grieved for him, a scar still as raw as Dr Arachchi's ruby branding. On the open page of Thomas' book John read '...though lovers be lost love shall not; and death shall have no dominion.'

Going back to Aberystwyth will only continue the madness.

Dr Thomas encouraged John's return.

'Student days are the best days of your life,' he said. 'Go and enjoy them.'

Early September

Before his heart problems John would make a pretty mean smoked mackerel pâté with unsalted French butter, lots of cream cheese and a dash of Tabasco or a dollop of creamed horseradish. It was the only way he could eat such a fishy fish; with sliced tomatoes – drizzled in olive oil and sprinkled with basil leaves – and thick slices of the oat and sunflower seed bread that Constance had taught him to bake all those years ago in Berkeley. With a glass or two of Chardonnay it made a good summer evening supper.

The new recipe, scribbled in Klaus's spidery hand in the margin of the well-thumbed cookery book, used fat-free quorn – butter no longer appeared on their shopping lists. The new pâté was better if the mackerels were peppered, but it lacked richness. He spread a generous layer onto a slice of crispbread; at least he'd be able to tell the zealous nurse in the rehab clinic that he was eating oily fish at least three times a week.

He was missing Klaus a lot more than usual; perhaps because this was the first spell on his own since coming out of hospital. Having the stent in his heart... well, the whole 'cardiac event' really – that's what the cardiologist had called it – was taking a bit of getting used to and he'd needed Klaus's reassurance, especially when he had the odd twinge in his chest. He'd felt for the GTN spray in his pocket a dozen times a day since he'd kissed Klaus goodbye at Manchester airport, a kind of second-guessing that told him he had a long way to go before he'd regain his equilibrium.

Eating alone, Klaus' absence was even more pressing.

He spread the newspaper across the table above his plate and read the obituaries. Those in the *Independent* were so much better than the ones that appeared in the other papers; he liked the variety of people and the quirky detail of their lives. An editorial note at the bottom of one column recorded the death of that particular obituarist back in 1999 and acknowledged additional contributions from a minor theatrical celebrity on the last years of the life in profile. This set him thinking about the obituarist's craft of writing about a person's life and achievements even before they were dead. Beca's words came back to him – about sitting with the family and saying something at the funeral.

What could he say about Elen Morgan?

After about an hour reflecting on her part in his life – and two more glasses of wine, which he wouldn't mention to the rehab nurse – he looked at the doodles on the notepad. There were four phrases caught in the web of his scribblings: *God finds us where we are... A kindness passed on... Crawling through thorns...* and *The journey is home.*

Night of the Laughing Man

Olwen Jones felt torn. 'Of course I want you to go back to university and get your degree,' she said. 'There's not much for you here, but —'

'There might be something going with the council,' Dai said.

'Don't be so bloody daft, Dai. The *council*? He's got too much brains for that.'

John caught a glimpse of himself in overalls, digging up the road and looking hunky. It made him smile.

'Dad and me, we both want what's best for you, *cyw*,' Olwen fretted.

'I know that's what you want, Mam,' he said. 'That's why I need to go back this week, so that I won't fall too far behind.'

'Just a few more days,' Olwen pressed. 'Don't go back to Aberystwyth too soon... please.'

Hearing the concern in her plea, he took a deep breath to stifle his impatience with her.

'What about spending this next week at home,' Dai urged. 'You need to make arrangements for a single room… or maybe you could even try to get out of that bloody Theological College.'

'Well, I suppose…' John conceded ambiguously.

It was a difficult week. When he escaped his mam's apron strings and got out of the house he felt the gawps prick and the intent looks linger. More than once he sensed that people were crossing the street to avoid him, and as the days passed he reconciled himself to being one of the fabled figures imagined by his community's erroneous beliefs about the Denbigh asylum.

He started driving again. The freedom to roam on the deserted dunes beyond Dyffryn, and get lost in the wilds above Cwm Nantcol – rambling over the rugged slopes of the Rhinogs – was a liberation. But with this independence, old ghosts returned and new ghosts emerged. Jatunga Arachchi's 'sweet nothings' harmonised with Adam's chanted verses of condemnation, and the Sunday Library Group's choruses were accompanied by the rhythmic buzz of David's shock box. With the hopes that he'd invested in the doctors now dashed, a more sinister whisper beckoned.

Friday dawned in a magical frost. Cader Idris glistened in the winter sun. Had the giant been sitting on his throne that morning he'd have seen all of Wales from Enlli to St David's Head. The lake at Tal-y-llyn was a sapphire set in a bed of platinum and even the grey slates of Corris were a shimmering silver. From the crest of Penglais Hill, Aberystwyth's rimed rooftops were a blinding white against the cobalt sea.

His new room E22 was in the roof, with beams, a sloping ceiling and a small window looking out over the bay. On his second journey up the five flights of stairs he met Stewart, with

Mai, one of the girls from the botany class. John was curious about the sparkle of intimacy in their eyes. They gave him such a welcome and offered to help carry his things.

'I'm glad you're alright,' Stewart said. 'Did you get our card?'

'Yes. It was nice that everyone put their names on it.'

'We've really missed you, John,' Mai said with a heavy south Walian accent. 'The practicals have been so dull without you fooling around.'

'Have I missed much then?'

'Not really, not in botany anyway,' Mai said. 'You're welcome to have a look over my notes if you like.'

'Some of the biochemistry was beyond me, John,' Stewart said. 'But the prof takes most of his lectures straight out of Lehninger so it's hardly worth you trying to decipher my scroll, just read the book.'

'Thanks, both of you. I've been a bit worried that I'll have missed too much to catch up.'

'You haven't missed anything really,' Mai said. 'And we'll help you, so don't worry.'

After another trip to the car, parked in Laura Place, and back up to E floor, John offered them coffee.

'I've got to go,' Mai said. 'I'm meeting a couple of girls in The Cabin.' She gave Stewart a peck on the cheek. 'Will I see you tonight then?' she whispered into his ear.

'Maybe, in the new union disco?' Stew said. 'But it'll be late. I'm going to the flicks with some of the boys.'

After Mai had left them, Stewart helped John rearrange the furniture in E22.

'I'm knackered after all those stairs,' John said as they shifted the bed against the wall. 'I'm on lots of drugs.'

Stewart's face lit up.

'No pot-head, not the sort *you* buy in the back bar of the Coopers'; prescribed drugs. I'll be on them for a while and they make me tired.'

'So, take a nap this afternoon,' Stewart urged. 'D'you fancy coming to the pictures tonight?'

'Yeh... what's on?'

'I don't know. There's a crowd going... meeting in the old union at half-six.'

They pushed the desk under the window.

'You've got a super view from here,' Stew offered in his plummy southern tone. 'It's a nice room, and not so small.'

'I like it a lot,' John said.

'New start,' Stew offered with a smile. 'And there's the lunch bell.'

Well... I suppose I've got to face Paul some time.

John was touched by the good wishes expressed by so many. The fact that Paul wasn't at lunch made those first steps easier.

He slept under a blanket on the bare mattress for most of the afternoon but was woken by a sharp rap on the door.

'Come in,' he said, fumbling with the switch of the bedside lamp.

Paul Wynne looked more handsome than before. His cropped haircut made him look so sexy. John took a sharp intake of breath, momentarily confused by the collision of feelings and thoughts. Was the anger rising in him really just the flip side of the longing he felt to reach out and pull Paul into his arms?

'Welcome back,' Paul offered. 'You've had a tough time of it then?'

'You could say that,' John said, suddenly shaking with anger. 'But it was made so much easier knowing that you were concerned about me; all those phone calls and letters —'

'Sarcasm doesn't —'

'Well fuck you,' John cut in, punching his fist into the pillow. 'Nothing, not a fucking word! You just couldn't be bothered, could you?'

'Is that what you really think?' Paul said, fingering the scar at his lip.

John shook his head and clasped both hands together to stop them shaking.

'If only you knew how many times I've wanted to get in touch,' Paul said. 'All the times I wanted to take you in my arms —'

Yes... take me, please.

'... and hold you.'

'Don't... please don't do this to me again,' John said, whimpering from the pain of their separation. 'You wanted to finish it – so just forget me.'

'Don't dismiss me like this. I care... a lot.'

John's anger drowned in a wave of needy yearning. 'How did you find out?' he asked, almost in a whisper.

'Elen Morgan phoned me. Wynne isn't so hard to find in the phone book, and she knew we were friends; I suppose she thought I'd have some news.'

'So... you've told her then?'

'Not everything,' he said pensively. 'I've got my call, John. I've got to protect my ministry.'

His words triggered a surge of rage and John vomited his resentment: 'Of course... your ministry... never mind how you fuck up people's lives.'

'I did tell her that I thought I'd done more harm than good.'

'That was big of you,' John spat.

'I didn't just stop loving you —'

'Are you saying all this just so that you can feel better, Paul? Is that it?'

'Oh dear God.' He sighed heavily. 'You must really hate me.'

'No,' John said, shaking his head and trying to calm the storm inside him. 'I don't hate you... it's just like you said; you don't stop loving someone that you've loved... that you still love.'

Silence wedged between them. They watched one another, but Paul's discomfort got to him first. He took a beige envelope from the inside breast pocket of his jacket: 'This is for you.'

John shook his head.

'It's a card from the Morgans. I had lunch with them today.'

'Please, go away.'

Paul tossed the envelope on the bed and left.

John lay back on the mattress and fingered the hard edges of the card through the envelope... then he placed it on the bedside table and set about making E22 more his own. Despite feeling unsettled by Paul's visit, his single-mindedness surprised him; he stacked his books on the shelf, stowed his clothes in the small chest and the slim wardrobe, and made up his bed. He remembered, too late, that he'd intended to meet Stewart in the old union, but was content to stay in and listen to the radio, and perhaps read a chapter or two of Lehninger... and he had his dad's old gramophone so he could listen to his new Elton John double album.

Adam and the Sunday Library group soon drowned out 'Candle In The Wind', accompanied by Jatunga Arachchi and David Jones on backing vocals. John felt wretched, and the starkness of his feelings stung. He turned up the volume on

'Saturday Night's Alright for Fighting' and held the envelope from the Morgans in his hands.

I won't open you yet. I'll save you for when things get really bad.

To escape this new loneliness he filled his days with busyness, copying up from borrowed notes between lectures and even reading the first four chapters of the dry biochemistry tome. Adam persuaded him that he was too vile to stain the Morgans' lives, so he stayed away from Peniel. He was offered personal tutorial time from staff in all his disciplines; the tutors were sympathetic to his situation and patient with him when his concentration lapsed. Busyness became the engine that drained his energy.

Most evenings he found himself stranded by exhaustion in the attic room with a sea view – with only harsh voices for company. When Adam's litany of hatred and Jatunga's dirty talk had worn him down, he opened the beige envelope. From the same series as the card Paul had given him, the Morgans had chosen a message written in bold, gold calligraphy.

> I said to the man who stood at the gate of the year, 'Give me a light that I may tread safely into the unknown.' And he replied, 'Go out into the darkness and put your hand into the hand of God. That shall be to you better than light and safer than the known way!' So I went forth and finding the hand of God, trod gladly into the night. And He led me towards the hills and the breaking of the day in the lone east.
>
> Minnie Louise Haskins 1875–1957

Elen Morgan had written a short welcome greeting, inviting him to call on them. He remembered their kindness.

And now you're urging me to put my hand in the hand of God.

Adam put the cord of Paul's dressing gown around John's neck and the Sunday Library Group played tug-of-war again. Jatunga whispered his malevolence while David flicked the switch. Buzz.

John tore up the card with the gold calligraphy. God's arms weren't wide enough to embrace people like him; he knew that now.

* * *

It was a bright, sunny Saturday morning. From his window, John could see the still inner bay and the blue line of the Lleyn peninsula across the open sea beyond. The roofs of the boarding houses along the prom were frosted and the morning sun dazzled in the windows at the end of the broad bay's sweep beneath Constitution Hill. He'd been back in Aber for two weeks and his life had become an exhausted, lonely blur. Up in the attic room, where Elton sang 'Funeral For A Friend' and 'Sweet Painted Lady,' Adam and Jatunga were John's only visitors – and they weren't welcome.

Walking along Great Darkgate Street for a ten o'clock appointment at the surgery in North Parade, he clutched the letter he'd been given in Denbigh to pass on to his GP. The doctor read with scowled concentration and paraphrased the main points to John's nodded concurrence.

'So, how have you been since you came back to Aberystwyth?'

'I'm alright.'

'You feel you're coping?'

'Yes. I've caught up well enough.'

'And you will be seeing the college psychiatrist?'

'Yes, I'm supposed to make an appointment —'

'And you'll do that?'

'Yes.'

The doctor wrote out a prescription. 'Come back and see me in two or three weeks,' he said, handing John the script. 'And be sure to make that appointment with the college doctor.'

'Yes, thank you.'

With two new bottles of pills in his pocket, he walked along the prom in the winter sunshine. For a while he watched some children throwing stale bread to the seagulls; then he kicked the bar. The walk back to Theol Coll was brisk and his rosy cheeks burned in the cold crispness. To the chink of cutlery from the dining hall he trudged up the five flights of stairs. He put the pills on the bedside table, slung his parka over the chair, and went down to the small student kitchen on D floor to make himself a drink; he carried the overfull glass of orange squash carefully back up to his room and placed it next to the small brown bottles. He bunched the sixty Nardil tablets into little heaps of five, and swallowed each with a gulp of squash. There were sixty-one pills in the Valium bottle. It amused him that the pharmacist had miscounted and as he swallowed the last, errant pill, he wondered about a 'note'.

Isn't there always supposed to be a note, to help the coroner decide that the balance of the mind is disturbed?

Dylan Thomas's collection of poems lay open next to the table lamp on a page marked by Paul's card.

'And death shall have no dominion' is a good enough sentiment to die by.

Feeling calm, he lay on the bed and waited to die. The voices

– Adam's and Jatunga's – were silent. He felt peaceful. It seemed right that he wouldn't be able to foul the world with his filthy life. Some faces came to him. Happy faces. Elen Morgan smiled, and he thought how good it was that he wouldn't sully her world for very much longer.

Everything was dark but he could hear the knocking. He couldn't call out, or raise his head, but the knocking seemed so urgent. And then the light hurt his eyes. And a voice. Shouting at him. But he couldn't see anyone. The light burned. It was Paul's voice – and someone was slapping his face. And then silence. And then the burning light, and shadows against the burning light. And more voices shouting at him... and slaps to his face. His arms pushed into his jacket.

It's cold in hell?

Knees giving way... his arms over their shoulders... his feet dragging. His eyes open again, and through the burning light lots of faces staring – and turning away.

So that's how it works! They turn their faces away and you go down.

Down and down. His shoes banging with each step. Down, into the darkness where his eyes didn't burn. And still someone slapped his face. There were sirens somewhere... and at the end of a long dark tunnel there were bright lights flashing blue. And then a rush of cold air. Being pushed into the brightness.

'Attempted suicide,' someone said.

'Anyone know what he's taken?' asked a different voice.

'These empty bottles were —'

And he knew what was happening. And it was the wrong kind of hell. In the ambulance they kept slapping his face.

'What time did you take the pills, John? How many did you take?'

And the lights were too bright, burning again. On a trolley, pushed quickly. Laid on his side. Mouth forced open... a pain in the throat... a strange ache in his chest. And still they pushed the rubber tube down. And there was bloody vomit and a horrible smell... and all the while they slapped his face and asked lots of questions.

'John! John! What time did you take the pills, John? Is there someone we can contact? We have to let someone know.'

And a softer voice.

'John lovey... who's your next-of-kin?'

No... no... no phone number... just let me go.

'We have to let somebody know, lovey. What about your parents?

'No...'

'We have to have a contact, lovey.'

'Elen Morgan then,' John whispered.

* * *

The warmth of a touch stirred him, but he couldn't open his eyes. His teeth ached, and his body was shot through with reservoirs of dull pain. In his fingers and toes there were sharp stabs of soreness, but the warmth of the hand holding his hand eased the jabbing. He heard the voice for some time before realising it was speaking a prayer... and still the warmth of the hand soothed his own. Then he saw those eyes, which were so alive. Rhys Morgan smiled, and held his hand.

But then Rhys Morgan was gone and a nurse stood with a doctor. The whiteness of the doctor's coat hurt his eyes.

'This is John Idris Jones,' the nurse said. 'He was brought in as an emergency on Saturday night.'

'Yes, the overdose,' the doctor said, scanning the notes. 'He's stable enough now though, is he?'

The nurse nodded.

'Good. Get him out as soon as you can, Sister. I need these beds for sick people.'

The nurse and the doctor had left the side room by the time the doctor's words had taken on their meaning. John felt everything boil up inside him.

'Have your fucking bed,' he howled, throwing off the cover and swinging his legs around. 'I didn't ask you to save me, you bastards! You didn't ask me if I wanted to live.'

He was on his feet, but unstable. In his upset, he made to kick the bedside locker, but he lost his balance. In a crumpled heap on the floor he looked up to see the nurse and the doctor at the door. They lifted him back into bed. John swore and called the doctor every bad name he could think of. Then, when he was alone, he cried for a long time.

Elen Morgan sat at his bedside for some minutes before he realised she was there.

'The hospital wants to discharge you, John,' she said straightforwardly. 'But you haven't allowed them to contact your next-of-kin so they don't really know what to do with you.' She smiled. 'You're welcome to stay with us, if you'd like to.' She spoke cautiously. A muscle at the corner of her eye twitched. 'You'd be very welcome, but because we're not your family you have to make the decision.'

'I made a decision on Saturday, Mrs Morgan,' John said, remembering how she'd smiled at him after he'd taken the pills. 'It was a good decision – the right one, but nobody took much notice of what I wanted then. They stuffed a tube inside me

202

and pumped out my stomach. Nobody asked me then if that's what I wanted.'

'We can talk about that, John,' Elen Morgan said. 'We can talk about all these things, but at the moment there's something more pressing because they need your bed. Would you like to come and stay with Rhys and me, even if it's only for a night or two?'

'Do I have any other choices?'

'Well, yes. You could go back to Barmouth —'

'No.' John shook his head violently. The force of the shaking set off small explosions of pain and shards of intense malevolence seemed to ricochet off his skull and implant themselves in his brain. 'Why did they save me? They should have let me die.'

'I'm glad they saved you,' Elen Morgan said, brushing her hand against his cheek. 'Now, will you please come and stay with us... we'd consider it a privilege.'

'Alright... just until things become a bit more clear.'

It was another sunny winter's day. Walking to the Morgans' car, John took some deep breaths of the cold morning air and tasted the salt from the sea. After the clinical heat of the hospital the day's freshness seemed to blow through the murk in his head and revive him. Feeling more alert, he began to wonder what the Morgans were thinking. Wasn't suicide, after all, the ultimate rejection of any faith in God and a denial of hope for the future?

In the car it was Elen who broke the silence.

'It's such a lovely day, and not too cold. Would you both like to go down to South Beach for half an hour before lunch?'

'I'd like that,' Rhys said. 'What about you, John?'

He didn't know what he wanted, but he recognised that being with them made him feel embarrassed and self-conscious. He said nothing for a few minutes. When the silence in the car screamed too loudly he spoke.

'I'm grateful to you both for caring about me, but I don't have a script for this bit of the story. Nobody was supposed to find me on Saturday night so this situation is difficult.'

Neither Rhys or Elen were certain enough of what they might say, so they both remained silent and hoped that John would talk. There was another silence.

'Yes,' John said to fill the void. 'I'd like to go to the beach for a while.'

They parked by the yacht club.

'Shall we stay in the car or go for a walk?' Elen Morgan asked.

'With this chest of mine I'd better stay in the car,' Rhys Morgan said. 'But why don't you two walk for a while?'

They strolled towards the castle. At first they were silent and apart, but eventually Elen Morgan put her arm through John's and he didn't reject her closeness. In a sunny spot, shaded from the breeze off the sea by the castle wall, they sat on a bench that overlooked the bay.

'Do you remember, earlier this morning in the hospital, when you told me you were angry with the doctors for saving your life?' Elen Morgan asked. 'I said that I was happy that they'd saved you.'

John felt himself tense up and braced himself for what might follow.

'D'you want to know why I'm glad you didn't die, John?'

'Elen... I don't —' How could he tell her that he didn't want her sermon?

'When you've been to our house, John, those few times —' Elen put into his awkwardness. 'Well, what Rhys and I saw was a bright young man who's got such a lot to give to the world. That's all I've got to say. That's why I'm glad that they saved your life, so that you – and what you've got to offer all of us – can still be offered.'

Her arm was still woven through his. They both looked straight out to the sea. Elen wondered if he'd even heard what she'd said. John, having heard what she'd said, couldn't see anything worthwhile that he had to offer. When she felt the tremors of his crying she hugged him. Wrapped in her arms he told her that homosexuals didn't deserve to live.

She held him close until his spasm of uncontrolled crying eased, and she thought carefully, knowing that the words she'd utter would carry a significance that might mean the difference for him between choosing life and choosing to die.

'We make life so very difficult for homosexuals,' she said calmly, though her insides were churned up. 'Even the word itself, it's like a label that alerts us... makes us uneasy.' She held him tightly to her. Even if the words she was speaking were unacceptable to him, at least she could hope that he would feel her warmth and know that she wasn't rejecting him. 'Of course, most of us never get to know the person behind a label like that. All of the fears we have – all of the stereotypes and myths that we think are attached to the label – get in the way.' She remembered a young man who'd studied with Rhys in Cambridge; they'd sent him down when his secret had been discovered. He was the only homosexual she'd met, though there were a number of men over the years that might have been. 'And do you know, John Idris... here, in Wales, I think we're more willing to believe the myths and be influenced by our fears, so we make it a very hostile place for people like you, and I'm so very sorry for that.'

'I don't want to be a homosexual, Elen,' John said, freeing himself from her embrace and wiping away his tears on the sleeve of his parka. 'I don't want to be a disgusting pervert.'

'But does being a homosexual automatically make you disgusting?' As she spoke these words she wished she could re-phrase them. 'What I mean is, I know that's what the label seems to conjure up, but... well, I wonder what it would mean for you to be a self-confident, self-respecting homosexual?'

'That's impossible,' he said, thinking of Adam and the Sunday Library Group, and Jatunga Arachchi's Aversion Therapy. 'Even the Bible says that's impossible.'

She took his hand in hers.

'I know there are some references to homosexuality in the Bible, John, and I know that, traditionally anyway, those are interpreted in a very negative way. Perhaps you'd better talk to Rhys about that. There are different ways to interpret things.'

John could hear Adam's litany and he shook his head.

'Listen to me, John,' she said, thinking he was rejecting what she was saying. 'God made you just the way you are. I know it's not easy for you to accept, but perhaps that's God's challenge to you, and to the rest of us; to discover what it might mean for you to live as a homosexual in a positive and creative way.'

John shook his head violently, seeing again Jatunga's pornography and feeling the electric shocks. 'It's impossible,' he said, rubbing the faded rubies on his wrist.

Elen put her arm around him.

'Well, John, perhaps it seems impossible this morning, but we've got time to talk about this, you, me and Rhys... if you'll give us the time and trust us enough.'

'I don't know who to trust any more,' John said.

'Perhaps, after a day or two, you'll feel that we've earned your trust.'

'Perhaps,' he said. And he smiled.

'We'd better go back to the car. Rhys will think we've got lost.'

Walking towards the yacht club, John was puzzled that her Christianity was so different to the Sunday Library Group's.

'I won't say anything to Rhys about what we've been talking about,' she said as they neared the car. 'But do feel free to talk to him as openly as you've talked to me.'

Driving to the manse, Rhys spoke directly about John's parents. 'If they were to phone Theol Coll for any reason, someone might tell them what happened on Saturday. That would be an awful way for them to find out, don't you think?'

'Yes,' John said. He twisted his fists into the car seat and let out a long sigh. 'It's going to be horrible to have to tell them what I did. They're going to be upset and they'll want to come here straight away – to take me home and wrap me up in cotton wool. Shit!' Immediately he was embarrassed that he'd sworn. 'I'm sorry for my bad language,' he mumbled. 'Just the thought of telling them makes me all panicky.'

'You can say that you're staying with us for a while,' Elen said. 'And if you'd like me to, I could talk to your mam, mother to mother... perhaps that would help them to give you a bit of time.'

John fisted the car seat, swearing under his breath. 'Perhaps I should phone them,' he said, yielding to the inevitable.

Elen showed him into Rhys' study.

'You'll stay, won't you?' John pleaded.

Elen watched him dial the number with a reassuring smile.

Dai Jones answered the phone. John said what he had to say in a very matter-of-fact way.

'Bloody hell,' Dai said after a long silence. 'We'd better come and get you.'

'No... I'm staying with Mr and Mrs Morgan —'

'You can't make trouble for other people, John. I'll be there in a couple of hours. You should never have gone back.'

'I don't want you to come,' he said. He thrust the phone into Elen's hand.

'Mr Jones... hello, Elen Morgan here. John can stay with us for a few days... he needs a bit of time, but we can stay in touch by phone.'

'Olwen and I can't put you to that trouble so we'll come and get him,' Dai said.

'But Mr Jones, John has asked you not to come to Aberystwyth,' she said firmly into the telephone.

'Don't let them come, Elen,' John mouthed as he fled the study.

Rhys Morgan was setting the table for lunch when John came through from the study. 'Everything alright then?' he asked.

'My dad's being difficult... but Elen is talking to him.'

'I see... well, did you have a good walk along the beach?'

'We didn't walk such a lot. Elen is easy to talk to.'

'And was talking helpful?'

'It's true that the Bible condemns homosexuals, isn't it, Mr Morgan?'

'Call me Rhys,' he said, to give himself a moment to reflect on how he might answer. 'There are some verses that refer to homosexual behaviour, that's true, and they can be interpreted that way.'

'Elen said I should talk to you. She said that if God has made me this way, the big challenge of my life is to learn how to have self-respect and live positively as a homosexual.'

Laying the cutlery beside the plates, Rhys recalled Howard, his friend at Cambridge. The discovery that he was a homosexual had been shocking; that the college authorities sent Howard down had caused great anguish and soul-searching. 'Interpreting scripture can be a real cause of conflict, John. Historically it's often led to schism within the church,' he said cautiously. 'We can talk about this... but it's not a five-minute conversation and I can't give you a definitive interpretation.' He saw an expression he took to be disappointment in John's face. 'But let me just say, straight away, that I'm grateful you feel you can trust Elen and me with this.'

'I don't know whether I'm telling you because I trust you or whether it's because, after Saturday, I don't feel I've got anything left to lose.' John thought about Adam and the Sunday Library Group, and Arwel Thomas's prayer for God's guidance with the Aversion Therapy. 'I might even be telling you so that you'll judge me too, and that'll just confirm that my choice on Saturday was the right choice.'

Rhys was taken aback by his candour. 'Well... we're not going to judge you, John. Elen and I... we've got too many specks in our own eyes to go looking for the splinters in yours. The Gospel I've been preaching for over thirty years is about how we respond to a loving and forgiving God. Judging other people isn't so difficult you know. There wouldn't be much to the Christian faith if its primary tenet was judgement. The real challenge, as I see it anyway, is how we set about loving God, and loving our neighbour, in the same way that we love ourselves.'

'But I don't even like myself,' John said.

'And you don't like yourself because you believe God finds you unacceptable because you're a homosexual?'

'It's not just God, Rhys,' John said with an edge of bitterness. 'The whole of society finds people like me unacceptable, that's why they gave me electric shocks in Denbigh... to make me normal.'

Rhys felt sickened by John's revelation. Society was indeed intolerant, but he thought they'd stopped doing that kind of thing in the sixties.

'God finds you wholly acceptable, John,' Rhys ventured. 'He made you in His image and He loves you. What God yearns for is that you become a fully alive human being who responds to His love.'

John's gesture suggested confusion – even incomprehension.

'Believe that God loves you,' Rhys urged.

'I'll try,' John said, biting his lip.

'It's not about trying, John,' he said. 'It's a simple choice. You choose to believe it – or you choose not to. But if you choose to believe, as an act of faith, your response to everything around you starts to change.'

Elen came through from the study looking flustered. 'I don't think I've convinced your father for one minute, but at least he's promised to get your mum to phone me when she comes in from work.' She sensed the tension between Rhys and John. 'Oh... I am sorry. I didn't mean to interrupt —'

'It's a conversation to be continued,' Rhys said, giving John an encouraging smile.

They ate a hearty leek and potato soup with thick slices of granary bread.

'I don't think I've grasped this whole thing about responding to God's love,' John said as he peeled the wrinkled skin off a manky looking apple. 'If I accept that God loves me, how should that make me respond to a society that rejects me?'

'Do you remember that we talked, before lunch, about loving God and loving your neighbour?' Rhys asked.

'Yes, the Great Commandment,' John said. Miss Gruffudd hadn't done such a bad job teaching him *Rhodd Mam*.

'It's a theme that runs through the Scriptures, John. God loves you, so you love God, and in loving God there's an implicit responsibility to love the neighbour – and through loving your neighbour you love God.'

'Yes,' John said, following the logic even if he didn't yet believe it.

'And many times in those ancient stories, different people and different communities asked God to help them identify their neighbour,' Rhys said, becoming animated. 'So, here we are on a Monday afternoon in February, and I'm sitting at the lunch table in the manse with you as our guest, and I ask myself, "Who is my neighbour?" And I say, "John Idris Jones is."'

'A homosexual neighbour,' John jibed.

'Right... and that's precisely my point, John. It wouldn't be difficult to judge you, but that would be to miss the fundamental invitation of the gospel; the challenge to love you as I love myself.'

'But what does that mean, Rhys?' he asked, not hiding his frustration.

'Another fundamental question. What is love?'

Elen smiled, recalling other conversations where the same question had been asked. 'In this day and age, with all this talk about "free love" and "making love not war", it's a very pertinent question,' she said.

'The New Testament is a good source of information on what people have understood God to mean when He talks about love,' Rhys continued. 'It's quite clear that *love* includes qualities like patience, understanding and respect. So, I'm invited to consider what it means to understand your situation as a homosexual, and to be patient in my deliberation about it. God is saying to me, "What does it mean for you to have respect for John's struggle in this situation?"'

John understood what he was saying, but it was so different from the way Adam and the Sunday Library Group saw things.

'The New Testament also talks about perseverance and tolerance, honesty and integrity, these things being the foundations of the relationships between people – the love between people if you like. Now… if these are qualities that I value for myself, and value them in my relationships with others, then I have to value them for my neighbour too, including my homosexual neighbour.'

Rhys looked at Elen and she smiled. John looked more confused.

'What you're saying is so different from the God Squad at Theol Coll,' he ventured.

'Let me try and illustrate what I mean,' he offered. 'For most of my lifetime, society has considered homosexual behaviour as something criminal. The church, in general, sees homosexuality as sinful and the medical community, given your recent experience, sees it as something that needs to be cured. Homosexuals have been – well, they are reviled by many.' He fell silent for a moment and searched for the illustration that he hoped would illuminate his thoughts. John looked perplexed. 'But – and there's always a "but" in theological debate, John,' he continued. 'Let's take a simple parable, the Good Samaritan.'

John remembered how Miss Gruffudd's false teeth would roll and acknowledged that he knew the story.

'Some clever lawyer asks Jesus that question about neighbourliness, "Who is my neighbour?" Jesus tells a very simple story about a Samaritan helping a Jewish traveller who's been beaten up and robbed. That clever lawyer wasn't happy with the story because in his day the Jews hated the Samaritans. They were reviled, and the clever lawyer is confronted with the possibility that his neighbour is his enemy.'

'Okay,' John said. 'God seems to throw up the unexpected.'

'Right,' Rhys said. 'So, let's re-tell the story in today's context. The traveller who's mugged is the minister of the local evangelical church, a real fundamentalist with a very rigid interpretation of the Bible. The person who stops to help him is John Idris Jones, who happens to be a homosexual. And I ask the God Squadders in Theol Coll "Who is the minister's neighbour?"'

'That's really subversive,' John said with a broad smile.

'Yes – but, in the age we're living, being a homosexual probably means that you'll always be on the edge of rejection by the wider community, John,' Elen said. 'That's why it will be important that you find a core of acceptance – inside yourself and amongst a group of people that you pull around you – so that when you face hostility you've always got that support to fall back on.'

'That feels heavy,' John said, the youthfulness of his features jaded. 'It's like you're telling me that I'm going to spend the whole of my life fighting for my place.'

'We're all on different journeys,' she said. 'In its own way, your journey may be more difficult than many, and you might even feel that you're never going to arrive. It's hard to think how the attitudes of a society might be changed; it might take a

213

generation. So perhaps, for you, John, the journey itself will be your home. If you can think about it that way there may be fewer disappointments.'

* * *

John stood on the pavement opposite Theol Coll's side door. *What if I meet someone who was there on Saturday night?* He took a few deep breaths to calm himself and hurried purposefully up to E22 to get a change of clothing and his toothbrush. *The door's locked. Who the fuck? Paul!* He hammered on the door of D6; Paul looked startled when he opened it.

'Have you got my keys?' It was more of a demand than a question.

'Yes,' he said, and reached into the drawer of his desk. 'I didn't know what to —' He placed the small bunch of keys into John's defiantly outstretched hand. 'It was me who found you and called the ambulance.'

'And you want me to thank you?'

'I'm glad you're alright,' he said, placing a hand on John's shoulder.

'Jesus, Paul!' He threw off his hand. 'You think I'm alright?' He kicked at the open door and sent it jarring into the metal bedstead. 'I'm completely fucking screwed up, and you should never have started meddling in my life.'

'I still care —'

'And you shouldn't have stuck your nose in on Saturday. I wanted to die!'

'No you didn't, John. You'll think differently in a while, you'll see.'

'Just... fucking leave me alone.'

214

The bedclothes hadn't been smoothed; it was as if he'd just been lying there. On the bedside table, Paul's card still marked Dylan Thomas' poem and the empty glass was ringed with dried orange sediment. He snapped the poetry book shut and tossed it into a Woolworth's carrier bag with a few essentials. What he wanted, more than anything, was for Paul to hold him, to breathe life into him again and make everything all right. He thought about the bag of laundry under the bed, and the magazine under the mattress – *Monica's Big Surprise*, the one Dr Arachchi had given him as a leaving present. The laundry would have to wait.

The chocolate cake was better than his mam's, and even better than Nana's.

'I talked to Olwen for about twenty minutes and I think I've persuaded her that there's no need for them to come down here straight away,' Elen said.

'Thank you,' John said, about to start on his third slice of death-by-chocolate.

'Mr Price, the psychiatric social worker, phoned too,' Rhys said. 'He's going to call sometime mid-morning tomorrow.'

'What do you think he wants?' John asked.

'He didn't say much, but after an attempted suicide there has to be a formal assessment, to be sure the person isn't going to try again,' Rhys said.

'So, it's just a formality then,' John said, licking his fingers.

'But you should give some thought to what you'll say to Mr Price, John,' Elen said. 'You wouldn't want him to... well, misunderstand your situation.'

'I will,' he said, wondering what there might be to misunderstand. He thought that they might talk again but the telephone in Rhys' study didn't seem to stop ringing and the conversations they'd already had were generating so many threads of ideas that his brain was racing. He sat with Elen in the cosy back room and was lulled to sleep by the crackle of the logs on the fire.

He had a crick in his neck from snoozing in the chair. 'What are you reading?'

'Do you know Waldo Williams' poetry?' Elen asked.

'He writes mostly in Welsh, doesn't he?'

'Yes, listen to this.'

She read *Pa Beth yw Dyn?* What is a Man? Perhaps, because belief and forgiveness had been two troubling themes for such a long time, a couple of lines gripped John's imagination: *'What is believing? Holding out until relief comes. And forgiving? Crawling through thorns to the side of an old foe.'*

Much later, unable to sleep, strands of the day's conversations wove with the lines of Waldo's poem. Adam seemed silenced by Rhys and Elen's love, and somewhere 'deeper inside' he found a quiet field where he could linger in their acceptance. Jatunga's pornography failed to play in his mind's eye, replaced by compassionate companionship and chocolate cake. He had hated himself for so long, yet it seemed that he'd yearned for the wrong kind of change. Was it too late to learn to like himself as a homosexual?

Adrian Price, the psychiatric social worker, was balding prematurely and combed a wisp of hair over his naked, gleaming scalp. He smelled of cigarettes and had a small tear in the sleeve of his tweed jacket. 'You're happy that Mr and Mrs Morgan stay for this interview?' he asked John after they'd settled in Rhys' study.

'Yes, we talked about it,' John said.

'Tell me then, in your own time, about the events that led you to try to take your life on Saturday,' he said, opening up a file on his knee.

John described what had been happening to him over the past weeks. Adrian Price clicked the end of his ballpoint pen and glanced furtively at his watch more than once.

'So, you were an in-patient at the North Wales Hospital until three weeks ago,' he said, summarising for the benefit of his file.

John thought he saw the trace of a satisfied smile pleat the corners of his mouth. 'Yes, I'm still under Dr Arwel Thomas.'

'And does Dr Thomas know about Saturday?' he asked, jotting down a note.

'I don't know,' John said, beginning to feel uncomfortable.

'I'll need to talk to him. You're still his patient so he's sure to have a view on this.'

John fiddled with his fingers.

'The ward sister told me that you were very angry and abusive towards the staff who saved your life. Is that true?'

John's fingers knotted.

Adrian Price looked at his watch again. 'Are you still angry with them?' he asked, seeking to interpret John's agitated silence.

John looked at Elen, who tried to reassure him with a wan smile. He wanted to say that he *had* been angry with them, but —

'Do you still want to die, John?'

Both Elen and Rhys shuffled in their seats. John watched the tips of his knotted fingers turn white.

'You're not telling me anything that persuades me you might not still be harbouring suicidal thoughts, John,' Adrian Price said with a little more warmth. 'I've got to be convinced that you won't try to harm yourself again.'

'I've been feeling better since I came to stay with Mr and Mrs Morgan.'

'We've talked about some of the things that have been troubling John,' Rhys put in.

'He can stay with us for as long as he wants to,' Elen offered.

'I'm sorry, Mrs Morgan, but it's not quite that simple,' Adrian Price said. 'The mental health laws give us the power to require someone in John's situation to be hospitalised, just for short periods, for their own protection and to help them over a crisis.' He turned to John. 'Do you understand what I'm saying?'

John nodded and untangled his fingers.

'I'm not certain enough that you won't try to harm yourself again, John,' he said with deliberate gravity. 'So I'm going to recommend that you go back to hospital for a while; back to Denbigh, so that Dr Thomas can care for you. D'you understand?'

John saw that Rhys' eyes had dimmed. Elen's expression was tortured, and gave him no clue as to how he should respond to the social worker.

'It would be better if you agreed to go voluntarily, John... otherwise I'll have to start off a process that will legally require you to go back to the hospital under a mental health section.'

Rhys looked disturbed by the turn of events. Elen was biting her lip and shaking her head slowly. John searched their faces. Adrian Price glanced at his watch... and to his great relief, John consented to the arrangements for his readmission to the asylum.

*　　*　　*

Dr Arachchi wanted to know if he was still bothered by 'that homosexual thing'. Fearing that they might begin the Aversion Therapy again he assured the doctor that the treatment had worked very well.

'So why did you try to commit suicide, John Idris?'

'Because I was exhausted by all the medication, and I got lonely and depressed when I couldn't join in with the other students.'

The new drug regimen left him listless, and by the third day his tongue was foul tasting and a sticky scum oozed at the corners of his mouth. Sometimes he sewed under Meirwen's watchful eye. Sometimes he played the piano or listened to the scratched Mozart recording of the clarinet. Sometimes he retreated to his 'deeper inside' and found the small field where Rhys and Elen accepted him and encouraged him to like himself. All of the time he felt that Chris Fisher, David Jones and Martin were watching him. When Dai and Olwen came to visit he told them he was a homosexual; after everything they'd been through it was time that they knew the truth.

'I don't know what that means for us all in the future, *cyw*... I don't know indeed,' Olwen said, seeing Bobby-Nansi in her mind's eye and remembering how he'd been found hanging from the newel post on the top landing at Wavecrest. 'But if I've got to choose between a homosexual son and a dead son... well, there's no choice is there? Come here and let me give you a big hug.'

Dai talked about Barmouth news – as if he hadn't heard what John had told them.

The Morgans sent a card or a short letter every two or three days. Elen even wrote out the Waldo poem that she'd read to him. They encouraged him. They nurtured his fragile sense of self. They were his guardian angels, sent by the God who threw up the unexpected. Often, when he lay in the small field of their love, feeling supported and sustained, he dared to think that he was acceptable to their God of surprises and wondered if he could risk belief. *'What is believing? Holding out until relief comes.'* Their talk of learning to like and accept himself – at first just a whisper – became a stronger inner voice; a voice that, sometimes anyway, even got the better of Adam and the Sunday Library Group. Still, he wrestled with the Morgans' God, and questioned whether those arms were wide enough to embrace him. But the cards and letters were a relief of sorts – tangibles in which he could have faith.

In the consulting room, where he'd been shown the pornographic photographs and experienced those electric orgasms, he sat before his doctors, who talked about him as if he wasn't there. Arwel Thomas seemed perplexed by his patient's withdrawal and interpreted it as a symptom of clinical depression.

'John Idris does not seem unhappy, Dr Thomas, not even when he is withdrawn,' Dr Arachchi said.

'Perhaps a short course of ECT might bring him out of it?'

'Electro-Convulsive Therapy is an option,' Dr Arachchi said cautiously, not wanting to antagonise his superior. 'But John Idris showers and grooms, and always dresses neatly; the nurses tell me that he plays the piano regularly and listens to music. That doesn't suggest clinical depression; he may be working something out in that head of his.'

'So you think we might continue to observe him for another week and then review?'

Jatunga Arachchi nodded his head and smiled.

John made sure that he played the piano every day and listened to the clarinet concerto. He cleaned up in the dining room after their meals and sewed just enough to keep Meirwen sweet. He talked with Chris and Martin – when they talked to him. But he still made time to bask in the quiet field. Adam didn't venture into John's tranquil enclosure; the sign on the gate said 'Beware of the Angels'.

By the end of the second week Arwel Thomas was in agreement with Jatunga Arachchi that John should be given as much time and space as he needed. After almost four weeks he was discharged into the care of his parents.

*   *   *

Dai Jones had taken the train to Aberystwyth, cleared E22 at the Theological College and driven the rusty Vauxhall Viva back to Barmouth, packed with the boxes that now cluttered John's bedroom.

'I've put some letters that came in the last couple of days on the chest of drawers,' Olwen called up after him.

Seeing his belongings piled high he wondered about Jatunga Arachchi's wank mag under the mattress, and what his dad had made of it. The letters distracted him. From the university registry came confirmation that the School of Biological Sciences was happy to hold his place open for the new academic year; from the finance department of the education authority there was a demand for the repayment of that term's student grant. Slumped on his bed he felt indifferent to the news contained in both letters. Dai called him down for supper.

'You'll soon get better now that you're home where I can

look after you, *cyw*,' Olwen said through the steam off her bowl of soup.

'It would be a good thing for you to cut all your connections with Aberystwyth too,' Dai said between slurps. 'Why don't you see if you can get transferred to some other university; Liverpool maybe, where Billy could keep an eye on you?'

To row with his parents was the last thing he needed. He listened to their concerns and came to realise that the shock of his suicide attempt was still raw for them. The fact that Elen Morgan had asked them to stay away from their son on that Monday in February had hurt them deeply.

'It would be better if you didn't keep in touch with the Morgans,' Dai said.

'But it was me that didn't want you to come to Aberystwyth.' *You'll never really understand what's going on, will you?*

The next morning he phoned Rhys and Elen from a phone box on the quay and asked them not to contact him. But he knew he still needed his angels, so he spoke to them often from that phone box.

Easter was early, the last weekend in March. It was a stormy weekend, but John's uncle brought a promise of spring.

Sam Idris Jones brought his new wife home to meet the family. Annie Jones liked Laura, and she was relieved that her son seemed happy after a second acrimonious divorce, but she wasn't sure about Laura's miniskirts, right up to her bottom! They were both teachers. Sam suggested that John consider volunteering as a teacher's assistant; there was a scheme running in Wolverhampton's schools. Laura's school was in such a deprived area they'd had no one volunteer for the scheme. She agreed to talk with her headteacher.

'If I can arrange it you can stay with Sam and me,' Laura said. 'The flat's a bit poky, but if you're willing to take us as you find us you'd be welcome.'

John liked his new auntie's Black Country accent and her down-to-earth common sense.

* * *

Just before the dinner bell on the Friday at the end of John's first week as his new auntie's classroom assistant, little Patrick Cooper, scratching his head and licking his top lip to dislodge the two columns of snot that seemed to hang permanently from his nostrils, began to distract the other children from their work. Through the week John had found him to be an angelic little demon.

'If you've finished your writing, Patrick, you can come to the reading corner,' John said, grabbing some tissues from the box on Laura's table.

'I luv you, Mr Joh-uns,' Pat said, as John wiped his nose.

'Come on, read for me, Patrick,' John said, his index finger under the first word at the top of the page of the book Pat had chosen.

'Are you coming next week, Mr Joh-uns?' Pat asked, scratching his head again. 'I wish you could be my teacher all the time.'

'But you like Mrs Jones, don't you, Pat?'

'Ye-eh, but she's never got time to sit with me like you do, Mr Joh-uns.'

'So you'd like me to come back again next week then?'

'Ye-eh... 'cos I luv you.'

'I'll have to come back then, won't I?'

Patrick smiled and began to stumble through the text of the story.

That evening, as John helped Laura prepare dinner, she noticed him scratching his head.

'There's a bar of Derbak soap in the bathroom cabinet that should get rid of them,' she said. 'We've had the nit-nurse in to see Patrick I don't know how many times!'

'You mean... I've got nits?'

John took a shower and only stopped rubbing the pungent smelling soap into his scalp when he heard Sam call him for dinner.

'Aside from the head lice, how was your first week then?' Sam asked with a chuckle.

'I've loved it,' John said.

'He's so natural with the children,' Laura said. 'You're a born teacher, you know. Have you thought of doing teachers training?'

'Not really,' John said, shrugging off Laura's lauding.

'You could do a lot worse,' Sam said. 'There's a shortage of men in primary schools and eventually that's going to have a negative kick back. Lots of kiddies don't have a dad at home and if they don't have any men teaching them either, they just don't see any positive male role models.'

Their confidence in him, and their willingness to share it, gave him a lift. Perhaps he could be a teacher.

Adam didn't seem to find his way to Wolverhampton, or perhaps it was just that John found his way easily into the quiet field where Rhys and Elen shepherded him. Perhaps it also had something to do with the fact that he'd started feeling more positive about himself, especially with the encouragement from Laura and Sam. During the three weeks of his stay, John thought more than once about talking to them about being a homo. What stopped him was the lurking possibility at the back of his mind that they would think he was unsuitable to be a volunteer classroom assistant.

They won't trust me with their boys if they know about me!

'I've made you a card, Mr Joh-uns,' Patrick Cooper said, his lower lip trembling as he fought back his tears. 'Will you come and see us again?'

'I don't think so, Pat,' John said sensing his own bottom lip quiver. 'I've got to go home tomorrow.'

*   *   *

In a blue peak-cap, a white shirt and trousers in a blue and white check, John looked the part and some of the kids even started calling him Fryer Tuck. He worked six nights a week frying fish and chips in 'Griff's Plaice'. On a quiet weeknight he'd be home just after eleven, but on Friday and Saturday he and Beti would do the salt and vinegar tango for the pub queue until about half-past-eleven and then they'd have to clean up.

For a few weeks this routine suited him. He didn't see much of Dad and Mam, so there wasn't too much family strife, and feeling buoyed up from volunteering with Laura he mostly felt good about himself. He phoned Rhys and Elen from the phone box on the quay on his way into work; even a five-minute chat was enough to sustain him.

He hadn't felt sexy in many weeks, but perhaps he was getting used to the new drugs, or maybe it was just that it was spring and the sap was rising. With the longer evenings, and the arrival of the tourists, he knew the places to find willing men and lads. On a night off from frying fish he went hunting.

As they played the staring game, John decided that the boy looked like Danno from Hawaii Five-O. Danno was definitely interested. John followed him out of the dank public toilet onto the prom where the sun looked huge as it fell behind Pwllheli.

'You got somewhere to go?' Danno asked in broad Scouse.

'No,' John said.

'We could go back into the bog and lock ourselves in the stall,' Danno suggested.

'Too many people around,' John said.

'I'm in a tent, on the site at the end of the prom,' Danno offered.

They walked together. John wished that Danno would talk about something because Adam had already started chanting. In the tent, after Danno's first kiss, Jatunga's dirty talk started. When Danno opened John's fly and sneaked his hand in there was nothing but the buzz of electric shocks.

'I'm sorry, I can't do this,' John said, zipping himself up.

'You're a fucking weirdo,' Danno jibed as John crawled from the tent.

With each successive day after the aborted hunting trip, John felt the new confidence and optimism sapping away. The sexual desires that had rekindled remained unquenched; each time he went to touch himself, Adam or Jatunga would start their mutterings. Once, when he ignored them, David Jones flicked the switch and buzzed him.

Barmouth was suddenly too small again, and frying fish felt like a dead end job. The thought looms began to weave failure into his mind and, fearing that he might be sent back to the hospital, he said nothing about the patchwork of negative thoughts when he saw the GP for a check-up. In late May, at Dr Thomas's clinic in Dolgellau Cottage Hospital, John put on a happy mask and acted his way through the consultation.

*   *   *

It was another glorious June day. Though he'd walked in the hills behind Barmouth on previous afternoons, and enjoyed the sun on his face, he hadn't been able to escape the gnawing sense of failure. Perhaps going for a drive would cheer him. The tyre on the back driver's-side wheel had been looking flattish for a while and though he'd checked the pressure and topped up the air a couple of times it was looking squidgy again. It took only a few minutes to replace the flat with the spare.

But the day was too warm to be in the car. After only twenty minutes he turned into a lane at Llanelltyd that led further up the Mawddach valley to Cymmer Abbey. Amongst the Cistercian ruins he lay in the sunshine on a grassy bank and watched the swallows dart through the three lancet windows in the towering east gable. Bees droned between the few remaining arches and dragonflies skimmed over a murky pool. In the next field, falling off to the river, late new lambs bleated.

With the smell of gorse and bracken, an idea was carried on an eddy of breeze so intangible that he barely noticed its emergence in his consciousness. He could leave Barmouth. Leave the fish and chips and his mam's overprotective intrusions. Drive away from the choking sense of failure. He'd already put 150 pounds in his Post Office book. He could start again somewhere else – and leave that person who'd failed at everything behind.

227

He drove out of Barmouth late in the afternoon, his rucksack on the back seat and his wallet stuffed with five-pound notes. The plain woman in the Post Office said that they'd run out of tens and twenties, but the wad of fivers felt like a lot of money, boosting confidence in his decision to leave and start again somewhere else.

But just along the Mawddach he began to second-guess himself. *If I'm miserable in Barmouth, won't I be miserable somewhere else? Won't I just take myself with me?*

He pulled into a shady lay-by, part of the old road that had been by-passed by the recent improvements between Barmouth and Dolgellau. Beyond the dry stone wall the hillside fell away to the river. He followed a sheep track and in a few minutes found himself by the river. On the opposite bank the pine forested hills rose quickly, and beyond four or five ridges Cader Idris looked austere against the cirrus-streaked sky. He sat for hours watching the water, trying to convince himself that he could leave failure behind.

Driving on through Dolgellau, the repetitive thudding that he'd reported to the garage, 'somewhere underneath, in the middle, at the back', suddenly stopped. Even the car had sensed a new beginning and decided to behave itself! The road narrowed and climbed steeply through an ancient oak forest, twisting on itself in sharp bends to ease the incline. On a hairpin bend, the rear of the car dropped with a bang. Sparks filled the rear-view mirror with the screech of grinding metal. One of the back wheels rolled beside the slowing car before taking a drunken turn, passing in front of him and bouncing down into the valley. The underside of the car gouging into the tarmac and the steepness of the hill brought him to a stop, almost off the road where the bank dipped into the trees.

He wasn't hurt. He was angry with the car and the stupid drunken wheel, and he was fascinated by the way the incident had played out in slow motion. He had enough presence of mind to check that the stranded heap wasn't a hazard to traffic on the poorly lit road. He left the side lights on; that the battery would run down didn't matter given the damage at the rear end – the car might be written off anyway. Cursing the wreck, he slung the rucksack over his shoulder and ran into the forest. He wanted time to think, and didn't want to be found with his vehicle.

The whoosh-whoosh of an owl in flight scared him so much he decided not to venture too deeply into the shadowy blackness, and he tried to stay parallel with the road. The headlight beams from the occasional car cast menacing shadows that danced around him. After an unnerving half-hour he emerged from the trees near the junction at the Cross Foxes Hotel. The road east passed over the mountains at Dinas Mawddwy and continued on through mid-Wales towards Shrewsbury. The route south would take him to Aberystwyth. He thought about Rhys and Elen; if he got a lift quickly he could be there in about an hour. He stood by the entrance to the Cross Foxes car park and stuck out his thumb.

After two cups of sickly sweet tea, his hands stopped shaking. With more coherence he explained what had happened. While Elen comforted him, Rhys went to the study and telephoned the police.

'The car has already been found and the police in Dolgellau have had it towed away,' Rhys said when he returned. 'They found an old envelope in the glove compartment with your Barmouth address on it, so they've talked to your parents.'

'Oh fuck,' John spat vehemently under his breath and hid his head in his hands.

'I'll talk to them for you,' Rhys said. 'If that's what you want?'

Before Rhys was back from the phone in the study a police officer arrived to take a statement. Elen knew him; his wife was one of the Sunday school teachers at Peniel.

'Will you have a cup of tea, Roger?'

'Just a quick one, Mrs Morgan, thanks.'

He listened to John's account of events.

'I've cut you a piece of chocolate cake too, Roger,' Elen said, placing the small tray before him on the table.

Rhys returned from the study.

'How do you both know John?' the policeman asked.

'He's been coming to Peniel since he came up to coll,' Rhys said.

'And in the last months we've become good friends,' Elen put in. 'John hasn't had an easy time of it recently.'

The police officer wrote out a brief statement of the events, as he'd understood them, interrupted by the occasional grunt of appreciation for the chocolate cake. John read the account and signed the statement.

'I have to tell you that the police in Dolgellau might press charges against you. Abandoning a wrecked vehicle in a situation that could cause injury to others —'

'But Roger,' Elen pleaded. 'In John's circumstances that's only going to make his life more difficult.'

'John's got to understand that he may have put other people's lives at risk tonight,' the police officer said. 'But I'm sure, when they take everything into account —' He looked at John. 'You may just get a very stern warning.'

After Roger Williams left the manse, Rhys recounted his telephone conversation with Dai and Olwen.

'They'll be here first thing in the morning, John. They're very upset about what's happened and your dad didn't hold back his views. He doesn't trust me or Elen.'

'I'm sorry if he was rude to you,' John said.

Rhys' face softened, but the glance he exchanged with Elen was troubled.

'Look... it's nearly three o'clock,' she said. 'Things might look a bit different in the morning.'

Olwen looked drawn; she hadn't even bothered to put on any make-up. Dai was angry and not about to bite his tongue. The coffee that Elen had prepared went undrunk and Rhys' quiet efforts at conciliation were cut by mistrust and Dai's glowering stares. The Morgans' offer of hospitality to John was rebuffed.

For perhaps ten or fifteen minutes at the beginning of their journey north, Dai chuntered his annoyances and frustrations about John's impact on their lives. John let his dad rant and he tried to find his way into the quiet field, but the path was blocked. It was lunchtime when they drove into Barmouth.

'I phoned Dr Roberts first thing this morning,' Olwen said. 'He'll see you at three o'clock.'

'I don't need to see him,' John said.

'Please John —'

Olwen's eyes teared up.

Dr Richard Roberts looked over his glasses, his face a contortion of concern.

'So you tried again,' he said.

'I don't understand what you're talking about,' John said with too much arrogance, because he was angry that Olwen and Dai had treated him like a naughty little boy.

231

'I'm talking about your car, and the fact that you tampered with the wheel.'

John hunched his shoulders against the accusation. 'What's this about?' he asked.

'It's not a joking matter, John,' Dr Roberts said, interpreting the shrug to mean indifference. 'You could have caused a major accident if the road had been busy. People might have been killed.'

'I didn't tamper with my car,' John spat, as the panic of realisation gripped him.

'Your mam told me that you changed one of the back wheels yesterday morning.'

'Yes... a slow puncture.'

'And you didn't put the spare back on securely because you decided to try to kill yourself again.'

'No, that's not true.'

Richard Roberts looked at John over the rim of his glasses and waited for him to capitulate.

'No,' John said with perhaps too much forcefulness. 'That's not the way it was.'

And still Richard Roberts waited for John to yield.

'No...' John yelled, jerking up from the chair and knocking it over.

'Don't make it worse for yourself, John,' the doctor said calmly. 'There's a car-ambulance outside to take you back to Denbigh. I've talked to Dr Thomas and he's keen to have you go back in for a while.'

Be calm and pick up the chair. Show him that you're rational and persuade him that he's got it all wrong.

'In the circumstances, John, we can have you sectioned. But it would be better for you if you went back to the hospital of your own volition.'

'This is all a misunderstanding,' John said, sounding more reasoned. 'Let's get my mam in here and we can sort this out. You've got it all wrong.'

'No, John. Yesterday you showed us again that you're a danger to yourself, and to other people.'

*   *   *

The ambulance men led him through the doors of the main hospital building. He asked the friendlier of the two men beside him why they were on the old site. The gruffer one said something about a late admission. And so they stood before the doors of Ffrancon Ward. He knew of its reputation. Everyone in the hospital just called it 'Male 6' – the locked ward for the really mad ones. The heavy locks echoed down the long corridor as the door opened before them. He couldn't co-ordinate his thoughts.

Male 6? The lock up ward? Why am I being locked up?

He was inside and the door was locked behind him, and still he couldn't grasp what was happening. His confusion became more acute as fear, fuelled by so many stories about the locked wards, clenched its grip. The nurse asked him lots of questions.

'But there must be some mistake,' John interrupted. 'I'm not supposed to be locked up. Why have they brought me here?'

The nurse kept asking more questions. John tried to answer them carefully, to co-operate rationally, so that they would realise their mistake and take him to Gwynfryn, where he'd been before.

After filling out all the paperwork the nurse led him to the dormitory area.

'But why am I locked up?' John asked again.

'It's alright,' the nurse said, trying to reassure him.

From the door of the dormitory, John saw that there were perhaps twenty beds. All of the windows in the cavernous room were barred. There were two other doors, one at each end of the room. Both were closed; their windows had bars on them too.

The nurse gestured towards a bed at the far end, against an internal partitioning wall. From about four feet up this partition was a large window. The thickened glass had a square wire mesh running through it. Beyond the windowed wall was a common room. The men in there, perhaps a dozen, looked curiously odd. They had a certain look about them. It was *that* look... And now he was amongst them!

God, am I mad? Do I have 'that' look too? Mad?

'Any neckties in your bag, John?' the nurse asked.

'Dunno... my mam packed it, so there might be.'

'I'm sorry, but you can't keep ties. I'll have to take your razorblades and your shoe laces too.'

Dazed with disbelief, John rummaged in his bag and gave the nurse what he'd asked for.

'You can put your things in the locker, then I'll put your bag in the store room,' the nurse said as he turned to go back to the office.

God, am I mad? Am I?

And John fell onto his bed and cried. The tears came in sobbing bursts, his mind spinning with thoughts.

Locked up. Madness. Sparks. The rolling wheel. Mad men. Locked wards. I've heard about people in locked wards...some never get out. And the rolling wheel, and the sparks, and the mad men. And me – a mad man.

His fear and claustrophobia were palpable.

After what seemed like hours alone, crying on his bed, the nurse, the one that had shown him to his bed, came to him.

'Will you get undressed now please?' he said, handing John a hospital dressing gown that was stained and had lots of holes from cigarette burns. 'The doctor wants to see you.'

He couldn't respond. He sobbed as the nurse undressed him.

'Why?' John blubbered through his tears. 'Please tell me. Why am I locked up? God help me... please tell me why! I'm not mad... am I?'

The nurse hugged John's head close into his chest for some minutes to comfort him. Then, after helping him into the dressing gown, which smelled musty and stale, he led him to the doctor – a stern looking man in a white coat.

'Why am I locked up?'

'I need to examine you,' the doctor said.

'Am I mad... is that why?'

'We're here to help you.'

John lay on the couch. The doctor's cold hands probed and prodded. After the brief physical examination the nurse took him back to the ward.

Slumped on his bed, John felt abandoned.

'Don't —' a young man, perhaps a little older than himself said, looking into his eyes from unnerving closeness. 'Don't cry. Moses will save us. He'll come... he will! He'll lead his people from adversity. Have faith.'

'Can you tell me why I'm locked up?' John asked through his tears.

'That's an easy one,' he said. 'You're mad.' The young man turned to leave the room. 'We're all mad here,' he said, over his shoulder.

The expanse of his bed became a vast and inhospitable wilderness.

Some time later the same nurse came back.

'Your mother's on the phone, John. Would you like to talk to her?'

'Tell her to fuck off! Shit! Piss off! Tell her to fuck off... to forget me. She told the doctor that I tried to kill myself. Fuck her. I hate her.'

The nurse left him alone without realising the depth of his despair. In the hardness of those words about his mother, John recognised that he couldn't even call upon the knowledge of her love to comfort him. *She betrayed me.*

Time passed and he had no more tears to cry. He found a pen, and on a piece of paper he tore from a lined notebook he wrote a hurried message to Rhys and Elen Morgan to tell them of this latest episode in his life. He explained how his mother had fabricated the story, and how the local GP had made arrangements for him to be locked up. Signing his name on the note he wondered if he might never see the Morgans again. He felt completely cut off from the sane world outside. He asked the nurse for an envelope and after addressing it in a barely legible hand, he asked that it be posted.

They were seated about the common room when he entered into their company; eighteen of them. Some were perched on the hard wooden chairs that reminded him of school, rocking back and forth. Others were lolling on the floor, and some slouched in the assortment of grubby lounge chairs. The sight of them frightened him and he sat at a distance on a chair near the door that led to the charge nurse's office. There were no nurses in the common room. He was alone with these men who all shared *that* look.

Might they kill me?

Through the tightness of his fear came laughter. A man with *that* look sat opposite him, smiling. He didn't stop smiling. Then he laughed, and laughed and never seemed to stop laughing. Another man across the room got up from the floor and removed his dressing gown; he began to urinate as he walked towards them, the grey-white of his underpants yellowing. He pulled off the sodden pants and sat naked on the floor at the laughing man's feet, still pissing a puddle around himself. Another man rocked in an upright chair so violently that he soon toppled over. And still the laughing man laughed. Two other men walked across the room... no, not to greet him, but to stare at him. And he sat, stared at and laughed at, and he felt powerless and alone.

But I am sane... I am sane... I am sane. But I'm locked up. Laughed at by this laughing man. Stared at by all these men with 'that' look. Do they see 'that' look in me? Is that why they're staring? Is that why I'm locked up?

And the thoughts went knit one purl one, knit one purl one.

And he tried not to think. Not to think about anything. He tried to create emptiness in his mind and close himself inside it. But the knit one purl one continued to produce a tight fabric of harsh threads.

Locked up. So maybe I am mad. I must be mad because they don't lock up sane people! So I'm insane. I'll probably never leave this place. Laughed at. Stared at. Are they staring because I have 'that' look too?

Knit one. Purl one. The knitted fabric of these thoughts closed over him.

The laughing man laughed. The man in the pool of urine, who'd been masturbating for some time, ejaculated onto a cushion.

So what now? Is all this the proof? Is this all I need to confirm that you don't exist... that you don't care, God? So what now?

And he heard himself speaking these words aloud and he became yet more convinced of his own madness.

Bedtime. The night staff had come on duty during his reverie and now they were gathering up the other patients and leading them through the doors, which would soon be locked, to their beds. The pool of urine was being wiped up but no one noticed the semen-stained cushion.

'You're the new one, are you? John Idris?' asked the night nurse.

'Yes, I'm John Idris Jones,' he said, trying to hold on to something he knew to be true.

'It's time for bed, lad, come on.'

'No! I'm not going to be locked in there with those nutters. I'll sleep here. It's quite comfortable, really. Please don't lock me in with them... please.'

'Don't be a stupid lad now, you can't sleep here.'

'No... I'm not going in there... not to be locked up with them. I'm afraid... I'm scared of them.'

'Scared? But there's nothing to be afraid of. They won't harm one of their own.'

'What's that supposed to mean?'

'They don't put normal people in here you know!'

His answer was chilling.

So I am mad. But I'm not!

'I'm not mad!'

'Aren't you?' he quizzed with a conniving smile. 'Well, okay, if you say so.'

The other night nurse came over to join his colleague.

'Having trouble, Don?'

'Yes. This is tonight's new admission, John Idris. He doesn't want to go to bed. He says he's afraid.'

'Afraid? Well, isn't that a shame,' he mocked. 'Come on you. I'm no soft touch like Donnie here. I won't have any nonsense. If you don't come quietly, like a good boy, we'll have to give you a jab to put you out, and when I give needles it can hurt!'

Stunned by the treatment he was receiving he went with the one called Don, who led him to his bed.

'What about night sedation?' the nurse asked. 'Do you want some Mistchloral or some Mogadon?'

'No... I don't intend to sleep in here with these loonies; I might not see the morning if I do. I'll just sit here on my bed and stay awake so that I can see what's going on.'

Before the nurse had a chance to say anything, the laughing man sat upright in the bed next to John's. He laughed, and laughed. The nurse turned to the laughing man and tucked him down into his bed.

'Okay Smiler, go to sleep now, go to sleep,' the nurse said lovingly.

Moving to his colleague at the door, the nurse turned and stabbed a pointed finger.

'You settle down, John Idris. We don't want any nonsense from you.'

The two nurses locked the door behind them. Through the glass partition wall, John watched them walk to the far end of the darkened common room and settle down in front of the television. And the laughing man began to laugh. Another

239

moaned. Someone else was crying, a sobbing cry. Bed springs creaked out the rhythm of someone's solitary comforting. Another man sang. John shivered with fear, and the knit one purl one continued to add to the web of thoughts that caused him to doubt his sanity. He felt stifled and anxious. The pitch of the concert of night noise seemed to crescendo. The knit one purl one in his head reached a fevered tempo. Frantic. Desperate. Desperate to be freed. Freed from the locked room and the incessant knit one purl one knitting its madness into his mind.

He tapped at the window of the partition wall. His eyes filled with the flashes of light transmitted from a television through the darkness, and they overflowed with bitter tears. He tapped the window again, but still the nurses didn't come. Inside him the chaos gathered its forces, the knitted patchwork quilt of insanity adding new stitches, new stitches, new stitches, knit one, purl one. His tapping gave way to banging, hitting, thumping the glass with his fists, and still no one came. And panic overcame. He threw himself at the locked door. He kicked at it, and banged at it, and shouted and shouted and shouted.

The nurse who could be cruel with needles unlocked the door.

'Back to bed! Now! Now, or I'll —'

'Please! Please let me out. I can't stand it in here. Please let me come out. Please —'

'Go back to bed, John Idris.'

The tears caught in his throat and through his weeping he gurgled his appeal to be released.

'Please!' he screamed.

The nurse called to his colleague and together they lifted John from the floor and dropped him, roughly and without compassion, back on his bed.

'Now,' said the one who could be cruel with needles. 'Go back to sleep. You get one more chance before I put you out with a jab.'

'God help me... please God! Help me.'

His screams disturbed some of the others.

But in time some calmness came. None of what was happening seemed to matter. The knit one purl one in his mind stopped. The fear ebbed. Tears dried up. The peace that settled over him seemed to embrace and protect. Night noises stilled and the laughing man's laugh gave way to the gentle purr of slumber. And something Rhys Morgan had written to him in a letter came back: '... and underneath are the everlasting arms.' He conjured them up, those everlasting arms – and lay in their security. He reached for God's hand... and felt its warm grasp.

*   *   *

After breakfast he quickly tired of being a spectator to the madness around him. In the office, the nurse refused to let him use the phone. John didn't know what his rights were under the mental health legislation.

'I'm a voluntary patient,' he ventured. 'I don't think you can stop me using a phone.'

'But there isn't a pay phone on this ward,' the nurse said.

'So, let me use the office phone.'

'Sorry, can't do that.'

John tried to size up the nurse, whom he sensed was just being awkward. He remembered that the previous evening he'd been invited to speak with his mam when she'd phoned. He chose sycophancy over abuse.

'I wonder if you'd be kind enough to phone my parents and ask them to phone back so that I can speak to them.'

'Yes, when I've got the time,' the nurse said. 'I'll call you.'

John swallowed back his resentment at the nurse's power game and smiled.

'Thank you. I'll wait just outside the office so that you don't have to come looking for me.'

He sat in the corridor holding God's hand for almost an hour until the nurse called him.

'It's John here,' he said into the phone to his dad. 'I want you to phone Griffin's Garage; see what Mr Griffin's got to say about the thumping noise at the back of my car. Then you can phone Doctor Roberts and tell him that Mam made a mistake. I'm going to discharge myself from here so you can come and fetch me if you like, otherwise I'll hitch a lift.'

'Don't be so bloody silly, John,' Dai said.

'I'm not being silly, Dad. I've never been more serious in my life. Just do what I've asked.'

'Look, John... I'll come up there. Give me a couple of hours.'

John glanced at the clock on the wall of the office.

'Okay, Dad, if you want to, but if you're not here by eleven I'll discharge myself anyway.'

He hung up the phone. The nurse in charge, who'd been listening to his conversation, sneered.

'You need our help, John. Try to discharge yourself and we'll section you.'

'No, I don't think so,' John said, shaking his head. 'If I stay here I'll lose everything. This psychiatric system seems to want to make people dependent on drugs and doctors, and conform to spurious ideas of normality.' *Don't stop holding my hand, God.* 'People like me aren't helped to find out who we are in a place

242

like this,' he continued, uncertain where the words were coming from but liking the sound of them. 'You're all trying to make me something that I'm not, something that I never can be, instead of helping me find who I am. The sooner I'm out of here the better.'

'You carry on talking that sort of gobbledegook and you'll just confirm to everybody that you're in the right place,' the charge nurse said.

'We'll see when my dad gets here.'

After showering and dressing – he remembered the importance Jatunga Arachchi had seemed to place on appearance and grooming – he sat for a while and reflected on his hours of incarceration. All that madness the previous night had touched him until he'd been embraced by those 'everlasting arms'... and then he'd dared to reach out – and found that God didn't snatch his hand away. With his hand held firmly he'd looked into the face of an insanity that demanded he become something that he could never become. Accompanied by the laughing man's snigger, he'd come to realise that his sense of himself would always be defined by the prejudices and misunderstandings of those who were so willing to bear false witness – if he remained silent. But the hand that held his seemed to lead to the brink of a new journey. *John Idris Jones, lover of music, lover of life, lover of men... you have a choice: the uncomfortable sanity of self-acceptance... or letting them destroy you.* And the warm hand that held John's tugged gently. *Go out and find your place in the world and make it your own with all the dignity you can muster. Search for your purpose within your community, and when you find it, fulfil it with intelligence and integrity. It'll take you a lifetime, but remember, the journey is home.*

When Dai Jones arrived he was visibly disturbed by the madness of it all.

'If you'd like to wait here, Mr Jones,' the charge nurse said offering him a chair. 'The doctor will be here to see you in just a few minutes.'

'It's all an awful mix-up,' Dai said. 'The wheel coming off the car had nothing to do with John.'

'Well, you can explain that to the doctor when he gets here, Mr Jones.'

*　　*　　*

The laughing man's guffaws silenced Adam and the Sunday Library Group. Jatunga Arachchi's whisperings and David Jones's buzzing shocks were drowned out by the noises of the night of the laughing man. The quilt of doubt about his sanity, so well woven, clung like a second skin. It had to be unpicked, stitch by stitch, over many months.

The Morgans helped. John stayed with them for a week at the end of June. They talked and cried together; they laughed and prayed. Rhys had bought a copy of Norman Pittenger's book, *Time for Consent*, from SCM Press. Elen had liked the book's sub-title: 'A Christian's approach to homosexuality'. The author wasn't claiming universal truths, but he was offering a new way of seeing. John devoured the chapters and Pittenger joined Rhys and Elen in the quiet field of angels.

One afternoon, walking along the prom to kick the bar, Rhys encouraged John to come back to Aber in the autumn and take up the place the university had kept open for him.

'I don't know,' John said. 'Aber's got so many bad memories for me.'

'You could lodge with us, if you'd like to… just to get you on your feet,' Elen said. 'There's a lovely room at the top of the house, all oak panelled. It used to be the minister's study before our day but it was so impractical, up all those stairs. It was Beca's room, before she left home.'

'I couldn't do that,' John said. 'It would be such an imposition. You've already done so much for me; I can never repay your kindness.'

'Kindness doesn't always have to be repaid, John,' Elen said. 'Sometimes it's enough – more important even – to pass it on. Rhys and I are offering you the room because we'd like to see you getting back to your studies and getting on with your life… so that all that latent potential can be nurtured – and shared. If we can support you in that then it becomes a privilege.'

Another afternoon, with too much of Elen's chocolate cake giving him a bellyache, John first heard about Taizé.

'Thousands of young people from all over Europe go there during the summer,' Rhys said. 'The simplicity of the brothers' lives and their straightforward spirituality seem to appeal to a generation pulled in so many directions.'

'And young people from so many different traditions, coming together and learning from one another can only be a good thing,' Elen said.

'Where is Taizé?' John asked.

'Somewhere down in Burgundy, not far from Mâcon,' Rhys said.

Back in Barmouth, John began to plan for his trip. There was no room in the plan for prescriptions and tablets. He emptied the contents of his pill bottles down the toilet.

*   *   *

Dai and Olwen believed that John's time would be better spent in the chip shop earning some money for when he went back to college, but they both, in their own ways, became reconciled to his departure. With a wink, Dai slipped him two crisp twenties across the breakfast table when Olwen was in the kitchen. Olwen, who went to the station to wave him off, pushed a tenner into his hand as he boarded the train.

Pulling out over the swollen Mawddach estuary, the swirling waters beneath the long wooden railway bridge unnerved him. The currents and eddies seemed to mimic his inner turbulence. With a thirty-hour train journey ahead of him – and who knew what other adventures – his enthusiasm and excitement for the trip were engulfed by doubts. *What if I don't find the inner resources to travel on my own in Europe? What if Adam comes back... or the laughing man?*

'If I can do this, I can do anything,' he said aloud to himself, clasping the document pouch that hung around his neck – with his passport, his Inter-rail ticket, and enough money to follow the student travel guide's recommendations for 'doing Europe' on five pounds a day.

Before the train reached Machynlleth he'd left his qualms behind. He thumbed the international train timetables and by the time he made his first change in Shrewsbury he'd sketched a provisional route for the weeks he planned to travel around Europe after Taizé. The possibilities seemed endless; international express trains could carry him from Paris to Rome or Amsterdam to Athens... even Barcelona to Berlin.

He was tired when he pitched his tent on a Burgundy hillside surrounded by Dutch, German and Italian pilgrims and a boisterous group from Yugoslavia. He'd slept little on the ferry or the night train, and because he'd been confused by the Paris metro system, and his grasp of French was so poor, he'd missed his connection at the Gare de Lyon. Venturing from the station's early morning gloom he'd walked along the Seine. Watching the sunrise over Notre Dame he wished he'd had someone with him just so that he could say, 'Isn't that lovely?'

'You're from Wales,' said a heavily accented, softly spoken voice as John unrolled his sleeping bag.

Turning, John saw a tall, fair lad about his own age, crawling from a large, three-man tent close to his own.

'I'm Arie,' he said. 'This is a Welsh dragon on your rucksack, no?'

John introduced himself. Despite a toothy smile and a crooked nose, Arie was confident of his good looks.

'How do you know the Welsh flag, Arie?' John asked.

'Last summer I walked the coastal path in Pembrokeshire,' he said. 'It's a very beautiful landscape.'

'Yes,' he smiled. 'What's your accent? I can't place it.'

'I'm from the Netherlands... Amsterdam.'

'You speak very good English.'

'Thank you. A little bit, yes. And some German and some French too.'

'I just do Welsh and English,' John said, feeling mildly ashamed of his bilingualism.

'This is my friend Henk,' Arie said.

The boy who walked towards them was taller than Arie. He wore shorts and a T-shirt and his skin was bronzed; the sun had bleached the fine hairs on his legs and arms. The hand he offered John was large, but his fingers were like the delicate fronds of a fern. When their eyes met they both recognised the struggle.

247

'If you're not with somebody you can come with Arie and me to the evening prayer,' Henk offered.

Like no other church John had ever seen, the Church of Reconciliation at Taizé had side walls that could be opened so that the thousands of worshippers outside could join the service. Arie pushed through the gathering crowd.

'It's more... how do you say?... atmospheric, if we get inside.'

They found some empty floor space and John sat between them. The white robed brothers processed in silence and knelt in two parallel lines down the centre of the sanctuary before an altar that was lit with hundreds of candles. On the west side of the building, the last of the sun's rays illuminated vividly stained glass windows: narrow oblique slashes of royal blue, disks of cadmium, squat squares of amethyst and lozenges of ruby red that appeared to have been scattered at random into the grey concrete like a frenzied, psychedelic pebble-dash.

'On Saturday it's the vigil of the resurrection,' Arie whispered. 'A festival of light.'

A solitary flute broke the hushed silence that had come upon the sanctuary as the brothers had settled. It played a simple melody and a single voice began to chant.

Ubi caritas et amor, ubi caritas, Deus ibi est. Ubi caritas et amor, ubi caritas, Deus ibi est. Ubi caritas et amor...

With each repetition, more voices joined the swelling mantra.

'Why is it in Latin?' John asked Henk.

'Because Latin doesn't belong to anyone now,' Henk whispered.

'But what are they saying?'

Henk put his arm over John's shoulder. 'Just sing. I'll tell you later.'

248

John leaned into Henk and took his hand. With the warmth of the evening and the press of people, the mesmeric chanting and the play of candlelight, John dozed, his head coming to rest on Henk's shoulder. Through a contented half-sleep he heard prayers being spoken, a stanza in French, a line of German... Russian, Spanish, Dutch.

Henk stroked John's wrist with his thumb, just where the palm of his hand opened. 'You've been sleeping,' he said with a hint of accusation.

John became alert with a start. 'I travelled all night.'

'So, you should go to bed,' Henk quipped.

'You won't get much sleep if the Italians are as happy as they were last night,' Arie said. 'They can drink so much and still be up early in the morning.'

They walked back to the field at the edge of the village where they'd pitched their tents. Arie and Henk had been in Taizé for a week already and they described the daily routine.

'If you can get out of the toilet duty you should do it,' Arie urged. 'With so many people coming here the toilets get blocked very often. It's not nice.'

'There are some jobs in the kitchen,' Henk said.

'I hadn't expected chants in Latin,' John offered. He recognised in himself traces of his father's anti-Catholic bigotry and was made uncomfortable by the recognition of such a latent prejudice. 'Because it's a dead language everyone can claim it, is that the idea?' John quizzed.

'At my school no one would agree with you that Latin is dead,' Arie said.

They all laughed.

'There are some pamphlets, for the worship,' Henk said, looking for words. 'The chants are sung in Latin, but the text is translated into many languages. The *Ubi caritas* means, where there is... *caritas*, charity... and where there is *amor* — ' He looked to Arie for help.

'*Where charity and love are present, God is also present*, or something like that,' Arie said.

Back at their tents, the Italians were already singing around a fire, but the Germans seemed to be in higher spirits. Arie spoke briefly with Henk in Dutch. Henk's open-handed gesture suggested uncertainty. 'Your tent is very small, John,' he said. 'Arie wants to know if you'd like him to sleep in your tent?'

John was puzzled for a moment. Then he realised that Arie wasn't suggesting they sleep together, but offering him the opportunity to sleep with Henk in their tent. He was taken aback by how up-front they were.

'I didn't mean to embarrass you,' Arie said, interpreting John's hesitation.

'I'm not embarrassed, I'm just surprised by your openness.'

'Ja... Henk is gay and you are gay... and my girlfriend is back in Amsterdam,' he said, laughing. 'I just want to make life easy for everybody.'

'It isn't that I wouldn't like to,' John said, holding Henk's gaze. 'But this was only our first date.'

Henk laughed, his hazel eyes sparkling in the glow from the Italians' fire.

'I don't know about Amsterdam,' John teased, 'but where I come from you don't sleep with someone after a first date. Maybe after the second or the third, but not the first.'

One of the gang of boisterous Germans called to Arie. He answered them in fluent German and then turned back to John and Henk.

'Okay boys, if you change your mind just put my sleeping

bag in the little tent,' he said before skipping off. 'Have a good night.'

Henk took John in his arms and hugged him.

'I would like it too,' Henk offered.

'My head's spinning with so many new things,' John said, and squeezed his new friend tightly. 'And I'm really tired.'

'So go to sleep, and in the morning we can have breakfast together and start a love affair.'

After a feast of hot chocolate, warm crusty bread and plum jam, they walked through fields of corn and sunflowers.

'I'm in seminary,' Henk said. 'But I think I'll have to leave. To become ordained I will have to hide that I'm gay, and tell lies, and that's not good.'

'What will you do?' John asked.

'I don't know just now. I came to Taizé to have some time to think, and pray about the future. I did one course at the university that looked at the relationship between theology and sexuality. In America, in California, there are some professors doing some interesting work. Maybe I'll go there to study for a while.'

In a street café in Cormatin they ate roasted chicken and salad, and shared a bottle of the rough local wine. On their ramble back to Taizé they lay together under a gnarled rowan tree and dozed away their wooziness. Late in the afternoon they climbed the steep lane that would eventually bring them to the Taizé hilltop.

'Will we put Arie's sleeping bag in your tent this night?' Henk asked.

John was puzzled by his response to Henk. He liked him, and he was attracted to him, but his body wasn't responding in a way that he could recognise. With Paul the sexual desire had become obsessive and he'd craved physical intimacy. Had Jatunga Arachchi's little talks, and all those electric shocks, made him incapable of loving anyone?

'I need to tell you about some of the things that have happened,' John said.

They sat on a rude wooden bench at the roadside, shaded by Lombardy poplars, and he told his story.

'I don't think this could have happened today in the Netherlands,' Henk said, his eyes brimming with tears. 'It's horrible, like the experiments the Nazis did in Buchenwald.'

'I didn't do the Second World War at school,' John said, not understanding Henk's reference. 'I know they tried to exterminate the Jews and did experiments on children with Down's syndrome.'

'Ja. Just thirty years ago we were... *Die Männer mit dem rosa Winkel*. I don't know how to say this in English, men with pink —' He drew a shape on his chest.

'A triangle?' John said.

'Ja... it's a German book. I read it last year... all about how the Nazis put tens of thousands of gay men in *Konzentrationslager*.'

'Concentration camps?' John said with disbelief.

'Yes, in Sachsenhausen... and in Buchenwald they did experiments... ach, my English is so bad.' He grasped his crotch. 'They cut off the *teelballen*, and with some men they gave operations to treat them with *hormoons*.'

'I didn't know this,' John said, plainly shocked.

'And in Great Britain in 1975 they give gays electricity shocks,' Henk said. 'It is not believable.'

They walked on in silence, up the hill into Taizé. In the field where they'd pitched their tents the Germans were playing volleyball over an imaginary net.

I wonder if their school system leaves out the Second World War too.

John slept in his own tent, lulled to sleep by *Ubi caritas*. He dreamed that the small field of his 'deeper inside' was filling up; with Rhys and Elen, and Norman Pittenger, he saw Henk and Arie... and thousands of angels with pink triangles.

He stayed in Taizé for nine days. Arie's sleeping bag never did find its way into his tent, but John tasted an intimacy with Henk that he'd never experienced.

'You'll come to Amsterdam before you go back to Wales then?' Henk asked, still hopeful.

'I'd like to come and visit you, Henk, and I'd like us to always stay in touch,' John said, wondering if he might feel more open to the possibility of a love affair after Venice, Athens and Salzburg.

At the service on Sunday morning in the Church of Reconciliation the Eucharist was celebrated. Henk offered his piece of bread to John.

'This is the Body of Christ,' he said. 'I hope it will give you the strength always to be honest about who you are. Eat it and be strong.'

*   *   *

Roving around Europe, he was troubled little by the laughing man's cackle or the Sunday Library Group's accusations. His head had been filled with *Ubi caritas* and Henk, the Grand Canal, the Acropolis and the Anne Frank House... and so many interesting people on trains.

But being back in Aberystwyth brought everything to the surface again.

Rhys and Elen were very tangible and immediate supports at times of crisis – like meeting Paul Wynne again for the first time and seeing Adam in Galloway's. Bumping into old classmates like Stewart hadn't been easy either; Stew had moved up a year and made firm friendships in John's absence, leaving him behind. Passing the hospital, where they'd pumped out his stomach, the events of the past winter seemed so much more vivid. He couldn't avoid passing the hospital on the hike up to the campus from town... an everyday reminder. But he did recognise a difference in himself; he had his field of angels.

In the oak panelled room at the top of the manse, John learned to be a disciplined scholar once again. On his dad's old gramophone he listened to Elton John and Beethoven, Simon and Garfunkel and his newest LP, *Chants from Taizé*. If Adam and the Sunday Library Group kicked off he'd let *Ubi caritas* wash over him and when the laughing man tittered and chortled, *Laudate omnes gentes* seemed to pacify him.

On a Sunday at the beginning of December, during the announcements by one of Peniel's Elders at the morning service, an advertisement from *The Cambrian News* was read aloud:

> A branch of the Samaritans will be established in Aberystwyth in the late summer of next year. People who think they might be interested to train as Samaritans are invited to write a letter of application by no later than Friday 9 January 1976. Interviews will be held during January and February and the training course will begin in March.

The next week in Galloway's bookshop a small bookstand appeared near the cash desk with copies of Chad Varah's *Samaritans in the 70's*. On page 174, under the heading 'Homosexual problems', a reasoned and positive essay outlined the Samaritans' befriending role: 'to help the homosexual come to terms with his or her constitution'. A leaflet that repeated the call for local volunteers had been folded into each copy of the book, giving a contact name and address. John wondered if his experiences would count for anything, and he wondered about the mysterious Barbara and her Post Office box number.

Early September

Klaus Hensel sat at the kitchen table and watched a charm of goldfinches feeding from the seed-feeders on the apple tree just outside the window. Occasionally he took an envelope from the small stack of mail that had arrived in his absence. Most of the correspondence was unsolicited junk, which he always tore into four pieces ready for the compost heap, unless there was a pre-paid return envelope; in such cases he circled his own details on any accompanying letter, wrote *please remove me from your database* at the end of an arrow leading from the circle, and mailed it back to the sender at their expense. For a while he watched a nuthatch make darting raids on the peanut feeder and carry its plunder to the wicker boundary fence where it wedged the nuts between the wefts. 'Did you go'n stay with that guy in the end?' he asked when John brought the coffee to the table. 'The one we met at the theatre.'

'Russell? Yes, I did. It was strange to be back there.'

'Where in Barmouth does he live?'

'One of the big houses on the hill – after the "cardboard castle". Remember, the place we used to go with Mam for Sunday lunch?'

'He's got money then,' Klaus cracked. 'You pay 50,000 just for the view up there.'

'He's got HIV and he's looking for friends.'

Klaus drew his eyebrows in. 'Don't you think you should hold off from being a Good Samaritan until you're feeling better?' He tore up a few more pieces of junk mail. John watched the nuthatch, but was thinking about Russell Talbert's Kyffins.

'How's the exercise going?' Klaus asked.

'I did some new things today – five minutes on a stepping machine.'

'And was 'gorgeous Mike' supervising you?' Klaus teased.

'No, one of the women.'

'So your blood pressure wasn't so high then.'

'A hundred and nine over sixty-five after my cool-down,' John quipped with a snigger.

'And that's good?'

'Very good.'

'And did you learn any new ways to prepare oily fish in your rehab class today?'

'I didn't go to the class, I saw Evelyne, the psychologist.'

'And —' Klaus said, part apprehensive about what he might hear and part encouraging.

'Well, I think I had one of those blinding 'road to Damascus' moments,' John said. 'Usually she just lets me talk... you know, about how I've been remembering things... all those crises that

I thought I'd resolved a long time ago that just keep coming back.'

'Ja...' Klaus said, offering his outstretched hand across the table.

John took the hand and squeezed it. 'Ev asked me why I was interpreting all this remembering as a revisiting of unresolved issues.'

'Hmm...' he nodded, his thumb stroking the back of John's hand.

'She's suggesting that maybe I'm re-living those old crises, not because they're wounds that have re-opened and need tending to, but because I actually coped quite well with them.' He stroked his chest. 'And now I'm searching for coping mechanisms for this huge crisis with my heart.'

'And does this make sense to you?'

'It makes more sense than believing I'm still screwed up about things that happened thirty years ago!'

'So, how does it make you feel?'

'Less heavy, and more hopeful maybe.'

'That's good.'

They drank their coffees.

'Did you ever go sailing on the lake in Effeld when you were a kid?'

'No,' Klaus said.

'Do you know about tacking and reaching?'

Klaus shrugged and shook his head.

'Evelyne's into sailing and she asked me if I ever got tired of tacking? That's when your sails are trimmed and you have to zigzag your boat so that you can move against the wind in a series of tacks. Apparently it's really hard work, but it's worth the effort because that's the way you manoeuvre yourself so that you can let out your sails and run before the wind. She said that the fastest and most fun part of sailing, when you sail across the wind, is what they call reaching.'

'So she gives you sailing lessons too?' Klaus chirped.

'No,' John said and laughed. 'After hearing me talk about my life these past few weeks she's started to wonder when I'm going to stop tacking and let the wind fill my sails.'

'And d'you think she's got a point?'

John heard an echo of Waldo Williams' poem. 'I've been crawling through thorns so long I'm not even sure I'd know how to let out my sails and reach into the future,' he said.

Klaus poured more coffee, unsure what to say.

'I missed you,' John said.

'I missed you too.'

'Why don't we go to bed for the afternoon.'

'What about your heart?'

'I'll lie on my back and think of Wales.'

Samaritans
and Slightly Christian Marxists
1976-81

Starting a branch of the Samaritans from scratch, Barbara Mitchell and her small working group needed more than 120 volunteers to open up a centre that would be staffed 24/7. They'd interviewed 164 possibles, and whittled them down to 114; this included half a dozen students that probably wouldn't be available for twenty weeks of the year. If she lost five or six during the training course the whole proposition began to look shaky. But she was a tenacious woman. She trusted that many of the new volunteers would be enthusiastic enough to do three sessions a month rather than the two they were expected to pledge, and once the new centre was up-and-running – the planning permission on the three-bedroomed end-of-terrace was a whole other kettle-of-fish – they could bring on new volunteers to make up the numbers.

Organising the volunteers' training programme had been a nightmare, and without the skills and experience gained from juggling the timetable during her fifteen years as headmistress of a girls' boarding school in Shropshire, she may not have pulled it off. It was only feasible to have all the trainees together for a couple of introductory sessions; most of the instruction was based on role-play and discussion, which could only be done in small groups. She'd worked on the basis of ten clusters of twelve volunteers, meeting every two weeks through the spring and early summer.

John was the only student in his cluster and, as far as he could work out, the only gay man. Three older men, in their forties and fifties, talked about rugby, wives, kids and mortgage interest rates during the breaks.

'You seem to be enjoying the training sessions,' Barbara said to John over their sandwich lunch.

'Yes,' he said, smiling. 'But I've had an easy time of it so far. I haven't had any really difficult situations.'

'Don't put yourself down like that,' she chided. 'You're very intuitive during your role-plays.'

He looked at the curling edge of his ham sandwich and felt himself curl up with embarrassment.

'I'd like to try something this afternoon that's going to get people's backs up,' she ventured. 'Would you help me with it?'

'What d'you have in mind?'

'You know that the Samaritans have a policy of not hanging-up on *anyone*?'

'Yes.'

'So, one of the things we have to prepare for is calls from masturbators.'

Her voice was so plummy it took John a second to register what she'd said.

'As a branch, we're going to need a few women, perhaps half

a dozen, who'll be willing to take calls from men who want to masturbate, and we have to train them.'

'And you want me to be a phone-wanker in a role-play,' John said, finally catching her drift.

'I'll be the volunteer,' she said. 'I was one of the women in the Shrewsbury branch who dealt with calls like this. There were four of us and we were all called *Brenda*. The regulars soon got the hang of the system and they'd always ask for *Brenda*.'

'Why me, Barbara?' he asked, his face crumpled into a scowl.

'Because you're very good at role-play,' she said generously. 'And because I remember your application letter. I think that some of the experiences you've had give you an edge over the other men in the cluster.'

He felt like saying he was a bit out of practice. For months he'd blocked such feelings and hadn't touched himself like that. For a split second he again felt the confusion wreaked by the flashbacks of David on the shock box when Henk had touched him. Henk had been so disappointed, and it had upset their time together in Amsterdam.

John searched Barbara's wrinkled face. He saw the integrity in the greenish-brown of her eyes, and interpreted the encouragement in her gentle smile. There wasn't even a suggestion of malice. 'Okay, what do I have to do?'

For the few minutes before they re-convened, she briefed him on the role she wanted him to play.

'Oh God! Didn't it make you feel like a prostitute, Barbara?' Julie asked after the role-play ended and John had come from behind the curtain to re-join the group for discussion.

'No,' Barbara said. 'I gave the caller active listening and befriending. *I* didn't give him sexual gratification.'

'But that's what he got out of it,' Phil said. 'Surely we should be able to put the phone down on perverts like that.'

'And if I'd hung-up on him, what might he have done?' Barbara asked, looking around the group and wondering if Phil was the only one not to have read and absorbed the *twenty principles*.

'He could have phoned someone at random, some vulnerable woman living on her own perhaps, and scared the living daylights out of her,' Meg said.

'Or he might have gone out and raped somebody,' Peggy suggested.

'Perhaps he'd have just opened up a copy of *Playboy* and ogled,' Mark said as a deliberate put-down to Meg and Peggy's notions; they were both too feminist for his liking.

The discussion continued for perhaps ten minutes.

'You're very quiet, John,' Barbara said. 'You role-played that very well, but what are you feeling?'

'Embarrassed,' he said. 'And a bit dirty.'

'Say some more, if you can,' she urged.

'Well... I suppose I'm embarrassed just because I role-played something that's usually a private thing,' he said, searching for words. 'I feel like I've given away something personal to the group.'

'You're feeling vulnerable then, are you?' Meg asked.

'Yes, I suppose... and dirty because what the guy was doing is so freaky. Doing it on the phone I mean; it's smutty, isn't it?'

'Do you feel you've de-roled enough, John?' Barbara asked.

'I know that I'm not that sad man on the phone, if that's what you mean?'

'Will you all show your appreciation to John for a really difficult role-play?' Barbara said.

There were claps, and a couple of the women got up and hugged him.

'We're going to have to come back to this at some stage,' Barbara said. 'We'll need to train up some women to be *Brendas* —'

'And what about men?' Mark interrupted.

'You wouldn't get women phoning up to do *that*,' Julie said with scorn.

'No, but you might get some sad poof wanting to get his rocks off talking to a man,' Mark said.

'And how do you men feel about that possibility?' Barbara quizzed.

'It's not my cup of tea,' Phil sneered.

'I don't think I can ever remember a masturbator who wanted to talk to a man,' Barbara said. 'But we did get lots of homosexuals looking for support. How would that be, Phil?'

'Well, as long as I was sure they weren't —' He closed his hand around an imaginary phallus and jerked it up and down.

'I'd have real problems talking to a homo,' Mark ventured.

'But you've talked to me about all sorts of things over the past few weeks, Mark,' John said.

The silence that cut between them couldn't have been for longer than a few seconds. Barbara smiled at John with what he interpreted as appreciation for his willingness to challenge Mark. Meg nudged Julie as if to say 'I told you so.' Mark became fidgety and turned bright red.

'We're really lucky to have John in this cluster,' Barbara said. 'He's got some experiences that we can all learn something from. Perhaps we can do some role-plays around gay issues next time; there's a small section in the book about befriending homosexuals that I'd like you all to read.'

264

*　　*　　*

The poster advertising for kibbutz volunteers showed people happy in their work. John fantasised about picking grapefruits and oranges, like the plump Jaffas in the supermarket. The groves, set in idyllic Biblical landscapes, would smell citrus sweet and he'd tan under a bronzing sun. Outside the students' union building a March gale was blowing in off the sea, rain lashing against the huge glass panels that fronted the building. He jotted down the contact details and hatched a plan for the three-month summer vacation; picking Jaffas was infinitely preferable to frying fish back in 'Griff's Plaice'.

He could only entertain the notion of spending the summer on a kibbutz because he'd been able to save from his grant; Rhys and Elen hadn't offered him the room at the top of their house so that they could benefit financially. 'Do something really worthwhile with what you save,' he remembered Elen saying when he'd pointed out that he was paying them so little.

'Going to Israel would be a wonderful experience,' Elen said over supper.

'I'll need to do some reading,' John mused. 'Aside from Bible stories, which might be a bit out of date, I don't know the first thing about Israel.'

'Lots of the kibbutzim were settled by war refugees, from the concentration camps,' Rhys said. 'Read some of the survivors' accounts.'

'And then there's the history of how the British relinquished their control of Palestine and how the modern state of Israel was founded,' Elen said.

At Galloway's the following day, John bought three books: *House of Dolls* by Ka-tzetnik 135633, *O Jerusalem!* by Collins and Lapierre and *Exodus* by Leon Uris. Through the spring, interspersed with all the science, John read the eyewitness account of the Nazis' camps and wondered at the real identity of the internee – the ka-tzetnik – who had number 135633 tattooed into his forearm, and got caught up in the freedom fighting campaigns of the Irgun and the Stern Gang, and the founding of the Haganah. He found reading about the birth pangs of the modern state of Israel both fascinating and confusing, and he wondered about the Palestinian side of the story.

*   *   *

The tabloid newspapers were full of it: Jeremy Thorpe had resigned as the leader of the Liberal Party because of allegations that he'd had a fling with a male model. The training workshop they did on homosexual issues took on an added sense of relevance. Meg did a brilliant role-play, making out to be the wronged wife who'd just found her husband in bed with another man. Mark, who refused the role of the volunteer, remained tight-lipped through the group's discussion. John noticed that since he'd come out to the cluster, Mark had avoided eye contact with him. Julie asked John if he'd meet her for a coffee sometime; she wanted to talk about her son, Harry. At seventeen, he'd never had a girlfriend, he'd always shied away from talking about 'relationships and things', and now he'd taped posters of David Bowie and Elton John to his bedroom wall.

*   *   *

Just days after his last exam, and confident he wouldn't be called for re-sits in September, John flew to Tel-Aviv. At

Heathrow, in the faltering queue at the El-Al security check, he found others who were kibbutz bound.

'I'm Michael,' said a lad with red curly hair and a freckled face when John introduced himself.

'And d'you know which kibbutz you're going to?' John asked.

'It's all up for grabs,' Michael said. 'I was there last year. They'll meet us at the airport; there's usually a list of kibbutzim that need volunteers and as long as the right number of people get sent to each place they don't really mind who goes where.'

They got seats next to one another on the huge jumbo jet and after five hours they'd struck up a friendship. 'Shall we stick together then?' John asked as they waited for the *fasten seatbelt* signs to go off for the last time.

'Sure thing,' Michael quipped.

Stepping from the relative cool of the air-conditioned plane into the dry heat of the late afternoon the air smelled of citrus blossom.

'Smell those oranges,' John said. 'I can't wait to get picking.'

'Forget it,' Michael sniped. 'Those fucking citrus trees have got thorns the size of one-inch nails. It's a nightmare... your hands get slashed to shreds.'

In the arrivals hall, where the air-conditioning was too cold, the twenty or so volunteers were herded into an alcove where the kibbutz representative, a tall, blonde woman in her late-twenties, held a clipboard. Michael talked to her in Hebrew. John rummaged in his rucksack for a sweater. 'She wants two men to go just east of Gaza,' he said as John pushed his head from his pullover.

'I thought kibbutzim were supposed to be egalitarian.'

'It's a big digging job, laying irrigation pipes in the Negev. What do you think?'

'So… I don't get my hands ripped by thorns,' John jibed with an openhanded gesture. 'They just get blistered swinging a pick and pushing a shovel.'

They strode over to the blonde with the clipboard. 'We'll go'n dig holes in the desert,' Michael volunteered, this time in English.

'Okay you guys,' she said with a strong American accent. 'This is a pretty tough job and after a month, if you want to, you get to go someplace else… that's the deal. Here's my card. If you decide you want to move you must contact me a week before – so in three weeks time – then I can fix you up.' She raised herself onto her toes to look over the small crowd of people around her. 'Some guys have come up from that kibbutz to take you down there,' she said surveying the arrivals hall. 'They must be here someplace.' She called out something in Hebrew and two swarthy young men came to her. They talked in a huddle for no more than a few moments and one of the men signed the papers on her clipboard.

'I'm Rafi,' said the shorter of the two, offering John and Michael his open pack of cigarettes. 'Welcome to Israel.'

'And I'm Avner,' said the one with film star good looks. 'We need to get on the road; it's getting dark already. Follow me.'

Michael climbed into the cab with Avner. John and Rafi sat opposite one another on the benches that ran the length of the rear of the truck and Rafi explained that he and Avner were doing their military service, which could include a stint on a kibbutz. John couldn't take his eyes off the two machine guns that lay on the floor next to where he and Michael had dumped their rucksacks; now and then the glow from a streetlight, or a neon advertisement at the side of the highway, would catch the black gunmetal.

'You guys will be working with Avner and me, and a couple of other soldiers,' he explained as they sped south along the coast. 'We get up at four and drive for about forty-five minutes into the Negev, but we're usually back by noon because it gets too hot to work.'

'Are there always guns?'

'The Arabs want to see all of us Jews dead,' he said without emotion. 'The kibbutz isn't very far from Gaza and we have to protect ourselves.'

'I've never seen guns like this before.' John wished he could see the detail of Rafi's face through the gathering darkness.

'You'll get used to them,' he said, reaching forward and squeezing John's knee lightly to reassure him.

'And when we go out into the desert?'

'Of course. Then we need guns more than ever.'

It was too dark to see much when they arrived. John was aware that they'd passed through a gate guarded by armed men, but he only realised the extent to which they would be living by the protection of guns the next morning, when he took in the high fence enclosure, the barbed wire and the perimeter patrols of men in shorts and T-shirts, machine guns slung over their shoulders.

After their third day digging trenches, Michael threw-up over the truck's tailgate all the way back to the kibbutz.

'You've probably had a bit too much sun,' Avner said. 'Go'n see the nurse when we get back.'

He spent the next days working in the laundry with a group of older women, their ka-tzetnik numbers tattooed on their forearms. When his stomach was still unsettled after a week he saw a kibbutznick who worked as a doctor in Sederot; she

269

prescribed antibiotics, but they made his runs even worse. 'If this keeps up I'm going to go and stay with my uncle in Jerusalem,' he said to John one evening. 'I can't work... and I just want to get better.'

Some days later Michael got a lift to Jerusalem with one of the kibbutznicks who was going to visit a university friend in the hospital, but his departure was overshadowed. Everyone buzzed with the success of the raid on Entebbe. The drinks in the bar were free all evening. John watched the reports on the television and was amazed that the Israelis had gone to such trouble to get their hostages back safely.

John had never really seen himself as one to enjoy hard, physical labour, but he thrived. After a week his muscles ached less and by the end of the second week he'd lost the slight roll of fat around his belly. The fact that Rafi and Avner often stripped to their pants when they were digging was an incentive when the alarm clock roused him at 3.50. That they all took a shower together when they returned from the desert, caked in dust and ripe with the smell of sweat, gave John something to fantasise about under the desert sun. Avner didn't linger in the open shower – a narrow, twelve-foot trough between two walls, with five sprinklers from an overhead pipe – but Rafi soaped and sponged long after the grime had washed away.

The first time he became aware of Rafi's loitering, John sneaked a look at the soldier's lean body and saw that he was hard; not a full erection, but hard none the less. Feeling uncertain, and afraid to out himself (he'd read somewhere that the State of Israel didn't acknowledge that any Israeli Jews were homosexuals) he dressed quickly and scurried off to the dining room for lunch.

Another day, when Rafi noticed John noticing him, he took the bar of ubiquitous green kibbutz soap and lathered himself until he was erect. John sensed his own arousal, which quickly became obvious. Rafi stepped towards him and began to soap John's back in slow circles.

'You don't mind?' Rafi asked over the hiss of the shower, his fingers probing.

'No, it feels good.'

Whether it was because all of that hard labour had pumped hormones around his body and infused him with vigour, or because enough time had elapsed... or just that he'd come too far away for Jatunga Arachchi and David Jones to reach him, whatever the reason, he was grateful to Rafi for releasing him.

John fingered the card the kibbutz representative had given him at the airport. With Michael gone, he was free to choose without considering anyone else. But he did think about Rafi. They weren't really having a relationship; they didn't spend any time alone together and they didn't sleep together, but he looked forward to their intimacy in the shower. For the first time in a long time he felt fully alive. Hadn't Rhys Morgan said once that 'the glory of God is the fully alive human being'? He put the card back in his wallet and decided to stay.

'You mustn't go into Gaza,' Avner said one day when they were digging.

'But I'd like to meet some Arabs... hear what they've got to say,' John said.

'Don't do that,' Avner said, his voice raised. 'They'll tell you lies about us.'

'But how can I be sure what you're telling me isn't skewed?'

271

'You're calling me a liar?' Avner's tone was menacing.

'No, Avi... no, I'm not. But when did you last sit down with any Palestinians and talk about how to live together?'

'You foreigners are so naïve... you just don't fucking understand,' Avner spat, throwing down his spade and walking away.

'His little brother was killed a couple of years ago,' Rafi said when Avner was out of earshot.

'By Arabs?'

'Of course by the Arabs!' Rafi spat. 'Palestinian terrorists took ninety hostages at a school in Maalot, way up in the north, and before our troops got them out, sixteen kids were killed.'

'Shit... I wasn't to know,' John said, throwing his shovel into the trench alongside Avner's. 'I'll go after him.'

'Leave it for now. Avi will be alright,' Rafi said. He walked over to John and put his arm around him. 'Look... if you really must go to Gaza, just go, but don't tell anybody; not even me, I don't want to know. Keep it to yourself... you might even be asked to leave the kibbutz if they find out.'

In the bar that evening John bought Avner and Rafi bottles of Maccabee beer; a gesture of reconciliation.

'You're going to Jerusalem?' Avner asked. 'What will you do there?'

'I'll go'n see Michael at his uncle's and then probably do what all of the tourists do; the Temple Mount and the Western Wall... Church of the Holy Sepulchre, Dome of the Rock.'

'Religious voyeurism then!'

'I'd like to spend some time at Yad Vashem too,' John said, ignoring Avner's dig.

'You shouldn't go there on your own,' Rafi said. 'I've seen tough soldiers crumple up and cry when they stand before the

272

eternal flame in *Ohel Yizkor*... the Tent of Remembrance.'

John took a bus from Jerusalem's central bus station, out to Mount Herzl, and walked to Har Hazikaron where Yad Vashem, the hilltop garden of remembrance, commemorates the 6,000,000 Jews murdered by the Nazis. In the shade of a Tabor oak, he turned the pages of his pocket Bible, the brittle tissue-like paper sticking to his sweaty fingers. In chapter fifty-six of the Book of Isaiah he read about God giving those who were faithful 'an everlasting name' – a *yad vashem*. Before the eternal flame, where tongues of fire seemed to rupture from amongst names carved into marble blocks on the floor – Treblinka, Flossenbürg, Dachau, Sachsenhausen, Auschwitz-Birkenau, Bergen-Belsen, Buchenwald – he watched tens of people give in to their grief, and though they were often huddled together he sensed how alone they were with their tears.

For a couple of hours, feeling numb, he sat in the shade of the oak tree. What he'd seen in the museums of Yad Vashem had shocked him deeply, but there had been nothing about the men Henk had spoken of – the men with the pink triangle – except for one stark sentence in one of the free leaflets: *Other Germans were incarcerated for being homosexuals, criminals or non-conformists; these people, although treated brutally, were never slated for utter annihilation as were the Jews.*

In the next days, digging trenches alongside Rafi and Avner in the Negev, John rationalised that Yad Vashem was a Jewish memorial. As with so much of his experience in Israel, he knew there was another story to be told, even if he wasn't sure who might recount it.

*   *   *

273

Being in Israel had stirred him in ways that had excited more than disturbed. Living amongst Jews, many of whom were holocaust survivors from across Europe, questions had arisen in his mind about identity, which invited him to question his own sense of self. How had his own family life in Wales shaped him? What were the imprints left by events, language and culture? What did he believe? What cause might he die for? And more fundamentally, after sitting under the Tabor oak on the Hill of Remembrance, he'd come to ponder how he'd been shaped by history... and by the untold story of the men with the pink triangle.

For 250 years his dad's clan had lived in the shadow of Cader Idris along the banks of the Mawddach. He had such a strong sense of place. These ancestors had subsisted as farm labourers and weavers, blacksmiths, washerwomen and ferry boatmen. His *taid*, Idris-Bloc, had been born to a single woman (who remained unmarried but bore five children) in the Dolgellau Union Workhouse in January 1901. At the age of eleven, Idris had been placed in Barmouth's harvest hiring fair and 'sold' into agricultural labour, from which he absconded at fifteen to enlist for the trenches. On his mother's side, the slate dust of Corris had caused generations of silicosis and hardship. He had a strong sense of his own people.

But in Wales, identity was bound up with princes over-thrown by the English and the Mabinogi, the Treason of the Blue Books and the Welsh Not. *Nain*-Corris had told him more than once that when she was a child she'd been beaten for speaking Welsh at school, the child ending the day with the Welsh Not slate hanging on a string around her neck.

Both languages were used on Dad's side, but neither was spoken well – except by Nana; she was from the English military class and spoke lovely English. Amongst Mam's tribe, English was as foreign as French or German. When Olwen had gone into service in Barmouth in 1945, when she was just 15, she could barely get by in English.

John and Billy had been put through the Welsh stream at Barmouth Primary School. Their headmaster, W. D. Williams, was a one-time winner of the National Eisteddfod chair who'd penned the table prayer *O Dad, yn deulu dedwydd* – recited by generations of children in school canteens throughout Wales as a grace before their school dinner. Mr Williams saw to it that they learned to appreciate their heritage. Miss Morris, who taught the infants, but had responsibility for music through the school, said John was a 'very special' boy soprano. She coached him in the boys' solo through years of *eisteddfodau* with considerable success. And there were youth camps with the *Urdd*, and all the fun of outdoor activity, midnight feasts and the *noson lawen*. By pedigree, anyway, he couldn't be more Welsh.

But at twenty he spoke the old language badly, despite his fluency. His vocabulary was limited, he confused the gender of nouns and he was utterly bewildered by the rules governing mutations. He hadn't worked his way into any of Aberystwyth's Welsh speaking student groups. Those living in the Welsh hall of residence, Pantycelyn, seemed cliquey, whilst the regulars at the *Llew Du* and the *Cwps* either drank until they were aggressively rowdy or talked too much politics – or both. He'd had one discussion about the Welsh Language Society's sustained campaign of painting out English language road signs with a group of Welsh speaking students and they'd accused him of betraying his language – and his soul. But English was his language too. He was articulate in English, and thanks to Miss Roberts, who'd urged her students to read and learn new words, he had a wide vocabulary that he used well.

But perhaps there was an even more fundamental betrayal of his Welshness? With a growing confidence in his sexuality, he found that he couldn't speak about being gay in Welsh; there seemed to be no language – and without language he didn't exist. Could he be Welsh and be gay? There were no role models; well, none that he knew of anyway!

And yet, for all of this complexity, he did exist... and Rafi had breathed new life into him, waking him up to new possibilities. So what did the sum of all the parts amount to? How did this 'identity thing' come together?

Sitting in the dingy kitchen of their three-roomed flat in Aberystwyth, his new flatmate, Steffan, suggested they only speak Welsh together. The arrangement with the flat suited them both; Steff, whom he'd met at Peniel, was older and already doing teacher's training, so for five weeks of the Christmas and Easter terms he'd be away on teaching practice and be back just at the weekends. They had their own study bedrooms and a shared bathroom along the landing.

'If we're going to be a Welsh flat then I'm changing my name,' John said. 'From now on I'm going to be Siôn Idris.'

Later that day, his first day back in Aberystwyth at the beginning of his second academic year, Siôn Idris wrote a letter to the Aber Gay Soc. After Rafi, he knew he was ready for a love affair.

Through the previous academic year he'd been on the fringes of many student circles, but he'd been wary of people getting too close. Being such a satellite, he was often left out and overlooked in arrangements, but not, he believed, through malice.

He did have all the support he needed from the crowd in the quiet field, but he'd often felt uncomfortably left out of things on a Saturday night and disliked going to the pictures on his own. Siôn reasoned, therefore, that he'd sign up for alternate Saturday nights on the Samaritans' roster. His volunteer name was Sam-76.

A single volunteer did the overnight duty, from 10pm to 6am, but there was always a duty leader for support at the end of the office phone. On his first Saturday night, Sam-76 befriended a teenage girl with an unwanted pregnancy (seventeen minutes), a beaten wife calling from a phone box after being locked out by her drunken husband (twenty-three minutes), and an older man swilling down aspirins with swigs from a bottle of Scotch because his business was on the rocks (one-hour-and-forty-eight minutes). Logging the calls in the way he'd been shown, Siôn recognised the warm glow of contentment that came from being able to contribute to his community.

Three weeks passed before he got a response from The Gay Soc. The letter was handwritten and barely legible, but it invited him to meet with some of the society's members in a bar at the Belle Vue Hotel. Excitement and anticipation flushed him with hormones, getting the better of any lingering anxiety, and though it was a weeknight, and he hadn't finished writing up his biochemistry lab report due the next afternoon, he spent half an hour in the bathroom getting himself ready.

The weeks of digging trenches in the Negev had left his body lean and tanned. When he took off his jacket in the smoky warmth of the Bay Bar after introducing himself to Simon, Jeremy, Trystan and Alun, he was aware that four pairs of eyes were ogling him. Siôn didn't pay too much heed to their attentions; he felt heady just meeting four gay men in Aberystwyth. In his own mind he recognised that he'd moved on from thinking he was the only one in the world, but four... all at once... in Aber!

'We've got about thirty names,' Trystan, who seemed to be the ringleader, said. He had a rugby player's build and his face was pocked with acne scars.

'But we never get that many coming along to meetings,' added Simon, who looked about sixteen, was slightly built and wore his hair long.

'When we have end-of-term socials a good crowd always turns up,' Alun put in. He was the one with the model's good looks. He reminded Siôn of an actor in *Coronation Street* – slim and fair, with a nice smile and lovely teeth.

After the introductions, Jeremy said nothing for a long time but Siôn was aware of his green eyes; whenever he found himself caught in Jeremy's gaze there was an invitation to linger and decode the nonverbal message.

'There are some staff members too,' Trystan said.

'And a few townies,' Alun quipped, remembering his tryst with the guy who worked in the architect's office on Pilgrim Street.

'What about another drink, Siôn?' Jeremy asked.

'Just another Coke then... thanks,' Siôn said. 'I've still got some work to do for tomorrow when I get home.'

'Shame,' Jeremy said, without shame.

'Oh, listen to you,' Trystan teased Jem.

Siôn saw the bitchy streak in Trystan's camp parody.

'I think Jem fancies his chances with the new boy,' Simon said, almost in a whisper, searching Siôn's eyes for clues.

Siôn walked home alone, feeling elated that there were

others like him in Aberystwyth. He worked until after three on his biochemistry lab report.

During the mid-morning break, he stood in the queue in the union coffee bar on the campus, his head fuzzy, an internal voice screaming for the buzz of caffeine after such a late night.

'Why don't you let me get this?'

Siôn turned. Jem's green eyes offered yet another invitation.

*   *   *

Siôn could hear The Carpenters singing 'Top Of The World' from the kitchen. He'd had a busy night at the Samaritans and 'There's A Kind Of Hush' would have been more appropriate. Steffan sat at the red Formica-topped table in his white Y-fronts and Aertex vest, eating toast with lashings of strawberry jam. Siôn thought he looked about as sexy as the Pillsbury doughboy from the TV advert and was grateful that he had no lustful intentions towards his flatmate.

'So, you're a closet Carpenters fan,' Siôn said in Welsh, squeezing the teapot into the mug he'd grabbed from the draining board. 'What happened to Hergest and Edward H?'

Steff munched his mouthful and shrugged.

'Aren't you cold, eating your breakfast half naked like that?'

'I wasn't expecting company,' Steffan said after washing his toast down with a slurp of tea. 'And yes, when you're out, I don't always stick to the Welsh rule. *Mea culpa.*'

Siôn smiled at the bead of jam in the dimple on Steff's chin.

'Anyway, I thought you'd be spending the morning after the night before with Jeremy. How is he?'

'I didn't spend the night with Jem.' His words sounded terse, though he hadn't meant to be defensive. He supposed that talking about his boyfriend would start to seem more natural the more often he did it.

'Oh... you've been on the helpline,' Steff said with dawning realisation. 'Does that mean you'll want to sleep all day?'

'I'll grab a few hours this morning. Are you going to chapel?'

'Yes, but this afternoon I've invited a few people around.'

'That's okay.'

'I was talking with Tim, from Theol Coll, earlier in the week. D'you remember him?'

Siôn recalled the tall, older, sinewy intellectual who'd been a monk.

'We're thinking of starting a discussion group,' Steff said. 'Just an excuse to meet up for tea on a Sunday afternoon really.'

'It won't be so lightweight if Tim's there.'

'When he was at university the first time around he was in the SCM.'

Siôn's wrinkled brow betrayed his puzzlement.

'SCM – The Student Christian Movement; it's at the opposite pole to the fundi-evangelicals! In the last couple of years they've been nicknamed the Slightly Christian Marxists.'

Siôn chuckled at the clever word play. He didn't have a clue what a Christian Marxist was but he liked the *slightly Christian* bit.

'We just thought it would be a good idea to have a group that can discuss serious political issues from a Christian stand-point without getting caught up in the literal meaning of this verse and that particular word. Did you ever go to the Sunday Library Group meetings in Theol Coll?'

Siôn smiled wanly; he hadn't thought about Adam and his crew for a while and their choruses had long stopped playing.

'We want to start a group that grapples with different views, without Bible bashing and falling back into the 'you're obviously not saved' argument,' Steff said.

'If they're coming for tea I could make a cake,' Siôn offered, recalling Elen Morgan's recipe and wondering if the paper shop in Northgate sold eggs and dark chocolate.

'You'd be interested to join us then?'

'If you don't mind?'

'Why should I mind? You see the world through different eyes, Siôn. Tim even suggested we could have a book club. Pittenger's book would be worth discussing, especially after the whole Thorpe affair.'

'I've read *Time for Consent*.'

'You have? Well, maybe you could lead a discussion then?'

'I couldn't do that! Not with people like Tim... and you; you've already graduated.'

'Don't keep putting yourself down like that, Siôn.'

'Well... we'll see.'

'And you'd be up for making a cake then? I bought some scones and teacakes from Spar, but something homemade would be great.'

Siôn didn't think that the chocolate cake was as good as Elen's, but Tim ran his bony index finger around the empty plate time and again to gather up the last crumbs.

'I've been to the SCM's centre near Bristol,' he said between licks. 'They've got community houses all over England, and one in Scotland, so I've been trying to persuade them to buy a house here in Aber, as a base for rejuvenating the Movement in Wales.'

'Do you mean the Wick Centre?' Steff quizzed.

'Yes,' Tim said. 'There's a community living in Wick Court,

281

it's a gorgeous Jacobean manor house, and some of the out-buildings, a coach house and some stables, have been converted into offices and a conference-cum-study centre.'

'What does the SCM mean by a community house?' Janice asked. 'It all sounds a bit hippyish.'

'Apart from Wick, I've only been to the ones in Oxford and Bristol,' Tim explained. 'They're all different, but the basic idea is that a group of Christian students live together. They eat a communal meal every day, and there's some time set aside for prayer. In Oxford they say compline together.'

'And do you think there's a chance that they'll set something up in Aber?' Siôn asked.

'They've asked me to look out for suitable properties,' Tim said. 'And a couple of people from Wick have agreed to come up in the New Year. They're really keen to get SCM going again in Wales, I know that much, but whether they'll plough money into buying a house remains to be seen.'

Before the group that gathered in Siôn and Steff's flat dispersed, they agreed to meet every alternate Sunday afternoon and drew up a rough schedule of meetings. Everyone agreed to read *Time for Consent* by the end of the Christmas vacation. Siôn was volunteered to lead the discussion at their first meeting in the new year.

The love affair with Jem lasted five weeks. They hadn't really got to know one another before tumbling into Jem's bed in a frenzy of passion. After a fortnight, Siôn already wondered if they had anything more than good sex binding them together. Jem was suspicious of Siôn's Saturday nights, and scurrilous about the fact he went to church; 'Organised religion is our biggest oppressor,' he'd said more than once. At the end-of-term Gay Soc disco, Jem danced with Douggie, who sang with the Elizabethan Madrigals. Siôn walked home alone, his heart only slightly broken... because he'd got to dance with the best looking man of the bunch – a tall, dark haired Canadian called Russ Talbert.

Over the Christmas break Siôn listened to the nine Beethoven symphonies that his dad had collected from the record club during the year and fantasised about an affair with Russ. To keep at bay any panic about leading the Sunday discussion group, he read, and re-read Pittenger's book. He took time with all the Biblical references, making sure he understood the arguments Pittenger offered: the mistranslations of words from the original texts, the consideration of context, the interpretations that were inconsistent with the way other verses in the same passages were read and understood. There were hikes in the Rhinogs too! It was the sunniest December he could remember, with clear, frosty days that made his breath steamy and his cheeks burn. On these rambles he reflected on Pittenger's *Ethic for Homosexuals*, a relatively short chapter towards the end of the book. Despite the sometimes-highbrow language, Siôn thought of it as a six-point plan on how to be the best homosexual he could be. With so much written that was negative and condemnatory, here was the first positive set of suggestions for how someone could be Christian and gay.

*   *   *

Siôn had expected Tim and Steff to go after all the Biblical stuff, but once Janice had asked him how he was so certain he was gay, the focus of the meeting became more personal than he'd anticipated. He detected no malice in their probing; they simply wanted to make tangible the things they'd read in Pittenger's book. After they'd eaten the remnants of a redundant

Christmas cake that Steff had brought back to college after the vacation, the icing rock-hard and the decorations looking tired, Tim cornered Siôn in the kitchen.

'You've allowed yourself to be really vulnerable with us; are you okay?'

'Yes... in a funny sort of way I feel flattered that you're all so interested.'

'Don't ever underestimate the impact of your own experience,' Tim offered. 'Most of us never get the chance to get to know someone gay, so all we ever have to frame our view are the stereotypes.'

'That's sort of true for gay people too you know,' Siôn said. 'Pittenger is the first, from a Christian perspective anyway, to offer something positive —'

'And you're the first to help me see the face of Christ in a homosexual,' Janice, who'd been eavesdropping, said.

Tim smiled and nodded.

Siôn was disturbed by Janice's comment, and by Tim's apparent agreement with her.

The Sunday tea group didn't have a name, but Tim passed them off as an embryonic SCM group when the delegation from the headquarters at Wick visited Aberystwyth at the end of January. The student president of SCM, a Scottish lad called Iain, stayed on in Aberystwyth for a few days after the others took the train back to Bristol; he slept on a mattress on the floor of Steff's room.

'If we can buy one of the houses we looked at, and establish a community house by the beginning of the next academic year I think we'll have a really strong base,' Iain said when Steff asked how he saw the future of the SCM in Wales. 'The

284

national executive committee, when it met in Wick before Christmas, decided that we should employ a Welsh travelling secretary to build up the Movement in Wales, and if that person could be based in an Aber community house... well, Wales would soon catch up with Scotland.'

'Who is it that decides these things?' Siôn asked.

'It's more or less been decided,' Iain said with a nicotine-stained smile. 'We all agreed on the house in Laura Place. I know it needs a lot of work, but the income it'll generate from ten students living there will make it financially viable. The basement will make a good venue for student groups to meet, and there's enough room to locate the Welsh secretary there; it's ideal really, and the Movement will always get its investment back on such a lovely house if it ever came to sell the place.'

'And how have other community houses gone about recruiting people to live in them?' Steff asked. 'Ten like-minded people won't be easy to find!'

'There may be folk from your own SCM group who'd like to join the community, and you could always do a trawl of the different Christian societies – Meth Soc, Ang Soc; you could even offer a place to an overseas student.'

Siôn's head buzzed with the possibilities, and a couple of days later, sitting on the wall of the Old Union in Laura Place with the weak winter sunshine warming his back, he gazed across the street at the proud Georgian terraced house with its FOR SALE board. He tried to imagine living there.

*　　*　　*

At The Gay Soc Valentine's disco it was obvious to Siôn that Russ Talbert and Simon Whatney were an item. If Simon, who looked about sixteen, was Russ's 'type', Siôn stood no chance. Jem was frosty with everyone, and especially with Douggie, who looked forlorn. Siôn drank too much and woke up the next morning feeling wretched... and naked in Douggie's bed.

For a few hours he felt nauseous and guilty in equal measure, but as the alcoholic, sickly feeling in his stomach eased he remembered something that Pittenger had said about one-night stands. His copy of *Time for Consent* was becoming dog-eared. He re-read the relevant section. Another new start then.

*   *   *

The purchase of 8 Laura Place went through quickly. For two weeks of the Easter vacation, Siôn joined the small team of students Tim had recruited to clean up and paint the inside of SCM Community House. Tim went to Wick for a couple of days and when he came back he announced that he was to be the new Welsh travelling secretary from July – and warden of the community to be founded at the house over the summer months.

There was never an actual discussion that Siôn could remember about him becoming a member of the community. The largest attic room, with its sloping ceilings and slender view of the sea between the castle and the tower of St Michael's, just came to be understood as his.

'Tim's going to buy decorating stuff and he wants to know what colour you'd like the beams of your room painted,' Janice called down the cellar stairs one day when Siôn was on his hands and knees cleaning one of the rooms that was to become the chapel.

'Milk and no sugar,' Siôn called back. 'I thought you'd never ask.'

'That sexist comment means you're ready for a coffee then, does it?' Janice quipped.

'I need something to clear the dust from my throat,' Siôn explained, emerging from the chapel shrouded in generations of spider's silk.

The cleaning crew sat in the enclosed backyard dunking biscuits into their coffees. Through the unwieldy limbs of a climbing rose that grew against the rear of the house, the diffused rays of the spring sunshine warmed faces that were streaked with oil and grease, cobwebs and magnolia emulsion from their varied jobs.

'You're not really going for this red are you, Elwyn?' Tim quizzed, fingering the paint chart.

'Liverpool's colours mun,' El said in his broad valleys burr.

'I like that mustard yellow,' Siôn said.

And so the core of the community at SCM House gelled: Tim, his girlfriend Jill, Elwyn, Janice and her soon-to-be-husband Huw, and Siôn.

*   *   *

It was all a bit of a rush when he got back from the lab after six. Steff had made a stew with liver and onions. It smelled good, but one mouthful left him in a quandary, it was delicious, but too garlicky. He didn't want to dash his chances with garlic breath, but he didn't want to offend Steff either.

'I think I might have a hot date tonight,' he said, deciding to be straightforward; he'd heard on the grapevine that Russell Talbert had dumped Simon Whatney. 'D'you mind if I scrape this back into the dish and have my share tomorrow?'

Steff gestured his agreement and grinned. 'Who is he?'

Siôn still hadn't reached a comfort level that made it easy for him to talk about boyfriends – or potential boyfriends. 'I'll tell you about him if things get to be a bit more solid between us,' he said, slicing bread to make some toast.

'There's some parsley growing just outside the backdoor.'

'What? Parsley on toast?'

'For garlic breath, stupid,' Steff laughed. 'Just in case that mouthful's left you tainted. The recipe said just one clove, but I put three and I wouldn't want my heavy-handedness to come between you and your quest for true love!'

In the shower, soaping all those hard to reach crevices and folds, Siôn chewed on the mouthful of freshly picked herb; then he shaved more carefully than usual so as not to leave any stubble that might be abrasive. He sloshed some Old Spice into his palms and winced as it stung his checks, and he dabbed a little amongst the hairs that edged down from his navel. Leo Sayer sang 'When I Need You' from the turned-down radio as he buttoned up his newest cheesecloth shirt and thought about Russ. After tugging on his new jeans, he eyed himself in the cracked mirror on the wardrobe door. The fine cotton fabric of the shirt outlined the muscles developed from the sweat and toil of the Negev in all the right places, but the line of his briefs spoiled the curve of his bum. He felt recklessly sexy leaving the house without underwear.

Despite his eagerness to attract Russell Talbert, he didn't want to arrive too early. The Gay Soc meetings were notoriously late starters and early birds could feel as conspicuous as a parrot on a perch, chain-smoking to make themselves look purposeful and feeling obliged to drink their pints too self-consciously. Being generally a non-smoker, that just left Siôn with the option of supping his beer too quickly and getting tipsy. He reached the prom by the King's Hall just before 8.30 and decided he needed another twenty minutes; he turned away from the Belle Vue, towards Constitution Hill. He'd kick the bar and watch the red streaks of sunset fade into the inky-blue.

The back bar of the Belle Vue smelled pungent and stale; yesterday's cigarette smoke, spilled beer and someone's patchouli oil. Siôn's heart thumped in his chest when he saw Russ standing at the bar; through the blue tinged swirl from the end of a cigarette, held between his ring and middle fingers, Russell pondered his pint. Between the thumb and index finger of the same hand he put the pack of Gauloises Disque Bleu through continuous somersaults.

'Another drink, Russ?' Siôn asked, sliding onto the bar stool next the tall Canadian.

'I'll nurse this one a while longer,' he said. 'But let me get one in for you.'

'Just a half of lager then. I try not to drink much on weeknights.'

'Don't the gay men in Aberystwyth piss you off,' he said, looking at his watch. 'Aber's such a stinking armpit for gay life, and yet, when there's a chance to meet, they all fucking stay at home.'

'Well... we're here,' Siôn said, pulling off his jacket. 'It's only just past nine.'

Over the almost pleasant smell of the French cigarette, Siôn caught the scent of Russell's body – a spicy mix more subtle than his own Old Spice, with just a trace of something akin to sweat, but which wasn't unpleasant. He felt the stirrings in his body and wondered if his tight jeans would betray his excitement.

'I looked for you after we'd danced at the Christmas disco,' Russ said.

'I was still with Jem then,' Siôn said, taken aback. He'd thought he was going to have to work much harder.

Russ caught the bartender's eye and ordered Siôn's drink; then he took the pack of cigarettes between his thumb and forefinger again and put it through more somersaults. 'I've just finished with Simon,' he offered, before tossing the cigarette pack onto the bar and taking a deep drag from his cigarette.

'Messy was it?' Siôn asked, seeking to empathise – and confirm the gossip.

'We didn't have too much in common.'

'It was a bit like that with me and Jem. The sex was good, but there's got to be more than that, hasn't there?'

'Simon didn't even like sex! He just wanted a teddy bear to cuddle.'

Siôn studied the young Canadian's profile. His hair was an anarchy of tight raven-black curls that glinted in the harsh fluorescent light from behind the bar. Lush sideburns cut deeply into the clear skin of his cheeks. He was clean-shaven, but the swarthy beard line was obvious enough. His face and nose were long, but he was a big man and neither looked out of proportion with the rest of him. Beneath his broad, clefted chin, through the open collar button, black hairs curled over the woven fabric of his shirt. A muscle quivered by Russell's ear, between the sideburn and that round protrusion at the ear's opening that Siôn thought might be called the tragus – though he wasn't sure. He wondered if Russ was nervous too.

'Trouble with gay men, seems to me, is that we're fucking one another before we even know if we like each other,' Russ said.

Siôn wanted to kiss the barely visible tremor – a tragus kiss.

'Doesn't have to be that way though,' he said, his words struggling against the flow of his lust. 'Whatever happened to good old-fashioned courtship?'

'You're kidding me, Siôn.' He took another long drag on his cigarette.

'How else d'you get to know somebody, Russ?'

'We don't have to ape the breeders,' he said with undisguised scorn. 'Gay liberation is about freeing ourselves from straight tyranny, not buying into their role models.'

'So, we have to explore new possibilities and try to create new ones,' Siôn said, surprising himself.

'Well, I guess so, but that ain't easy.'

Siôn took a long draught from his drink. 'I suppose it depends on what we want,' he said into the silence that settled between them. 'Casual sex isn't so hard to find, even in – what did you call this place? A stinking armpit?'

They both laughed.

'But if we're looking for long-term relationships,' Siôn said more seriously, 'It might help us if we had a common understanding of what we think we mean by a relationship – especially with the Gay Lib lobby being so opposed to us mimicking the straights.'

'I guess I'm looking for companionship and good sex,' Russ said after a moment contemplating the end of his cigarette before stubbing it into the ashtray. 'I'm not sure in which order of priority they come.'

Siôn smiled. 'But what does companionship mean for you, Russ? It can mean different things to different people. Does it include faithfulness... sexually, I mean? D'you want a companion to be your best friend? Someone who likes what you like and does everything with you?'

291

'Oh God no, there's got to be spaces in the togetherness, but I get your drift – and what's good sex for me might not be for someone else.'

'Exactly, which brings us back to some kind of courtship – or whatever name we want to give it – so that two people have some time to come to understand one another's needs and expectations.'

'Sounds like hard work.' He lit another cigarette. Through the blue smoke he said, 'Maybe it is just casual sex that I want after all.'

'And maybe that's fine, as long as that's what the other person wants too, but —' Siôn swallowed his words in another mouthful of lager because he thought what he was about to say might sound as if he was moralising.

Russ turned, capturing Siôn's gaze in the deep slate-blue of his eyes and holding him like a magnet. 'But what?' he coaxed.

'Well... I think... when people have casual sex... I think there's more chance of someone being used.'

'Oh, come on! Two people choose to have casual sex... so they *use* one another for mutual gratification. Sounds pretty egalitarian to me.' And still holding Siôn's gaze his face broke into a smile. 'My God, you've got the bluest eyes.'

'But where sex is concerned, people don't always recognise the different levels of intention and motive that they have,' Siôn said, pretending to ignore the obvious pass. Grateful that he was seated on the barstool, he felt sure, had he been standing, that his legs would have turned to jelly.

'I don't know what you're saying, Siôn.'

'I just believe that sometimes people say yes to something because they think it's what they want, and only later do they realise they actually had a much deeper yearning; a much more

292

fundamental need if you like.'

'I still don't get it,' he said, his eyes asking other questions.

'I think it would be very nice to have sex with you, Russ, and I'd certainly like the opportunity to find out how nice it might be, so I can see a situation where I'd say yes if you asked me back to your place. But at another level, deep inside me, I know that I'd feel bad after the event because I believe that sex between two people should be an expression of... depth and friendship... and —'

'Love?' Russ said cynically into Siôn's floundering for words.

'Yes... that too. Gay Lib might find the whole concept of love a bit outdated, but I do believe that sex should be an expression of love... ideally.'

'And you're an idealist.'

'I didn't say that.'

'But you'd like us to fuck?'

'I'd like the chance to get to know you better.' Siôn smiled at him. 'And yes, I'd like to fuck you.'

'But ideally it should be an expression of love.'

'Now you're mocking me,' Siôn said, searching deeply into the slate-blue pools. 'And through a little chink in this gorgeously attractive exterior I can already see a little bit of you that I don't like – and we're right back to the beginning of our conversation and the importance of spending time getting to know one another.'

'And how long would our courtship need to be before I can invite you home?'

Siôn laughed nervously. 'Would that be an invitation for good sex or for exploring the possibilities of companionship?'

'I don't see them as mutually exclusive, Siôn.'

They held one another's gaze. Pittenger's ethics struggled against the flow of Siôn's desire.

'Can I kiss you?' Russ asked, almost in a whisper.

'What? Here at the bar?'

'We've paid to hire the place so it's our territory tonight,' he said, moving closer and placing his hand on Siôn's hip.

The muscle by Russell's ear quivered again. Siôn stroked it with his thumb.

*   *   *

Russell leaned into the pillows and crooked his right leg slightly at the knee to stop himself slipping down the bed. He lit a cigarette and drew deeply. For a while he watched the rise and fall of Siôn's belly, and the glint of the flickering candle dancing between the hairs on the dewy film of sweat across Siôn's chest. It had been much too good, especially after the disaster with Simon, to bracket off as casual sex. He reflected on the conversation they'd had in the pub just a few hours before. He'd thought then that Siôn was a bit too intense – all that crap about sex being an expression of love and needing to be sure you weren't using the other person – but now he found himself hoping for something with Siôn that would last beyond a few hours of frantic tumble.

Siôn stirred and his hand came to rest beneath the top of Russell's arched leg. As he woke from a deep but short slumber he felt, against his fingertips, the heaviness of his new lover's balls. He let his fingers play.

'Thank you for my first legal fuck,' Siôn whispered through the half-light.

'What d'you mean?' he asked, enjoying Siôn's finger-teasing and shifting his leg a fraction to give him freer access.

'I was twenty-one the day before yesterday.'

294

Russ dropped his cigarette into the ashtray on the bedside table and hunkered down to take Siôn into his arms.

'Happy birthday,' he said. 'See... I have a present for you.'

Siôn felt the hardness joshing at the inside of his thigh.

Over the next hours, Siôn, who'd had plenty of sex over the years but had never experienced such lovemaking, recalled a fragment from Pittenger about how the quality of sex could be so different 'when love entered the bed.'

'I think I'm falling in love with you, Russ,' he said through the half sleep that came after their fourth orgasm.

'I love you too,' Russell sighed, reaching for another cigarette.

For days Siôn went around with a smile on his face, and despite the livid bulges that ripened like damsons under his eyes from too little sleep, the blue of his irises sparkled.

'I've got exams in a couple of weeks,' Siôn said one morning after a long night of lovemaking.

'You worried about them?'

'No, but I'm going to have to knuckle down and do a bit of work.'

'Which means you have to ration the time I have to ravage your body I suppose.'

Siôn thought he detected an edge of disdain in Russell's tone.

'Something like that,' he quipped lightly. 'I need more sleep... and I'll have to do some revising. Can't we arrange some times to see one another, just for the next few weeks?'

'Why can't you come here when you've finished studying?'

'Because we'll end up fucking.'

Russell nodded his head and smiled.

'I can't keep up that sort of pace and prepare for my exams, Russ.'

'Please yourself then,' he said somewhat coldly.

'Don't be like that.'

'So what's my ration? Three nights a week? Two afternoons?'

'It'll only be for a few weeks, Russ. Why are you being so unreasonable?

'I've already said you can please yourself, but I thought we were in a relationship. If you want to cool things —'

'Oh fuck! Come on, Russell... I haven't said anything about cooling the relationship. I love you... and it's been wonderful.'

'Past tense already!'

'It *is* wonderful, Russ... but my life's been a little bit out of balance these past three weeks. I've missed a couple of nine-o-clocks because we've stayed in bed; I can barely make it through an afternoon in the lab because I'm so knackered. I've started to make stupid mistakes... and I've pulled my first 'C' in biochemistry because I didn't put enough time and effort into my last lab report.'

'Okay... I'm sorry. I guess being a research student has made me forget what it's like to keep up with course work.'

But the spell was broken.

It was the middle of the night after Siôn had finished his last exam. Russ was propped up against the pillows smoking; he always smoked after sex.

'I'm going back Ottawa for the summer,' he announced.

'But I thought we were spending the summer together here in Aber,' Siôn said, suddenly wide-awake.

'I changed my plans.'

'But we decided —'

'I need a change and my dad offered to pay.'

'Shall I come with you?' Siôn offered, not sure whether his savings would stretch that far.

'No... like I said, I need a change.'

There was no more to be said. Siôn dressed quickly and left.

*   *   *

Tim was happy for Siôn to move into the attic room with the view of the castle at the end of June – rent-free for the summer as long as he worked for a couple of hours every day. Next to the bare mattress on the dusty floorboards, he found the tins of mustard yellow gloss, all-purpose undercoat and magnolia emulsion that had been bought during the Easter vac. He could start with his own room! But he needed a paying job too. The chippy on Bridge Street needed a fryer for the lunchtime shift – eleven 'til three, six days a week, and the Marine Hotel wanted someone in the residents' bar from eight until the last of the guests went to bed.

He slipped easily into this routine and it carried him through the weeks of disillusion after Russ. When he felt at his bleakest, he'd set the Leo Sayer album on the turntable; *When I Need You* seemed to help. On sunny days, if he felt less down, he strolled along South Beach in the afternoons and daydreamed about the bronzed men in skimpy swimming trunks.

By the middle of August the house was buzzing. Elwyn had moved in and was getting on with the hall, stairs and landings, Jill was making curtains and spending lots of time at local auctions buying furniture from house clearances, Huw cooked the evening meals, pruned the climbing rose and cleaned up the yard, and Janice finally got the cellar sorted.

It was approaching midnight and all the windows in the upstairs residents' bar of the Marine Hotel were thrown open to capture the faintest hint of breeze off the sea; it had been a sizzling day. Two middle-aged couples sat at a table in one of the bays playing contract whist. One of the women was badly sunburnt, her shoulders all blotchy with calamine lotion; maybe they wouldn't stay up too late. The only other drinker was a man in his thirties who'd come in for a nightcap; a commercial traveller type, his boxer's build and the slightly effeminate swagger of his hips contradicted one another.

'Elvis is dead,' he said. 'It was just on the radio news.'

Siôn wasn't always good at these impromptu conversations. He'd never liked Elvis Presley and he didn't know what to say.

'He was such a good-looker before the pills and booze got him,' the man said.

And Siôn decoded the message.

'D'you live in?' the man asked as the two couples ended their game and got up from their table.

'I've got to clean up here before I'm off duty.'

'God, you've got the bluest eyes,' he said.

'So I'm told,' Siôn quipped, and straight away wondered if he was being coquettish.

'I'm Nick... room 23.' He dangled his key so that Siôn could see the number tab clearly. 'If you're interested... after you've finished down here of course.'

Their sex was raw – hurried and rough. Siôn bled, on and off, for three days. To assuage his remorse he read Pittenger again, and decided that his life would be more straightforward if he were celibate.

Another new start then.

He chose embryology, immunology and animal physiology as his three final year modules, and it was agreed that his honours research project and dissertation would be something immunological. He thrived, despite the necessity to pith frogs and gas pregnant rabbits for his experiments. Notwithstanding the mediocre results he'd achieved in that summer's exams, his tutors predicted that he'd scrape an upper-second, if he worked hard.

Conflicts between members of the community in SCM House were minor, to everyone's surprise. They took turns to prepare the evening meal, which was daunting for many, and everyone was expected at the table, though as the months passed they became more relaxed about such 'rules' and missing the odd dinner for rugby practice, a late night in the library or an invitation to share food at someone else's table was accepted. On Saturdays and Sundays it was a free for all, but Tricia cooked Sunday dinner once a month and that became a fixture. Whoever cooked had to say grace, which was often an imaginative expression of resignation, especially on 'disaster' nights; Pete's toad-in-the-hole was more of a turd-in-a-puddle, Janice burnt a lasagne and Siôn's pizza had to be scraped off the kitchen floor in soggy pieces. In the cellar, the chapel service rota changed regularly so that no one would find attendance a chore; sometimes there'd be a week of morning or evening prayer, occasionally a hunger lunch, a Bible study series on Sunday afternoons for a month, a meditative half-hour on an evening once a week through Lent... short term commitments that seemed to suit most people and were always well attended.

Being celibate wasn't easy for Siôn. For a few months he didn't even touch himself and he often woke-up on a wet patch after nights of lurid dreams that featured attractive strangers he'd passed in the street or seen on TV. But one troubling dream recurred; Dali's Jesus, from the print that had hung above Paul Wynne's bed in Theol Coll, came into his bed and made love to him.

After the first time, Siôn had thought hard about this dream. He concluded that the *Gay News* blasphemy case must have jogged the memory of his one reading of Kirkup's poem about the centurion. Throughout the *Gay News* trial, the prosecution had repeatedly linked all homosexual acts to child molestation, and in the days after the verdict in July the papers had been full of it. Back then he'd been too broken-hearted over Russell Talbert to pay it much attention, but by the autumn his sexual frustration was palpable – like toothache... hard to ignore – and his subconscious was seeking release. It was an easier explanation, anyway, than believing he was fucked-up.

One wet Sunday morning in November, buying a copy of *The Observer,* in the small newsagent's at the top of Market Street (after chapel), he saw a gay magazine amongst the top shelf tits and bums. He'd come a long way since Dr Arachchi's photographs and electric orgasms. Over the next months he bought half a dozen magazines: *Honcho, Stud, Mandate...* and *Zipper*, which he liked a lot. The discomfort he sometimes sensed about using pornography was balanced by the feeling of equilibrium and wellbeing that settled within him... and the fact that Dali's Jesus stopped coming to his bed.

Despite the forecast of an upper-second, Siôn knew that he didn't want to be a career scientist and wouldn't consider any of the master's courses advertised on the notice board in the Science Block common room.

'I've decided to do teacher's training,' he told his immunology tutor one day by the coffee machine.

Filling out the application form for a PGCE course hadn't been so straightforward. Over tea with the Morgans, Rhys urged him to be open and honest when answering the question about 'any history of mental ill health.' Elen was less ingenuous.

'It's Christian fundamentalism and society's sick attitude that got you into trouble, Siôn,' she said in protest against the consequences she secretly feared, should he follow her husband's guidance. 'I don't think you were ever mentally ill.'

'But on the application form I've got to sign that I agree to release all of my medical records for scrutiny by the medical interviewing panel,' Siôn said. 'Somewhere, gathering dust in a file, all the case notes from my gap year in the Denbigh asylum are just waiting to be rediscovered. I don't even think a white lie is an option... and besides, if I try to conceal everything that's happened it would be like I was ashamed of my struggle or something, wouldn't it?'

The journey is home, Elen thought, offering him more chocolate cake.

*   *   *

The appointment for 'the medical' arrived in the same brown envelope as the slip of paper saying that his chest x-ray was clear. Sitting alone in the small waiting room, thumbing through a *Woman's Own* from 1972, he remembered the first time Dr Arachchi had examined him; then the slight Sri Lankan doctor had pulled down the waistband of his pants, squeezed each of his testicles gently and pulled back his foreskin. He hoped the doctor who was about to examine him wouldn't be a gorgeous young man... just in case he got a stiffy.

The consulting room smelled of pipe tobacco. Siôn thought he could see a last wisp of smoke hang in the shaft of dust-speckled sunlight that streamed through the large window.

'I'm Dr Emmanuel,' said the round old man in Welsh. 'Please sit down.'

Beneath a gaping white coat, stiff with starch, he wore a greeny-brown tweed suit. The gold chain of a pocket watch spanned the expanse of his belly where the buttons of his stained waistcoat strained against his bulk. On the desk, Siôn saw only a thin, buff coloured file. He felt himself relax; they seemed not to have bothered to trawl his medical history.

Dr Emmanuel's hands were cold, and the physical examination seemed perfunctory. Indeed, it had hardly seemed worthwhile going behind the screen and stripping off.

'There's no physical reason for me not to recommend you,' Dr Emmanuel said in plummy English, when Siôn had dressed and seated himself opposite the doctor across the desk. 'But I have some concerns about your mental health.'

Siôn felt his stomach churn.

'I've had a note from Dr Arwel Thomas at the North Wales Hospital. He tells me that you discharged yourself – when was that, May or June '75? – and that subsequently you've ignored all of the outpatient appointments he's sent you. Is that correct?'

'Yes, that's right,' he said over the thudding of his heart.

'You decided you didn't need psychiatric help then?' Dr Emmanuel quizzed.

'Yes.' He tried to calm himself and discern exactly how much he needed to tell the doctor.

'And you feel qualified to make that decision?'

'I knew that being treated by Dr Thomas wasn't right for me.'

Dr Emmanuel shifted in his seat and looked over imaginary

glasses. 'Hmm... not right for you,' he said, tapping his chin with a crooked index finger.

Siôn held the doctor's eye, but said nothing.

'Do you get any medication from your GP?' he asked after a moment, the index finger now curled around a wart on his cheek. 'Any anti-depressants for example?'

'No. I haven't needed any pills to get me through. I don't get depressed... I don't have any suicidal thoughts.'

'You would conclude that your mental health is good then?'

'Yes.'

'And you are a practising homosexual, Mr Jones?'

'I don't really think that's anybody's business but my own, Dr Emmanuel,' he said, trying to stifle the wave of nausea that came over him.

'Oh... I think it is my business, Mr Jones.' He looked again over his imaginary spectacles, his index finger tapping his temple.

'Why is that something you need to know about me?' Siôn asked, wanting to seem reasonable and giving himself a further moment to think.

'If you are a homosexual, I would have to think very carefully about your application to be a teacher, wouldn't I? Working with boys and impressionable young men —'

Siôn felt as if he was choking for air as he drowned in the realisation of his worst fears.

'Why would you want to put yourself in the way of such temptation, Mr Jones?' The crooked index finger stroked beneath his chin.

'I'm sorry, but I don't understand what you're implying, Dr Emmanuel,' Siôn offered with as much conviction as he could marshal against the old man's allusion.

The doctor's chair creaked as he shifted again in his seat and leaned his belly against the desk. His head moved forward conspiratorially, the index finger tracing small circles in the air between them. 'Don't pubescent boys excite you?'

That's it then. There's no chance —

'I'm shocked by your insinuation, Dr Emmanuel,' Siôn said, his voice clear and strong. 'I like men, not boys. I am a homosexual – a gay man, *not* a paedophile. I'm disturbed... and, quite frankly, disgusted that you don't seem to know the difference.'

'And you think that the teaching profession will find people like you acceptable,' the doctor said, apparently unruffled by Siôn's attack. 'You think that parents will be happy that you teach their boys.'

'I believe the teaching profession will judge me on my merits as a teacher, not on who I choose to go to bed with,' he said... but as soon as he'd spoken he wasn't so sure he really believed it.

'I wish you every success then,' Dr Emmanuel said. He lumbered from the chair and offered Siôn his hand.

'Thank you,' Siôn said, taken aback.

Some minutes later, sitting on a bench in the hospital grounds looking at the crimson tulips sway on a breath of air and feeling the spring sunshine warm his face, Siôn sensed the stew of emotions begin to boil over. *It's just not fair that even educated people like Dr Emmanuel should equate being gay with being a monster that abuses children. But...that's one of the arguments they used against* Gay News *for God's sake! So... sensible people, and parents, really believe those myths.* And he chewed on the ambiguity of Dr Emmanuel's final words.

Nearly three weeks elapsed before the letter confirming that he'd passed the medical arrived, three weeks in which self-doubt ploughed him up and sowed a harvest of suspicion. And then came the invitation to meet one of the lecturers in the Education Department for what the letter described as 'an informal interview'.

Siôn recognised Dr Griff Edwards from Peniel. It seemed natural to speak in Welsh. They drank coffee and talked about teaching.

'Have you thought about training to teach through the medium of Welsh?' Griff Edwards asked.

'But all of my formal education has been in English.'

'That's still true for most people, Siôn. But, you know, the number of first language Welsh schools is increasing and there's a crying need for Welsh medium science teachers. Your Welsh is fluent enough.'

'Would I have to do the coursework in Welsh?' he asked, knowing his grasp of the grammar was weak and anticipating that this might pull down his grades in any written work.

'At the moment that wouldn't even be possible because we don't have enough Welsh-speaking staff, but you could do your teaching practice in a Welsh, or a bilingual school, and your tutorials could be in Welsh.'

Siôn's look must have betrayed his misgivings.

'And you'd have absolutely no problems getting a job if you could offer to teach in both languages.' Griff Edwards became animated by Siôn's possibilities and his enthusiasm carried Siôn through the remainder of the interview. 'Is there anything you want to ask... about the course, or teaching in general?'

Ask him about the profession's views on gay teachers.

'I don't think so,' Siôn said with some hesitation.

'Now's your chance,' Griff Edwards said.

If Dr Emmanuel hasn't told them I'm gay, why should I?

'No… really, I don't think there's anything.' But leaving the Education Department, Siôn wondered if Griff Edwards would be so enthusiastic if he knew; would he think Siôn was a paedophile too?

*　　*　　*

He was satisfied that he couldn't have worked any harder, but the upper second eluded him. There was no hiding his disappointment. Elen Morgan helped him put his achievement into perspective.

'Do you remember that morning when we fetched you from the hospital?' She coaxed the memory from him. 'We sat by the castle and you told me some of your story —'

'Yes,' he said.

'And just before we left the hospital —'

Those bleak days, for a second, were juxtaposed against his present.

'Yes, I do remember. I told you that I'd made the right decision on that Saturday morning when I took all those pills.'

'Siôn *bach*, come here,' she said, her arms wide to embrace him. 'Try not to measure the success of your time in Aberystwyth by the class and division of your degree. You've rebuilt your life, and for what it's worth, Rhys and I believe that your achievements these past three years are beyond a first class honours, and we're so proud of you.'

For the fraction of a moment in his mind's eye, Siôn was back on the locked ward in the asylum and the laughing man was laughing at him. 'Yes,' he said, recognising how far he'd come.

*　　*　　*

He knew, from all the harping over coffee in the staff room, that the two other students on placement were having a hard time; discipline problems were turning their classes into battlefields. He believed that the fun he and his students were having was due to the fact that biology was so fascinating; he couldn't see that they liked him. Neither could he acknowledge that he had a presence in the classroom that aroused interest, encouraged respect and sometimes even inspired. He prepared his lesson plans with an almost fussy care and developed a delivery that was relaxed and engaging.

'I've rarely seen a student enjoying teaching practice so much,' Griff Edwards said after sitting in on a couple of Siôn's lessons. 'Perhaps you could watch out for all those 'Okays'... and I know that you were worried about your Welsh, but you needn't be.'

Siôn broke into a smile.

'The profession needs people like you, and we need you to stay in Wales.'

During a lunch break in the staff room, Siôn read the grim details of the mass suicide amongst the members of an American religious cult, the People's Temple, in Guyana. He was supervising a fifth form class for a teacher on sick leave later that afternoon; if the students had no work to get on with they could have a discussion about cults.

'What do you think about that pop group, Village People, Sir?' a pretty blonde girl asked just after the class had settled, and after Siôn had ascertained that they'd been left no work.

'We've been having an argument about whether they're all really gay,' another girl put in.

''Course they're all queers,' one of the boys jeered.

'Ho-mos... ho-mos... ho-mos,' came the low chant from a scrum of boys on the back row.

'Since you haven't been set any work,' Siôn said, 'I'm happy for us to have a class discussion about something, but it's got to be well behaved or I'll just have you all get on with some homework.'

His authority surprised him as the chanting stopped.

'So... what about this cult in Guyana?' he asked, almost tentatively. 'It's been on the TV news and it's all over the papers.'

There was some foot shuffling and a couple of girls started to plait strands of their hair and look out of the window.

'Okay,' Siôn said, and almost bit his tongue as he recalled Griff Edwards' gentle chiding. 'Religious cults don't seem to grab your interest. Homework then, is it?'

'Oh Sir,' half the class croaked in unison.

'Alright,' he said, quite conscious of his use of language. 'There was a question about Village People; about whether they're gay.'

The class looked instantly more focused, though some of the boys grimaced. Then the 'ho-mo' chant began again.

'That's enough,' Siôn said, catching the eye of the boy he thought was the chorus leader. 'What's your name?'

The chanting stopped.

'Meurig, Sir.'

Siôn remained silent for fifteen or twenty seconds, his eyes moving slowly from Meurig to the other boys on the back row, holding their gaze until they surrendered. Cruising men had trained him well for holding a stare!

'That's better,' he said when he'd won their attention. 'I'm all for having an adult discussion as long as you can behave like adults. Village People then; does it matter if they're gay?'

'It does if you fancy one of them,' said the blonde girl,

whose name was Eluned.

Lots of the girls giggled.

'Oh, it's disgusting,' said one of the boys next to Meurig. 'They're all bum boys!'

'Seems that there's a bit of prejudice amongst some students in this class towards people who are different,' Siôn cajoled. He looked at the rows of faces and wondered how many of them might be struggling as he had struggled.

'What d'you mean, Sir?' quizzed another of the back row boys.

'Let's explore this notion of difference for a while,' Siôn said. 'I want you to work with the people next to you, just three or four of you together. I'd like you to come up with a list of obvious differences between people... let's say five things.'

Chairs scraped and noise level rose as the students clustered.

'I don't expect complete silence when we work this way, but I can't have you disturbing the classes next door, so let's keep the volume down please.'

They worked well for a few minutes and when each group around the room had five differences, Siôn asked them to share their lists. Along with hair and eye colour, left-handedness and acne spots, the class had come up with gender and skin colour, mental and physical disabilities, whether or not someone was gay and a person's religion. The back row boys thought a significant difference was the like or dislike of rugby!

'Let's take one of these, then,' Siôn suggested. 'Which one?'

'Gender,' said one of the girls next to Eluned.

He wrote 'gender' on the blackboard in large capitals and then wrote 'women' and 'men' as column headings divided by a line.

'How do the differences between women and men get highlighted in our society?'

'Jobs,' said one of the boys. 'You don't get many women engineers.'

'And you don't get many male nurses,' a girl in the front row offered.

'Women earn less too,' someone called out.

'And we have to say that we'll obey when we get married,' a girl voiced.

'And girls don't play rugby,' said one of Meurig's crowd.

'So... society expects men and women to play different roles,' Siôn said.

'And there seems to be more value on what men do than on what women do,' a different girl said.

'Good point. Can somebody expand on that?' Siôn solicited.

'You can see it in school, Sir,' Eluned said. 'The girls aren't allowed to do woodwork and metal work... or technical drawing. We get to do cookery and needlework and we're just supposed to become meek little wives who stay at home to look after kids and cook the dinner.'

'Can you think of any women who've broken out of these more traditional roles?' Siôn asked.

'Mrs Thatcher's the leader of the Conservatives... and there's a lady doctor working in the surgery now,' one of Eluned's group said thoughtfully.

'There's that Mrs Castle too... she's something with Labour,' a boy's voice croaked.

'And Germaine Greer,' Eluned said. 'My sister's read *The Female Eunuch*... and she says that marriage is just a kind of legalised slavery so she's living with her boyfriend. My *nain* says they're living in sin.'

'So some women do break the mould,' Siôn encouraged.

'But there aren't many,' Meurig said in a way that suggested he wouldn't like to see too many more.

'Okay,' Siôn said to the echo of Griff Edwards' voice, which threw him off his stride.

'Even here in school there are more male teachers than female ones and the women just teach girly things,' Eluned said.

'What do you mean by "girly things"?' Siôn pressed.

'Just look at the sixth form,' she said with agitation in her voice. 'Physics, Chemistry, Maths, they're all taught by men and it's mostly boys that do those subjects for A-level. Then Welsh and English, Scripture... and Music are taught by women and there isn't even one boy doing Music A-level.'

'That's because it's sissy,' the boy next to Meurig quipped.

'Let me ask the boys a question,' Siôn said, regaining his balance. 'How many of you can see yourselves working for a woman boss sometime in the future?'

'No way...' and 'Never in Europe!' they chorused.

'What's all this got to do with Village People, Sir?' a girl at the front asked.

'Who can answer that question?' Siôn put to the class.

'We're exploring how the differences between people can lead others to expect certain things based on those differences,' Eluned said.

'So if Village People are gay, what do we expect of them?' Siôn quizzed.

'That they're all child molesters,' Meurig said.

'Where does that association come from?' Siôn asked.

'What d'you mean, Sir?' Meurig asked.

'Well... what I mean is, why do some people think a gay person is more likely to interfere with kids than a heterosexual person?'

'Because that's what being gay is, Sir. They're all arse bandits and into little boys.'

Siôn scanned the students' faces, though he wasn't sure what he was looking for. 'Does everyone in this class think that way?'

'It's what the papers say, Sir,' Meurig said.

'Yes,' Siôn said, scratching his head. 'I know that's what the papers say.' He wanted to say that he knew, from his own experience as a homosexual, that what the papers said wasn't always true. But of course, he couldn't do that.

'Maybe we should be more critical of what we read in the papers,' Eluned offered.

Siôn moved the lesson on, encouraging the class to think about how society stereotyped black people and disabled people. When the bell rang he was confident that he'd managed to get them to start looking at the assumptions they made about others, which was perhaps all he could have hoped for without a thought-through lesson plan.

Most of that evening, he considered how he might have been more focused in the discussion on difference and stereotypes. One thought kept hijacking his reflections – that he'd joined the oppressors. Because he'd felt unable to use his own experiences to challenge the assumptions that the students were making about gays, he'd hidden behind his closet door. He remembered looking at the sea of faces after Meurig had asserted so forcefully that being a homosexual and a paedophile were synonymous; then he'd wondered what he was looking for... now he knew he'd been searching for the one or two who could see through his lie as he pretended to be one of the enemy.

'You're either very brave or very naïve,' Beryl Watkins, one of the Welsh teachers said during the break the next morning.

'What did I do?' Siôn said, putting up his hands in a gesture of surrender.

'Meurig, in 5W. He's my youngest,' she said.

'We had a very lively discussion.'

'You'd do better to stick to homework when you're covering for someone, Siôn *bach*,' she said, her tone patronising. 'And you certainly shouldn't encourage fifteen-year-olds to think that sexual perversions are something we should accept.'

He searched Beryl Watkins' face and saw the malice ingrained in her wrinkles. 'Thanks for your advice,' he said with a nod. 'I'll be more careful next time.'

* * *

More than once, Siôn thought he might talk to Griff Edwards about the classroom discussion – the misconceptions, the prejudices, and the warning from Beryl Watkins – but he kept second-guessing himself. During his second stint of teaching practice, Dr Edwards sat in on only one of Siôn's lessons.

'Dr Ffred ap Dewi will be coming to observe your classes next week,' he said as he packed his briefcase ready to leave.

'I'm border-line then?' Siôn said, biting his lip as he recalled some distant tutorial, and the criteria for a visit by the external examiner.

'He likes to see the best and the worst so that he can get a feel for the range of ability.'

'I can't think that I'm one of the poorer student teachers.'

'Siôn *bach*,' he said, patting Siôn's shoulder in a warmly appreciative, rather than patronising way. 'When are you going to realise just how damn good you are? It's been a privilege to supervise you and watch a really gifted teacher grab those children's attention and spark their imagination.'

How could he tell Griff Edwards that every day now, when he

stood before his classes, he searched for the one or two who could see through his lie as he pretended to be one of the enemy?

In June 1979 John Idris Jones – he couldn't be Siôn Idris on official documentation – graduated with distinction in the practical skill of teaching. Griff Edwards was baffled by Siôn's decision not to take up a teaching post and genuinely angry by Siôn's seeming inability to give a plausible reason for turning his back on the profession.

*　　*　　*

They travelled together on the train to Birmingham. Tim's feet were already itchy, and since that day in March, when the Theological College in Llandaf had accepted him to train as an Anglican priest, he'd found it hard to sustain an interest in his work as Welsh travelling secretary of the SCM. He was hoping that the Easter conference at Aston, with the theme of *Vessels for New Wine*, would inspire him through the last months of his contract. Siôn, always ill-at-ease with Tim's intense intellect, concentrated on his book.

'Only one person has applied for my job,' Tim said as the train pulled slowly over the Dyfi bridge.

'You're not leaving until July though, so there's still plenty of time, isn't there?' he said, squinting over his book but not really committing himself to a conversation.

'All the members of the Welsh Council will be at *Vessels* and we'd hoped that we might interview the candidates; that would save us convening the Council later on.'

Siôn laid the book on the seat beside him and gave Tim his attention. 'Is the applicant a strong contender?'

314

'He's committed enough, and he's got good communication skills, but he doesn't speak Welsh. He'd be interrupting his studies too.'

'I can see why not having Welsh is an issue, but it wouldn't matter if he took a sabbatical, would it?'

'I think we need someone who'd be willing to do two or even three years.'

'Why's that?'

'Well, all I could really hope to do in my term was generate interest, and I've done that. There are embryonic SCM groups in all the colleges now, and there are a few denominational groups that might consider affiliating, so what we really need is someone who can consolidate everything and capacity build; nurture the babies and bring them on if you like.'

'Sounds like an ad for a child-minder,' Siôn quipped.

Tim laughed. 'And the national exec has decided it would be good to hold the student congress in Wales sometime in the next eighteen months to raise the Welsh Movement's profile, so whoever gets the job will need to coordinate all of that too.'

'A child-minder and a conference organiser; that's a tall order.'

'Then there are the plans for a study tour to visit Christian groups behind the Iron Curtain; the ESG, the SCM in East Germany, is really keen to host a visit. I've been working on it with Derek, from Bristol. We're exploring some possibilities in Czechoslovakia too.'

'All that on top of being warden of the Aber house; you're asking a lot of someone.'

'Yes… but it's an interesting job.'

They both read for a while.

'How was your teaching practice?' Tim asked, distracted

315

from his reading as the train slowed into Welshpool. 'You must be relieved that it's over.'

'I loved being in the classroom, but it's not easy being a gay man in teaching,' he said, surprised that he was opening up to Tim. 'I've had to fight with myself and God to get comfortable about being gay, and now I feel that being a teacher is going to force me right back into the closet.'

'You don't have to wear it like a badge, Siôn. People don't like having their faces rubbed in something that they find even slightly uncomfortable.'

'So what do I do if people assume I'm straight? Do I live that lie just so that I don't upset them?'

'Depends who the people are, and how important the relationship between you is, I suppose.'

'That's no way to live, Tim, always having to decide who you'll tell, and remember the reasons you've decided not to come out to others. That only gets you caught up in a web of misinformation.'

'I guess I haven't considered that.'

Tim was thoughtful for a while. Siôn watched the spring bursting through the grime of the train window and felt himself sink again into his doubts about taking up a teaching post. His first interview, for a job teaching Biology, General Science and Health Education at a small comprehensive school in rural Clwyd, was only a fortnight away.

'So are you thinking that maybe you won't go into teaching?' Tim ventured.

Siôn knew that if he answered Tim he'd choke up.

Tim sensed Siôn's struggle and reached into his briefcase for a slim folder. 'Here, read this. Perhaps you should apply for my job?'

The man from the Gay Christian Movement had a really cheeky smile. He was running a workshop on the second afternoon of *Vessels*, and despite the organiser's assumption that there wouldn't be many participants, the twenty-odd students who turned up had to move from the small, stuffy room into the bar area. He was older than Siôn, maybe twenty-five or twenty-six, and he was muscular – though not like a chunky weightlifter, more like a regular swimmer. Siôn felt instantly attracted to him.

'Pull the chairs around into a circle,' the handsome swimmer directed. 'I don't want anyone to have to look at the back of someone else's neck.'

When a loose ring had been formed, and everyone was seated, he looked around at everyone, his pert smile offering all the welcome that was necessary. 'Hello everybody. I'm Richard. I'm homosexual. I'm a Christian. I work for GCM.'

Siôn was hugely impressed by his honesty, and by the way he presented his gayness as something so ordinary.

'We're a small enough group, I think,' Richard said. 'Would you all like to introduce yourselves and say why you've chosen to come to this workshop?'

'I'm Siobhan,' said the woman to his left. 'I'm a lesbian, and a feminist, and I'm really struggling with this whole misogynist Christian thing.'

'I'm Euan and I come from Glasgow,' the boy next to her said. 'I've come to the workshop because homosexuality is a difficult issue in our chaplaincy.'

'And you're a gay man, Euan?' Richard asked.

'No... sorry. I like girls,' he said with a look of discomfort. There was a ripple of gentle laughter, which wasn't meant to be unkind. 'Do I have to be gay to attend this workshop?'

'Of course not, Euan,' Richard said with a gentleness that

317

belied any sense of a put-down. 'I just didn't want to make any assumptions about you.'

'I'm Polly,' said the woman across from Euan. 'Like our friend from Glasgow I like women too.' The laughter around the circle was heartier. Euan laughed loudest, indicating that he hadn't taken offence. 'I'm here because I need support,' she said. 'My father's a vicar. He and my mother are evangelicals... let's just say things aren't too great at home.'

'I'm John,' Siôn heard himself say. 'I'm training to be a teacher and... I'm gay... and what I'd like to take away from the workshop is the sense that I have a community.'

'Do you live somewhere rural, John?' Richard asked.

'Aberystwyth is the gay capital of Wales,' Siôn said. The laughter around the circle was raucous.

After the introductions, Richard shared bits of his own story and encouraged others to share theirs.

'How would you suggest that I introduce this back in my chaplaincy and get a constructive dialogue going?' Euan asked. 'We're quite evangelical, so it's all a bit hostile towards gays. We haven't got anyone who's actually come out either, but I think a few people are struggling. We just don't have any of the powerful stories like the ones we've heard this afternoon.'

'You could invite Richard to come to one of your meetings,' Polly said.

'You could indeed; it wouldn't be the first time I've been a Daniel,' he said. 'But there are other things too; what about a discussion group for a few weeks? Or a book club?' He searched in a box beside his chair and drew out a book. 'This new one, *Is the Homosexual my Neighbour?*... two evangelical heterosexuals have written it, which makes it difficult for straights and fundamentalists to dismiss out of hand.' He passed the book around. 'It'll be available on the GCM bookstall tomorrow afternoon in the agency fair along with other gay books that you probably won't find on the shelves in your local bookshop.'

Siôn didn't doubt that Richard, playing the salesman, could have sold him anything!

At the end of the workshop, the group was slow to disperse. People thanked one another for sharing their stories and struggles; they swapped addresses, flirted and filled out GCM membership forms. Siôn realised he was besotted.

'I've got a boyfriend,' Richard said, after Siôn had bought him a drink and tried to chat him up.

Reading Mollenkott and Scanzoni's *Is the Homosexual my Neighbour?* over the next days helped push the disappointment of lost opportunity with Richard from his thoughts. Excitement about becoming the next Welsh travelling secretary of the SCM helped refocus Siôn's mind.

* * *

The Bristol printer with the contract for SCM's stationery duly dispatched the Welsh order to Aberystwyth. Siôn saw straight away that Heather in the central office at Wick had used his given name: John Idris Jones, Welsh Regional Secretary. For tax, insurance and pension purposes it was the name he'd given her, so the misunderstanding was genuine. It was surprising how quickly Siôn Idris was left behind.

One of the groups Tim had urged John to nurture was the large chaplaincy group in Swansea called Open Door, which he visited in November. The forty or so students who'd come to the meeting listened to his presentation with polite attention, but no one asked a question and the chairman moved the meeting swiftly on to a Bible study. John was disappointed by the lukewarm reception and it became obvious, as the Bible study progressed, that the majority were evangelicals. Back in Aberystwyth, rereading Tim's notes in the file marked 'Swansea', John concluded that Tim never saw a glass half empty.

Then, just days after his visit, a letter arrived: Open Door slammed the door shut on affiliation to the SCM, its members' hearts and minds closed where homosexuality was concerned. A couple of articles on sexuality, which had appeared in the SCM's bimonthly magazine, *Movement*, had stirred them up, and the presence of GCM at *Vessels* had upset the chaplaincy delegates. The letter went on to criticise the SCM Press' publication of pro-gay books like *Is the Homosexual my Neighbour?* and Pittenger's *Time for Consent*, and whilst the letter didn't allude to the sexual orientation of the Welsh Regional Secretary, he couldn't help feeling it personally. Open Door didn't even wish to retain any links with the Student Christian Movement for as long as it took such an un-Biblical stance on sexuality.

Some dark days followed. Adam and the Sunday Library Group's choruses disturbed his sleep and the laughing man laughed – mocking him. Even Jatunga Arachchi started talking dirty again. John convinced himself that the SCM wouldn't grow in Wales under his stewardship; homosexuality was too difficult an issue. But it wasn't an issue from which he could disaffiliate – so perhaps the Movement's fortunes in Wales would be better served by a new regional secretary?

All of the national staff team urged him to stay, and each of the regional secretaries talked with him on the phone to offer their support. Heather, in the Wick office, reminded him that the SCM Press was a completely separate entity to the SCM, and that neither he, nor the Movement, had any influence on what the press chose to publish. The Welsh Council, meeting in Carmarthen at the beginning of December, agreed with unanimity that the Movement in Wales should retain its radical edge, even if that did mean a small membership. All of the Council's members rejected John's offer to resign.

Walking the cliff path north from Aberystwyth towards Clarach on a crisp, frosty day so clear that he could see both Bardsey and the Pembrokeshire coast, he wondered how he might better have dealt with the whole Open Door crisis. Perhaps, if he had a more formal theological education? It was something he'd talk about with Rhys Morgan.

*   *   *

With the Gay Christian Movement's newsletter there was always a booklist; Richard was ever the salesman. The English translation of Heinz Herger's *Die Männer mit dem rosa Winkel* finally appeared nearly five years after Henk had talked about it in Taizé.

In John's memory, Buchenwald had been the camp where gay men had been incarcerated and experimented upon... and Buchenwald was just a few kilometres outside Weimar, one of the cities on the itinerary of the East German trip. It was this supposed connection that had convinced John he'd join Derek in leading the study tour – he wanted to stand at the place where that forgotten history had happened and be a witness. But Buchenwald wasn't mentioned in the book, which left John wondering what other sources Henk had found in German, French or Dutch, yet to be translated into English, that had become conflated in Henk's own retelling of the story. The camps featuring most prominently in *The Men with the Pink Triangle* were Sachsenhausen and Flossenbürg. John remembered the names from *Ohel Yizkor*, the Tent of Remembrance in Yad Vashem.

Herger's account of life and death in these camps didn't shock him in any kind of numbing sense; perhaps, subconsciously, he'd replayed the tapes from the conversations with Henk and revisited the photographic record on that memorial hill above Jerusalem so many times that the horror of what was done had been blunted. After reading about the brothel that was established in the 'special block' at Flossenbürg, and the weekly 'cure' visits that the men with a pink triangle were forced to pay to the prostitutes, under the close scrutiny of the camp commander, watching through specially drilled holes in the walls of the brothel's rooms, John wondered about the similarities between the Nazi doctors and his own at the Denbigh asylum. It didn't matter that Buchenwald wasn't mentioned in Herger's account; he still needed to go there.

Derek, the southwest regional secretary based in Bristol, did most of the planning for the East German trip, through direct contact with the ESG's office in East Berlin and with some support from the World Student Christian Federation's office in Geneva. For four weeks in the summer of 1980 a small group of students from all parts of Britain caught a glimpse of life through the eyes of Christian students living under the totalitarian regime of the German Democratic Republic. It was a confusing glimpse.

There was no briefing meeting about the visit to the GDR before the group gathered in Dover, though Derek had been efficient with mailings. In the bar on the ferry, pitched by a fierce summer storm, a couple of the students who weren't being seasick wanted to know if there were any topics they shouldn't raise with their East German hosts.

'We'll have an escort from the moment we cross the border into the east,' Derek said. 'His name is Ewald; he works for the ESG... and we don't want to compromise him in any way. We are an officially invited group so the *Stasi* know about us... and we'll probably be spied on. I don't think we should consider that any topics are off limits, but we should probably accept whatever answers we get without too much probing... and if someone doesn't want to answer a question we shouldn't push them.'

Had the sun been shining when they crossed the border perhaps John wouldn't have felt like they were a bunch of extras in a fifties black and white spy film. The heavily armed border guards, and the display of military hardware, disconcerted and intimidated some of the group. John remembered how uncomfortable he'd been the first time he'd been close to a machine gun, in the back of the truck with Rafi when they'd driven from the airport in Tel Aviv. 'After a few days you'll hardly notice,' he said, hoping his experience would reassure them.

Ewald Kleißmann, their escort from the ESG's office in East Berlin, was in his mid-twenties. His curly ginger hair fell like a lion's mane between the blades of his broad shoulders, and an infectious smile beamed from a freckled face of clear skin. His outgoing temperament and fluent English eased the tensions that had mounted in the minibus during the slow passage through the checks at the border and the mood of the group quickly took on a holiday feel. John noticed Ewald's hazel eyes; how they held his gaze as long as any cruiser might. Though not instantly attracted to him physically, John allowed himself to fantasise

323

and sought to interpret the meanings of the lingering looks. Later, remembering that Derek had suggested they'd be spied upon, John wondered if Ewald might be that informer. He made a conscious effort not to catch Ewald's eye again.

On their fourth day in the East they made a short trip to visit the Schloss Cecilienhof, where the Potsdam Conference had taken place at the end of the Second World War, and the Schloss Sanssouci, Frederick the Great's fabled retreat. They were a group of about twenty, the British visitors and a handful of East Germans.

John became aware that Rolf, a slight boy of eighteen or nineteen, was always close by. With cropped black hair and pallid skin, he looked fragile, and never seemed to be without a cigarette between his lips or his heavily stained fingers. They'd met briefly at the welcome reception that first evening in East Berlin.

'You want a smoke?' Rolf asked as they started to climb through the series of terraces up to the Orangerie in Sanssouci Park.

'I don't, but thanks.'

'I'm not very fit,' he said, breathing heavily. 'Shall we sit on the wall for some rest?' The members of their party continued past them up the stone steps. 'We have only a few minutes,' he said after everyone had passed by. 'Ewald will come to find us soon. He won't like it that we talk this way so we must be quick. Here... take one so it looks like we just smoke.'

John puffed on the lighted cigarette.

'The other night, in the small group, you ask about homo-sexuals.'

'Yes,' John said. 'I was surprised to hear that the GDR has more liberal laws than the west. It's amazing that under your civil partnership laws two men or two women can legally register.'

'That's the official position,' Rolf said. 'But it is difficult for us. There is no place for us to meet so many *Schwule* join church groups. The *Stasi* keep *Rosa Listen*; if they know about me they put my name on the pink list and try to make me talk... to pass informations about others.'

John looked up the flight of stone steps for any sign of Ewald, and choked on his cigarette.

'Many *Schwule* apply to leave the GDR and many...' he searched for a word, 'self-murder... so it's not such a good situation for us. When it becomes known that you are *schwul* it is possible to lose your place at the university... or your job. Most of us don't show it.'

'Do you have any gay friends?' John asked, remembering what it had been like to feel like he was the only one in the world.

'I have a friend —'

'*Los. Beeilt euch doch mal was!*' Ewald called from the top of the steps.

'Yes... we come,' Rolf shouted.

They climbed towards Ewald, who stood waiting for them by one of the lion's head waterspouts in the retaining wall of the top terrace.

'Is there anything I can do?' John asked Rolf, still far enough away for Ewald not to hear.

'Please forget that we talked like this.'

There were other walks in other parks, on riverside promenades and in busy streets – in Dresden, Freiberg and Karl-Marx-Stadt, in Naumburg, Erfurt and Weimar; and other snatched conversations that no one could eavesdrop... about food shortages and the inability to be openly critical of the State, travel restrictions, censorship of western literature and the personal, practical, everyday costs of Christian discipleship under an atheist regime.

The wrought-iron gates in Buchenwald's gatehouse bear an inscription *Jedem das Seine*. 'It means something like 'to every man his due',' Ewald explained when questioned.

'Didn't stop them killing women too,' Alison, a student from Cambridge said, almost under her breath.

John remembered Heinz Herger's list of the coloured triangles stitched onto the inmates' uniforms to denote their 'offence': brown for gypsies, purple for Jehovah's Witnesses, red for political prisoners, yellow for Jews... and pink. The morning sun was warm. He pulled off his sweater, under which he wore the pink T-shirt he'd bought especially for this visit. Passing through the gatehouse, past the inscription on the gate, he reflected on what life expected of him. Thirty-five years earlier, to pass through that same gate would have meant almost certain death.

'We need to stay together to look around the exhibits, but I think in this place you will want to spend some time on your own... with your own thoughts,' Ewald said.

After the 'tour', that included the disinfection station – where the arriving inmates had all of their hair shaved off before being forced to bathe in disinfection baths, the pathology department – where corpses were plundered of anything deemed valuable, including tattooed skin for lampshades, and the crematorium where remains were burned, John wandered around the camp. He followed the line of the barbed wire, counting the posts that carried the electrified fence. Then he stood before the hanging post where inmates, their hands tied behind them, were hung by the wrists for hours – sometimes days. Sitting on a low wall that enclosed the stump of Goethe's Oak – so named by the inmates because Goethe had visited the area often and walked in the Ettersberg forest close to the camp – he read long sections from *The Men with the Pink Triangle*.

They did this to people like me.

Jedem das Seine... to everyone their due.

*　　*　　*

Back in Aberystwyth, John read some Bonhoeffer. In one of the mailings Derek had sent before the East German trip there were photocopies from *Letters and Papers from Prison*. The Lutheran pastor and theologian had been involved in resistance to the Nazis, and after being linked to a plot to overthrow Hitler, he'd been imprisoned. In the first months of 1945 he was incarcerated at Buchenwald, before being transported to Flossenbürg, where he was hanged. Whilst John had been reading Herger's testimony by Goethe's Oak, Derek had sat against the hanging post reading excerpts from *Letters and Papers*.

It was Bonhoeffer's writings that helped to crystallise John's thoughts about studying theology. Rhys Morgan doubted whether there was anywhere in Britain doing any gay studies under the broad banner of what had become know as Liberation Theology. 'You might have to consider going abroad,' he said. 'America seems the most obvious place. I've just been reading a book by Robert McAfee Brown called *Theology in a New Key*; he's one of the theologians trying to interpret the new ideas coming from Latin America and understand their significance for us in the rich western nations.'

'And in America there are feminist theologians; women like Rosemary Ruether,' Elen said. She paused, searching her

327

memory for other names, but couldn't locate them. 'These women are suggesting that the way we understand the Christian tradition has been skewed by male interpretation and we need to start looking through women's eyes and women's experience.'

'So there may be people over there who are encouraging us to look through gay eyes and gay experience,' John mused.

'There's sure to be someone in SCM... or the SCM Press, that knows about the possibilities,' Rhys said.

At the three-day staff-training meeting in Wick in the first days of September, John had the opportunity to pick people's brains. Barry, the regional secretary in Scotland, suggested that he contact the World Council of Churches. 'There's a scholarship programme that not many people from Britain apply for because there's a perception that it's mainly for third world people to come to Europe or America. I can't think of the name of the laddie you'd need to talk to but I can find out and let you know.'

John spent four days over the application forms from the World Council of Churches Scholarships Office in London. Mailing off the bulky envelope he wondered whether he'd been too expansive; would anyone bother to read so many pages of outpouring?

Late September

The radio voices were almost a whisper. John watched the high branches of the birch trees outside their bedroom window sway almost imperceptibly on the breeze; high above the nervous leaves, whipped cream clouds were splattered across the sky. Klaus snoozed. His lovemaking had been more energetic – more like it used to be. He was becoming more confident that John wasn't so fragile after all.

The phone rang. Klaus shifted and said something in German.

'Let the answering machine get it,' John said, snuggling up to Klaus.

John heard a voice, muffled by distance and the bedroom door, leave a message.

Klaus poured himself some *Rioja*. After swirling the weighty red around the large glass and smelling the rich raspberry and plum fruitiness he resisted that first sip, setting the glass down so that the flavours could ripen. He grated a carrot into a dish of shredded celeriac and after mixing the amber and orange shards he made up a simple dressing with lemon juice, olive oil and a fat clove of garlic crushed with a little fine rock slat. Despite the obvious breeze that agitated the leaves in the grove of birch trees at the end of their garden it was still warm in the house after the day's sun. His muslin dressing gown gaped revealing a belly that he'd resolved to flatten; with John's new dietary restrictions he had an incentive to lose the odd kilo.

'Did you listen to Russell's message?' John asked as he came into the kitchen dressed only in shorts.

'Another invitation to Barmouth,' Klaus said.

'He's keen to get to know you.'

'Hmm… are you sure he's not desperate?' Klaus took a mouthful from his wineglass and savoured the oaky complexity.

John set the table.

'Exactly how sick is Russell?' Klaus asked.

'You saw him at the theatre: he's got that gaunt look. D'you remember Ranley?'

Klaus peeled the strips of smoked salmon from their vacuum packing. 'But that was years ago,' he said, remembering those bleak months of hospital visits and all their efforts to help Ranley die with some dignity at home. 'I thought the new combination therapies had stopped all of that.'

'When Russell looks at you sometimes his eyes are too big in his face… and his cheeks are all hollow.'

'So you don't think he's got very long?'

'Who knows?'

'And you think we ought to get involved?'

John thought again about Elen Morgan's challenge, all those years ago, about passing kindness on; he'd pondered it a good deal in the last days... but the Kyffins were muddling his judgement. 'It's not a *should* or an *ought* Klaus, but Russ would like our friendship.'

'You know how much I like going to Barmouth,' he said with a smile.

'Okay... so why don't *you* phone him back then?'

'No time like the present,' Klaus said and left the kitchen.

John poured himself some wine. Wondering why they were drinking red with smoked salmon he felt himself being pulled back again into the mire of memory.

Before the interview for the Liverpool job, the only one he'd applied for in the weeks after his return from California in the late summer of 1984, John had decided not to lie about being gay. If they asked, he'd tell them the truth. But of course, they hadn't asked. Some on the interview panel were curious about why he wasn't in the ordination process, but they seemed content that he was still 'wrestling with the sense of call'. A couple on the panel even suggested that appointing a theologically and pastorally trained lay person to the post of Merseyside Welsh Chaplain would be a novel solution to the desperate shortage of clergy. After all, offering the job to one of the other candidates would mean that a cluster of churches in Wales would lose their minister and create a whole new set of problems.

Within days of his appointment, John knew that once the celibate phase he'd moved into after contracting hepatitis-B in the Berkeley bathhouse came to an end, whenever that might be, he'd be living a lie – and then he'd met Klaus. If they became lovers... when they became lovers, he knew he'd find living that lie impossible. Perhaps he'd confide in Gwil, and hope that Gwil's God had broad enough arms to embrace such difference.

Gwil ap Dylan was from an almost completely fractured branch of the Presbyterian Church of Wales that still believed in a radical Gospel – one that required the church to engage with everyday life as lived in the last quarter of the twentieth century, socially relevant and politically challenging, inviting faith that was spiritually grounded and Biblically based, and yet free from literalism. Gwil appreciated the freshness of John's theology; he'd even said that John seemed *cutting edge* when compared with the dribble of new clergy coming from the Theological College in Aberystwyth, most of whom were touched by evangelical fundamentalism. John liked him, and believed they got on well together.

John's report for the Home Mission Board, on the first eighteen months of the Merseyside Welsh Chaplaincy, had been submitted to Gwil's Cardiff office almost a month late. It had taken much longer than John had anticipated, typing away on his old Adler manual. Describing the pastoral work with convicted drug dealers and armed robbers, a double murderer and hundreds of sick people, had been straightforward enough. John's account of the reflective process, born of these pastoral relationships, had proved more difficult, and he worried that he was exposing aspects of his personality that might give too much of himself away. After all, the double murderer was a handsome, sexually confused twenty-something, who'd decapitated his ultra religious parents after they'd discovered him masturbating with a gay porn magazine.

The completed dossier for Cardiff, which included worship bulletins from services in the prison and various hospitals, the texts of half a dozen sermons and photocopies of every letter of appreciation that came back to him from Wales ('...it's all evidence of the value of this ministry,' Gwil had urged) was stalled further by its progress through the Liverpool Presbytery. The chairman asked for an English translation of the narrative sections, and knowing that the renewal of his contract depended on a favourable local response, John had banged away on the Adler for another few days.

'We need to meet,' Gwil said into the phone in his heavily accented Carmarthenshire Welsh. 'I've got meetings in the Theological College in Aberystwyth next Thursday afternoon. Could you make a morning meeting, say at ten?'

'Is this a meeting I'll need to prepare for?' John quizzed. He didn't want to ask directly if the Home Mission Board had got problems with his report.

'There's unanimous support for you, John,' Gwil said. 'But the Board has asked me to talk to you about the work you're doing with the Mersey AIDS Support Group. You didn't say too much about it, and I got the impression it's something you've chosen to do in your own time, but they'd like us to talk through your time-management.'

'Am I not supposed to have any spare time?'

'The Presbytery wants you to do more Sunday services for them, and take on a couple of evening things; the Stanley Road Chapel would like to start a weekly Bible study, and Laird Street, in Birkenhead, want a mid-week prayer meeting once a month.'

'But the chaplaincy is already more than a full time job, Gwil, and I already give the Presbytery two Sundays a month.'

'And they pay your rent and rates, and contribute generously to your gas, electricity and phone bills,' Gwil said.

'But the congregations are —' John wondered how blunt he could be. He no longer knew what to say to the meagre

333

gatherings of elderly expatriates who were more Welsh than the Welsh for an hour in church on a Sunday, but who lived their daily lives as salt-of-the-earth city dwellers and spoke Scouse as well as native born Liverpudlians. Indeed, many were natives, the sons and daughters of those early twentieth century migrant workers. But they clung to a sense of Welshness that no longer existed, not even in the Welsh-speaking heartlands.

'Don't you think I know what it's like?' Gwil said. 'Let's talk about it next week.'

On issues of sexuality, Gwil ap Dylan proved to be a conservative. 'I can't really say that I'm surprised,' he said after a long pause. 'You talk so passionately about AIDS victims, and how you see your work with the Mersey AIDS Support Group as part of your ministry.'

'People with AIDS,' John said.

Gwil looked confused.

'Those people who are antibody-positive, and those that have gone on to develop AIDS, they don't like to be thought of as victims... so it's important that we say *people with AIDS* or *positive people*.'

'If you hadn't said anything,' Gwil began, ignoring John's assertion and becoming distracted by the new set of problems John's departure would cause.

'If I hadn't said anything, I'd be betraying the struggle I've had for half a lifetime to become myself,' John interrupted. 'And if the Gospel is about anything at all, it's about being true to yourself.'

Gwil raised his eyebrows in a gesture John interpreted as questioning doubt.

'I can't begin to love my neighbour as myself if I'm living

without self-respect, and I know from experience that if I start living a double life it won't be long before I'm filled with self-loathing.'

'What will you do now?' Gwil asked after another long silence, confirming John's sense that the offer to extend the contract would be withheld.

'I'm going back to San Francisco in August, just for a month, with a film crew from S4C. We're going to make a documentary about how the different institutions have responded to AIDS; the health services, the church, the civic administration, the huge gay community. Maybe that'll open some doors in the media. Or, if I decide to stay in Liverpool, there's work to do with the Mersey AIDS Support Group.'

'If only you hadn't said anything, John. Nobody would have asked.'

'No Gwil. If that's the sort of double standard the church expects then I'm better off outside it.'

Mid October

Klaus thought that Russell Talbert's new oil painting was too grey and heavy, but then, what did he know about landscape art? Shirley Bassey bawled the gay anthem 'I Am What I Am' from the speakers of the Bang & Olufsen. It wasn't his idea of pre-dinner drinks music. Russell, who'd suggested that Klaus try a glass of chilled white port as an aperitif, had gone back into the kitchen and John, who'd slept for an hour after their arrival, was still enjoying a soak in the gold-tapped sunken bath. Klaus read the name of the painter and decided that should he and John ever be in a position to buy original artworks he'd be sure not to give Kyffin Williams any wall space.

'When John was here a few weeks back he talked about the work he's been doing with the police,' Russell said, walking back into the lounge carrying a bottle of *Ramos Pinto*, the green glass heavy with condensation, and three delicate crystal flutes on a small silver tray. 'Is his interest in gay politics your doing?'

336

'No... he was already into HIV and AIDS work when I met him in Liverpool. I think the time he spent in San Francisco is what really politicised him.'

Russell poured out the port and handed Klaus the glass. 'And didn't I read something in *The Post* a while back about him doing something for the Assembly in Cardiff?'

'In 2000 he became the joint-chair of the Wales LGB Forum,' Klaus said, wondering why Russell hadn't asked John himself about it. 'The Welsh Assembly needed an advisory group on lesbian and gay issues, and John's really good at bringing people together, despite their differences.'

Russell's eyebrows arched over his dull grey eyes, lengthening a face that already seemed too long and thin. Klaus interpreted the gesture as a sign that Russell hadn't understood him. 'There were meetings of LGB communities across Wales, in Cardiff and in Aberystwyth, and I think in Llandudno, and it quickly became evident that the Welsh speaking queens had never really spoken to anyone who didn't speak Welsh, the lesbians didn't talk to the boys, Cardiff had more in common with Bristol than Llandudno, and the supposedly sophisticated city gays thought that their brothers and sisters in the rural areas were just country pumpkins!'

Russell laughed. 'Bumpkins,' he said. 'Country bumpkins.'

'Ja...' Klaus quipped, not sure his relationship with Russell was sufficiently personal for such a correction of his use of English idioms.

'So Welsh gays and lesbians had never spoken with one voice,' Russell said.

'That's right... and the Assembly was saying 'please come and talk to us about equality and gay rights'.'

'And what about Stonewall, or are they too London based?'

'You'll have to ask John about this,' Klaus said. 'Stonewall is somewhere in the picture, but you must have lived in Wales long enough to know how complicated it is between the Welsh and the English.'

Russell sipped his port. 'D'you like it?'

'It tastes like a very dry sherry,' Klaus said.

'But four times as expensive, my dear,' Russell sniped.

Klaus wanted to like him, but he wasn't making it easy.

'So who's holding the fort while John's off sick?'

'I don't know the term "holding the fort", but I suppose it means 'in control' or something?'

'Yes, what's happening to the LGB Forum?'

'John's a team player,' Klaus said. 'Okay, so he often gets to be the spokesman – you know how much he can talk... and sometimes he even talks sense – but the work with the police and with the Assembly wasn't John working on his own. Like I said, he's good at bringing people together and getting them to focus.' He sipped his port and decided that he preferred a good dry sherry. 'Anyway, John stood down as the chair of the LGB Forum in the spring; he was doing that, and the police work, on top of his full time job and it was too much.'

'It's a bit ironic that he should get heart trouble after he'd started to slow down,' Russell said.

'Perhaps... if he'd still been doing all that work, he might not have been so lucky.'

'And when he's fully recovered —' John's footsteps on the stairs cut him off. 'We were just talking about you.'

John came into the lounge carrying a small package wrapped in pink paper. 'It's just something small,' he said. 'Last time I was here I saw that you liked musicals.'

'Lesley Garrett, 'I Will Wait For You',' Russell read after

338

tearing the wrapping away from the CD.

'It's a mixture of show tunes and opera,' Klaus said.

'If you're opera queens you might find the CDs in the bottom left hand cupboard to your taste,' Russell offered. He got up and moved to the B&O. 'She's so gorgeously brash, don't you think?' he quipped as he ejected Shirley Bassey. 'What about Bellini's 'Norma'? I've got a digitally re-mastered recording of Maria Callas at La Scala in Milan from 1954.'

'That would be wonderful,' Klaus said. 'We just saw 'Norma' in Düsseldorf with my brother last May.'

Russell got down on his knees and opened up his 'opera' cupboard. 'I don't listen to these much anymore,' he said. 'Opera's such hard work. I know that Midler and Streisand and Minnelli are just brain candy, but they keep the silences at bay.'

'So, you like Wagner,' John said as he hunched down at Russell's side and scanned the rows of CDs.

'In the late eighties I went to the Bayreuth Festival three or four years on the run and when I lived in London we were regulars at Covent Garden.' The bell of a timer rang out in the kitchen. 'Time to put my pinny back on,' he said, rising to his feet. 'Dinner will be about ten minutes. Why don't you choose the music; whatever you like... and help yourselves to the port.'

Klaus knelt next to John before the impressive CD collection.

'And... thank you both for coming to stay,' Russell said, standing at the door. 'It means a lot to me.'

The Streets of
Francisco
1981-84

Through September, looking from the roof garden of 1815 Arch Street in Berkeley, the sun falls into the Pacific Ocean between the palm trees that grow lower down the hill on Spruce and Walnut, and the uprights of the Golden Gate Bridge on the distant horizon. The large bay window of John's room in apartment 303 faces directly west across the Bay. Above the bristled scarlet and yellow flowers of a bottlebrush tree, San Francisco's skyscrapers fill the two left panes, the bridge spans the middle one and Mount Tamalpais rises behind Sausalito in the centre of the two on the right.

The curtains weren't heavy enough to keep out the red glow of the sunset; he twisted beneath the damp cotton sheet, wondering about the woman whose song and soulful voice had woven with his dreams: *'Filling up and spilling over, it's an endless waterfall, filling up and spilling over, over all. Filling up and spilling over....'* He'd slept for just an hour. Still exhausted by jet lag and the unforeseen overnight delay in the departure lounge at JFK – because Freddie Laker's Sky Train had been forced to refuel in Newfoundland causing him to miss his connection – John hauled himself from his bed, pulled on his jeans and a T-shirt, and made for the roof.

The woman sat on a slatted table, her bare feet on a bench, and strummed her guitar:

"Sometimes it takes a rainy day
Just to let you know everything's gonna be all right.
I've been dreaming in the sun, won't you wake me up someone
I need a little peace of mind, oh I need a little peace of mind..."

She stopped singing when she saw him approach.

'You don't get too many rainy days in California,' he said. He tried to stifle a chuckle as he remembered Alan, one of the men who'd met him at San Francisco airport earlier that afternoon, telling him about the drought... and the 'restroom code': 'If it's yellow, let it mellow.'

'Well hello there,' she said, a jolly smile jarring with the mood of her song. 'You must be my new neighbour from Wales. I'm Bonnie Beck, but everyone calls me Bee-Bee... or just Bee. I saw you when Alan and Perry brought your bags up. I'm in 302.'

'I think I must be just underneath here, so when I heard you singing I came to explore. I'm not intruding, am I?'

'No,' she said, pushing back her long, dark hair and shaking her head into the sky as if she were trying to throw off the melancholy that dulled her hazel eyes. 'The September sunsets are spectacular. Usually there are more people up here, with a bottle of wine or a few beers.'

John took in his new landscape. He'd grown up with sunsets

341

over Cardigan Bay, but from this vantage point, high in the Berkeley Hills, he got the first sense of what people meant when they talked about America's big sky.

'You're so lucky,' she said. 'To have the room right below us, I mean. Just about everyone covets that room. You've got the best view at Pacific School of Religion.' She twisted to her left and pointed to the tall clock tower that poked through the eucalyptus trees in the near distance. 'I look south across Cal campus. That's the Campanile, and in the trees there you have the main buildings of UC Berkeley. I've got to screw my neck out my window to see the City and the Trans-Am.' She pointed across the Bay to the pyramid skyscraper, its whiteness tinged pink, some of its windows aflame with reflections of the dying sun. 'And that's mega-bucks land over there,' she said, gesturing to the northern end of the Golden Gate. 'Marin County. Some folks reckon those guys are the wealthiest in the state, and lots of the houses along the shore are just awesome.'

'Aren't there some redwoods over there? I'd love to see some Sequoias.'

'Sure, Muir Woods is just the other side of Mount Tam. They're the closest, I guess, but you know – there are redwoods all the way up the coast, so go north if you get the chance, otherwise you'll just have to mill around with all the tourists off of the tour busses from the City.'

'It's quite a spectacle,' he said, taking in the vista again.

For a few moments they watched the Pacific Ocean engulf the sun. He was astonished by the swiftness of the dusk. Before his eyes, as if someone higher up in the Berkeley Hills had thrown handfuls of diamond into the Bay's basin, lights began to twinkle.

'There's a group of us going over to La Val's on Euclid for

pizza and beer,' Bee ventured. 'Why don't you join us?'

'I'd like that,' he said, reflecting that his desire to get to know people was greater than his need for sleep.

'I'll call by in about forty-five minutes and we can go on over there together; it's only a ten-minute walk.'

They strolled beneath the line of California fan palms that grew along Ridge Road. Thick grey-ringed trunks thrust into the clear night sky. Sixty feet above them the leafy crowns, like giant feather dusters, buffed the stars until they gleamed.

'This is the new library,' Bee said pointing out the sleek glass and concrete building to their right. 'And on the left, just along here, is the Episcopalian school. You know that all of the seminaries on Holy Hill are part of the GTU... the Graduate Theological Union?'

'I saw that in the prospectus but I'm not sure what it means,' John said.

'Well, each denomination likes its own students, especially if they're ministry candidates, to be registered with them. Most of the Episcopalians will be at CDSP, the Baptists go to ABSW, Lutherans to PLTS and so on. You get to work out the acronyms, and there are lots of them!' She laughed. 'I was so confused by it all when I got here, but this way each denomination ensures that their own future priests and ministers have a core curriculum that's acceptable. Beyond the basic requirements, students can take courses at any of the seminaries.'

'But Pacific School of Religion has people from all denominations, doesn't it?'

'That's right; it's interdenominational... and celebrates diversity in more ways than one.'

'Oh-kay,' he said, looking curiously at her. 'But I'm not sure

343

I'm picking up on all of what you're implying.'

'Because PSR isn't bound to a denomination it's probably the most radical seminary in the west,' she said, with what John interpreted as considerable pride. 'We've got black and Asian teachers, and lots of women on the Faculty – and lots of women students too, Roman Catholic women especially; they don't get too many opportunities in the Catholic seminaries.'

'Right, I'm with you.'

'And then there are folks like you.'

'Overseas students?'

'Yeh, lots of people from overseas, but also gays and lesbians.'

'Am I *so* obvious?' he asked, more intrigued than troubled.

'You're a celebrity, Mr World Council of Churches Scholar for 1981!'

'No, Bee. You're pulling my leg.'

'I'm not touching your legs,' she said, her hands raised above her shoulders.

'You're teasing me,' he protested.

'No,' she said, shaking her head. She mimicked someone John had yet to meet: "This year's WCC scholar is a gay man from Wales who's come to California to study the American churches' response to gays and lesbians".'

'It's public knowledge?'

'I guess PSR is proud to have you,' she quipped. 'It's only my impression, for what it's worth, but I do two afternoons' work-study in admissions and you've been the focus of gossip once or twice. Alan thinks you're hot; he was smitten by the photographs you sent.'

'Those snaps... for all of the different ID cards? They were awful; from a Woolworth slot machine.' He recalled the tall, fair-haired man whose smile revealed gleaming teeth and whose muscular arms bulged and strained the cotton print of his shirtsleeves when he'd lifted the suitcases into the trunk of the car. 'You're not serious are you – Alan fancies me?'

'You can bet your bottom dollar that the Admissions Secretary doesn't make the trip out to SFO to meet all of the overseas students,' she said.

'So... are there lots of gay students?' he quizzed, trying not to think about Alan.

'Maybe three or four who've come out in the last year or two – but, you know, if you're in the ordination process, that closet door stays slammed shut.'

'It's hard for me to believe that being gay is such a novelty, in California of all places.'

'Outside the Bay Area they're pretty red-neck,' she said, sternly matter-of-fact. 'They voted Ronald Reagan governor for heaven's sake. And – this *is* seminary. Homosexuality is still a difficult issue here.' Her words seemed to create a sense of threat she hadn't intended. 'Of course, MCC sends students here to do the M.Div.,' she added to lighten things up.

John's face betrayed his curiosity; he knew she wasn't talking cricket.

'You don't know about the Metropolitan Community Church?' she asked, her face lit up with surprise. 'Most folks think it's a gay denomination, but officially I guess it's gay and lesbian friendly. You should go along to some of their services; they're real interesting. The minister at the San Francisco church is such a fine preacher, and they get congregations of two or three hundred every Sunday. MCC's been sending students here for three or four years now, and those guys have fought so hard to get into married student housing. There's a lesbian couple in one of the apartments on Le Conte and two cute boys live together over on Virginia.'

'So I shouldn't expect too much hostility on campus, being such a celebrity I mean,' he said with a cheeky grin.

'Look, John, I may be wrong,' she offered, much too seriously. 'I didn't mean to put you on tenterhooks, and I'm sorry if I've spoken out of turn, but I do think you're probably the first student to come to PSR specifically to look at gay and lesbian ministry, and with the WCC scholarship and all, it gives you profile.'

'Yes, I can see that... and I can see that I might add an extra notch to PSR's radical credentials.'

'But you've got balls enough,' she quipped with a grin. 'You must have weathered a few storms to get this far.'

'I guess I'm a survivor,' he said. He smiled to himself – but he wasn't sure if it was because he was slipping so easily into Americanisms like *I guess*, or because he heard Elen Morgan say 'the journey is home even when you're crawling through thorns.'

'So... this is Euclid Avenue,' Bee said as they turned into a bustling street block. 'There's a pharmacy just here, and the Seven Palms over there is a small grocery store. All of the restaurants are good and not too expensive. At the bottom is Hearst Avenue; if you cross over down there you're immediately on Cal campus and it's just a ten or fifteen minute walk right over to Telegraph.'

He was amazed just how lively it was on that 400 yard stretch of Euclid between Ridge and Hearst. Flashing neon signs beckoned attention and a dozen strains of music suggested atmosphere in the different establishments. Tanned young people in T-shirts, jeans and cut-offs milled along the broad sidewalk. Outside Swensen's ice cream parlour there was a good-humoured queue.

'The Dynasty has really good Cantonese food,' she said, pointing across the street.

He laughed; her pronunciation was such that he heard *Dine-nasty*. 'They have seagull traps on the roof, I suppose,' he quipped, recalling all the rumours about Aberystwyth's only Chinese restaurant.

'I'm sorry,' she fired back. 'What did you say?'

He heard the barb in her tone and opted not to explain his snide remark. 'It's nothing. I must have misheard you.'

'The Bagel Factory over there serves Peet's Coffee,' she offered, regaining her tour guide poise. 'You should try some; it's the best coffee on the whole West Coast... probably all of America!'

'I drink tea.'

'Peet's do some teas as well; Oolong and China Black, and lots of herbal blends,' she said without pronouncing the 'h' in herbal.

'If I can find a supply of Ty-phoo somewhere I'll be happy.'

A frown drew her sad hazel eyes deeply into her face behind puffed cheeks. 'But we Americans are coffee drinkers, John! You really should try Peet's Sumatra; it is to die for.'

He shrugged, and thought of all the jars of instant powder and granules on the shelves of the Co-op on Terrace Road in Aberystwyth.

'Why don't you come by for breakfast in the morning?' she coaxed as they reached La Val's. 'I always keep some of Peet's house-blend in the refridge; a small pot is all you need when you're pulling an all-nighter on a term paper.'

'I'm so jet-lagged that once I get off to sleep I'll probably need someone to knock me up in the morning, so I'm not promising —'

Her shrieks of laughter cut him off.

'What did I do?' he asked with a bemused grimace.

'Don't go asking your room-mates to 'knock you up' Honey,' she said through her mirth. 'Not unless you want a black eye.'

*   *   *

Wesley and Irvin were about to begin their third year on the joint M.A./M.Div. programme. Most of their belongings were already boxed-up, and apartment 303 didn't have much of a lived-in feeling. They were moving off campus, Wes to a studio apartment on Arch at Virginia and Irv into a duplex with his partner, a physician at Alta Bates Hospital who could afford the rents around Oakland's Lake Merritt. John hadn't seen much of Irv but he'd talked to Wesley, a tall, striking man from Georgia who was perhaps in his early thirties; in John's mind Wes was Sidney Poitier in *To Sir, With Love*. The mid-Wales coast was pretty white; he'd served the occasional day-tripper in the chip shop and the bar of the Marine, but Wes was the first black man he'd ever spoken with beyond courteous pleasantries and being doctored to by Jatunga Arachchi.

'I sure am sorry this place is such a mess,' Wes said. 'Irv and me, we're going camping up to Yosemite for a couple of days before the semester starts, so we need to get all of this stuff packed up and ready to move.'

John didn't make too much of an effort with his two roomies once he'd realised they were leaving, and despite the clutter, he could see a reason to be grateful that they were moving out; at least he and any new room-mates would be able to start as equals in a neutral space.

He let the orientation schedule arranged by CAPSR, the seminary's community association, carry him through the first exhausting days. The week-long programme of events, seminars and group work, intended to ease new students into PSR and Berkeley life, was full and tight. John found himself in Bee's 'breakfast cluster' – a group of eight students that included Ann and Nathan, two of the people he'd met that first evening in La Val's, and Denny Paltridge, one of the few openly gay men on campus, already in his senior year. The cluster didn't just meet for breakfast of fresh-squeezed orange juice, Peet's coffee and doughnuts in the roof garden at eight-thirty every morning, but came together at different times to consolidate information, discuss and problem-solve. They thrashed out the details of the work-study programme, student loans and course registration, and as orientation week progressed, they gathered anecdotes from middlers and seniors about the teachers and courses that were a must – any of Lebacqz's ethics classes, Chaney and Coote's seminar on the Prophets, Bob McAfee Brown's course on theology in Wiesel's novels and Foster's Bonhoeffer colloquium. John particularly liked the sound of Albie Smith's practical symposium on Non-traditional Ministries, and the San Francisco Urban Ministry Programme run by a woman called Hope. He made appointments to meet with a number of the Faculty; some of the courses he wanted had prerequisites for students in the regular masters' programmes, but Alan, on their ride in from the airport, had said that as the WCC Scholar, he'd be able to register for any course that took his fancy, as long as the course leader was willing to take him on.

Ann had a broad, southern accent and John loved the sing-song way she greeted them on the roof at breakfast with 'How you all doing this morning?' He'd warmed to her when they'd talked over that first pizza and beer in La Val's. In less than fifteen minutes, he'd learned that she came from a long line of lawyers and teachers; an established Dallas family of not inconsiderable means, he'd concluded. Ann had done her undergraduate years at Duke and then worked for a couple of years up in Boston doing community organising. She explained that the Episcopalian bishops in her home state were mostly opposed to the ordination of women. To become a priest, she'd have to go back to North Carolina, or someplace else in the South; she couldn't see herself settling in a northern Yankee state.

John also heard about her 1971 Dodge Demon with the wrecked air-con. Driving from Dallas to Berkeley had taken Ann and her sister four days, and motoring through New Mexico and Arizona in the late summer without air-conditioning had been a sweaty nightmare! 'Now that I'm a student again, I guess keeping Ma Dodge is an expensive luxury,' she said.

Wondering whether the car's nickname had anything to do with a daemon mother back in Dallas, John suggested she think about sharing the car, and all its costs, with one or two others.

'You bright man,' she said, taking him aback. 'Why didn't I think of a car co-op?'

At that point Nathan had joined their conversation and the three of them began to explore the possibilities of sharing Ma Dodge.

John had overheard Nathan telling Bee and the others that he came from New Jersey. He played tennis, liked running and had degrees from Brown and Yale. He also liked to travel, and especially loved Spain, though his Spanish was bad. John noticed the Taizé cross hanging from a leather thong against his tie-dye T-shirt with a pang of nostalgia. Seeing the way his shirt strained against the muscles of his chest, John had become aroused.

But Nathan had such bad skin. The knot of the leather thong at the nape of his neck nestled amid a small cluster of angry red volcanoes, their yellow caps seemingly ready to erupt. His cheeks were pockmarked from a decade or more of acne, and on his chin a shiny red swelling suggested a further breakout in the near future. Travels in Europe, and an experience at Taizé, should have given them common ground on which to be easy with one another, but John was confused by the forces of attraction and repulsion vying inside him.

Nathan was such a natural raconteur that by the middle of orientation week John failed to notice the pustules that had burst open on his chin. They sat on the shady deck at the rear of the refectory after a sandwich lunch and talked about Taizé. Nate's greenish eyes had a way of holding the gaze, which left John wondering about possibilities – but Nate had given no clues, despite John's stories about Henk and *The Men with the Pink Triangle*. Later that day, watching the sun set from his room, John wondered about the nature of sexual attraction: Nate was lovely, even handsome – once you got past the zits.

Denny Paltridge's blemish free face wouldn't have been out of context in a *GQ* ad for some lavishly expensive skin-care products pitched at the modern man. He wore pastel coloured, short-sleeved shirts with button-down collars and a cheeky green crocodile on the pockets, khaki chinos, and what John would have called deck shoes and Denny called Topsiders. It was a look John came to recognise as common amongst the undergraduates at UC Berkeley; walking across Sproul Plaza with Ann, she'd described the style as 'preppy'. Denny's hair seemed a bit *big*; too thick, too long and too well groomed, and he held himself in too feminine a manner, his gestures often seeming affected, like a teenage girl trying to be sophisticated. But he was powerfully built. Gym-worked muscles, bulging from his shirtsleeves, confounded the illusion of effeminacy and the cotton fabric of his chinos hugged the contours of beefy buttocks.

'What kind of self-respecting faggot are you anyway?' he quizzed the first time they were alone together on the roof. A gleaming smile blunted his sharpness. 'You're so straight.'

'I come from Wales, Denny,' was all John could think of in riposte.

'I'll have to take you under my wing then, won't I?' he said with a seditious wink. 'We can start by doing some shopping. What d'you say we go over to the Castro one Saturday afternoon and get you kitted out?'

'That'll be a challenge on my budget.'

'Well Honey,' he said, and bit his lip. 'The thrift stores may be alright for the Berkeley hippies and the street-people, but you need a make-over.'

Feeling uncomfortable, John folded the cardboard doughnut tray ready for recycling and considered Denny's motives. Was he just being a bitchy queen?

'If you got rid of that beard,' he continued, pushing John's chin from side to side with a gentle flick of his index finger. 'And maybe you could brush a bit of mascara into that excuse for a moustache. Hmm, that might work!' He paused. 'You got anything against wearing hand-me-downs?'

John shrugged.

'I was a clone for a couple of months, and I've got a dozen check shirts I won't be wearing ever again. You might even get into the Levi's.'

Denny interpreted John's blank expression.

'Oh my God – this is worse than I thought.' He brought his hand up to his mouth and rested his chin in his palm. 'When I take you up to the Castro you'll see all these guys that look the same: Levi's, check shirt, heavy moustache. They're called *clones*. I don't know what got into my head, turning myself into one of them. I looked hideous with a nailbrush under my nose.'

'I'm not sure I came to California to become some kind of parody,' John said, deciding that Denny had overstepped the mark.

'Okay, Honey, so maybe the mascara was pushing it too far.' Denny offered an appeasing wink. 'You're welcome to come see what's in my closet. Some of the shirts will suit your colouring; and besides, you're a cute Brit so you'll get away with anything. I tell you, some of the guys in the Bear Pit will be creaming themselves just listening to you talk!'

Constance Matthews managed the kitchen. 'So you're the boy from Wales who needs a job,' she said.

'Yes… in Admissions they told me that foreigners don't qualify for the work-study jobs so I'm stuck with janitorial or groundwork.'

She described the chores of a cleaning job; an hour every weekday to make sure the rest rooms in the dining block (staff and public) were all in order, and seven hours at the weekend to give the dining hall and kitchen a good going over. He duly expressed his interest in the position, mainly because he could fit the hours in to suit himself.

'You'll need to fill out this form,' she said. 'The job's yours.'

*   *   *

353

Professor Albie Smith sucked on his pipe and gazed through the blue smoke. 'Your scholarship sees you through to next summer, right?'

'Yes, but the finances are all a bit tight and I have to work twelve hours a week. I've got a cleaning job in the kitchen.'

'You and ninety percent of the other grad students at PSR,' he said. 'I guess, coming from Great Britain, you don't have much experience of paying your way through school.'

John smiled a nod and wondered about the professor's accent.

'Are you certain you couldn't raise the funds to stay? I think, from what you've told me, you'd gain a lot from the master's programme, and if you could do the M.A. as well as the M.Div —'

'I don't qualify for any student loans in this country, Dr Smith.'

'Albie,' he said. 'Call me Albie.'

John warmed to him. None of his teachers back home had ever invited such familiarity. Albie leaned forwards into a shaft of morning sunlight, which caught the tight black curls on his head. John saw the glisten of hair gel and for a fleeting second he found himself wondering why a man in his forties would slick his hair.

'Couldn't you borrow money from your family? Fifteen thousand dollars, maybe even as little as ten if you could find a job that pays more than being a janitor. It'd be worth it.'

'I don't know whether I can even start thinking about that, Dr — Albie.'

'I guess I'm getting too excited for you,' he said, and sucked on his pipe.

'I've got this year, that's clear in my mind. I want to make the most of it, and I'd really like to do your class.'

354

'And you're thinking about the Urban Ministry Programme in the City with Grace Hope?'

'Yes.'

'Hmm... listen John.' He grasped the pipe from his mouth and waved it before his face. 'I'd be prepared to supervise you in what we call a private study. You see, my Non-traditional Ministries symposium only touches on homosexuality, and most of Grace's work centres around the Tenderloin district – and you won't see too many gay folks down there amongst the pimps, hookers and pushers. But as the WCC Scholar, you don't have to be tied to specific courses, so maybe you could be linked to Grace's programme in San Francisco, but have the freedom to look at all of the different aspects of ministry to gays and lesbians in the City. It would be a jointly supervised private study for the whole semester. What do you think?'

John tried to frame Albie's idea, but found himself distracted by the different shades of blackness on the palms of his hands, the inside of his forearms and the folds of his ears.

'I could talk to Grace, if you like?' Albie encouraged.

'It sounds exciting,' he said, uncertain what the proposition might entail, but finding himself trusting Albie Smith's faith in him, and his enthusiasm for the possibilities.

When Albie came off the phone he was beaming. 'Grace wants you to call her; she'd like to talk with you before she commits herself, but she's not antagonistic to the idea.' He scribbled her number on a piece of paper and handed it across the desk. 'I want you to read Nouwen's book, *The Wounded Healer*, and after you've been over to see Grace come back and see me; I'll have a book list for you and we can talk up some objectives.'

John rode BART into the City and got off at Powell, just as Denny had suggested. Reaching the top of the stairs from the underground station, he saw the city's skyscrapers rear up along Market Street. He searched the skyline for the Trans-Am pyramid but couldn't see its sleek white form amid all the smoked glass and steel. Turning onto the wide sidewalk at the top of the escalator, the clanging of a bell drew his attention and he watched as a cable car pulled onto the turn-around at the bottom of Powell Street. Its bell continued to clang as it revolved through 180 degrees in readiness for its journey back over the hills to Fisherman's Wharf. Scenes from countless episodes of *Streets of San Francisco* flooded his memory; Michael Douglas and Karl Malden were surely just around the corner, staking out some seedy residential hotel before a drug bust.

Denny had said that the walk into downtown Berkeley, and the ride on the Bay Area Rapid Transport train into the City, would take about an hour. He'd given himself two hours to be safe; he didn't want to be late for his meeting with Grace Hope. Finding himself with more than an hour to kill, he walked along Eddy Street as far as Jones and located the building that housed the Urban Ministry Programme. In the lobby a small plaque announced the SFUMP's suite of offices on the sixth floor. Feeling secure that he'd have no problem finding the building again he decided to explore the district.

In many a doorway, prostitutes in miniskirts, faux furs and feather boas touted for business, and at most of the intersections, drug dealers sold their powders and pills with impunity. The garish lights of pornography stores flashed a welcome, and bored-looking men behind glass screens sang the praises of the latest clips in the twenty-five cent movie booths.

He quickly realised that each store had its speciality – big black women, lesbian follies, Latino transsexuals, well-hung men and even anal pleasures. The windows of the stores were blacked out, and though most entrances were draped with curtains, he caught glimpses of the brightly lit interiors; a display of dildos, life-like but overstated in length and girth, a blow up doll, her staring eyes reminiscent of some cartoon character – Betty Boop or Olive Oil, a shelf of rubber vaginas with tufts of pubic hair in different colours. The streets of Aberystwyth hadn't prepared him for the Tenderloin.

And there were street-people. Bedraggled bag-ladies lugged their possessions in discarded carrier bags from Gumps and Nieman Marcus – one so rich in material belongings that she pushed a wobble-wheeled Safeway's shopping trolley brimming with the jetsam of her existence. And shabby men, grasping paper bags from which bottle necks protruded – glass phalluses that ejaculated hard liquor to numb the knocks from the street's hard edges. One vagrant with no shoes, his trousers stained crisp, the rancid smell obvious even from the safe distance of a wary pedestrian, ranted at the passers-by. John remembered how Bee had berated Ronald Reagan's past administrations in Sacramento for closing down the long-stay mental hospitals throughout California without any thought to the provision of community care.

Grace Hope was a diminutive woman. She wore no make-up and her face was wrinkled; mid-fifties, John thought, but her hair was still blonde, and not the bottled kind.

'Here at the SFUMP our ministry is devoted to the people of the Tenderloin,' she said after the briefest of introductions. 'Albie Smith tells me you're interested in gays and lesbians.'

357

John shared his proposal, more refined now after the talk with Albie.

'We believe that vital Christian ministry moves beyond church walls,' she said. 'We have to reach people where they live and work, on the streets out there, in the residential hotels, the brothels, the porn stores. Most of the gay life in this district is hustling; a lot of the male-to-female transsexuals pay for their hormone treatments and surgery by prostituting themselves. Those that have developed breasts already, but haven't had their genital surgery yet... well, let's just say that there are guys who come to stay at the St Francis and the Hilton who'll pay big bucks for an hour of their company.'

'I guess it's really important to take Jesus to such places,' John said, a bit surprised by her candour and shocked by her words.

'That's a very triumphalist... a very colonial, nineteenth century view of mission,' Grace accused, after a moment in which she'd seemed to disbelieve what she'd heard. 'Every one of those folks on the sidewalks down there has been given gifts for the common good; our work seeks to draw out and affirm those gifts through personal, face-to-face ministry.'

'I see,' John said, his discomfort obvious.

'How well d'you know your Bible?'

'We had to learn tracts every week for Sunday School.'

'"But seek the welfare of the city where I have sent you into exile, and pray to the Lord on its behalf, for in its welfare you will find your welfare,"' she quoted in a slightly preachy tone.

'One of the prophets I'd guess,' he said, feeling his grasp on the interview slip away. 'Amos... maybe?'

'Jeremiah twenty-nine, verse seven,' she said. 'What do you think it means?'

The image of a full-breasted *man* with a penis invaded his

358

mind's eye and he couldn't concentrate on Jeremiah's words.

'Think about it.' The trace of a smile on her face suggested she was content that he was so discomforted. 'Jesus is already walking those streets, John,' she said, her tone more compassionate. 'We just need to be open enough to see his face in the pimps and hookers, and in all those street-people.'

And John was back in the flat he'd shared with Steff in Aberystwyth. *And you're the first to help me see the face of Christ in a homosexual*, Janice had said. He remembered how her words had troubled him.

* * *

Connie Matthews stood behind the long, woodblock-topped unit that ran down the middle of the kitchen for half its length, the blue wrap-around apron tight against her impressive bosom.

'It can get real cold in the City at night,' she said, and continued to chop a head of celery. Her ampleness exaggerated the slicing motion of the professional cook and the earrings that dangled almost to her shoulders swung erratically whilst the bangles on each of her forearms clinked and jangled.

'Ann said I could borrow her ski jacket,' John said.

'And how you going to get home safe at four o'clock in the morning?'

'We've worked out a deal so I get to use her car.'

'You and that pretty yellow rose of Texas got something going on?' she quizzed, her tone light and singsong.

'You know I'm gay, Connie,' he said, not really knowing that she knew.

'You are?' she shrieked. The motion of her chopping faltered. 'My... that's real white of you,' she said just loud enough to be audible across the kitchen.

John busied himself, but remained silent; he heard Connie's knife regain its rhythm against the woodblock worktop. He pushed the gallon drum of bleach back onto the shelf beneath the sink and wondered if the reference to his whiteness was a negative.

'You're doing a fine job in those restrooms,' she said. 'And I don't ever remember this worktop looking so good. Maybe, as the semester moves on, I could find you some more work helping in the kitchen... if you need the money?'

'Well... yes, I guess I could manage a few more hours.'

'I get to cater for lots of weddings, birthday celebrations and the like; it wouldn't be regular... not every week, but maybe once a month I could give you five or six hours general kitchen duties; and I could pay you a dollar fifty more an hour than PSR pays you.'

'That'd be just swell,' he said, mimicking one of her often used phrases.

'You get on out of here,' she yelled with a golden-toothed grin. 'Some of you white boys are too cheeky for your own good.'

John blew her a kiss and dashed off to shower before his first class of the day.

Professor Robert McAfee Brown pushed back the lock of white hair that fell across his forehead.

'We need to see the *doing* of theology as a process,' he said. 'And I introduce that word with some hesitation because I don't want you to get confused with the process-philosophy of Alfred North Whitehead.'

John had never heard of Whitehead and not for the first

time, since he'd started to attend classes, he began to wonder whether he had the breadth of knowledge necessary to warrant his place at PSR.

'To avoid any confusion, I'm going to preface the word 'process' with a few adjectives,' Bob Brown continued. '*Doing* theology has to be an open-ended process and a corporate process; it is also, I suggest, a self-correcting process and an engaged process.'

The lecture room was too full for comfort, but then all of McAfee Brown's classes were over-subscribed. John felt the trickle of sweat dampen his collar, but despite the airlessness, everyone seemed to hang on the professor's words.

'We can no longer assume that theology will come to fixed positions, that will be securely defined and nailed down for generations of inspection. As an open-ended process, theology will involve ongoing reflection, alternating between looking at its past conclusions and reviewing them in light of the present world seen from the standpoint of the oppressed.' He paused and looked over his audience, wondering if they were beginning to grasp the implications of his assertion. 'For us in North America, that means we have to start listening to the experiences of the oppressed peoples in our own society; women and blacks, native Americans, gay people... the illegal migrant workers picking the fruits in the Central Valley just over the hills out there.'

John tried to stifle the shock of excitement that caught his breath. Perhaps he'd misheard what the professor had said, or just not understood. The Sunday Library Group's choruses echoed in that piece of himself that resided in Aberystwyth and Arwel Thomas was kneeling at his side in the Denbigh Asylum saying a prayer that was inaudible over Jatunga Arachchi's sweet talk. He forced himself to concentrate on Bob Brown's words.

'*Doing* theology is a corporate process in as much as the input will come from many sources and many disciplines. And it will be an engaged process; from start to finish, those of us who choose to 'do theology' in this fashion, theology in a new key if you like music metaphors, must be doing it with our lives as well as with their heads and minds. Theology in a new key is not so much an activity of the classroom but an engagement in the arena of human need, immersed in the stuff of politics, engaged in the struggles of all oppressed peoples, and being open to personal risks for the sake of those whom the world counts as nothing.'

John sat in the roof garden and allowed his awe at the view to distract the thoughts that had vied through the day since Bob Brown's lecture. The vehemence of Adam and the Sunday Library Group's attacks, and the vividness of the flashbacks to Denbigh – after so many years – had distressed him. Just before the sun set, Ann joined him. Over a six-pack of Budweiser he told her his story.

'No wonder those old ghosts have been assailing you all day,' she said. 'They obviously can't cope with having you learn a different song in a new key.'

* * *

Connie had been right about how cold it could be on San Francisco's streets at midnight during the Fall. When Ann had reached for the red, overstuffed ski jacket from her wardrobe and handed it to John on a semi-permanent loan, he thought he might look ridiculous, enfolded in its downy bulk. Walking beside Troy Liddell up Polk Street towards the Empress Hotel, snugly insulated from the chill, he made a mental note to buy Ann a couple of six-packs as a gesture of his gratitude.

Troy was a short, stocky man with lots of hair. Under his chin, the line of his beard was indistinguishable from the chest hair that spilled over his clergy collar. A small, but sturdy, silver ring pierced his left earlobe, and around his right wrist, where a watch might normally have nestled, he wore a two-inch wide, silver studded band of black leather. On previous visits to the Tenderloin, catching glimpses through the curtained doors of the porn stores, John had come to realise that burly, hirsute men had their own genre of titillating magazines, and he found himself wondering if Troy was *a bear*.

'Did Grace Hope fill you in on the Night Ministry?' he quizzed.

'She told me that you're funded by the San Fran Council of Churches, and that you and a small team of clergy serve the city, all night, every night.'

'We're a ministry of presence,' he said. 'I'm a United Methodist. I guess I'm the head honcho, the only one that's paid a full time stipend. My colleagues are a Lutheran, a couple of Episcopalians and one of the brothers from the Society of St Francis.'

'What do you mean by 'a ministry of presence'?' John asked, remembering how Grace had scorned his notion of mission; he didn't want to make any assumptions, or make a fool of himself again.

'We just try to keep the mystery of God present to all these folks who aren't tucked up in bed,' he said. 'Every night, one of the team is out walking, meeting people on street corners, in bars and all-night coffee shops. Tonight we're going to the

Empress to be with a group of transsexuals that have made it their home while they're in the City. Every month I offer them a communion service. As you can probably guess, when you're still in the process of gender reassignment, local church congregations don't find it so easy to be welcoming.'

'Not even at Glide?'

'Ah... you've been to hear the Reverend Cecil Williams already?'

'Glide was an experience, so much more than just hearing an amazing preacher,' John said, surprised by Troy's derisory tone. 'I've never been to a church with such a diverse congregation, and their jazz group is spectacular.'

'Glide does some impressive work, I grant you, but it's not to everyone's taste. Some white folks can find it intimidating, and those that are less liberal in their worldview just get blown away.'

They passed one of the porn stores and John thought about the transsexuals. 'The people we're on our way to visit, for how long are they —' he searched for words. 'How long are they in-between?'

'How long is a piece of twine, John?'

'Grace was saying that a lot of these guys work as prostitutes.'

'Sure, and some are minor porn stars,' he said with a chuckle. 'There are a couple of stores over on Leavenworth that specialise in trannies; it might be an education if you dropped by.'

Under a plastic palm tree, in the gloomy lobby of the Empress Residence Hotel, five girls sat on two mock leather sofas. The upholstery on the arm of one sofa was torn and the yellow foam padding bulged from the tear like a huge, ripe zit. They could have been models, awaiting their troll along a catwalk: immaculate hair, polished fingernails, and carefully-done-though-heavy-make-up. It was just the Adam's apples that gave them away.

'Hi Troy,' a girl in a pink T-shirt straining across her bust called out in a gruff voice as they approached.

'How's it going, Mandy?'

'Good,' she said. 'Who's your cute friend?'

After everyone was introduced, Kristel fetched coffee, which they drank from polystyrene cups.

'One of Angel's tricks turned on her,' Mandy offered. 'He agreed to pay her 150, but after he was done he couldn't find his billfold.' There was a sharp edge of scorn in her tone.

'She got beat up real bad,' Rose said.

'She in the hospital?' Troy asked.

'No. They patched her up in the emergency room,' Mandy said. 'She doesn't want to come down tonight, not with her face all blue and puffy.

'But I think she'd like it if you'd call on her, Troy,' Rose said.

'Sure thing,' he quipped.

'What's the latest on this gay bowel syndrome scare?' Kristel's question cast John back to the day he'd been met at the airport by Perry and Alan; hadn't they talked about some diarrhoeal illness affecting gay men? 'Most of my punters want to fuck me, and they're welcome as long as they can afford the price tag on my butt,' the coarse man lurking inside Kristel said. 'But there's been a lot of talk on the street again; they're saying it's something to do with using amyl.'

'And some guys are so big you just gotta use amyl,' Mandy quipped.

'I only know what I read in the *Bay Area Reporter*,' Troy said. 'Maybe you gals should get yourselves on their mailing list.'

'One of the girls living over at the Dalt has had diarrhoea for a month,' Rosy said.

'She may have just picked up some amoebas,' Troy offered, trying to calm any hysteria before it broke. 'You all are still getting yourselves checked out regular for common sex diseases, aren't you?'

The girls nodded. There were a few half-hearted 'Yahs' and a 'Sure thing'.

'So, did someone remember to bring bread?' Troy asked into the awkward silence that had ensued.

'I walked all the way over to North Beach to buy this olive ciabatta,' Mandy said, taking the flattish, slipper-shaped loaf from a brown paper bag. 'It's five years this week since my Mamma died and I wondered... can we say the Mass for her, Troy?'

'Sure thing, Mandy. Was your mom from Italy?'

'No,' Mandy said with a trace of a chuckle. 'She lived all her life in Winnemucca, Nevada, but the one time she came to visit me in the City, this was the bread she liked best – with peanut butter and strawberry jelly.' Some of the girls laughed. 'Is it the wrong sort of bread for Mass?' she asked Troy, a look of panic in her eyes.

'Mandy, olive ciabatta is just perfect. Did someone bring wine?'

'Here,' Kristel said, passing over a half-full bottle of Paul Masson Merlot.

Troy flattened the brown paper bag in the centre of the sticky-stained, cigarette-charred coffee table and placed the rustic loaf on the makeshift tablecloth. After downing his coffee he poured a slug of the Merlot into the polystyrene cup, sloshed it around, drank the dregs, and filled the cup to within a centimetre of the rim with the deep plum-coloured wine.

'Would someone like to read?' he asked.

'If I can choose a bit, I'd be happy to,' Kristel said. 'I really like the story of the Samaritan woman at the well in John's Gospel.'

No one objected and Kristel thumbed through Troy's dog-eared Bible.

'After I've said the communion prayers we'll serve one another the bread and the wine, the way we usually do, passing the elements around the circle,' Troy said. 'When you offer the bread to your neighbour, you say "This is the Body of Christ" and when you offer the wine, you say "This is the Blood of Christ", and after you've received, you offer it on.'

Mandy, her huge breasts heaving under her pink T-shirt, served John, and he, in turn, offered the consecrated olive ciabatta and the Merlot in a polystyrene cup to Rosy.

Driving Ma Dodge back to Berkeley over the Bay Bridge at 4.30 in the morning, he wondered if the sacrament they'd shared in the Empress Residence Hotel wasn't perhaps closer to Jesus' breaking of bread during that last supper than any a silver-chaliced Eucharist, presided over by a priest in silk and lace, or the dour Calvinistic ministers' *Cymun* in the rude chapel on the wind-swept hill above the Mawddach.

For a few nights, after that first visit to the Empress Hotel, Dali's Jesus visited John in his dreams... well, a version of Dali's Jesus: the face was the same, but he had breasts and a penis, both exaggerated in the way that dreams can distort reality. Janice, from Aberystwyth, and Grace Hope joined this Jesus to drink Ty-phoo tea from polystyrene cups. They had a conversation about seeing the face of Christ in street people, in-betweens and homosexuals.

367

* * *

After scanning a copy of the *Bay Area Reporter*, and finding nothing about gay bowel syndrome in its columns, John decided to ask Denny about it.

'It's just a lot of rumours and whispers,' he said, looking into the sunset and sipping his wine.

'And what's amyl?' John quizzed.

'Oh, my dear boy,' he intoned with the melodic disdain of a Wagnerian diva.

'Just cut the crap, Denny. Aberystwyth's on a different planet to San Francisco and I'm an alien here; at least, that's what it says on my visa!'

'Amyl comes in little bottles, under all kinds of fancy names like *Rush* and *Locker Room*,' he began, a bit school-ma'amish, but trying his best to appear serious. 'It's also called *poppers*, because after inhaling from the bottle, the little ring of muscle in your tush just 'pops' open to let a fat dick in.' He burst out laughing.

'You're not a nice person, Denny Paltridge.'

'Oh, come on, naïve Welsh boy... I'm just not used to such innocence.'

John wished he could think of some witty response, but couldn't... so they watched the sky turn red.

'You've started going to the baths, haven't you?' Denny accused after a while.

'The baths? No... I've been so bombarded by new experiences and ideas these last six weeks... and then, with cleaning the kitchen at the weekend and all, I'm too exhausted most of the time to even think about sex.'

'Then it's time you came out on a hunting trip to the Castro,

368

before your balls burst. What are you doing for Halloween?'

'It's not such a big deal for us Brits. I've hardly even thought about it.'

'I'm going to a party in the City. I could get you invited.'

'Okay,' John said, surprising himself.

'Come see my costume,' he offered, jumping up with excitement. 'I don't have all the accessories yet, but... come see what you think.' He skipped on ahead, down from the roof to apartment 211. Reaching the open apartment door he called back to John: 'Sit in the lounge while I change... and help yourself to the wine on the table.'

When he heard Denny's feet pad along the hallway, John looked up from the pages of *The Advocate*.

'I still haven't found the shoes I want,' he said, doing a graceful turn in the middle of the floor, his arms outstretched.

'Oh my God... you can't go to a party looking like that.'

'Isn't it just beautiful?' he said, smoothing his hands down his slender waist and allowing them to rest on his hips.

'A leather corset and fishnet stockings,' John said, gawping at the obvious bulge in the crimson silk bikini briefs Denny wore beneath garters that hung from a lacy belt slung around his hips.

'It's an underbust Victorian basque,' he said, contemptuous of John's derision. 'Black leather with red leather appliqué and a silk lining. Isn't it just divine? I want some classic pumps with four-inch heels, slingbacks even, but they're not so easy to come by in a Size Eleven. And I was thinking of a studded, black leather collar, or maybe a feather boa.'

'I'm not sure I should come to this party,' John quipped.

'You will too,' he said, pointing a finger. 'And I'm going to help you find just the right costume for your coming-out ball.'

For a few days before the Halloween party, John walked around the decorators' debris in apartment 303 in the pair of green stilettos Denny had bought for him from a thrift store on Telegraph Avenue. He was surprised how easy it was to get the hang of them, and he quickly grew in confidence. The green and black PVC corset, however, remained in its box until Halloween afternoon.

'I look ridiculous,' John said, staring at the slightly scary, slightly erotic image of himself in the mirror on the inside of the wardrobe door.

'Honey, you look so sexy you'll have them crawling on their knees to lick the leather of those cute pumps. Crack that whip again and pout those moistened lips.'

'But what happens if we get pulled over by the Highway Patrol?'

'It's Halloween in the Bay Area, John. Anything goes!'

It was a balmy evening in the Berkeley Hills. Despite his earlier bravado, Denny showed up in a full-length raincoat, belted tightly and with the collar turned up. The feather boa, the whip, the studded collars and the high-heels were stowed in the trunk of his Mustang. John's fishnet-stockinged feet looked incongruous in his best black leather shoes.

'You might have to come back on BART,' Denny said as they approached the Bay Bridge toll plaza.

'I can drive, if you want to drink.'

'I was thinking more along the lines of what you'll do if I find a hot man,' he said as they drew towards the pay booth.

The toll collector, a woman in her sixties, wore pumpkin earrings that dangled to her shoulders. 'Happy Halloween, girls,' she said, as Denny handed her a dollar bill, his fingernails crimson to match the leather appliqué on his basque.

'Happy Halloween to you too ma'am,' he said, unbuttoning the raincoat and thrusting his leather sheathed torso towards the chuckling grandmother.

'And what if I'm the one who finds a hot man?' John quipped as they drove out over the Bay.

'Then I'll be jealous as hell.'

The two blocks of Castro Street between Market and 19th, closed off to traffic for the night, pulsed to the music from bars along the sidewalk and the pheromones of thousands of men in party mood. There were hundreds of scary drag queens with big hair, their gowns in sequins, taffeta and shantung. A muscle-bound Latino boy wore a feather – and nothing else. An eight-foot python, coiled around a black guy with a sapphire nipple ring and a G-string that didn't cover too much, flicked its forked tongue here and there on the marijuana-scented air. A posse of cowboys, in Levi's and chaps, swilled Budweiser from bottles and flirted with the queens. Others wore chaps without the Levi's, their bare muscled bottoms fondled and fingered by hands of anonymous strangers in the squeeze. White-faced nuns with lip-gloss and eye shadow – the Sisters of Perpetual Indulgence – rattled collecting boxes for the homeless gay teens who fled to the City from Red-neck country; and there were enough men in corsets to stage *The Rocky Horror Picture Show* in every theatre west of Lake Tahoe, and time warp the entire state.

By 11.30 the crowd had thinned as the revellers moved on to private parties. John sat on the curb outside the garishly lit up Castro Theatre, slipped off his high heels, and dug his thumbs into the soles of his aching feet.

'They're a bitch, aren't they?' Denny sympathised.

371

'I don't care,' John said. 'I don't think I've ever felt so alive and so... well, that I belong.'

'Welcome to paradise,' Denny said with a broad smile. 'You going to be able to walk the few blocks over to Scott's place? We've got an ice swan's chance in hell of getting a cab tonight.'

'I'm fine.'

Pushing his swollen feet back into the green stilettos, he pinched himself hard. *I must always remember what tonight feels like.*

The house on Sanchez Street, an Italianate Victorian with Corinthian columns on the porch and fancy carving on the façade that reminded John of the gingerbread houses in fairytale picture books, was lavishly decorated. The walls of the two large rooms on either side of the hallway at the front of the house were painted deep red and dark green, and the soft furnishings were of damask, velvet and rich brocades. On the polished mahogany, rosewood and lightly figured curly maple of occasional tables, buffet servers and lowboys, there were vases of tropical flowers the like of which he'd never seen: Birds of Paradise and Jungle Queen Ginger, Porcelain Roses with red, white and pink Anthuriums; Stromanthes, Jacquinii and Oncidium orchids.

The sumptuous opulence of Scott and Bill's home made him feel uneasy; what if he spilled something on the oriental rugs, or knocked over one of the flower arrangements? But Scott, dressed as Elizabeth Taylor's Cleopatra, quickly put him at his ease. 'You might be more comfortable if you slip off those heels,' he suggested in a voice heavy with Bostonian vowel sounds. 'I don't want you to break your ankles, and they do nothing for nineteenth century Ningxia and Kansu rugs.'

John sipped his non-alcoholic fruit punch and began to enjoy the company. As he milled amongst the guests, who seemed to be mostly lawyers, bankers, and health care workers, he learned that Scott worked as a physician at San Francisco General and had a national profile in chest medicine, while Bill, who was 'old money from the south', did something high up in Bank of America. For a while, he talked with an Episcopalian priest called Frank who was dressed in a gold lamé gown that clung to his slim, toned body. 'I'm a chaplain at SF General,' he said, and went on to say what a good preacher Scott had become in the couple of years since he'd trained as a lay Reader.

John's head spun with the possibilities that gay men in San Francisco had realised for themselves, and more than once he wondered how Denny, who'd 'disappeared', had found his way into this circle.

Frank circulated. John ladled himself another cup of fruit punch and caught himself eavesdropping the conversation of two middle-aged men with pallid, hairy bottoms constrained in leather harnesses. They were discussing the cut glass punch bowl, which reminded John of the prizes at the rifle range in Barmouth's summer fair.

'It's an American Brilliant,' the stockier of the two men said. '1880s or 90s.'

'Must be from Bill's family,' the hairier man said.

'In pristine condition, one like that would sell for 1,200 today.'

'You're kidding me.'

'No... just look at the complex patterns; those hobstars for instance – the more points they have the finer the piece. And look at all the swirls in that pinwheel.'

'I didn't know you knew so much about glass, Matt.'

'It's got lattice work too,' Matt said. 'Now, that makes it a real desirable item for a collector. I shouldn't wonder if they could get 1,500 bucks for it if all the cups are in one piece.'

The hairy man realised that John was listening and he smiled. John returned the smile and turned towards the French doors. *Bare bottomed men in chaps and harnesses discussing crystal glass, and a chest specialist dressed up as Cleopatra. San Francisco really is on a different planet. And there's Troy Liddell, and the in-betweens at the Empress... and a 'straight A' from Albie Smith for the reflection paper on* The Wounded Healer... *and Bob Brown inviting me to share my views on oppression as seen through pink-tinted spectacles – inviting me to sing in a new key. I've arrived! I've become a fully alive human being. I belong.*

Surfacing from this reverie, John found himself gripping the cut glass punch cup so firmly that the tips of his thumb and finger had turned white. He placed the ugly cup on the low boy, next to the vase of Bird of Paradise flowers. *Welcome to paradise* he heard Denny say again.

Denny's eyes were glazed, and his left stocking was held up by only two of the four garters. 'Have you visited the dream room yet?' he asked, readjusting the basque, which seemed to have slipped up and to the right.

'This whole night is a bit like a scene from a dream,' John said.

'Down the hall on the left,' Denny pointed with a wink, before Scott took him by the arm and led him towards the French doors that led out onto the garden deck.

Candles on two elaborate silver candelabra lit up the dream room. The floor, and what John assumed were two divan-type sofas, were covered with white sheets. A naked black man lay on one of the divans, and three men in various states of undress were taking pleasure in his, and one another's bodies.

On the other divan, a muscled drag queen, his sequined ball gown hitched up around his waist, was fucking a muscle bound Latino boy. John recognised the single ostrich feather that lay on the floor beneath the divan.

One of the half-dressed men, a cowboy, John supposed, from the unbuttoned check shirt and bandanna knotted around his neck, was fondling the nipple of another between his thumb and forefinger. He beckoned John over with a wink and a sideways nod of his head. John lingered at the door, first watching the Latino boy inhale the fumes from a bottle of Rush, and then, as his eyes became accustomed to the uneven light and the dancing shadows, he focused on the burly cowboy, who had the smallest erect penis he'd ever seen. The naked man on the divan raised his head, smiled, and blew John a kiss. Recognising the sapphire nipple ring, John wondered where the python might be lurking.

The cowboy with the small penis stepped forward and reached for the obvious distension in John's skimpy green briefs. His fingers played. At the same time, the snake man with the sapphire nipple turned onto his belly and slithered, like his python might have done, down from the divan and along the floor to John's feet. His tongue was warm against John's ankle. Fingers traced the length of John's leg before dextrously snapping open each garter. With a soothing, stroking motion, the stocking was peeled away and the flicking tongue made languid upward progress.

The other stocking followed the first, and then the snake man, whose tongue had reached the top of John's leg, tugged at the elasticated waistband of the green briefs with his bared teeth. John felt them snag on his erection, but the snake man's tongue soon freed them.

'Uncut – and so cute,' the snake man said, and fed hungrily.

John was only partially aware of other hands and other tongues. Someone kissed his neck, and a moistened finger teased its way between his cheeks setting off little tremors of pleasure. The corset fell away and his lovers, by unspoken code or intuition, led him to the divan. He was kissed deeply by a man whose tongue tasted of strawberries, and as his head was laid gently to rest on a silk pillow, he thought about the fruit punch, and the fruit bowl trophies in Barmouth's fair. And then he watched the python, its head bobbing in the flickering candlelight, part coiled and part draped over the high curtain pole, its forked tongue sensing the amyl spiked air.

*   *   *

After Wes and Irv moved out of 303, he'd expected new roommates to move in. Alan, from the Admissions Office, looked flustered when John opened the door to him just a few days into the Fall semester.

'They really didn't give us too much notice that they were moving off campus,' Alan said. 'I'm real sorry that you've found yourself on your own here, but in the circumstances, we can offer you a room in another apartment.'

'But what about my view?' John carped.

'We were thinking maybe it would be a good time to refurbish this apartment, John. It needs new drapes and carpets throughout, and all of the paintwork needs attention. A new shower, too.'

'Can't we do a deal, Alan? Can't I just stay here and let the work go on all around me?'

'I guess... if you're okay with that,' Alan said with a shrug of

376

his broad shoulders. 'Maybe we could give you a small rent rebate; it wouldn't be much, because you're turning down the offer of another room... but... are you sure you don't mind living here on your own?'

And that's how John found himself without roommates until the beginning of the winter semester.

Late one Sunday evening in November, after John had spent the day cleaning in the kitchen, Nathan called by. He was looking good; all that jogging, the vegetarian diet and the gentle Berkeley Hills climate had done wonders for his skin.

'What's with the lemons?' Nate quizzed, when he saw the bowl of squeezed and torn rinds on the new coffee table in the refurbished lounge.

'My hands stink of bleach and lemons seem to neutralise the pong.'

'I've been thinking,' Nate said, as he slouched into the cushions on the new sofa. He paused, and seemed suddenly agitated. He wound the leather thong of his Taizé cross around his index finger and looked around the room. 'You've got nice new drapes.'

'You've been thinking about my new curtains?' John offered with a barb.

'No,' he laughed. 'I've been thinking that I'd like to get to know you better.'

'Better?' John quizzed, remembering how sexually confused he'd felt about Nate in those first days. 'Better than what?'

'Better, like in the Biblical sense of knowing.'

John sensed the stirrings, and wondered why Nate had waited so long.

'Shit... I haven't misjudged this, have I?' Nathan said, interpreting John's thoughtfulness as hesitation. 'It's just that I thought you were interested in me.'

'And I thought that I'd read you wrongly because you didn't respond to those early overtures.'

'It's not easy... being in the ordination process. There's such a lot at stake.'

'Yes,' John said, recalling something Bee had said, and remembering the destructive relationship with Paul Wynne.

'I'd like us to be lovers,' Nate offered.

'You sure that's what you want?' John asked, excited by the physical possibilities.

Nate looked confused.

'I guess what I'm hearing is that you'd like us to have sex, and I've no doubt that would be interesting.' John smiled, and his thoughts flitted back to Halloween. That last night of the year in the old Celtic tradition had been like a rite of passage into a new understanding of his possibilities. 'But I'm also hearing that a relationship with you, as a lover, would have to be kept a secret.'

'There'd be no need to broadcast it.'

'No, Nathan,' John said with a certainty that took Nate aback. 'We'd have to keep it a secret because you want to be ordained, and I'm not too happy with my sexuality being pushed back into that secretive realm, not after the struggles I've had to get free.'

Nate slumped back into the cushions feeling dejected.

'Be a bit more honest with yourself, Nathan,' John said after a tense few moments. 'We can have sex if you like – how do you Americans put it? We can be fuck-buddies. But you don't really want to be somebody's lover; there's no place for that in the life you've got mapped out.'

'But *that* kind of sex sounds so detached, John; so devoid of relationship. I could pay a hustler for that.'

'The church demands some pretty stark choices from the people it calls.'

'But I need human touch, John. I need closeness and warmth… and sexual intimacy.'

'And the church demands celibacy in singleness and fidelity in marriage.'

'That's not helpful!' Nate spat.

'So, go to the bathhouse down on Fifth Street. It's all there – the human touch, the intimacy… and you won't be asking anyone to keep secrets.'

'I went to the baths once, in Greenwich Village, when I was doing an internship in New York. I felt so bad afterwards.'

'And if we become fuck buddies will you feel bad afterwards?'

'It's not easy, John.'

'Tell me about it, Nathan.'

'Just hold me then?'

John moved to the sofa. Despite the nagging thought that he wasn't sure he could trust himself, he took Nathan in his arms.

'You're hard,' Nate said after they'd lain beside one another for a while.

'So are you.'

'I want this so badly, John.'

'Me too,' John said, knowing that desire was clouding his judgement.

*   *   *

They both wanted more, in different ways.

Nathan yearned for 'their relationship' to be recognised as a creative force that was making him feel happier and more fulfilled. Something so good couldn't be so wrong, despite the time-honoured Biblical interpretations of just a few verses and the tradition of hundreds of years. John wanted not to have to keep second-guessing whether his gestures were giving too much away. He'd like to have been able to hold Nathan's hand when they walked back from La Val's after a few beers, to be more spontaneous – a kiss, a smile, a touch. He wanted to wake up beside him in the morning, and for Nathan not to have snuck off, like a sexual outlaw, before dawn.

They both knew that after the Christmas vacation two new people would move into apartment 303 and it would be impossible to be so clandestine about their sleeping arrangements.

'When you come back, things will be different,' John said after Nathan had declared his intention to fly home to the East Coast for the holidays.

'Yes,' Nate said. 'I'm sorry.'

'Sorry that things will be different?' John pressed, not wanting to misinterpret Nate's words and gestures.

'No... sorry I pulled you into my need to hide.'

'I didn't take much pulling; you've nothing to be sorry for on that count.'

'Then... I'm sorry that I can't be more free to love you.'

'Yes. I'm sorry about that too.'

On his return from dropping Nate at San Francisco airport, John joined Bee for breakfast.

'Are you sure you won't reconsider?' she asked. 'My folks' house is on Pismo Beach and it's —' She stopped herself and reached for John's hand across the table. 'Oh, hell, John! I hate to think of you spending Christmas on your own.'

'But I won't be on my own. I'll have the cats for company and on Christmas Day I'm helping with the Urban Ministry Programme's Christmas Dinner for street people.'

'So you've agreed to house-sit for Catwoman,' she said unkindly.

'Summer Star has only got three cats, Bee, and I know people think she's a bit strange, but she's really very nice. Her apartment is lovely; she's got a television, and a stereo system with a huge collection of LPs, and her bookshelves just sag. I'm going to really enjoy kitty-sitting.'

'And what about the New Year holiday? You could come down for a couple of days, couldn't you? My Mom and Earl always have a big party on New Year's Eve. Last year, it was such a lovely night... we all went skinny dipping.'

'Y'know, Bee,' he said, his brow wrinkling. 'The days around the turn of the year aren't my best time. I thought I might go and explore Point Reyes, and maybe drive up the coast to find some redwoods.'

'On your own?'

'It's a time when lots of old ghosts come a haunting and I do better on my own.'

'Sounds scary,' she offered.

'No, Bee, it's not so scary,' he said, refusing to rise to her bait. For as much as he liked her, he didn't want to tell her his story. 'Just some old demons that try to regain their hold.'

'Well... I'll give you my mom's number so you can call me if you change your mind.'

Summer Star's apartment was in a building lower down the hill on Le Conte, just a few minutes from Arch Street, so John didn't pack too many things; he just slipped home when he

381

needed a change of clothes. She'd introduced him to the cats when he'd called around to receive his instructions, the evening before she flew up to Alaska. He'd paid more attention to the quantities of cat food he needed to place in each bowl, and to which plants needed watering from the bottom only, so whilst he remembered that the cat's names were Serendipity, Gentle Breeze and Loveday, he couldn't identify them. One was white, thin and mean looking, and did a fair bit of hissing. He rarely saw the orange tabby with white tufts here and there. The third cat, the one he thought might be Serendipity, was handsome; a fluffy black and white creature that purred and seemed to smile when he was fondled. He had jagged ears. John found it hard to imagine one so docile being involved in street fights, especially when he cuddled up for hours on the sofa while John watched the TV, or read the well-thumbed book about California coastal trails he'd found on a shelf in the hall amongst a collection of travel guides. He'd never especially liked cats, but Serendipity became a good friend.

Playing Summer Star's LPs, John realised how much he missed being able to play music. Perhaps, if Connie continued to give him wedding jobs, he could save a bit, and buy a cheap stereo system. Summer Star's taste was eclectic; the Rolling Stones, the Mamas and the Papas and Fleetwood Mac, Sinatra and Andy Williams, some Chopin and lots of stuff in French – Edith Piaf, Jean Ferrat and Jacques Brel. John supposed that Brel was her favourite *chanteur*; there were five of his records, and one compilation of his songs sung in English by an assortment of singers. He recognised 'If You Go Away', 'Seasons In The Sun' and 'Port Of Amsterdam' from these cover versions without ever realising that Brel had made them famous. And he discovered

'Jackie', which he played over many times. The next time someone said that his accent was 'cute', or that his butt was 'cute', or that he was 'cute', he had a ready riposte; the Brel put-down: 'Cute, cute, cute in a stupid assed way!'

More than once, lying on the sofa with Serendipity, whilst Piaf or Brel or Mama Cass sang to them, John wondered about the Welsh ghosts. They'd returned annually, between Christmas and New Year, to commemorate his first stay in the Denbigh asylum. He wondered how he'd ride out their haunting. When he'd begun to explore theology 'in a new key' with Bob Brown, and acquired the tools of redaction criticism as an approach to Biblical texts in his Bible classes, Adam and the Sunday Library Group had come on strongly for a few days. Then they'd fallen silent, and John suspected they might be consolidating for a major confrontation. By the morning of New Year's Eve, when he drove Ma Dodge over to the coast to look for redwoods, they still hadn't made an advance.

After an early start on a clear, sunny day, he reached Jenner before lunch. The guidebook, which Summer Star had pressed him to keep, suggested a number of trails, and the Armstrong Redwoods State Reserve wasn't too far away. The town was no more than a few houses, a couple of restaurants and a general store, clinging to a hill above the water where the Russian River spilled into the Pacific Ocean. There were some expensive inns too, where city-weary San Franciscans fled for weekend breaks. He'd decided to sleep in the car and didn't pay them too much attention.

With no one to please but himself, and with no sense of passing time, he watched the river from a sun-drenched grassy bank. An otter fished for its lunch, and some dog-faced harbour seals played chasing games. An osprey, its white breast almost dazzling in the afternoon sun, soared and swooped, and after hovering over the gilded surface of the water for a few seconds, it wheeled away over John's head, a large fish twisting in its talons. And there were pelicans!

He remembered a visit to Chester Zoo. The keeper had thrown fish into the air and the large birds had caught them in their long, orange bills. The fish had wriggled in the pouches, until they were swallowed, and many in the audience laughed. But in their natural environment, these huge birds inspired admiration and respect, not laughter. Their spanned wings must have been seven or eight feet across, and they skimmed, just inches over the estuary's currents, their heads tilted, their bright yellow-orange bills scooping up the water like oversized shrimping nets. John quickly realised that the three birds were working together, gliding over the water in a V-formation, to herd the schools of fish towards the shallows where they could feed more easily.

With the sun warm on his face, and awed by the wonders of nature, he thought about Rhys and Elen Morgan's letters – the first ones they'd sent him at Denbigh's asylum, folded in the original envelope, safely zipped in the inside pocket of Ann's overstuffed red ski jacket. Perhaps he didn't need to read them, though it had become an annual ritual. Perhaps it was time to recognise that whilst those memories were part of an important past, they didn't have to embitter the new possibilities of his life in California.

In the dripping, damp cool, deep in the Coast Redwood grove at Armstrong State Reserve, John marvelled at the 1000-year-old trees, which rose 250 feet into the dark green canopy, eclipsing the blue sky. He'd seen no one for an hour or more and felt confident he wouldn't be overheard.

'I'm leaving you all here,' he shouted into the forest as he visualised their faces: Jatunga Arachchi and Arwel Thomas, Adam and the Sunday Library Group. 'When I walk back out into the sunshine I'll be free of you... and I'll never let the likes of you get to me again.'

* * *

Denny turned up the volume on his new Kenwood sound system.

'I never had you down as an opera queen,' John sniped.

'Scott's the real diva,' Denny said. 'Bill gets corporate tickets for the San Francisco Opera through the bank, but he hates it; d'you know, he even called Maria Callas a Wailing Witch after hearing a recording of her sing 'Norma'! He's a barbarian... but it suits me because I get to go with Dr Scotty.' He lowered the stylus carefully into a groove, about an inch in from the edge of the revolving vinyl LP. 'Just listen to this. It's called 'Song To The Moon'.'

A harpist plucked arpeggios up and down a scale; the tone was bold and clear, but the mood created was subdued. John closed his eyes and saw wisps of dark cloud pass over a bright, full moon, only to be blown away by the breeze of woodwinds. The strings began to quiver a melancholy refrain on the warm night air, a melody quickly taken up by a rich soprano voice that carried him off with its longing.

'Wasn't that just awesome?' Denny said, as he lifted the stylus carefully and drew back the arm to its stop position.

John was pulled back to the lounge of apartment 211. 'She's got a stunning voice.'

'Some Spanish woman, I think,' Denny quipped, as he searched the record sleeve for her details. 'Her name is Pilar

385

Lorengar; recorded in Rome in 1966. And what about the composer?' He flicked his fingers with impatient anticipation.

'She wasn't singing in Spanish,' John said.

'Czech,' Denny cued.

'Hmm, I don't think I know any Czech composers.'

Denny hummed a melody, which John recognised from the *New World* symphony.

'I had no idea that Dvorak had written operas.'

'And what do you think of the sound reproduction from my new Kenwood?'

'I'm envious. Was it a Christmas present?'

'Yeh, from Dr Scotty.'

And John found himself wondering again about the relationship between Denny Paltridge and Scott Rashford, but it didn't seem right to query.

'What have you done with the old one?' John heard himself ask.

'One of the speakers had a bit of vibration, so it's ready for the trash collector.'

'You won't mind if I salvage it then?'

For the best part of a week, John played, and replayed *Rusalka*'s 'Song To The Moon', until his new roommates complained.

Todd and Mitchell were easy going enough, and John liked them. Neither was registered at PSR; Todd was at the Unitarian seminary and Mitch was with the Lutherans. They cohabited harmoniously enough, but didn't become close friends.

Nathan flew back a week late, and missed the beginning of the January Intersession.

'I needed some thinking time,' he said, as John pulled Ma

Dodge onto the Bayshore Freeway outside SFO and headed for the Bay Bridge. 'I've decided that I'm called to be celibate.'

'If that's what your inner voices are telling you, I guess you have to be true to them,' John said.

They drove towards the City in silence, but as the skyscrapers came into view, Nate became animated.

'I met up with one of my friends from Brown over the holidays; Jed's studying medicine at Columbia now, and he's real interested in this new disease affecting gay men.'

'Gay bowel syndrome?' John quizzed, remembering the conversation with the *girls* at the Empress.

'Hmm… I think different groups, in different places, are calling it by different names; Jed talked about KSOI.'

'You Americans and your acronyms!' John quipped. 'What's that supposed to mean?'

'I don't remember,' Nate said, biting his lip. 'The OI bit is Opportunistic Infections, but I just can't think what the KS bit is now. Some obscure cancer, I think. Jed was saying that by last spring eight gay guys in New York City had been diagnosed with this KS thing, and then, during the summer, five more guys in Los Angeles were diagnosed with some kind of strange pneumonia.'

'And they're all gay?'

'That's what's so weird about the whole thing, John. They're all young gay guys who seem really healthy, except that they've got these little-known infections.'

'Did Jed mention that it might have something to do with amyl?'

'What? Like using poppers causing an immune overload or something? It's all foreign to me… remember, I'm liberal arts, not science.'

'Developing opportunistic infections would fit with some

387

kind of immune system breakdown.'

'Listen to Dr Jones,' Nate teased.

'I did study immunology as an undergraduate,' John said, with some irritation.

'You never told me that.'

'It would be really fascinating if something about being gay, or the way gay men live their lives, is causing an immune deficiency that allows infections that usually don't bother non-gays to develop into fully blown diseases.'

'That's not fascinating, John; that's damn scary.'

When John pulled the car into the parking bay in the Arch Street lot, Nathan reached over and stroked his arm. 'I am sorry things have turned out this way between us.'

'No hard feelings, my friend,' John said.

He whistled his way through *Rusalka*'s song at least a dozen times as he swept, and scrubbed in the kitchen, mopping and scouring through a gloriously sunny Saturday. Throughout the day, too, he reflected on Elie Wiesel's short autobiographical novel, *Night*, a Holocaust witness account that had carried John back to Buchenwald, Yad Vashem and *The Men with the Pink Triangle*. He'd read *Night*, cover to cover, the previous evening, in preparation for Bob Brown's advanced theology seminar, Theology in Wiesel's Novels. In the introductory blurb to the seminar, Brown posed some questions: How do we react in faith to monstrous moral evil? How can we continue to believe in God after Auschwitz? How do we hear stories like Elie Wiesel's, and respond to them with honour? These questions pushed their way into his scrubbing and whistling, and thus distracted, he tipped a drum of bleach over himself.

'I know I said I'd come with you to the Castro tonight,

Denny, but —'

'You're taking a rain check, aren't you?' Denny accused into the phone.

'Denny, I'm sorry, but I stink of bleach and no amount of rubbing myself down with lemon rinds is going to get me smelling sweet.'

After a fourth shower, and spraying some of Todd's French cologne over himself, John settled down to an evening in. He curled up on the sofa with Wiesel's first fictional novel, *Dawn*. As he read, he quickly realised that in as much as *Night* had been the personal account of a victim, in *Dawn*, through his young protagonist Elisha, Wiesel was exploring the psyche of the executioner; might it not be better to kill, and survive, than be the victim and succumb?

That night he had wild dreams. In pleasant, landscaped grounds, a firing squad marched towards a man chained to a wall of honey-pale stonework. John recognised Arwel Thomas. Where the chains rubbed, and pulled at the psychiatrist's wrists, there were bloody weals. At the officer's command, John raised his rifle. Gunshots resounded down the corridors of Denbigh's asylum. He woke up tangled in his sheet, shaking with fright. He knew that Elisha would execute John Dawson at the end of Wiesel's novel. He knew, too, that to kill and survive would give no respite to the horrors of night.

Feeling the walls of his room close in, John fled to the roof garden to watch the sun come up over the Berkeley Hills.

'I've been looking for you,' Bee said when the sun was already up. 'Denny's been in an accident.'

'Is he okay?'

'He's dead, John.'

'I've told him more than once that he drives that Mustang of

389

his too damn fast,' John said, not really registering Bee's words.

'He was crossing the street somewhere near the Castro; a couple of kids, joyriding in a stolen car, ran him down.'

'They must be feeling pretty cut up.'

'The cops haven't found them yet. It was a hit-and-run, but there's a witness, so maybe they'll get them.'

'I've still got his opera LP,' John said, his eyes focused on the glint of the morning sun reflecting off the Trans Am pyramid. 'We were supposed to be out on the town together last night.'

'The witness said that after they knocked him down they reversed back over him, and then drove off, laughing.'

'There's trouble in paradise then,' he said, as the tears rolled down his cheeks. *How long will homosexuals keep having to be the victims?*

Two weeks passed before the funeral rites.

Scott Rashford's eulogy at the memorial service filled in the gaps about Denny's life that John had often puzzled over.

'He was hustling, like so many of the gay teenagers who run away from small town America, to escape the taunts and the beatings, and the scorn of family and star-spangled-banner-apple-pie society. To begin with, he was suspicious of me; he thought that I wanted *favours* in return for my *kindness*, but over time, Denny became like a son to me.'

Scott looked up from his notes and laughed quietly.

'But Denny never forgot who his parents were, and he tried more than once to be reconciled with them, so, of course, I never was his dad; more of a big brother really... and the little SOB would keep calling me 'Dr Scotty'!'

Laughter rippled through the large congregation.

'He was a bright, intelligent boy. When he decided to go

back to school, it was just such a privilege for me and Bill – yes, I'd met Bill by then, and fortunately for me, Denny approved.'

Laughter again.

'We were so privileged to encourage and support him, and we were so proud when he graduated *magna cum laude* from UCB, just across the Bay there, and when he decided to enrol at Pacific School of Religion.' Scott looked over the congregation, to where the contingent from PSR was seated. 'Bill and I, we're real grateful that the president of the seminary, a number of the teaching faculty, and so many of Denny's fellow students have come along today. Thank you. It's been a real comfort to us to hear you all talk about Denny so warmly, but then, you couldn't not like Denny Paltridge.'

At the graveside, John found himself appalled by the sanitised American way of death. Denny's high gloss casket – Bee was quick to rebuke him for calling it a coffin – was lowered into a hole lined with plastic grass that was too lime a shade of green, and at the 'ashes to ashes, dust to dust' bit, Scott got to sprinkle earth onto Denny's remains from a silver platter with a small, silver shovel. Leaving the Cypresstree Eternal Memorial Park – 'they can't even call the place a cemetery,' John said to Bee – it seemed that no one had to kick dirt from their shoes.

Back at the house on Sanchez Street there was fruit punch, served up in the American Brilliant punch bowl, and enough exotic flowers to open a flower stall, but this time, most of the guests wore sober suits and black ties, and the dream room had been transformed into a calm, elegant sitting room.

'This was Denny's,' John said, handing Scott the opera LP. 'I borrowed it and —'

'You're John, from Wales, aren't you?' Scott interrupted.

391

'You were here for the Halloween party... and caused quite a stir in the dream room, I gather.'

John blushed.

'Denny was so pleased that you were getting such a lot of pleasure from his old record player, and that you liked the aria from *Rusalka*. You know, he was taking the credit for turning you on to opera.'

'I hadn't appreciated how close you and he were until today,' John said, realising that Denny had talked to Scott about him. 'I'm so sorry.'

Scott's lip quivered, but he took a sharp intake of breath and smiled.

'I want you to have Denny's new record player, and any of the records you think you might like, including this one,' Scott said, handing back the opera LP.

John, not sure enough of the social codes, looked slightly dazed.

'And in a few weeks, when we're all in more of a party mood, I'd like you to come over and have dinner with Bill and me.'

*   *   *

Bob Brown had led the class in a discussion on Wiesel's third novel, *The Accident*. Ghosts haunt Eliezer, a survivor from the death camps – ghosts from which the tortured young man yearns to flee. During the class break, John sat in the sun on the lawn of the quad, outside the Mudd Building, and considered the notion of *flight* as a possible option for dealing with a destructive history. *Am I running away from my own past by 'escaping' to California... trying to deny my history by casting those ghosts from Denbigh and Aberystwyth into the redwood forest?*

392

'I saw you at Denny's funeral.'

John looked up into brown eyes that held his gaze.

'I'm Theo,' a slight man of perhaps thirty said. 'How are you liking Wiesel?'

'He makes me think, and it's uncomfortable sometimes,' John said, wondering why Theo had come to class in clergy garb – and how he managed to get the lines of his beard so sculpted.

'So, you're the guy from Wales.'

John smiled, but felt his mouth go dry. 'Don't tell me; you recognised my *cute* accent,' he said, longing to use the Brel put-down.

'I'm not impressed by cutesy things,' Theo said, returning John's smile. 'Denny talked about you sometimes.'

The students started to move back into class.

'Have dinner with me sometime,' he said. 'Please... and let it be soon.' He turned and joined the press of students. John watched him go, his heart thudding in his chest. Before taking his seat, John looked around the classroom and saw Theo sitting towards the back. Those brown eyes held his gaze again.

The shady avenues on the Cal campus were heavy with the smell of eucalyptus as they walked over to College Avenue on a beautiful spring evening. Theo shared some of his recent history; undergraduate years at Amherst College, where he'd studied philosophy, and then a master's in theological ethics at Union Theological Seminary. He enthused about his involvement with the New York City and the San Francisco chapters of Integrity, the Episcopalian gay and lesbian lobby group. 'At the moment I'm trying to swing an internship at the Parsonage on Castro Street, but the Field Ed people are being a bit sniffy.'

'I visited there a couple of times, before Christmas, as part of a piece of research I've been doing,' John said. 'It's amazing that the San Francisco diocese is so upfront about it's ministry with the gay community. Why have your Field Ed people got reservations?'

'The diocese established the Parsonage as a lay-ministry and all of the workers are lay people; I've already been ordained into the diaconate.'

'You'll have to explain your Anglican structures,' John said, recalling Theo's clergy outfit, but also remembering the ancients who sat in the *sêt fawr* in the chapels at home; they were called deacons too.

'We ordain people as deacons first, and then a year or two later a deacon is ordained as a priest. The Catholics do the same, except they exclude women.'

'So, what can a priest do that a deacon can't?'

'I can preach and teach, and marry and baptise, but I can't celebrate the Eucharist or give people absolution.'

'Oh... I see,' John said, further mystified by the church's traditions.

Over the starters, John selectively potted his history. Theo wanted to know about Celts, the Welsh language and Joseph Parry. '*Aberystwyth* is one of my favourite hymn tunes,' he said.

As a steaming dish of spaghetti was placed between them by a glad-eyed waiter, Theo seemed keen to discuss the fourth novel in the Wiesel sequence, *The Town Beyond the Wall*. John hadn't found Michael's story an easy read; the notion that one could choose to be a detached spectator in the face of huge moral evil troubled him. As Theo tried to draw him, John realised that he hadn't even begun to frame any responses to Wiesel's themes in *Town*.

'D'you agree that the person who chooses the role of spectator is the most morally culpable?' Theo quizzed.

'I don't know what to think,' John said, fearing that Theo would find him shallow.

'You don't strike me as intellectually lazy,' he said. His fork, dripping *Carbonara* sauce, glided through the space above his plate like a conductor's baton. John was taken aback by Theo's candour, but he was also beginning to realise why *Town* was so troubling to him. 'By choosing to be a spectator, you're willing to let others do the dirty work that you're not willing to do yourself,' Theo pressed.

'Yes.'

'And you must see that that makes you morally corrupt.'

John couldn't hold the inquiring gaze of those brown eyes and he found himself staring at the small gold ring in Theo's left ear. 'I guess so,' he offered.

'What do you mean? "I guess so".' Carbonara sauce from Theo's fork spattered onto John's shirtfront but Theo didn't seem to notice. 'The spectator is never neutral,' Theo whispered. 'By your silence you're complicit.'

John wiped the eggy spots on his shirt with his napkin. *It's not that simple when you've been there... to the edges of night... and seen what I've seen in the asylum's locked wards. I nearly went mad... but chose to disengage... to watch.*

'And what did you make of the suggestion that one of Michael's options could be to go mad?'

John thought about the string of unhinged characters in the novel; Martha, the town drunk who'd invited the eight-year-old Michael to make love to her, and Moishe, Varady and Kalman. 'I think I've got more of a handle on madness as an option,' he said.

'In the world of night, where everything seems mad and

395

babies are burnt by lovers of opera and fine literature, who's to say what madness is?' Theo said.

And in the world of the laughing man, where an eighteen-year-old is shown gay pornography and given electric shocks...who's to say what sanity is?

'Wiesel's novels have aroused some memories that I thought had been comfortably tucked up in bed,' John said. 'Can we talk about this another time?'

Theo smiled... and wondered... and changed the subject. 'Denny told me that he'd got you hooked on to opera; what are your favourites?'

'He introduced me to Dvorak.'

'Ah... the Czechs. D'you like Janacek too?'

John had never heard of him. 'I don't even know the whole opera; *Rusalka* I mean,' he offered, believing by now that Theo must be thinking he was a real jerk. 'Denny lent me a compilation of women sopranos.'

'Sir Geraint Evans is singing in the City later this spring, one of his famous roles; Leporello I think. Perhaps we could get some tickets?'

John knew, of course, who Geraint Evans was... but Leporello?

He quickly came to appreciate Theo's superior intellectual rigour; so steeped was he in the Classics, philosophical thought, literature and music, he could so easily have found himself intimidated. But then, beneath a palm tree on Ridge Road, as they were about to say goodnight, Theo kissed him.

Within a fortnight of their pasta supper they became lovers. In the frenetic weeks that followed, when lust and love were so entangled, their lives had a raw edginess from the sexual pleasuring that deprived them of sleep. Theo bought John small gifts. The first was a single white carnation; no one had ever bought him flowers before and he cried. This was followed in a couple of days by a macramé friendship band. 'Susan Finster showed me how to make it,' he said, fastening it to John's wrist. 'She's so clever with her hands; she has little origami birds flying all over her room.'

'Susan's the blind girl at the Baptist seminary?'

'She's Baptist and she's blind, but she hasn't been a girl for at least fifteen years,' Theo quipped. 'I'm surprised that six months in Berkeley hasn't liberated you from your sexism.'

John learned quickly that Theo was more prepared to be political than polite.

He wrote John poems too. Handwritten, in an elegant script, he sought to express the spiritual and emotional aspects of the physical chemistry that had ignited between them. These verses were presented inside Sierra Club cards, depicting America's wondrous nature. John didn't understand many of the words Theo used, let alone how he'd strung them together. Sometimes, when their bodies came to rest against one another, spent and salt-bitter, Theo would recite these poems from memory and John would think that he understood something of his lover's depths.

On Easter Saturday they went to a secluded beach, an hour south of the City on Highway One. Driving down University Avenue towards the freeway, Theo found a station playing classical music. They'd both been silent for a while, a piece by Sibelius drowning the traffic noise and John's thoughts about Britain's war with Argentina over a group of islands he'd never even heard of. Passing beneath the first bulky, grey portal of the Bay Bridge's gantry, John shifted in the passenger seat and laid his hand on Theo's thigh.

'I'm really struggling with *The Gates of the Forest*.'

'Takes a while to realise who's who,' Theo said.

'Wiesel's got such a lot to teach us, but —' John sighed, and looked down on a small armada of colourful sailing boats bobbing in the Bay. 'Even the opening sentence threw me.'

'"He had no name, so he gave him his own".'

'Exactly! How the heck d'you straighten out all those personal pronouns?'

'I liked that whole opening section,' Theo mused. 'I got the sense that Wiesel wanted me to know that confusion... the turmoil... that complete dislocation – call it what you will; that feeling of being on your own, and not even knowing who you are any more because of the horrific events that you've been through.'

Another piece by Sibelius swelled from the radio when they emerged from the tunnel on Treasure Island. It cast John back to Wales; for a split second, suspended high above San Francisco Bay, they all came back... those ghosts he'd cast into the forest. The speakers crackled as the skyscrapers began to interfere with the signal. John watched the City grow below them as they neared the centre of the second span. A hymn that they'd sung to the radio's melody streamed through his consciousness, but it couldn't displace his own night – or Wiesel's conundrum.

'D'you sing any hymns in Welsh to *Finlandia*?' Theo asked.

John felt his heart thud against the walls of his chest and he knew it wasn't nostalgia. He didn't want to talk about Welsh hymns sung to Sibelius' tune. 'I need to tell you a story.'

*   *   *

There were about a dozen cars parked on the bluff, high above the turquoise ocean's vastness. John leaned against the dented body of Theo's old Ford Vega and traced the dust-yellow ribbon of Highway One through squinted eyes as it fluttered its way south through the shimmering heat, pitched and heaved by the quake-scarred coastline. Before opening the trunk to fetch the cool-box, the travel blanket and their beach things, Theo came around to the passenger side of the car. Taking John in his arms, they kissed for a long time.

'That was nice,' John said, feeling his body respond.

'We can find a quiet spot that's not overlooked.'

Descending the cliff path they began to pick out the men on the beach below. In the central sandy crescent, three athletic types played Frisbee whilst a fourth lay on his back in the sun surrounded by his friends' backpacks. In amongst the rocks at the north end of the bay, perhaps 300 yards away, were a number of solitary men; one practised *t'ai chi*, casting spider shadows onto the white sand. Nearing the beach, the shingle at the base of the cliff came into view. In amongst the driftwood – that included two tree trunks – small hollows had been established over time. A T-shirt or a towel, hanging from a bleached branch, indicated that someone had taken up residence for the day. The south end of the bay, where the sand gave way to an expanse of pebble beach, seemed deserted. They made for a rocky outcrop that would offer them some seclusion.

'You were very quiet in the car,' John said, rubbing sun cream into Theo's back, and putting extra on the pale skin of his buttocks.

'I was afraid that if I said something I'd interrupt your flow.'

'I'm sorry. It was just like a dam bursting.'

'You've nothing to be sorry for,' he said, taking the tube of sun block. He squeezed an inch of the pink cream onto the back of John's neck and began to massage it into his shoulders.

Almost without either of them noticing, the movements of Theo's hands became the touches of a lover.

When there was quiet between them again Theo said, 'Over the weeks I'd guessed you were working out some heavy stuff... I didn't ask because I had a sense that you'd say something when you were ready.'

'What do you think about it all?'

'Makes me think that psychiatry sucks,' he said, stroking John's thigh. 'And even the Devil can cite Scripture.' His finger traced the fine hairs around his lover's navel. 'And it makes me realise again how important it is that gay men find solidarity with one another. I don't think what you've described could have happened if you hadn't found yourself so isolated; they can't pick us off so easily when we're one of a group... and when that group becomes a movement that can articulate its cause and argue its case, the bigots start to be seen for what they are.'

John took Theo's hand and held it.

'Elie Wiesel's books have given me a —' He searched for words. 'His novels, the way his characters work through the awful things that happened to them, it's like he wrote them for me.' Then he sensed something he interpreted as discomfort seep through Theo's body. 'I don't mean that their story is my story, Theo.'

'No.'

'No. What happened to me is nothing to what the Nazis did to all of those millions, but Wiesel's given me a way to work through my own night, and despite all of the upset and confusion of the last few weeks, I feel —' There were no words again. For a moment John watched the sun dance on the water.

Theo squeezed his hand gently. 'You feel free to embrace the

400

future unencumbered by the shackles of the past?'

'That sounds like a quote from a book,' John quipped.

'Sorry,' he said before laying his head on the flat of John's stomach.

John played his fingers through Theo's beard and felt heavy with gratitude.

'I've bought you an Easter present,' Theo said after a while. He pulled himself up and rummaged through his backpack. 'I noticed that your ear is pierced, but you never wear a ring or a stud in it... so I bought these,' he said, opening a small velvet-padded box. 'One each!'

John held up the gemstone ear stud to the sunlight. As he twirled the post between his thumb and forefinger, golden Pyrite stars twinkled in the opaque blue depths. 'Lapis lazuli,' he said.

'Some cultures believe it's the stone of truth and friendship,' Theo offered. 'It's supposed to bring concord to the relationships of the wearer.'

'Truth and friendship then,' John said, pushing the post gently through the hole from which Theo had just removed the small gold ring he'd worn since they'd met.

'And harmony between us,' Theo said, putting the other stud in John's ear.

John lay back, resting his head in Theo's lap. Being loved by Theo Jeffrey sharpened each sensation.

*   *   *

On the notepad by the phone in apartment 303, Todd had scribbled a message from Scott Rashford. John was apprehensive about meeting him and Bill again; he barely knew them,

401

but they'd been so generous, and he enjoyed their gift of music every day.

'If you like, John, you could join Bill and me for the eleven o'clock Choral Eucharist at Grace Cathedral a week from Sunday,' Scott said in his warm New England burr.

'I'd like that,' John said.

'Then maybe we could go over to The Patio on Castro Street; we could stand you brunch, and maybe go for a walk in Golden Gate Park. Have you been to the Conservatory of Flowers yet?'

After hanging up the phone he wished he'd said something to Scott about Theo; he'd have felt more comfortable going to brunch as two couples, but then, Theo was tied up at St Mark's most Sundays.

Bill had lost some weight. Both he and Scott looked tanned and relaxed.

'When you hit fifty it gets harder to work off all those corporate lunches,' Scott teased.

'And because I hate going to the gym with all the Muscle-Marys we tend to do a two or three week stint at a health farm every spring so that I can at least get into some kind of shape for the summer,' Bill said.

'We've found a lovely gay resort in the desert near Palm Springs; Bill's fallen for one of the personal trainers down there who can actually get him exercising for three hours a day.'

Bill laughed.

The over-muscled waiter offered them a choice of sparkling English elderflower pressé or a California 'champagne', and after pouring the bubbly, pink-tinged wine into their fluted glasses, he set the bottles on a side table and handed them each an over-large menu card.

'Today's brunch special is smoked wild Alaska salmon with Eggs Bénédict and fresh strawberries,' he said. 'Or maybe you'd rather make your choice from our regular breakfast menu. All our bread is handmade and baked on the premises; today we have sesame seed finger rolls, a multi-grain malted batch and a walnut and mushroom bread baked in a ring form.'

Though The Patio was only a few doors away from The Parsonage, John hadn't ever paid it much attention. From the street it looked like a small bistro; the few times he'd passed by, no one ever seemed to be at the tables visible from the sidewalk. Seated in the shade of a bottlebrush tree at an elegantly set table on a small deck above a pool where fat black and orange koi swam, John supposed that only those with time for a quick sandwich ever sat inside. The garden was lush and the shrubs and trees offered privacy and intimacy to diners; he estimated that there were more than thirty tables and only one that he could see wasn't occupied by groups of men. He wondered if over-developed muscles were a prerequisite for The Patio's waiters.

'Tell John about all these guys going down with pneumonia,' Bill said after some small talk about the Choral Eucharist.

John remembered that Scott was a chest specialist at the hospital and began to recall the conversation he'd had with Nathan on the way back from the airport.

'Have you been following the reports in the gay press about this new health scare?' Scott asked as he smeared a curl of whipped butter onto his sesame finger roll.

'No, but I've heard bits and pieces,' John said. 'Are you starting to see gay men with that weird pneumonia?'

'Since Christmas I've had half a dozen referrals. PCP – Pneumocystis carinii pneumonia – is such a rare lung infection, something that we only ever had to worry about

403

with transplant patients or very old folk, but all of these new PCP patients have been gay men in their twenties and thirties. A couple of the guys had obvious Kaposi's sarcoma too, which again I'd only ever seen in much older people, and the majority had a generalised lymphadenopathy.'

John's look betrayed his lack of comprehension.

'Swollen glands – everywhere,' Scott said. 'And KS is a relatively benign cancer, but it can look really unsightly, especially on the face.'

'So they are immune compromised in some way,' John said.

'There seems to be an acquired immune dysfunction,' Scott said with raised eyebrows.

'Didn't Denny tell you? I majored in immunology.'

'He told us stories about you, John... all the time,' Bill said. 'But I guess he didn't tell us that.'

'And is using amyl still a prime suspect?' John asked, putting curiosity about Denny's tell-tales aside.

'Nobody rightly knows, but I doubt that inhaling poppers could damage the immune system in such a fundamental way,' Scott said. 'Seems more likely to be some kind of infectious agent.'

'What? Some other bug getting at the lymphocytes or something?' John quizzed, striving to recall the immune mechanisms he'd studied back in Aberystwyth.

'Yeh... and God forbid that whatever the bug is, it doesn't turn out to be sexually transmitted.'

For a fleeting moment John was back in the dream room at their house on Sanchez Street; the cowboy with the small cock and the snake man with the sapphire nipple were driving him crazy with pleasure and the muscled drag queen was fucking the Latino boy. 'Is that a serious possibility?' John asked, his mouth suddenly dry.

'I was at a convention down in LA last Tuesday and had lunch with a couple of gay medics who suggested as much,' Scott said.

'That scenario doesn't bear thinking about,' Bill quipped. 'Not when you think about what goes on in the bathhouses of every major city across this *great* nation.'

'Can any of these opportunistic infections kill you?' John asked.

'KS won't. And as long as you hit PCP with a ten-day course of pentamidine the patient does pretty well. But doctors don't expect to see PCP in young people, so there's every chance they'll be misdiagnosed and not be treated appropriately; then they die.'

John was fascinated by the biology – and horrified by the potential human tragedy. 'And presumably, if whatever bug they discover messing up the immune system does its job effectively, people will get sick with all sorts of things as their immune system fails —'

'Two brunch specials and scrambled eggs on an English muffin,' the waiter announced, cutting John off. 'Help yourselves to the salad bar; there's a fresh blue cheese dressing... a thousand island... an Italian herb... a Vinaigrette... and a classic French. Today's house coffee special is Peet's Arabian Mocha-Java and the decaf is Sumatra. Do you guys need some iced water?'

After the waiter's fussing, and the trips to the salad bar, the flow of their conversation was lost.

'Have you been able to extend your stay beyond the year of your scholarship?' Bill asked.

'It seems that Denny did tell you a lot about me,' John said, certain that he hadn't mentioned this to Scott or Bill.

'I think he wanted more than he was able to articulate,' Bill said.

405

'More, in what way?'

'He wanted for you and he to be lovers, but he couldn't say so,' Bill said with a smile that was tinged with sadness.

'No! Denny didn't have too many problems saying just what was on his mind,' John insisted. 'He wasn't interested in me. I was too — rural. Too naïve for him.'

Scott smiled, and sipped the pink champagne from his replenished glass. Then he leaned across the table and put his hand on John's arm.

'He talked about you all the time, John. He was smitten. But, for all his bravado, he was as insecure as hell. If I'm not mistaken, I think he thought you were much too decent.'

John laid down his fork and looked at his hosts in amazement. 'Too decent for what for goodness sake?'

'Denny just didn't think he was good enough for you,' Bill said.

They fell silent. Their knives and forks began, slowly, to chink against their plates again.

'So, will you be going back to Wales at the end of the semester?' Scott pressed.

'My parents have offered to lend me some money, but it's not enough... and my brother and his wife are wanting to start a family so he's good for a few hundred now and then, but —'

'But you would like to work for an M.Div., wouldn't you?' Bill asked.

'I'd love to be able to stay.' *Especially now that I've met Theo.* 'But I'm twenty-six years old and I've got to —'

'Go back to Wales and be a school teacher?' Bill quipped cynically.

An awkwardness engulfed their table. John looked at the strips of smoked salmon on his plate and then at a fat orange koi as its gaping mouth gulped at the surface of the pond.

'We'd like to make you an offer,' Scott said. 'Perhaps you can imagine, Bill and I have got a sizeable joint income and we'd rather not have to give Ronald Reagan our hard earned dollars to build more nuclear weapons.'

John wasn't good in this kind of situation. He thought how ugly the koi were.

'I'm sorry,' Scott said. 'I didn't mean to embarrass you.' He took Bill's hand in his own. 'You're the one who's used to talking money, Billy. Why don't you spell out our proposal to John?'

He rode the BART back to Berkeley. A couple of times he pinched himself, just to be certain he wasn't dreaming. He was wide-awake. Scott and Bill were going to pay his tuition fees for the M.Div. programme and he was barely able to contain his excitement.

*   *   *

John spent the evening cleaning the dining hall. He and Connie had catered a wedding the day before, which had gone on past midnight and the revellers had left the place in a mess. He'd called Theo when he got back to Berkeley to tell him about Scott and Bill's offer. They agreed to meet later for a beer.

'I've brought the course catalogue with me so that we can figure out how I'm going to meet the core requirements,' John said after they'd settled at a table. 'When I go to the Dean's office tomorrow I want to have a fair idea of what my options are. D'you think they'll recognise my private study towards the Field Ed requirement?'

'Slow down,' Theo urged. 'The first thing you need to think

about is whether you can swing this financially. You've still got to live for the next couple of years; it's not just about the course fees.'

'Connie's already said that I can have the breakfast cook's job if I stay on.'

'What's that? Six 'til 8.30, five mornings a week?'

'Yes, and it pays more than cleaning! The weddings keep coming too, and some of your crazy compatriots have been paying me to leave English butler type announcements on their answering machines; some guy over on Spruce gave me thirty-five bucks for five minutes work and said he'd pass my name on to some of his cronies!'

'And your folks have offered to lend you some money too?'

John smiled and his body quivered with exhilaration. 'This is going to happen, Theo.'

'You won't have any denominational requirements, I guess,' Theo said, scanning the list of basics in the catalogue.

'I'm not in the ordination process, so I guess not.'

'But the M.Div. is the professional qualification for ordination in most Protestant denominations, and if you're not going to be ordained, why don't you do the M.A. and avoid all the Field Ed requirements?'

'Because I —' John stopped himself and thought about Grace Hope's Tenderloin ministry and Troy Liddell's work with the girls at the Empress. He recalled the joyful, thought-provoking services at the Metropolitan Community Church, and the Episcopalian outreach work at The Parsonage. 'Because I'm trying to stay open to whatever the possibilities might be.'

Theo raised his glass. 'To possibilities,' he said.

Their beer mugs clunked and John's excitement raced ahead. 'You did a CPE didn't you?'

'Ten weeks in a Reno hospital during the summer wasn't such a good choice for Clinical Pastoral Education,' Theo quipped. 'Cardiac rehab was maybe not my forte and the air-con was downright cold. I had a miserable summer!'

'When I was scrubbing the floor in the dining hall I was thinking about something Scott Rashford said at brunch; he's started seeing sick young gay guys, y'know, with this new immune deficiency disease. Seems that it might be caused by something that's sexually transmitted.'

The brown of Theo's eyes turned autumnal. 'That could mean tens of thousands getting sick just in the Bay Area and the choruses from Bible Belt will be all hellfire and damnation,' he said after John's words had sunk in.

'I was wondering whether there'll be a specialised CPE programme next year or the year after. So many gay guys escape to the City, just like Denny; they're either estranged from their family, or their folks don't even know they're gay. Someone in that position becoming terminally ill will need a huge amount of support.'

'And it's a sad fact that they won't always be able to rely on their gay friends. The Castro can be such a bitchy meat market!'

John looked down the columns of courses on the open pages of the booklet seeking to distract himself from such a bleak scenario. 'Anyway,' he said. 'It looks like I'll be spending the next twelve to eighteen months cooking breakfasts and doing lots of Bible, church history, systematics and ethics, just to get the basics in.'

'And there's Hebrew and Greek.'

'I don't think so! That's two good reasons not to be in an ordination process.'

Theo smiled. 'How are you at American breakfasts – over-easy eggs and apple streusel muffins?'

'I guess I'm headed for a steep learning curve.'

*   *   *

By the end of that summer, when Theo and John headed up
the coast to Bodega Bay for a short, mid-week vacation at a
beach house owned by someone in Theo's church, John had
completed his scholarship report for the World Council of
Churches and spent some time preparing for the hectic year
ahead. He'd read Bright's tome on the history of Israel, Perrin
and Duling's introduction to the New Testament, Frend's
hugely readable book on the early church and Hans Küng's
not-so-readable *On Being a Christian*. He'd washed lots of
windows too, in some fabulous houses in the Berkeley Hills,
thanks to Bee's eccentric aunt, who'd recommended him to
her equally eccentric circle of friends. One wrinkled,
bejewelled grande dame, whose house was so large it had
taken two days to wash all of the windows, inside and out,
paid him 150 dollars. Despite protesting that she'd paid him
too much she'd sent him on his way with a smile. Within
hours, he received three calls from her neighbours, wanting
him to wash their windows too.

The Malvinas war had come to an end. Italy beat the West
Germans in soccer's World Cup final in Spain – though the
Americans barely noticed, and Diana produced an heir for the
House of Windsor, which got lots of press. Despite the joyous
celebrations at the arrival of a new prince, all was not well in
Britain's royal household; the Queen's bodyguard, Michael
Trestrail, resigned after admitting to a homosexual affair. In

410

Poland the Solidarity demonstrations continued and Lech Walesa was becoming a household name, whilst in Washington, after being found not guilty of trying to kill Ronald Reagan on grounds of mental instability, John Hinckley was sentenced to indefinite detention. And the new disease was finally given a name, Acquired Immune Deficiency Syndrome.

With the American's fondness for acronyms, people were calling it AIDS. Very little was known about the agent that caused it, or how that agent was transmitted. Gay life in the City continued much as before, though the boys in the bars could now begin to name their anxiety.

For those last few days of August in Bodega Bay they forgot about the world outside of their own life together. They sunbathed and combed the strand line along the beach, made love in the afternoon and then slept until five or even six o'clock. After simple suppers of chicken or fish with salad, some good sourdough bread and a bottle of Napa valley wine, Theo read John erotic poems from an anthology he'd picked up in Cody's on Telegraph Avenue.

John read *The Oath* by Elie Wiesel. Silence betrays the victims of events by allowing them to be forgotten – and in that forgetfulness, bad things can happen again to good people – so silence betrays the living too. A promise to remain silent, an oath, has to be broken because the language of silence always leads to betrayal. John scribbled notes in the margins of two pages alongside Wiesel's narrative that seemed to speak to him during those sun-filled, love-filled days at the beach:

'God needs man to manifest Himself, that we
know. Whether to affirm His power or His mercy,
He does so through man... we are all messengers.'

411

'God must be lived, my boy. You must live Him, not study Him in books, between four walls!'

He remembered the conversation with Theo over beer at La Val's on that Sunday evening, after Scott and Bill had offered to pay his tuition fees. That God might actually be 'calling' a gay boy from Wales to be a minister was absurd. But then, thinking about the likes of Rahab, the Samaritan woman at the well and even Jesus himself, John concluded that God's relationships with people often seemed unreasonable. He talked about 'calling' for a long time with Theo. They both agreed that God had a keen sense of humour.

* * *

In September, apartment 303 became the international corner of 1815 Arch Street; Malosi was a squat, muscular Samoan in his late twenties with a smile that could melt your heart and an evangelical missionary zeal. Dirk, a fair, blue-eyed German, was in the Lutheran ordination process and had come to PSR for the media studies programme; he had a fondness for Beck's beer, the occasional spliff and 'gin-tonic'. The rapport between the three of them was easy and warm, and Dirk and John quickly became Malosi's brothers. After a couple of weeks, Theo became a brother too. John often wondered how one who seemed so theologically conservative could hold it all together with such grace, and though they often talked about their cultural differences he shied from asking Malosi about the Samoan attitude to gay relationships.

Sometimes, on a Friday night, they'd sit with a group of friends in their lounge, the lights dimmed so that they could watch the City twinkle, and drink Tanqueray or Bombay Sapphire with lemons from one of the campus trees. They'd talk until late. After Christmas, these soirée's became a regular affair known as 'lectures', because everyone thought 'salon' was too pretentious!

John settled quickly into the new routine. Getting up at 5.30 wasn't difficult, as long as he got to bed by ten, but his days were long. He didn't have the luxury of carrying a light class load; he needed to pack all of the basics into two semesters, the January Intersession and the summer school – forty-eight weeks of a calendar year. If all went to plan, that would leave him clear in his senior year to enrol on the new year-long programme that Grace Hope had set up in partnership with PSR: a supervised, half-time inner city church placement (for which he would be paid) that would challenge the theological education of the class room to be practical and relevant, running in parallel with a new module of seminars in Bible, theology and ethics that would underpin and inform the city ministry. If he completed all of that, he'd be on course to graduate in June of 1984.

Cooking breakfasts was a much more sociable job than being a janitor. Within minutes of opening up the dining hall, John usually had company in the kitchen; a non-residential student who'd driven to campus before the rush-hour or someone who'd been up all night on an assignment, a member of the faculty needing a coffee fix before an early lecture or the couple of regular early birds who came for breakfast before the official opening time because they needed to ride the BART into the City for their CPE placements.

It was through Judy Francis that John got a more positive outlook on CPE. He knew Judy from a sexual ethics class with the Dominicans the previous semester. Throughout that Fall she came into the kitchen four mornings a week for her bowl of granola, scrambled eggs with fresh chives and one round of cinnamon-raisin toast – and at least four cups of coffee!

'One of the guys in my CPE group came out yesterday,' she said one morning, about a month into the semester.

'Had you sussed him out already?' John quizzed with a broad grin.

'I'd kind of thought he might be. Tell me, why it is that all the best-looking guys are gay?'

They smiled at one another and John shrugged; how she'd complained, the previous spring, about the dearth of datable straight men in the Bay Area.

'Was he planning to be ordained?'

'Not if this gets back to his denomination,' she said with a harsh edge. 'It makes me so angry. Craig is such a good pastor; he's got such rapport with his patients and so much empathy.'

'So, why did he come out? Has he just made the discovery?'

'No, I think he's well adjusted,' she said. 'We've got three gay guys with AIDS on one of the medical wards; they've got PCP and Kaposi's. My CPE group were having a discussion with Richie, our supervisor, about the fact that lots of the medical and nursing staff are real uncomfortable about them, and some of the cleaning staff have even refused to clean their rooms. Craig asked if it would be okay if he went to see them in his role as a chaplain.'

'Oh Judy, that's just the kind of CPE placement I'd like.'

'You wouldn't believe the grilling Craig got from Richie. He really pushed to get at his motives, and Craig was so focused. Seems he was bullied a lot in college and even beaten up on, so he's got a real sense of what it feels like to be excluded and scapegoated.'

'So is he getting to meet them?'

'Richie fixed it up for tomorrow.'

Judy made a speedy exit to catch BART over to the City. John, continuing to prepare breakfast, decided to apply for the summer CPE programme at University of California Medical Centre.

The Clinical Pastoral Education programmes offered in the City hospitals were popular and always over subscribed. Theo suggested that he talk to Scott Rashford, who might be able to pull some strings at SF General, but John wasn't comfortable with that kind of nepotism. In the spring of 1983 he applied for five programmes, but was only offered a place at the Contra Costa County Hospital in Martinez, a small city on the Sacramento River about 40 minutes from Berkeley. Reflecting that there wasn't much chance of working with AIDS patients out in Martinez, he stalled his response until he knew for certain that he'd got a place on Grace Hope's new year-long programme in San Francisco that she'd called 'Exiles in the City'.

The interviews for 'Exiles', with Grace and Lynn Bridges, the professor of Field Education at PSR, took place in the SFUMP's offices on Eddy Street in the City. He'd been thorough in his preparation; he'd re-read the papers he'd written for Grace and Albie Smith during his private study and through Judy, he'd got to talk with Craig from her CPE group about AIDS ministry.

'I can't promise you a placement with a church that's lesbian and gay affirmative,' Grace said, after John had shared his hopes and expectations for his senior year.

'And we won't be able to confirm your place until we've

415

secured you a church,' Lynn added. 'We've got an interview lined up for you with Parkside Presbyterian Church in the Avenues, just a block from Golden Gate Park.'

'Do they know I'm gay?'

'It's not our policy to out any of the personnel involved with SFUMP,' Grace said. 'But all of the churches that expressed an interest in offering a student internship as part of this programme have received our business pack, so they all know that we're an affirming ministry dedicated to working with, and alongside marginalised people.'

'What are the Avenues' neighbourhoods like?' John asked.

'I guess you'd call them professional people, probably mostly white and mostly families; at least that's the case around Parkside,' Grace said.

'They're especially interested in hiring someone who can work with their youth group and develop the Sunday school curriculum,' Lynn offered. 'And what with you being a trained teacher, we thought you and Parkside would match up well.'

Grace saw the misgivings in his face.

'We have to work with the churches that come forward, John. I don't have the luxury of handpicking them. Parkside is the best match we can come up with right now.'

'I appreciate that, Grace. I guess I just need to adjust my expectations. What's the next step?'

'They'd like you to go along to their 10.30 service on Sunday,' Lynn said. 'You can meet with people during coffee hour, and the minister and a couple of elders will informally interview you over a sandwich lunch.'

The bus from downtown dropped him two blocks from Parkside Presbyterian Church, which stood on a corner lot at a busy junction. The large double doors were at the foot of a squat, square tower dominating the front of the building, minimising the impact of the arched, stained glass window in the gabled west wall. Many San Francisco churches built in the fist decade of the twentieth century had a similar plan, the tower proclaiming the local church as a community gathering place, symbolically calling the people to worship, though Parkside's was built of brown bricks that looked grimy from the exhaust fumes of cars that idled at the busy intersection and gave the building a less than welcoming aspect.

Crossing the street, John decided not to introduce himself as the prospective intern; as a casual visitor he'd be better able to assess Parkside's openness to strangers than if he made the greeters at the door aware of his presence. In the porch, two smiling middle-aged women met him with effusive good mornings; one handed him a worship bulletin and the other offered him a hymnal. The sanctuary was gloomy, the stained glass of the windows too heavily pigmented – or just too grimy to allow much of the bright sunshine in.

John counted thirty people seated indiscriminately. He checked his watch, almost twenty-five past ten. A choir of seven, swathed in royal blue robes, shuffled out from a small side door behind, and to the left, of the pulpit; they lined up, adjacent to the organ console, and began to sing a piece that he judged to be technically beyond their ability. The organist-cum-choir master reminded him of Troy Liddell – a cuddly bear! They sang two more pieces, with difficulty. Congregants continued to arrive. He smiled at the latecomers, those that caught his eye, but barely got a response. At almost a quarter to eleven, the minister emerged from the shadows beneath the organ pipes, mounted the pulpit and announced the call to worship to a congregation of perhaps sixty. But where were the children and the young people from the youth group? The teddy bear played the introduction to a rousing opening hymn; the congregation responded with a less than tuneful mumble – to all five verses!

John estimated that the minister was in his fifties, a balding man with heavy framed glasses. Grace's words came back to him more than once during the long, badly constructed, poorly delivered sermon; 'We have to work with the churches that come forward John. I don't have the luxury of handpicking them.' His expectations would need to be re-examined yet again.

The 'coffee hour', lasting no more than twenty minutes as people seemed eager to get away, was a joyless affair. The minister, who introduced himself as Hal, had deduced that John was 'the student'. Not a difficult deduction; he'd been the only one in that morning's congregation under thirty.

'There will just be the four of us,' Hal said. 'Kitty, she was one of the greeters this morning, Dean, who's our music minister, and you and me.'

In a comfortable, wood-panelled room with a red, thick-piled carpet and a faint smell of furniture polish Hal made the introductions.

'And this is John Idris Jones, our possible student intern,' he concluded.

'So, you're from our sister church in Wales,' Kitty said. 'How interesting. My family come from York-shire, but that's five generations ago.' She giggled. John wondered what response he was expected to make.

'But you're not in the ordination process back home, are you?' Hal put in.

'No, I'm still wrestling with that angel,' John said, sure that Hal, at least, would get the allusion to Jacob.

'And what gifts do you believe you'll be able to share with us at Parkside?' Dean, the teddy bear, asked.

I could lead a bit of congregational singing instead of having that awful choir sing pieces that are out of their league... and I could teach you a thing or two about preaching a well-crafted sermon.

'I understand that you're looking for someone to develop your Sunday school curriculum. I think I can help you there, but I'm curious because I didn't see too many kids this morning.'

'It's the Sunday school we want to develop,' Hal said. 'We've got lots of families with kids on the books and we feel that a good Sunday school will bring them in.'

'And the same is true for the youth group?' John quizzed, wondering as he spoke whether he could have phrased his question with less accusation.

'We have about a dozen teens who come on a Wednesday evening, but we don't have an education programme for them,' Hal said.

'One of those silly girls got pregnant this last winter,' Kitty sallied forth. 'We need someone who can work on their self respect. What is it that Nancy Reagan says? 'Just say no'?'

'That's a drugs message, Kitty,' Dean said.

'They need educating about that too,' Kitty fired back. 'The room those kids use smells of marijuana after they've been in there.'

'Nonsense, Kitty,' Hal spat.

'It does too,' Kitty insisted. 'I know what it smells like!'

There was an uneasy silence.

'So, if you're struggling with your sense of call, what do you see yourself doing in five years?' Hal asked, trying to get the interview back on track.

'I think that this whole AIDS thing is going to present the church with a huge challenge in the next two or three years,' John said, conscious that this might be provocative, but how much of himself was he expected to hide?

Kitty began to tut, and Hal shifted uncomfortably in his seat.

'How do you see that challenge in the context of a local church like Parkside?' Dean asked.

John wondered if Dean went to the same bars as Troy, to meet other bears.

'AIDS seems to be hitting the most marginalised people in society and my reading of the Gospels would place Jesus right in the midst of AIDS sufferers,' John said.

Kitty tutted some more.

'But homosexuals have put themselves at odds with Scriptural teaching,' Hal said. 'This new disease is a sure sign that God is punishing them.'

'Well, Hal, I think that's kind of an Old Testament view of God,' John said, conscious of using the minister's name. 'The Jesus story puts him in amongst those folks that his society was seeking to push to the edges. I don't think any of us can begin to imagine what AIDS is going to mean in the next years, but I believe we have to be beside those who are suffering.'

'We don't want any more fags coming to Parkside,' Kitty said. 'That last bunch caused so much upset, trying to get us to be a lighted-up church.'

'A "More Light" congregation,' Dean said. 'Do you know about this, John?'

'Dean, let's not go there,' Hal said with a blunt edge.

John searched Hal's face for an explanation to the conflict that was obvious between the two men.

'The congregation voted not to become a More Light church

and we lost about half a dozen members,' Hal began, realising that he had to say something by way of an explanation.

'We lost fifteen gay men who were regular attenders and whose annual contributions came to more than 10,000 dollars,' Dean snapped.

Hal shifted in his seat again, his discomfort palpable.

'I guess it's important that you realise from the outset that we've had some difficult times here at Parkside,' Hal said. 'The More Light Movement within the Presbyterian Church nationally seeks to challenge and encourage congregations like ours to be more open to homosexuals – but it didn't sit well with us. We're a conservative community, and more traditional in the way we understand the Scriptures.'

'That will be quite a challenge for me,' John said.

'You're not a fag, are you?' Kitty ventured.

John looked long into each of their faces. 'I'm sorry, I think I've wasted your time here this afternoon,' he said.

Hal and Kitty both looked at their reflections in the polished tabletop and said nothing. John got up to leave.

'I'll see you out,' Dean said, his face full of disappointment.

Late the following afternoon, John picked up his mail from the Admin Building and found a note from Lynn Bridges in his mailbox. She looked harassed as he sat opposite her across a cluttered desk.

'Parkside has pulled its offer to take an intern, so we're in deep trouble.'

'I'm sorry,' John heard himself say, not really grasping the implications of their withdrawal, but feeling he was responsible.

'Hal Taylor talked to me this morning, but someone called Dean Fellows, who says he's the music minister at Parkside, talked with Grace and gave a startlingly different report of your interview. D'you want to tell me what happened?'

John described the events as faithfully as he was able.

'I guess Grace and I screwed up, John. I'm real sorry we put you through that. We obviously didn't do enough homework with Parkside, and we certainly didn't know that they've been in a civil war over the More Light ministry. If we'd known they'd be so hostile we certainly wouldn't have exposed you to that.' Her eyes caught John's and they held each other's gaze. 'Are you okay?'

John nodded.

'Really?'

But a flood of tears burst, surprising them both. Lynn moved quickly to kneel beside him, and held him until the spasm subsided.

'I'm fine now,' he said, drying his eyes. 'I guess I hadn't really appreciated how upsetting the whole thing was.'

'I'm afraid I'm going to have to add to your upset,' she said, and dragged over a chair so that she could sit close to him. 'We don't have another church to offer you right now, so we can't confirm your place in the 'Exiles' programme.'

'I'd guessed as much.'

'Are you still stalling on CPE at Martinez?'

'Yes.'

'I think you need to accept their offer, just in case we can't come up with a church for you. I've taken a look at your transcript, and the CPE, along with that special study you did, will leave you just four credits short of the basic Field Ed requirements for the M.Div.. You should be able to pick those up easily enough with a Weddings and Funerals workshop and a Death and Dying practicum.'

'And what do you think the chances are that you'll find me a church?'

'I think the chance is slim. A half-time stipend is a lot of money to find.'

'And I'm not an easy person to place.'

'You've got some unique gifts, John. You preach well, you've got wonderful people skills, your writing is clear, well argued and incisive. Grace is real keen to have you in the programme; she thinks you'll make a good pastor.'

John felt his face flush.

'We'll pull out all the stops to find you an internship, but that's the only promise I can make.'

That evening he wrote a brief letter accepting the Martinez offer.

* * *

The schedule of the CPE programme was simple; Monday to Thursday the group of seven seminarians, six from the Berkeley schools and one guy who was studying at Emory in Atlanta, met in the classroom at 8.30 with Nick Reid, the programme leader. Despite the 'classroom' sign on the door, it was more of a lounge, with a couple of sofas, four matching easy chairs and three huge, garishly patterned floor cushions. The first to arrive in the morning made sure there was Peet's coffee brewing and for an hour they'd talk about the previous day's experiences or discuss the articles and books on the recommended reading list. From 10 'til 3.30 they spent time on the wards, and during the last hour of the day, when Nick held individual supervisory meetings, they could write up their reflective journals, work on case histories and laboriously re-create from memory the verbatim reports of significant pastoral acts they had participated in during that day. Fridays were set aside for the group to attend to its process.

There were no AIDS patients in the Contra Costa County Hospital and John drew the short straw in the ward allocation.

'Acute psychiatry's a real interesting challenge, John,' Nick announced. 'We've got some folks locked up in there who see spiders creeping from the electric plug sockets and snakes peeking out from the faucets, and there's usually at least one Jesus Christ and a Virgin Mary.'

He decided not to say anything about his time in Denbigh's asylum all those years ago, but he realised that working on the locked ward would probably awaken difficult memories and possibly rekindle some long suppressed emotions. Perhaps it would all come out, with Nick in a supervisory session, or as part of the group's process.

In Denny's LP collection, amongst the many divas singing Puccini and Verdi, John found a couple of Dvorak symphonies. Over the months he'd come to like the seventh, and especially its second movement, the *poco adagio*. Despite the record sleeve's contention that the D minor was the most sombre and austere of the composer's symphonic works, he found this slow movement melodic and uplifting; the flutes and piccolos were even cheerful and the blasts from the brass blew away the most stubborn cobwebs. Listening to the strains of the *poco adagio* drift through the pink-tinged evening to the roof garden from the open windows of apartment 303, he reflected on the events of his first day in Martinez and chuckled to himself at God's sense of comedy.

Possessing a set of keys to the secure unit made all the difference, he could get out whenever he needed to. The nurse in charge, Charlene, was pleased to see him.

'They're bouncing off the walls today,' she said. 'Must be the full moon on Friday!'

John's face gave away his surprise.

'You stay here long enough and you'll start to see the patterns,' she said. 'I'll put ten dollars on it being like a rest home for dignified old ladies next week, but for the next few days it'll be a circus.'

Charlene peered over her huge breasts, which strained the buttons on her pinafore dress, and checked off a number of points on some paperwork. It was a task that needed little of her attention and she continued to talk to John.

'You going to be doing a service in the day room every day, like the last chaplain did?'

'If that's a useful thing to do, then yes,' John said. 'Is there a fixed time for that?'

'It's better in the afternoon; mornings are crazy here with the doctors' rounds and the case conferences... and you'll probably be going to some of those anyway.' She got up from the desk. 'Let me show you around.'

An extension to an older, red brick building that housed the day clinics and doctor's offices, the secure unit was all concrete, steel and reinforced smoked glass. It was light and airy, with a constant hum of air conditioners. The patients had their own rooms, which circled a central open area where a few sad looking shrubs and trees grew from a parched, lawned area, more brown dust than grass.

The patients, more women than men, more blacks and Hispanics than whites, fit the stereotypes of the mentally ill. A

425

woman with wild eyes, seated on a high-backed chair, rocked her body from the waist up – back and forth... back and forth; a man near a window, standing to attention like a soldier, occasionally swatted an imaginary fly with his right hand; a lad of perhaps twenty, his complexion sallow, stared vacantly into the middle distance; an anorexic girl with scarred wrists braided and unbraided her hair. Nothing had triggered any discomfort or dislodged a memory despite the deep pulls on John's empathy.

They turned the corner in the corridor and came towards a black man who sat on a chair reading a baseball magazine.

'We've got two secure rooms here too,' Charlene said. 'Since last night we've had to put one of the women in a straightjacket because she was trying to hurt herself.' She pointed at the black guy. 'Donald's been tied up here all morning. When we've got someone in restraint we have to keep them under constant observation.'

Donald stood up as they approached.

'This is the new chaplain, Donny.'

'Good morning, sir,' he said, standing at least 6ft 6 and thrusting his huge hand towards John.

'Hello,' John said, already distracted by the straightjacketed woman he could see through the open door, who lay, motionless, on a low bench. 'I'm not sure we do this to people back in Britain,' he continued, picking through the surge of memories that began to flood his senses.

'It's a useful tool when someone's violent and threatening to self-harm,' Donald said.

'If they're just being violent we put them in here,' Charlene quipped. She opened the sturdy door to her left. John peered into the small, empty room; it smelled rancidly of piss. Its walls were lined from the floor to the ceiling with thick padding, clad in a canvas type material that was heavily stained in places. 'After thrashing around in here for a few hours they soon get exhausted and we can let them out, but we haven't had anyone in there since the last full moon; our sedation regime is pretty effective most of the time.'

Later that day, a white man with broken teeth and an armful of tattoos was confined to the padded cell. John wondered if his violent mania was as a consequence of the waxing moon.

Missing Theo, who'd left the previous Saturday for a month-long retreat at a monastery on the coast near Carmel, John spent a couple of hours that evening doing some yoga breathing. He let the *poco adagio* wash over him and tried to convince himself that some of the sights from the secure unit, and the plight of some of its inmates, hadn't unduly upset him.

Because the title intrigued him, he chose a work by Thomas Szasz for his first book review. In *The Myth of Mental Illness*, the author seemed to be suggesting that psychiatry in the 1960s and 70s had become a tool to control undesirable behaviours. Whilst neurologists dealt with diseases of the brain, Szasz maintained that psychiatry had developed into a discipline that was concerned with the 'problems of living' and had little to do with demonstrable biological pathology. Classifying certain behaviours as illness offered society a way of controlling undesirable people – medicalising their undesirable behaviour – so that they could be detained and medicated, often involuntarily, to prevent them from behaving in ways society found intolerable. In unguarded moments, over the few days it took to read Szasz, the pornographic photographs and electric orgasms, and Jatunga Arachchi's sweet nothings, came back

427

with vivid clarity. Walking down Euclid, John saw, in a squabble between two drunks, the Jenkins boy kicking Bobby-Nansi on the pavement outside the tobacconist's shop in Barmouth. Then he remembered all those newspaper reports, where 'homosexual' was used as a noun alongside other nouns like thief or criminal, blackmailer, alcoholic or murderer, pervert and even unstable psychotic. The Sunday Library Group's interpretations of scripture whispered with their chanting. And Dr Arwel Thomas wanted to pray with him again, and medicalise what society perceived to be an undesirable lifestyle.

The *poco adagio* soothed the anger that surfaced, but he knew that such a virulent rage couldn't be appeased for long.

Nick Reid scratched his chin through the luxuriance of his black beard.

'That's quite a story my friend. D'you want out of acute psychiatry, is that it?'

'No Nick, not at all. I've told you all of this because I don't know what to do with the anger that's all bottled up inside me.'

'I guess I don't need to tell you that anger can be real destructive, but y'know, there is something positive to hold on to.' They caught one another's eye and Nick held John's gaze. 'The fact that you're angry says that you know they were wrong to do what they did, and you can only know that because you've reached some peace inside yourself about who you are. Against the story you've just told me, that's a huge achievement.'

John thought about what Nick was saying and felt embarrassed. Nick interpreted John's silence as doubt ridden.

'You're a very strong man, John, and I don't just mean those muscles that buldge when you flex your arm.'

They both smiled.

'I've been watching you these past four weeks. You're passionate about ministry, about being *there* for people, and you've got a depth of experience to draw on that gives you qualities of empathy that are rare, believe me.'

'Thank you,' John mumbled, his embarrassment now palpable.

'You don't have to thank me, John,' Nick said, almost dismissively. 'I want you to be aware of your strength. I want you to value your struggle so that any anger you feel about the way the world treated you gets used as a source of energy for making change... for touching lives in meaningful ways and for doing good.'

'But right now the anger feels too raw, and almost too unwieldy to tame.'

'So, you need to get some therapy, my friend.' He reached back across his desk and lifted the red card index box onto his lap. His fingers flicked the cards with manic precision. 'There's a real neat woman I know; I think she's in Oakland.'

'Therapy doesn't come cheap and I'm on a pretty tight budget.'

'The music and the yoga breathing you described are just a pacifier, John. You need help to develop the skills that'll tame that beast, otherwise it'll get you.'

Nick jotted down a name and a phone number, and then tore the sheet from the note pad with a flamboyant swipe of his hand.

'Anger destroys people's lives, John. Anger causes tumours. Anger makes people drink and take drugs. Anger screws up relationships.' Every time he said 'anger' he said it louder than the time before. 'You're too bright to let the lack of money be an excuse not to get this sorted.' He pointed at the paper John

429

clutched between his fingers. 'Cindy Coleman is good. She'll have a sliding scale, but she doesn't come cheap.' He reached forward and brushed John's knee lightly with his hand. 'You can't really afford not to.'

It took John only a couple of days' reflection on the conversation he'd had with Nick Reid before he called Cindy Coleman.

*   *   *

Theo had been back a few days and they were enjoying one another. When the telephone rang, just after seven in the morning, it woke them from a deep sleep. Disorientated, John grasped that he was running an hour late, and felt the anxiety rise within him as he snatched up the phone.

'Sorry to call so early,' he heard Grace Hope say through the earpiece. 'I wanted to catch you before you left for Martinez. How's your CPE?'

'Fine, thanks,' he said, his voice husky, his tongue thick with tastes of Theo.

'Can you get over to the City tomorrow evening, say about 6.30, to meet with me and some folks at Shiloh United Methodist Church?'

'You've found me an internship?'

'It looks promising,' she said cautiously. 'Dots Shober, the minister, had really wanted Shiloh to be in the programme this year but when she got pregnant she didn't think it would be fair to take an intern.'

'She miscarried then?' John said, trying to sound sympathetic.

'No, she's due sometime around Christmas. The story's all a bit convoluted, but Dean Fellows, the music minister at

Parkside, knows the organist at Shiloh and talked to him about you. I think his name is Tom – and something Italian, like Bellini, or Cherubini. Anyway, this Tom talked with a group of the gay guys in the congregation and they persuaded Dots to reconsider, and between them they've come up with almost all of the year's stipend already.'

John watched the seconds tick away on his alarm clock and knew there were questions he ought to be asking. 'Six-thirty will be tight, even if I drive straight over from Martinez,' he said. 'Can we make it seven?'

'Okay, I'll fix that up. The church is on Sanchez Street. D'you know that part of town?'

'Yes, quite well,' he said, wondering if it was near Scott and Bill's house.

'I'm not sure which block, but it's right next to a parking garage with a big blue sign. If you reach Army Street, driving away from Market, you've gone too far.'

'Thanks, Grace,' he said with a gravity that surprised him.

'I want you in the 'Exiles' programme, John,' she said. 'See you tomorrow... and try not to be late.'

Shiloh United Methodist Church served a richly diverse part of the city with a significant, hard-working, Filipino community. There was a sizeable population of older, white professional people too, some of whom were wealthy – though, since the boom in house prices most were just rich on paper, especially the higher they lived on Diamond Heights. Then there were the gay men; fifty-five registered on the church roll, a rainbow coalition of races and ages, exiles from redneck communities across the nation. Of the fifteen gay couples, six were well-heeled. With their considerable joint incomes, they'd bought up and renovated

431

once grand Victorian houses and turned them again into 'painted ladies'. This 'pink power base' at Shiloh (as John once heard them called) clearly understood that their place in the church community could be secured by regular attendance, a willingness to sit on various committees, and being prepared to serve on the coffee hour group and flower rota. Sometimes, the flower arrangements for Sunday worship were just too over-the-top! These men knew, too, that a readiness on their part as individuals to pledge a regular weekly amount of money, which came to hundreds of dollars per head over the course of a year, made a substantial pink contribution to the church funds and muted any expressions of latent homophobia.

There were 187 members on the church roll and Dots Shober often said, with some pride, that they carried no driftwood. Liturgy and preaching were a quality product at Shiloh, and it was rare that the main Sunday service didn't pull in between 90 and 100 'bums-on-seats'. It wasn't uncommon to have more than 120 in the congregation. Aside from the dozen shut-ins, who were visited on an as-needs basis, every member on the roll attended at least once a month, and seventy-nine percent of the members pledged their annual offering, so the finances were secure, even if they weren't a wealthy church.

There was a lively children's Sunday school. To John's considerable relief it was run by a single mum – one of the few young white women in the church, and a Filipino gay dad, both elementary school teachers. There was a well-attended adult Bible-study-cum-discussion group that met at 9.30 on Sunday mornings from September through May and a sometime women's group that met for a few weeks, now and then, to discuss a book, cook up recipes from the different cultures represented in the church or make costumes for the Christmas show. A monthly potluck lunch, an ad-hoc choir coming together for the festivals, and an annual children's trip to the zoo or Golden Gate Park as a 'reward' for working so hard on a play or a concert – all this testified to a healthy and vibrant life together.

After Tom Cherubini's conversation with the music minister from Parkside, he talked to some of Shiloh's gay cohort before putting his idea to Dots. She was a confident thirty-something with degrees and diplomas from some of the finest schools in the nation. Despite being a good, careful listener, she often spoke her truth quietly and clearly. Her outspokenness didn't always sit well. With Tom, she seemed willing to reconsider the positive aspects of taking on an intern and together they figured out a way of ensuring that whoever came to work for them would be well supported when she was off on maternity leave. Dots had already talked to Travis Gunderson, who'd been worshipping at Shiloh for four years; he and his partner had moved to the Bay Area from Seattle. Travis, an ordained minister who worked as a psychotherapist at a gay men's health cooperative, had already agreed to preach once a month during her absence, and take any funerals, should the need arise. Tom suggested that Travis might be able to supervise the intern; a proposal to which he knew Travis wasn't hostile because they'd already talked. After Dots had conferred with Grace Hope, she became quietly excited about the possibilities offered by the seminarian from Wales.

John was slow to grasp that Shiloh wanted him, and that he didn't have to work too hard at the interview to impress them. Tom and Travis liked him instantly, and Travis sensed that they'd get along just fine. Dots appreciated his candour, his sharp intelligence and his grounding in Bible. What she initially interpreted as a streak of arrogance, she quickly reinterpreted as oozing self-confidence, and liked him better for it. Myrtle McFadden, her antique pearls milky against her navy blouse, found him charming... and anyway, she thought it was time they had a man on the ministry team! Juni Dimaapi, not sure whether he'd been invited to the meeting as the token Filipino or to represent the interests of the Sunday school, appreciated John's teaching background and hoped that he'd at least show some interest in the curriculum developments planned for the Fall.

At the end of a meeting that had lasted almost two hours, where all of the duties Shiloh expected of an intern had been itemised and discussed, Dots asked John to take a walk around the block. On his return he found them all smiling. Dots offered him the job. Grace Hope beamed with pleasure and satisfaction.

Driving back to Berkeley over the Bay Bridge, the radio tuned to a local network, his excitement about the internship at Shiloh was tempered by a report about AIDS on the news bulletin: 'Transmission of this new disease has become a major issue in San Francisco in the past two months and even the SFPD has equipped its patrol officers with special masks and gloves for use when dealing with what the police call a suspected AIDS patient,' the dusky voice of the woman reporter said. 'This is what one police officer, patrolling the Castro district, told us this afternoon: 'Many of the officers are concerned that they might catch this mystery bug and take it home... so the whole family gets AIDS.' Tonight, no one from the Mayor's office was available for comment.'

The last weeks of CPE passed quickly. John was attacked by Randy, a new admission on the secure unit, a boy in his early twenties who'd addled his brain with phencyclidine, an addictive street drug commonly known as angel dust... though the assault did take place on the afternoon of the full moon! Had Donald not lifted Randy into the air like a bundle of straw in his huge hands, John may have suffered more than bruising around his throat from the boy's wrench-like grip. Still shaken by the experience, he carefully prepared a verbatim report of the incident to see if he could fathom a reason for Randy's behaviour; perhaps he'd said something to upset or offend the boy? Nick Reid agreed that the conversation leading up to Randy's violent outburst was innocuous.

A while later, Charlene was short with John for not filing a report of the incident in Randy's notes. Scanning the entries in the thick wad of paperwork from previous admissions, John saw references to delusional behaviour, hallucinations and paranoia, and a history of violence against other patients and staff going back many months. Later that afternoon, Randy floored a patient who was seriously concussed when her head hit the wall as she fell. Randy spent the remainder of the day singing to the moon in the padded cell.

Back in Berkeley, still shaken up by Randy's violence, John thought about the poor woman who'd been knocked unconscious, and reflected on his own good fortune. The *poco adagio* soothed his fretful soul and Theo soothed his trembling body.

During the last personal supervision meeting with Nick Reid, after they'd gone through John's learning contract for the CPE and both agreed that all of the objectives had been met, Nick asked about Cindy Coleman.

'She's working me really hard,' John said.

'I'm happy that you took my advice,' Nick said. 'She's a damn good therapist. You're such an able minister and hugely gifted in the way you offer pastoral care. You mustn't let all that negativity inside you jeopardise that.' He reached out and touched John's knee. 'Don't look down at the floor when I say good things about you. Look me in the eye.'

John held Nick's gaze with some discomfort.

'You're a man who's destined to be dealt with,' he said.

'What's that supposed to mean?' John quipped.

'You think about it,' he said, and winked.

John took the hand that was offered and shook it with a sense of triumph that he'd successfully completed the CPE programme.

'Now get the hell out of here,' Nick jibed with a broad smile.

*　　*　　*

Tom Cherubini took such delight in John's arrival at Shiloh. He persuaded Myrtle McFadden to bake banana bread for the coffee hour on John's first Sunday. Travis Gunderson brought along his renowned double chocolate brownie – *sans* hashish, and Juni Dimaapi made Buko Pandan, cubes of green 'jelly' with a distinct, but hard to describe taste – sort of fresh hay and nutty – in a deliciously creamy-sweet coconut sauce.

John's first impression of Tom, on that August evening of the interview, was that he was buoyant, funny and thin as a rake. His eyes, recessed beneath high cheekbones, were a foggy grey, and his fringe was combed forward over a deep forehead. He wasn't an easy man to age. John thought he might be forty, but then his hair was dull and silvering and his skin was sallow.

During that first coffee hour, his head beginning to buzz from too much caffeine and an overload of sugar – he'd had to try all of the goodies so as not to offend anyone – Myrtle talked him through the gallery of church members' photographs exhibited on the wall of the church hall.

'And these are from last year?' John asked.

'I think maybe the last eighteen months,' Myrtle said. 'The idea first came up at the Thanksgiving potluck two years ago; we had a run on new members through that Fall, and I guess the photos were taken over the three or four months after that.'

Tom Cherubini's fuller face beamed from a photograph, his brown hair glossy and swept back, his skin tanned. He looked no more than thirty.

By the middle of October it was obvious that Tom wasn't well.

'Have people in the congregation noticed the decline?' John asked Dots during one of their weekly supervision meetings.

'Sure they've noticed,' she sighed and rested her hands on her pregnant belly. 'But Tom's got a reputation for burning the candle at both ends. He's come to church straight from a night at the baths before now.' She bit her lip and swept her burnt blonde hair back. 'Well... maybe they don't know about his visits to the bathhouses, but they know he likes to party. I guess people just think he's burning out.'

'And is that what you think?'

'I read the papers, and I had a long talk with Travis one day,' she said, and winced as the baby kicked her.

'And you're sure you want me to go to the hospital to visit him?'

'Until they know what's wrong with him, yes, it might be better if you go.'

'And he won't be upset that you've sent me.'

She shifted in her seat to try to settle the baby into a more comfortable position.

'I think Tom knew —' She sipped some iced water from the glass on the coffee table. 'Back in July, I mean, when he came to see me about you. He was so keen to get a gay man on the staff. I guess he just felt that it would be a safer option for him to have someone he wouldn't need to explain himself to in the months I'm off caring for this little one.' She rubbed her belly as the child inside her settled.

'And if it is AIDS, how will the folks at Shiloh respond?'

'People really love Tom,' she said, her face broken into a smile. 'I've got every confidence that we'll be there for him —'

'But what?' John said into her hesitation.

'Well, I guess with all these rumours about casual transmission. Jeez, d'you know that the cops have even been issued with plastic gloves now?'

'And that's why you'd be happier if I went to see him?'

She made a simple open-handed gesture.

'But then, if AIDS is so easy to pass on, we might have already picked it up from him, or any of the hundreds of others —' Somewhere in his head John heard Denny's voice over the hubbub of the street party in the Castro that first Halloween: *'Welcome to paradise.'* 'God forbid!' he said under his breath.

'What?'

'In a city like San Francisco there could be thousands of people like Tom.'

'If I wasn't so hormonal maybe I'd see a clearer picture,'

Dots said after a moment's pause. 'I'm not usually the type to get hysterical about things.'

'I'm not judging you, Dots. The whole thing is damn scary.'

She smiled, appreciating that her gay intern from Wales was so discomforted; it made her feel that her own unease wasn't such a betrayal of Tom. 'I guess I'm hoping the community at Shiloh won't be freaked by it,' she said.

'I don't know people yet... to get a sense of how we need to play it.'

'I've always been direct and to the point,' she said, becoming the proficient clergywoman again. 'If we don't address it face-on, the gossip and the rumours will do more damage.'

They both reflected for a moment.

'Okay, Dots. I'll go to the hospital on my way back to Berkeley, and if that rasping cough that Tom's got has been diagnosed as PCP —'

'Then we'll know that he's got AIDS.'

'I'll call you later,' he said as he left.

He drove to Scott and Bill's house. The door was opened just seconds after he'd pressed the bell.

'John, how good to see you,' Scott said, a bundle of mail in his hand, his leather briefcase carelessly abandoned on the Oriental rug that ran the length of the hallway. 'Come on in; don't trip on my bag there.'

'I'm sorry to call unannounced,' John said, perhaps a bit too formally.

'You're lucky to find me in,' he said, opening his arms to hug him. 'I've only been home a few minutes. Bill won't be home for a while yet, but you'll stay and have some dinner with us, won't you?'

They embraced, and John felt himself relax after the tensions of the meeting with Dots.

'I'd love to, but I can't, not today. I'm on my way to visit someone in the hospital.'

'My hospital?' Scott quizzed, gesturing that they go through to the kitchen.

'Yes. One of the guys from church.'

'So, how are you liking your job at Shiloh?'

'It's only been a few weeks, but I like it a lot.'

'I'd better not offer you a gin and tonic then, had I?'

'No, some iced water maybe?'

Scott piled ice cubes into two large crystal tumblers. 'So, one of your jobs at Shiloh is hospital visiting?'

'Yes. Are you still seeing gay guys coming in with AIDS?'

'A couple of new cases every week now; it's getting real heavy.'

'So it may be that the guy from church is one of your patients and I don't want to —'

Scott handed him the iced water. 'What do you want to know?'

'I haven't come to ask you about Tom Cherubini, but there's so much fear in this city about how AIDS is transmitted —'

'And you've come to ask me if I think that just visiting Tom in the hospital will put you at risk?'

John felt embarrassed that his motive was so transparent. 'Dots Shober, the minister at Shiloh, has asked me to go'n see Tom because she's heavily pregnant; I guess I want to be able to reassure her too.'

'Well... what can I tell you?' Scott began, running his hand over the day's growth on his cheek. 'We still don't really know for sure. I work on the basis that whatever it might be is blood borne, so the only precaution I take is wearing gloves, and only

440

then if I'm dealing with body fluids.'

'So the police department isn't so stupid after all,' John quipped.

'So long as they're willing to wear their gloves with every person they find bleeding, or vomiting or pissing over themselves,' Scott said, his tone derisive. 'They can't know who's infectious just by looking at them.'

'And the scientists haven't come up with anything?'

'There was a report out of France this past May; the Pasteur Institute has isolated a new virus, but over here we've tended not to give that too much credence.'

'What's wrong with French science?'

'I guess we Americans are sometimes a bit too scornful of old Europe.'

'But surely AIDS is too big for that kind of pettiness!'

'AIDS is so big that whoever discovers the causative agent, and then goes on to develop effective diagnostic tests and treatments, will get very rich indeed. They might even get a Nobel prize.'

John reflected for a moment on human avarice.

'If it's any help, you can tell Dots that I don't lie awake at night thinking that I'm going to get AIDS just by being sociable with these guys... or by percussing their chests. My gut tells me it's not a casually transmitted thing. Blood borne... it may be. Sexually transmitted? Hmm, now that would give me nightmares!'

Tom Cherubini was in a single room on the fourth floor with views across Potrero Hill to the skyscrapers in the financial district. He was sitting up in bed, his back against a stack of pillows. From a flimsy plastic mask, askew across his nose and mouth, came the gentle hiss of oxygen. A machine above his head bleeped at regular intervals and from a drip, set up at his side, a steady flow of drops passed down a tube and into his body through a needle embedded in his forearm.

'D'you get to take the mask off so that I can give you a kiss?' John asked as he dragged the only chair in the room a little closer to Tom's side. He heard the echo of Scott's reassurance that it probably wasn't casually transmitted, and fought against a baser instinct to leave the chair by the window and visit with Tom from a distance.

'Just a peck on the cheek then,' Tom said, pulling the mask away.

Surprised by the clarity and strength of Tom's voice, John proffered the peck and noticed two small, raised, blue-black *bruises* on his forehead, under a thinning fringe. So that's what Kaposi's sarcoma looks like, John reflected, recalling some of the articles he'd read. Tom's sinewy fingers released the plastic mask, and the elastic band that passed around his head pulled it back over a face that was already an old man's.

'Here, hold my hand,' Tom muffled through the oxygen hiss.

John took the cold, clammy hand in his and felt some of his apprehension dissipate. Tom was still Tom!

'The drip's only got a few minutes left to run,' he said.

'That's okay,' John said, aware that the simple routines of hospital life could take on a disproportionate significance. 'If the nurse comes to unhook you I can just step out for a few minutes.'

'This pentami-stuff is wonderful. I feel so much better already.'

'That's great,' John said and squeezed Tom's hand. He could just figure out the name *pentamidine* on the drip bag's label. 'You'll need to be on it for a while though, I guess,' he said, recalling something that Scott had said when they'd first talked about AIDS. 'So you'll need to be a patient patient.'

Tom's thin lips edged into a tight smile, scarcely visible through the transparent plastic mask. 'Patience isn't one of my virtues,' he grumbled.

The veins on the back of Tom's hand, like the tributaries of a river across a broad delta, were raised ridges of blue. John stroked one of the tracts and watched it disappear momentarily under the slight pressure from his thumb before surging back. The bleep of the machine above Tom's bed seemed to fill the room. Through the course of the CPE programme, John had become easier with the silences that could happen when words weren't easy. Holding Tom's hand in silence seemed to fit with his developing understanding of the pastoral nature of ministry. He was more confident now, and unless he was clear in his own mind that he knew what he wanted to say, it was better to say nothing, allowing gestures, touches and closeness to speak.

'You must tell Dots not to come,' Tom said, his eyes tearful, his tone straightforward.

'I think she'll appreciate your concern and understanding,' John offered with a gentle squeeze of his hand.

The bleeps seemed louder.

'I've had a note from Myrtle already,' he said, pointing to the only card on the windowsill.

'She seems to be a grandma to everyone at Shiloh.'

'Myrtle's alright,' he said. 'Her bark is worse than her bite.'

'I haven't seen that side of her yet.'

'Get her on your side, John; she'll carry the twin sets and pearls with her.'

'Thanks... that's useful to know.'

'Can you bring me Communion?' he asked into the bleeps.

'I guess so. I can't do the Sacraments myself yet, but Dots and I can figure a way... and if I can't do it, then I'm sure Travis would come on over —.'

'You're my minister now. You and Dots can fix something.'

'Sure we will. Do you want us to pray together... now?'

'No, that'll just embarrass me.' The bleeping machine seemed to shriek. 'There's an envelope amongst that clutter there someplace,' he said pointing at the bedside locker. 'I've put down the arrangements for my funeral; the music I want... the readings... a few things about my life that might be worth a mention in a eulogy.'

'That's very thoughtful of you,' John said, his voice cracked. 'Let's hope that I won't need —'

'Don't give me any platitudes, John Idris Jones!' Tom cut in. 'We both know better than that. If the PCP doesn't get me this time it will be something else... next week or next month.'

'Okay Tom,' John ventured, searching his grey eyes. 'We do this straight down the line, hmm?'

'Straight down the line. No bullshit.'

John pushed the sealed envelope with Tom's no bullshit directions between the pages of the small book of prayers and readings that he carried with him on pastoral visits.

'The drip's almost through,' Tom quipped. 'On your way out you can ask one of the nurses to come and unhook me... and see what you can do about that Communion.'

'Is there anything practical you need right now?' John asked as he stood up to leave. 'Laundry, or... shopping? Cookies or potato chips?'

'Oh, sure. A case of Michelob,' he said, pulling the oxygen mask from his face anticipating a kiss. He smiled broadly and John tried not to flinch at the sight of his bleeding gums. 'Or

444

a gorgeous man to cuddle up with! Or some homemade ravioli from Sturani's in North Beach and some sourdough from the little Jewish bakery on Haight... and maybe just an ounce or two of weed.'

'I think the weed is probably off limits,' John said with a chuckle. 'But I'll see what I can do about the gorgeous man.'

Tom laughed – a guffawing, rasping laugh that seemed to mock his past life. And then he began to choke, spattering spots of bloody saliva onto his stained T-shirt and the pale blue cotton sheet. John reached for his hand again but Tom snatched it away. 'Don't get my blood on you,' he urged as he recovered from the spasm of coughs, his voice edged with panic.

John wanted to touch him, to show that he wasn't scared and reassure him that he wasn't one of the new untouchables that the religious right's TV evangelists had been bad-mouthing. The bleeps from the machine screamed... and a voice inside his head pleaded to get out of Tom's room.

'Maybe I'll just settle for the ravioli,' Tom said when he was calmer.

'Sure thing,' John quipped.

After listening to the messages on the answering machine, John took Tom's instructions from between the pages of his little green book. He fingered the envelope, made from cheap, thin paper, and felt the folds of the enclosed sheet. It wasn't a self-sealing envelope, but one that had had to be licked. He saw Tom's bleeding gums and the bloody saliva spattered on the sheet, and he heard Scott's words of prudent advice; 'the only precaution I take is wearing gloves, and only then if I'm dealing with body fluids'. And the spit-sealed envelope in his hand became the focus of all the anxieties and fears he harboured

445

about AIDS. He threw it to the floor.

I've touched Tom… even kissed his cheek. And those bleeding gums…and all that coughing, spraying bloody saliva.

John stood under the shower, his skin red from the heat and the scrubbing, wanting to believe he was being ridiculous but not able to stop himself.

'But when you were with him you were calm and rational and gave him no reason to believe you were uncomfortable in his presence,' Theo said after John had cried about at betraying Tom.

'I hope that's true, Theo, but when I came home, when I held that envelope in my hand —'

'So, let's open it together right now so that it doesn't become an even bigger stumbling block.'

'D'you think I'm an awful person for reacting like this?' he asked as he took the envelope and tore it open.

'I'll tell you when I've met someone who's got AIDS.'

*   *   *

After a lot of prayerful thought, Dots Shober decided not to include any mention of AIDS in her sermon. It didn't fit with the text from John's Gospel anyway, and she felt that any reference to it would seem forced; she didn't want anyone to think she was making a token gesture. She'd acknowledge Tom's absence, due to illness, during the announcements at the beginning of the service, and ask whoever was leading the prayers to include a petition for people with AIDS in the prayers for the sick. After checking the prayer rota, and discovering that Travis was signed up to be prayer leader, she talked with him a couple of times on the phone and felt confident that he'd be thoughtful and sensitive in his choice of words. Reflecting on her preparations for that Sunday's worship she quietly congratulated herself that she'd hit exactly the right note.

Overhearing derisive remarks about Tom Cherubini at coffee hour, she felt dismayed, but after mentally registering those few individuals who'd made the almost whispered comments, she decided not to jump in, all guns blazing; she'd employ a little tact and diplomacy and pay them a pastoral visit.

The depth of disquiet amongst the community at Shiloh only became apparent when Juni Dimaapi came to the church office after coffee hour as Dots and John were discussing how the next week's responsibilities were to be divided between them.

'I've just had three parents tell me they're real uncomfortable about Tom coming back, if he gets better I mean,' Juni said. 'They're already talking about taking their kids out of Sunday school. One even said it will only be a matter of time before other gay guys in the congregation get sick and —' Juni looked at the floor.

'And what?' Dots snapped into his awkwardness.

'Well... infect everybody.'

'But that's stupid,' Dots retorted, more from frustration that she'd so misjudged her congregation.

'We're all frightened by AIDS,' Juni said quietly. The calm simplicity of his words reminded Dots of her own fears.

'I'm sorry, Juni, I was out of line for snapping at you like that. Thank you for coming to tell me. I guess I'd better call a meeting of the church council so that we can figure out a way to get through this.'

'D'you want me to resign from the Sunday school?' Juni asked.

'Oh Juni... no, of course I don't want you to resign. Has somebody said something?'

'Not directly, but I'm one of the gay men they think is going to infect everyone else.'

'You're doing a great job with the Sunday school, Juni, really. And I won't have you, or any of the other gay men hounded out of this congregation.'

'Thank you, Dots,' Juni said, his voice strong. 'I'll be happy to work on the Filipino families, if you think that's appropriate.'

'Myrtle will carry a lot with her too, won't she?' John said, sensing that a strategy was beginning to come together.

'And Travis is hugely respected; he gets on with the straight guys because he's so into baseball,' Dots chipped in, as she scanned her diary. 'Can you two make Wednesday evening?'

By the end of the afternoon, Dots had talked with everyone she needed to talk to and the meeting was set for Wednesday at seven.

Riding under the Bay on BART, and reflecting on the day's events, John decided he would offer to give up his already agreed preaching slot on the following Sunday. It wasn't that the prospect of preparing and delivering a sermon that would have to address the community's fears about AIDS was daunting to him, he just wanted to give Dots the chance to preach that slot without forcing her to claim it back.

'That's good of you to offer,' she said into the phone. 'It did cross my mind... but you've already been to visit Tom, so you'll be able to speak from a position that I can't. It's your slot, but if you can see your way to letting me read your sermon before you preach it. Not that I want to vet it... but it would just help to know what you're going to say.'

'Thanks,' he said, grateful she hadn't pulled rank. 'I like

working with you, Dots Shober.'

The Gospel reading for the following Sunday was again from John, the fourth chapter. He'd heard many a sermon expounding on the 'water that gives eternal life', but John also recalled this same passage from the Communion service with the in-betweens at the Empress Hotel; Kristel's choice – the Samaritan woman at the well.

He read the passage through a couple of times and wondered about the woman in the story. Why had she gone to the well on her own, and in the middle of the day, the hottest time? Wasn't drawing, and carrying water, work that women did communally in the hours after dawn, before the day became too hot? And what did it mean that she'd had five husbands? Was that a Biblical euphemism for saying she was a harlot, the reason she was alone maybe, shunned by the other women in her community? And why her surprise when Jesus asked her for a drink?

John scanned the footnotes in his Oxford Annotated and read that Jews held Samaritans in contempt, and that rabbis avoided speaking to women in public.

'So Jesus is going against his tradition by inviting this relationship,' he said to the open pages of his Bible as the spark of an idea flared in his mind.

He spent the evening in the library doing a thorough exegesis of the passage and was so excited by his interpretation of the text that he decided to ask Bee and Ann to check out his findings and conclusions. With this sermon there was no way he could afford to read into the text something that just wasn't there.

The meeting of the church council was a polite affair with no raised voices, no hysterical outbursts and no expressions of overt anti-gay sentiment. Myrtle, who insisted that she be called *madam chairman* when she chaired a meeting, had thought long and hard about her opening remarks. She'd talked to Travis at some length, been to visit Tom in the hospital, and read some of her journals from the war years, when she'd been a young nurse in Europe's battlefield hospitals.

'And if AIDS does turn out to be casually contagious?' she said, before throwing the meeting open. 'Well, I guess it won't be enough just to leave Shiloh will it? We'll have to leave San Francisco! Go and live someplace out in the boondocks, or maybe join Sally Ride and take a trip on that Challenger space shuttle.' She smiled quietly. 'But I guess you all who have plans to leave had better be real careful about who comes along with you. I visited with Tom for an hour this afternoon in his hospital room. He held my hand and we said the 23rd Psalm together, and when I left I kissed him on the cheek.'

The impact of Myrtle's compassion and common sense was obvious in people's faces, and John, whose sermon was shaping up, wondered if she'd stolen his thunder. By the end of the meeting there was a general agreement that the Shiloh community would commit itself to learning more about AIDS and seek to understand the challenges it presented, and the people present pledged to do whatever was necessary to support Tom and any others in the congregation who fell sick.

Dots read the draft of John's sermon. She smiled when she handed it back, but said very little and offered no suggestions despite being invited to do so. He asked Scott to read it, and when Bill said that they'd both come along to hear it preached he was a bit taken aback. Then Ann asked if she could come over to Shiloh with a couple of people from her preaching class;

doing four or five sermon critiques was a requirement of their preaching course and she really wanted to hear what he'd made of the exegesis he'd asked her to check-out. Preaching *'Who is the Samaritan woman at the well?'* became a personal challenge as well as a professional one.

In the first minutes, John saw that he had the congregation with him and this knowledge fed his confidence. He knew, too, that the sermon was a good one; Biblically sound, contemporary and challenging. He just needed to preach it well. For years he'd watched preachers carefully. Many looked from their pulpits into some void in the middle distance, and failed to hold their listener's attention; a congregation, he believed, didn't like to be talked-at. Other preachers seemed to talk down in an all-knowing manner, while some still ranted in that old fashioned way. In Wales it was called 'getting into a *hwyl*', though some of the black preachers he'd heard had made that style seem appealing. John was striving for a more conversational technique. He'd choose six or eight people in the congregation and look at them often, imagining that he was speaking directly to them, and he used silence, often after raising a question or proffering a challenge, so that the listener could begin to formulate a response.

Beginning his conclusion he knew that he'd preached well.

'Because it is only through my relationships with others that I can reflect God's love for me, and my love for God, so Jesus offers me an example of what it means to take risks in forming relationships. Jesus risks the wrath of the religious institutions of his day by engaging with this woman… a Samaritan, a member of a tribe that the Jews hate because of their worship of false gods. Jesus risks the anger and resentment of his own community by speaking with her – because she's a woman – a woman who isn't a member of Jesus' family, which means he's forbidden by tradition to speak with her. And Jesus risks being made unclean by allowing her to hand him a cup of water... for not only is this woman's sexual history dubious, Jesus has no way of knowing at what stage this stranger is in her menstrual cycle.'

Travis nodded his head thoughtfully. Myrtle twisted her finger in her pearls. Ann was writing notes in her notebook. Scott smiled broadly.

'This past week I came upon a modern day Samaritan Woman at the well. My encounter was with a man that many in contemporary society express hatred for, because of the *tribe* he belongs to. Some would even go so far as to say that the sexual freedom in the gay community is like the worship of a false god. I was challenged by my fear of what people would think and say, and how people might shun me, because of my contact with this man. I was challenged by notions of being made unclean – frightened by the myths and misconceptions that are being spread in this city, and around the world, about AIDS.'

A shuffle of discomfort in the congregation distracted him. Travis gently tapped the back of the pew in front of him with his finger in time with his nodding head. Myrtle smiled, her eyes twinkling. Ann was taking in the response of the congregation. Scott silently mouthed 'Go for it'.

'As someone who's new to Shiloh, it has been my clear impression, in the last weeks, that Tom Cherubini is well liked in this community. He might indeed be the first man we know to have developed AIDS, but Tom is still Tom. Despite our present lack of knowledge about this disease, we are being assured by scientists and doctors that casual transmission is unlikely. Both Myrtle and I, when we visited Tom in the

452

hospital, were not asked to wear special clothes, or required to visit with him through a glass screen. We could hold his hand. We could kiss his sunken cheek.

'The religious right in this country is bellicose in its ranting about AIDS being the wrath of God directed at sinful people. If those TV evangelists are right, we have to ask some fundamental questions about the nature of a loving and forgiving God, and to be consistent in our thinking, we would need to see cancer, and heart disease, even appendicitis, as God's punishment too.'

In a pause that seemed eternal John shook his head slowly as he eyed people in the congregation.

'In exactly the same way that Jesus took risks in his relations with the woman at the well, so I am invited to take the risk of relationships. And so are all of you.'

Myrtle nodded her head. Scott was whispering into Bill's ear; they were both smiling. Travis winked when John looked at him.

'We need to stay faithful to our relationship with Tom if we are to remain faithful in our relationship with God. Amen.'

*   *   *

Only one family left Shiloh in the days after the church council meeting and the sermon on the woman at the well, but the numbers attending worship on proceeding Sundays rose steadily. The grapevine spread the news that Shiloh was a better than okay place to be for gays and lesbians – and for people with AIDS. With a growing sense of being in the right place, at the right time, and doing something thoroughly worthwhile in a community that valued him, John was thrown off balance by an ambush he couldn't have foreseen.

'Have you ever thought about writing any of these characters a letter?'

He was in Cindy Coleman's office, a small room with minimalist décor he found austere. The sun, streaming through a large window that looked onto Oakland's Lake Merritt, caught her eyes; they flashed green and brown.

'Sending them letters?'

'Writing, not necessarily sending,' she said.

He hesitated, not sure he was grasping the implications of her suggestion.

'From what you've shared with me over the last weeks, I get the sense that you'd have plenty to say to Jatunga Arachchi and Arwel Thomas if you wrote each of them a letter.'

'A few pages of ripe cussing, I guess,' he said, his tone dismissive.

She smiled, but because of her tooth brace it was a self-conscious smile. 'You could write them what you think, and feel, about the way they treated you. How what they did has haunted you all these years and how it's left you with all this pent up anger.'

'I'd have to write a lot of letters,' he said after a moment, recalling some of the many events and people that had made him feel bad about being gay during those early years.

'Think about it,' she said. 'It's an exercise that works for some people. Putting down all of that grievance on paper can be a way of letting it go, but you have to want to let it go.'

He searched her face for any trace of malevolence, but saw only encouragement. 'You mean that some people willingly hold on to such negativity, despite the harm it does them?'

'Maybe not always consciously, but it's worth asking yourself if you're holding on to it for some reason.'

'Like what?' He felt the muscles in his stomach begin to clench.

'I don't know, John, but perhaps you can think about that too.'

For a long time they considered one another in a silence marred only by the traffic noise that was just audible over the hum of the air-conditioner.

John searched the labyrinth of his mind and came upon doors that had been slammed shut so long he'd forgotten they were there.

Cindy leaned forward in her chair and decided to trust her intuition. 'Sometimes, when the demons have tied us up in knots for years and years, it can take a long time to untie those bonds. We might think we've done a good job of releasing ourselves, but actually we're still being held back.'

Putting his ear against a rediscovered, tightly bolted door, he heard the whisperings of jibes that could still hurt him. Through a keyhole, the stench of stale urine evoked the shame of those anonymous encounters with men in public toilets. The Sunday Library Group sang a chorus that echoed over Jatunga Arachchi's sweet-nothings, and guilt rattled a door that was slightly ajar further along a now seemingly endless corridor of doors. 'But I don't feel bad about being gay,' he said, surprising himself that he felt the need to say it.

Cindy raised and lowered her open palms in a contrary motion, mimicking a set of scales. 'On balance that's probably mostly true, but y'know, most of us gays and lesbians grew up absorbing and internalising homophobia every day of our lives, and those residues can cling to us like the burnt bits on a casserole dish, no matter how much we think we've cleansed ourselves.'

'So you think I may be clinging to my anger because a part of me is still filled with self hatred?' he blurted.

'That might be much too simple an analysis —' She stopped

herself saying any more when John's face seemed to contort like a rubber Halloween mask.

'But maybe I need to think about it,' he said, feeling the tears hot on his cheeks.

The *poco adagio* from Dvorak's seventh symphony did little to calm the chaos that broke out in his head. Theo held his trembling body.

'But you're strong now, John; strong enough to be able to deal with that shit,' he whispered into the candlelight.

'Maybe... I'm just so surprised that those feelings are still there,' John said after a while.

'Perhaps they never really go away,' he offered, recalling his own struggles. 'But we can find ways of making a different sense of it all. You've got a community that's supportive now, that validates you and values your contribution, and you've got all the tools you need to reinterpret that history.'

'But all that filth is still there, Theo,' he said, remembering the steaming baths in Theol Coll.'

'No, John,' Theo said, pulling him more tightly into their huddle.

'I'm still rotten at the core.'

'No... think about Wiesel's characters. You know what capacity a person has for both good and evil, and you know about forgiveness and redemption.'

He sensed the shift in Theo from lover to priest.

'You have a different set of choices now, John. You're not in the same position you were back in Wales.'

John pulled himself from their knotted tangle and lay on a cooler piece of the sheet. 'Of course, I know you're right,' he said after a while. 'At least I've got a handle on the theory.'

Theo reached through the flickering candlelight and stroked John's appendix scar.

'And if I don't really believe that faith in a loving God can transform lives then what the fuck do I think I'm doing at Shiloh?' He caught the glimmer of a smile in Theo's face. 'I guess I need to let Cindy help me open up those doors and let the *ruah* blow through them.'

'Fancy *you*, who didn't want to do Biblical languages, remembering that the Hebrew concept of the Holy Spirit is the breath of God, blowing its creative powers over chaos,' Theo said as he nestled closer against his lover's body.

* * *

Tom Cherubini was sitting up against a stack of pillows. Nestled against his arched knees was a dog-eared paperback, and scattered over the bedcover were copies of *The Advocate* and the *Bay Area Reporter*. His cheeks had colour, but his lips were crusted with scabby sores.

'You're looking better,' John said, dangling a small package in front of him. 'I hope you're feeling well enough for some of Sturani's best.'

'You trolled all the way over to North Beach for me?' Tom said with a campness John hadn't witnessed before.

'I hope there's a microwave here someplace; cold ravioli isn't my idea of a treat,' he quipped as he set the package down.

Tom thrust his arm forward, limp at the wrist, offering the back of his hand. 'With all these herpes, I'm only taking kisses here,' he said with a flutter of his fingers.

John pecked the proffered hand. 'I know how painful cold sores can be.'

'These aren't so bad,' he said, gesturing to his lips with his fingers. 'But my cock's on fire and my tush feels like someone dripped hot wax into it, and I've got shingles all around my middle that itch and burn like crazy.'

'But at least you're not on oxygen all the time,' John sallied, his hands on his hips mimicking some camp diva.

'So, you think I should be grateful for small mercies,' Tom jibed, his face breaking into a smile that cracked the crusty carapace of his lips.

'The KS looks like it's fading too,' John said, moving some magazines and a cassette recorder from the chair so that he could sit down.

'It's just a bit of foundation; Dr Scotty, my chest physician suggested it.'

John decided not to acknowledge that he knew Scott Rashford.

'As older men go, Dr Scotty is very... gorgeous,' Tom said with a swoon.

'But is he a good doctor?'

'He's the best... and it's easier when the doctors and nurses are gay; there's just so much that doesn't need to be said.'

John lifted a small medicine bottle from his carrier bag and placed it next to the ravioli.

'You brought me some herbal potion too?' Tom asked, the glimmer of a twinkle in his dull eyes.

'It's communion wine. Dots already did the prayers over it, and that's the only screw-top bottle she could find.' He set a chunk of bread, wrapped in clingy plastic, alongside the wine.

Tom shifted himself into the pillows, a movement that seemed to change his mood to a minor key. 'I know I asked you to bring me communion, but —' His eyes teared up and he sniffed back his upset. John took his hand. 'With all this "God's wrath" talk, I've been thinking —' Tom said. John squeezed his hand gently in the hesitant silence. 'Reach me the cassette recorder please,' Tom said after another long sniff. 'There's a song I want you to listen to.'

He fiddled with the rewind and play buttons. Staccato strains of a woman's voice pierced the silence between them until he found the beginning of the track he was looking for. 'I think Joan Armatrading might be from England,' he said, laying his head deep into the pillows and closing his eyes as drums and a base guitar played an introduction. In a richly mellow voice, the woman sang what John interpreted, on first hearing, as a love song to a girlfriend. "Shelter in a storm',' Tom sang quietly as the music faded. He pressed the stop button and repeated the short phrase over and over. John sat quietly as Tom whispered what seemed to have become his mantra... and waited.

His head looked small against the pillows, his cheeks hollow, the skin liverish against the pale blue covers. Along his scabbed lips, speckles of blood clung like autumn berries in a hedge of briars. John thought about Cindy Coleman, and all those rediscovered locked doors behind which he'd tried, so unsuccessfully, to keep his past from seeping into his present. *And if I don't really believe that faith in a loving God can transform lives then what the fuck do I think I'm doing here at Tom's bedside?*

'All this talk about God's wrath, and AIDS being a punishment,' Tom said. 'I don't want to believe it. It doesn't fit... but if they're right, I can't do communion.'

'I don't believe that they are right, Tom,' John said, feeling the rush of the *ruah* blowing through him and sensing surprise at the force of his certainty. 'They're just the words of frightened bigots.'

459

'God's always been a shelter in a storm for me,' he said.

'That's such a good image to hold on to my friend.'

Tom sighed a long sigh. His face softened, and John got the sense that he was expelling the breaths of doubt.

'Myrtle was all fired up by your sermon,' he said, his eyes suddenly more green than John had ever noticed. 'She said it helped a lot of people.'

'And preparing it helped me to get my own thoughts clear on this.'

'You're afraid that you'll get AIDS, aren't you?' he said, stretching out his arm and offering John his hand.

'Yes, I am.'

His skeletal fingers gripped John's hand and sought to sooth the fear, but after only a few seconds he became uncomfortable with the apparent reversal of roles. 'So you think it's okay for me to sing along with Joan,' he said, releasing John's hand.

'Yes,' he said, grateful for the gift Tom had given him.

'And you don't think I'm unworthy to take communion?'

'"We are not worthy so much as to gather up the crumbs under thy table",' John said, echoing the Eucharistic prayer. 'That's why we must share it, Tom.'

'"But thou art the same Lord whose nature is always to have mercy",' he said, picking up on the prayer.

'Why don't we play Joan Armatrading while we do it,' John offered, peeling the clingy plastic off the dried out piece of bread.

'There's a mug in the sink for the wine.'

Remembering how, with the in-betweens at the Empress Hotel, they'd served one another, John suggested they do the same.

'I was kind of hoping that you'd go through the whole

460

communion service from the prayer book,' Tom said.

'But I don't have the credentials to do sacraments, Tom – and Dots already did the magic.'

'Please,' he said, his eyes filling with tears. 'You're my priest now.'

*   *   *

On Boxing Day, Theo and John drove to the house in Bodega Bay.

'D'you think we'll get to see any whales?' John asked into Theo's uncharacteristic silence as they sped along the almost deserted freeway.

'Maybe, if we go out to Point Reyes one day. But I was hoping we wouldn't do too much driving around.'

'Are you just knackered after the run up to Christmas?' John felt his question hang on the tension that had been tightening between them for some time.

'Yes... and I've been thinking about when you graduate.'

'We've never really talked about what happens when my student visa runs out,' he offered, hoping that Theo would articulate the thoughts that he'd also begun to harbour about their future together.

'I talked to the woman in our international office. We get lots of Anglicans from England and Africa coming to study at CDSP and she told me that if you were in the ordination process, and could get a church to employ you, even part time, you'd be able to change your visa status.'

'That might not be as simple as it sounds, Theo. This AIDS backlash has triggered so much anti-gay feeling in all of the denominations... it's scary.'

'Couldn't you talk with Dots Shober or Grace Hope?'

'Dots and I talk a lot about ordination. I'd have to lie through my teeth all the way through the process. I wouldn't be too comfortable about that.'

'You wouldn't be the first,' he said, recalling his own evasions.

'But I've been completely out these past years at PSR, and all through my time at Shiloh. It's a fair bet that the fact I'm gay would get back up through the hierarchy to someone who'd find it a problem.'

'Celibacy in singleness,' Theo quipped.

'And fidelity in marriage,' John said. 'And despite my faithfulness to you, gays can't get married, not even in California.'

'What about Elaine and Jo?' Theo said after a while.

'What... about Elaine and Jo?'

'Are you still talking to Elaine about making babies?'

'I'm still their prime suspect,' he said with a hybrid chuckle-snigger that reflected his ambivalence about fathering a child.

'So, you could include a marriage of convenience clause as part of any parenting deal.'

'I'm not sure I want to donate my sperm to two dykes and play at being happy families.'

'Not even if it means you can stay in the US?'

John heard the subtext in Theo's question about the possibilities for their life together. He stared out over the Pacific Ocean; an artist's palette of blues and greens, with blotches of white, teased his eyes.

'I won't think badly of you if you decide you want to go back to Wales,' Theo said after about ten minutes. 'I know how important family and roots and language are.'

'Oh Theo... even just thinking about my life without you

hurts too much.' John reached for his lover's hand. 'I don't know about going back to Wales,' he said, feeling reassured by the warmth of Theo's hand in his own. 'I've been wondering... if I go back, whether I can still be the person that I've become these past couple of years.'

'We're always in the process of becoming who we are,' Theo quipped, imitating some lifestyle guru he'd heard on the television.

They both laughed out aloud.

Highway One undulated like a rollercoaster with the careless topography of the northern coast. Theo pulled off the road onto a bluff, hundreds of feet above the ocean, and they watched for whales.

'What we've shared has been such a rich gift,' Theo said. 'Too precious just to slide on through the winter and spring and not make conscious choices.'

'I don't see why we just can't go with the flow.'

'Come on, John,' he said in a tone John had come to recognise as calling for a reality check. 'We'll get back to Berkeley and our busy lives will take over. We'll end up getting to June and just be pulled apart by circumstances. That's what'll happen and you know it.'

'But there's still six months... to carry on with what we've got.'

'I can't function like that. If we're about to set off in different directions, I want us to be able to celebrate what we've had, and then I'll need to do some grieving for what we're going to lose. I want us to be able to say goodbye as friends.'

John scanned the horizon and decided there were too many white caps to see any whales.

*　　*　　*

During the first days of 1984, Tom Cherubini started to have headaches – terrible headaches with blurred vision and dark shadows that floated intermittently across the line of his sight. On Epiphany, a bout of diarrhoea started... and didn't stop. He noticed a vague ache in his back that progressed, over three or four days, into an acute pain. And then he developed a fever that peaked at 104. He was back in San Francisco General as an emergency admission by the middle of January. 'They think I've gone and gotten tuberculosis in one of my kidneys, and cytomegalovirus is chomping away at my retinas,' he said, when John had settled in the chair.

Tom's sunken eyes, all clouded and vacant, startled him. The bones of his cheeks were too sharp under skin that looked like dull tissue paper. He wondered if Tom's matter-of-factness might suggest that, like himself, he hadn't really understood what he'd been told. Could TB develop inside a kidney? John thought it was a lung disease. 'What's this cyto-what-did-you-call-it?' he asked with a lightness that he hoped would disguise his upset at the deterioration.

'CMV? It's one of the herpes cousins. A lot of people carry it and it doesn't do a thing to them – but with me? It's eating away at my eyesight.'

John pondered Tom's words and realised what a keen grasp he had of his situation.

'And the KS has gone into overdrive,' he said, flicking open the jacket of his pyjamas. His chest was covered with blue-black lesions, like the ones on his forehead; some were smaller than dimes, but there were many that were larger than quarters.

'But you're breathing easy,' John said. 'No sign of the pneumonia coming back.'

464

'There you go again, trying to get me to think I should be grateful for small mercies,' Tom jibed… but this time there was no smile.

*   *   *

With the new semester's class load and assignment deadlines, the day-to-day routine at Shiloh, visits to Tom at the hospital and being excited with Dots and Gavin on the arrival of their new baby boy, there really weren't enough hours in the days. But John found time to miss Theo. There wasn't the aching hurt that he'd anticipated, but perhaps that was because there were too many drains on his emotions. He missed Theo's touch, and the way he'd often read a poem when they lay beside one another in bed. He missed his unruffled common sense. He missed their regular sex. In rational moments, he accepted their decision to stop being lovers. 'I need this transition time,' Theo had said on the beach at Bodega Bay. And because he loved Theo, he knew he had to give him up sooner rather than later.

But there were many less rational times.

One evening in late February he drove back from the City and pulled off University Avenue onto Fifth Street. The Waterworks bathhouse wasn't difficult to find. He let himself be folded into the arms of the first handsome man to offer him a wistful smile.

Going to the baths a second time was much easier than the first, and the third time he didn't even second-guess himself. Anonymous sex sated an appetite, even if it did leave a gaping emotional hole. Despite the *ruah's* airing of all those closed up rooms in his mind, John managed to find a door behind which to lock the visits to the baths.

The addictive quality of sex with a stranger in the relative safety of a dark room, a pine scented sauna box or swathed in the mentholated swirls of a Turkish bath's steam, only became apparent when the visits became regular and the duration of each visit stretched into the early hours of the morning. In bleak moments, when he felt the need to justify himself, he reflected on the gentleness of those passing intimacies; the warmth of human touch, the mutual willingness to trust and be vulnerable, the sharing of pleasure.

In late April, Margaret Heckler, the Health and Human Services Secretary in Reagan's administration, announced that Dr Robert Gallo at the National Cancer Institute had isolated the virus that caused AIDS. They'd called it HTLV-III, a blood borne virus that could be sexually transmitted. In San Francisco, the Department of Public Health closed down all of the gay bathhouses. Across the Bay in Berkeley the Waterworks was busier than ever.

*   *   *

Every Wednesday morning through the spring the 'Exiles in the City' met in Shiloh's schoolroom for a theology seminar, led by Bob McAfee Brown. The ten-week course was, in effect, a meditation on the verse from Jeremiah that underpinned the work of the San Francisco Urban Ministry Programme: 'But seek the welfare of the city where I have sent you into exile, and pray to the Lord on its behalf, for in its welfare you will find your welfare'. One of the recommended texts was a dense, but readable book called *Suffering* by the German theologian Dorothee Soelle.

Reading a short, but thickly referenced, chapter entitled *A*

466

Critique of Christian Masochism, John found himself cast back to *Calfaria* – where Miss Gruffudd taught in the Sunday school and Barmouth's perms-and-pearls-brigade paraded their lavish hats as Enoch Lloyd got into a *hwyl* in the pulpit. He recalled the succession of washed-out clergymen; how their incoherent ramblings had jaded his sense of the religious and stifled any desire to explore his own spirituality. It had all seemed so much doom, gloom and hellfire. And he remembered how guilty he'd felt after the pleasure boat disaster at Penmaen Pool – and after Aberfan.

He was gripped by a disquiet that left him feeling nauseous as he read Soelle's appraisal of the widely held view that suffering is a trial, sent by God, which individuals, and sometimes entire communities, have to bear. This sadistic understanding of human suffering, with its proposal that a just God, the mighty ruler of the world, sends suffering to punish, to test or to instruct, was a theological view he'd rejected intellectually for years. But with the *ruah* airing all of those closets in his mind over the last weeks, it was as if he'd been subconsciously laid open, and old truths laid bare. Over a couple of hours, reading and re-reading Soelle's analysis, he started to understand. The notion that all suffering could be attributed to God's chastisement had been planted so deeply in his psyche that he still wasn't free of it. Cindy Coleman was right about the burnt bits on a casserole dish.

For two weeks, the 'Exiles', guided by Bob Brown, discussed and debated 'the suffering city' in light of Soelle's work and John sought to exhume and exorcise all the residues of that childhood legacy. Particularly helpful was a Bible study, led by Grace Hope, on the 'When did we see you a stranger and welcome you, or naked and clothe you?' passage from Matthew's Gospel.

467

'What we learn from this text, I believe, is that God expects us to love him not as an immediate object, but rather through other people,' Grace offered. She cast a smile around the circle of students. 'I'm real sorry about the male personal pronoun; you all know I've said, more than once, that in San Francisco today we're just as likely to see God in the black Hispanic lesbian sitting in her wheelchair in the food line outside St Boniface. My point here is that God becomes immanent in historic reality – in the relationships you and I forge with one another.' She pushed back her thick blonde hair and looked carefully into the faces of a couple of students. 'In this passage from Matthew:25, I really believe that we're being challenged to give up all of our notions of God as some all-powerful being that directs everything from on high. This text suggests to me that if we are to be faithful to God, we're asked to be in open and honest relationship with people in our communities – we share food where people go hungry, *and* do all that we can politically to ensure that we eradicate poverty so that people aren't hungry; we visit those young gay guys dying of AIDS in the hospital, *and* do all that we can to challenge the bigotry of those who say AIDS is God's wrath; we support the transsexuals in their struggle to become who they believe themselves to be, *and* do all that we can to get the health care system to offer treatments at affordable rates so that those guys aren't forced into prostitution or the clutches of the porn movie directors to fund their surgery.'

Grace paused, picked up her battered Bible and poked her glasses back up her nose.

'"Truly, I say to you, as you did it to one of the least of these my brothers and sisters, you did it to me". God becomes immanent in the realities of the suffering that is *here* and *now*; it's clear as day – "I was hungry... I was thirsty... I was a stranger".'

John spent a day at Muir Beach. Watching the Pacific waves roll in, he let Dorothee Soelle and Bob Brown scour the last of the stubborn burnt bits on the casserole dish. Grace Hope and the 'Exiles' joined them... scouring... scouring. Troy Liddell and the in-betweens at the Empress lent a hand, whilst Charlene and the patients in the secure unit at Martinez pointed to some tenacious bits that clung under the rim. Tom Cherubini's skeletal fingers were thin enough to get to the places others couldn't get to. The wind off the ocean and the *ruah* freshened even the closet where John had hung his visits to the baths. *'I was hungry... I was thirsty... I was a stranger'*. And Theo came to him... and John took him in his arms and celebrated the rich gift they'd shared.

He'd never felt so free... and never been so clear about the ministry he was being called into.

*   *   *

He sat on the only chair in the small, airless room, quietly cussing the architects who designed buildings with windows that didn't open and air-conditioning that was unreliable. Tom lay unconscious, beneath the pale blue of a frayed and torn San Francisco General Hospital sheet, hooked up to machines that hummed and purred and bleeped and buzzed. From visits to Yad Vashem and Buchenwald, photographic images of wasted people kept coming into John's mind now, whenever he looked at Tom.

469

He was grateful that Jonas and Randall had agreed to go home for a few hours; they'd been there for most of the day. Jonas had rallied a clutch of Tom's friends to be at his bedside after a doctor had said, perhaps in an unguarded moment, perhaps carelessly, that he thought they were moving into Tom's last days. But it had been more than a week already, and many of the younger men had found it impossible just to sit and watch their friend die.

Myrtle still called on Tom – every day during this grim period; she'd taken to phoning John after each of her visits – to update him, and to carp on about getting in touch with Tom's next-of-kin back on the east coast. They had the same conversation at least a dozen times.

'I'm a mother, John,' she'd whine through the telephone. 'I'd want to know if my son was dying in some hospital bed.'

'But Tom made it clear he didn't want that, Myrtle. His family completely rejected his lifestyle – *they* cut *him* off.'

'She still has the right to know that her son's dying. It should be her choice, to come or not to come.'

'Tom has his family around him, Myrtle,' John assured her. 'The people he chose. Jonas and Randall are so faithful, and you're there from his church family.'

'Have any of the doctors or nurses said anything to you?' she asked with uncertainty in her tone.

'They're between a rock and a hard place,' he said, not wanting to confide in her that he'd spoken with Scott Rashford. 'Tom didn't get power of attorney sorted out, and whilst *we* are his family, none of us are his legal next-of- kin, so they're really reluctant to say too much.'

'But it's not looking good, is it?'

Scott had explained to John that there was an infection, and possibly multiple infections, overwhelming Tom's system. They were doing all they could to identify the hostile bugs, so that they could medicate more specifically, but Tom's immune system was just so weak now.

Until Jonas returned, just before eleven, shaved and in fresh clothes but still looking weary, John read to Tom; poems from the anthology Theo had bought him from Cody's on Telegraph Avenue – Allen Ginsberg, Winston Leyland, Gerrit Lansing... and a few Psalms. And he'd played Joan Armatrading, singing 'Shelter in a Storm'.

He talked with Jonas a while, and after agreeing to come back in the morning, he headed back across the Bay Bridge. By midnight he was seeking to affirm life, in the face of death, in the arms of a nameless man at Berkeley's Fifth Street baths. They were compatible lovers and spent a couple of hours together.

Tom died at ten minutes to two in the morning with Jonas at his side.

*   *   *

Dai and Olwen Jones made the trip out to California to see their son graduate with a master's degree in divinity from Pacific School of Religion. Olwen had written every fortnight over those three years, and only missed once because of a bad bout of flu. She always tried to make her letters interesting, snippets of the family saga, life in Barmouth, births, marriages and deaths... and who'd been up before the magistrates. Dai had sent him copies of *The Cambrian News* every now and then, and tapes of the music he'd been listening to. John had written them no more than a dozen letters, telling them of the places he'd visited; a

471

trip down Highway One to Carmel and Monterey, Napa's vineyards, Hollywood, tea on the Queen Mary in Long Beach, camping in Yosemite where bears had sniffed around their tent — But nothing about his life. Olwen had looked forward to his monthly phone calls, which usually came late on a Sunday afternoon, but when they finished chatting she'd realise again and again that she didn't really know her John Idris. After all that business in Denbigh, he'd gone back to college in Aberystwyth and just seemed to get on with his life. One day he'd told them he was off, halfway around the world, on a scholarship, but didn't tell them what that was all about, not even when he'd asked for money to help pay for it all. She remembered how embarrassed she'd been when she'd talked a few times with Elen Morgan in Aberystwyth; the Morgans seemed to know so much more than she did.

John was pleased they'd come. They'd get the chance to see him in a place where he'd grown into himself, and where he was happy. He planned an itinerary, a mix of things they could do by themselves in the City, and days out together to see the redwoods, the wine country and some of the coast. And he fixed up some social things, so that they'd get the chance to meet people: Scott and Bill, Theo, folks from PSR and Shiloh.

More than once, Olwen offered an 'If I were you John, I'd...' to which John responded, perhaps too forcefully, 'But you're not me, Mam!' She called him *cyw* a couple of times too, to which he clucked like a chicken until she got the point. Dai looked down his nose at the men holding hands on Castro Street, and averted his gaze in an exaggerated way if two guys kissed one another. But then, a couple of lesbians nuzzled up close in a booth at the IHOP sharing a stack of buttermilk pancakes and scrambled eggs seemed to fascinate him. Of course, it was nothing they could talk about.

They spent a couple of hours in the redwood grove at Muir Woods and then Olwen insisted on an hour's window-shopping in Sausalito's expensive boutiques. At a restaurant on stilts, out over the water, a friendly waiter seated them at a table by a window with a panoramic view across the Bay to Alcatraz and the City's skyline. They watched the Trans Am pyramid turn pink as the sun set.

'You remember that I've got a funeral on Wednesday, so you'll have to entertain yourselves all day,' John said over a silver platter that heaved with lobster and langoustines.

'I thought we'd go to Golden Gate Park,' Dai said. 'I've been reading all about it; there's a Japanese garden and a big glasshouse with exotic flowers.'

'Is it someone from your church that's died?' Olwen asked.

'Yes, our organist.'

'And are you doing the funeral?' she quizzed.

'Dots Shober, the minister, is just back from her maternity leave so we'll be doing it together.'

'Was she old?' Olwen enquired. In her experience, church organists were always women.

'No, Tom was only thirty.'

'It's more sad when someone dies young,' she said. 'Was it an accident?'

'No. He had AIDS.'

'That's that new disease, isn't it?' Dai said. 'There was something in the *Daily Post*. Don't they call it the —' He cut himself off and took a slurp of wine to conceal his discomfort.

'Some of the papers call it *the gay plague* over here too,' John said, not sure whether he was trying to open up a conversation or humiliate his parents.

'I don't know whether it's these candles,' Olwen said into the embarrassed silence. She reached across and touched John's chin. 'Just turn your head a bit, *cyw*.' She drew closer to him and looked into his eyes. 'I think you might be a bit jaundiced,' she said. 'The whites of your eyes look really yellow.'

He got the results of the blood tests the day after he'd put his parents back on a plane bound for Heathrow.

'Hepatitis B is an infectious disease, so I have to report your case to the County Medical Officer,' the doctor at the gay men's health co-op said. 'In gay men it's usually sexually transmitted. D'you go to the baths?'

'Yes.'

'Well, you'll be infectious for a while so you'll need to give sex a miss until the bloods show you're clear. We'll need to do tests every week.'

'For how long? I'm leaving California sometime over the summer, back home to Britain.'

'How long is a piece of twine? You'll really need to have shed the virus before you go. Could be a matter of weeks, could be a few months.' The young doctor smiled to encourage John. 'I guess the fact that you're not feeling unwell may mean that you've picked up a really mild dose, so let's hope for the best.'

'Do I need any medication?'

'It's viral, so it just needs to run it's course, but we'd best do some more tests. If you've picked up Hep B from sex in the baths you might have picked up some other sexual infections.'

'Like AIDS and stuff,' John said.

'Yeh, or gonorrhoea, syphilis, amoebas. You'll need to drop your pants so that I can take some swabs.'

November

The narrow streets around the chapel were double-parked. 'Just as well we're in good time,' John said, turning back into Queen's Road.

'Why don't you try the prom?' Klaus offered. 'It looks as if the rain might keep off and I could do with a walk after two hours in the car.'

The waves, whipped by a storm that had raged since the previous afternoon, splashed over the road by the pier where John had once parked his rusting old Vauxhall Viva. Will Young and Gareth Gates sang their cover of 'The Long And Winding Road' from the pier amusement arcade as they drove by. 'The journey is home,' he heard Elen say. He felt for the folded sheet of paper in his pocket, the one on which he'd doodled that evening in September, after Beca had asked him to say something at the funeral. In amongst the squiggles and scribbles, he'd written the four phrases that Elen had offered, and which had become his lifelines.

Theol Coll's upper floors, judging by the cracked and broken windows, looked abandoned, but the ground floor was lit up. In one of the bays, two smartly dressed women, septuagenarians with tinted hair – one a little too blonde and the other a washed-out purply pink – drank their morning coffee from elegant china cups. A sign at the gracefully arched entrance declared that the Cambrian Tea Room was open.

The chapel was filling up. Bethania was much smaller than Peniel, which had been demolished some years before to make way for a fitness centre. Walking down the aisle to the pews reserved for 'family', many a familiar face, some so ravaged by wrinkles and age spots that recognition came with a jolt, allowed meagre funeral-smiles of acknowledgement. John raised an eyebrow here and there, sometimes nodding his head or mouthing a silent hello. He and Klaus turned into the last of the reserved seats, five rows from the front. After only a moment, Klaus, who was more comfortable in chinos and open-necked shirts began to fidget; wearing John's 'second' suit, which was tight at the waist, and a tie that choked him, he felt oppressed by more than the Welsh Calvinist's 19th century austerity. John tried to remember the names of Elen's nine (or was it ten?) grandchildren, and kept telling himself that this funeral was a celebration of a life well-lived. The flower arrangements reflected this celebratory theme, though the less cheery chrysanthemums and the chapel's sombre polished oak tempered the showy loudness of the season's last dahlias.

In the hours after Beca had phoned to let him know that Elen had died, John had wept with little self-control. But then the tears had dried up and he'd recalled the lifelines she and Rhys had thrown him, and remembered times in his life when her words had helped him make choices about plotting his course. He knew that he'd probably cry during the service and he hoped that Klaus wouldn't feel too self-conscious to wrap an arm around him.

The minister talked about Elen Morgan as a woman whose life had been put to the service of others, and to the advantage of her community, without counting cost. John bit his tongue hard to stop himself weeping, and he wondered about the wisdom of a life given to serving others. Evelyne, the psychologist at the rehab clinic, interrupted the minister. *'You say that you're not stressed, John, but you can't tell me that living your life as an openly gay man and challenging prejudice and ignorance in the way that you've done for half a lifetime... in the church... in education and the health service... and chairing a national LGB rights group to advise ministers in the Welsh government on LGB equality issues... you can not tell me that wasn't stressful. And stress, as you now know, is a huge factor in coronary heart disease.'* If he believed what she was saying then his own willingness to serve his community had almost cost him his life. Klaus poked an elbow into his ribs. 'Didn't you hear the minister announce you?'

John walked to the lectern that stood next to the coffin. He remembered the last time he'd seen Elen, in the hospital, her head of wispy white hair barely making an impression on the pillow. The folds in the piece of paper he took from his pocket were sharp and for a couple of seconds he fingered the creases, but he couldn't get the sheet to lie flat. He knew the four phrases he'd written amongst the doodles by heart so he crumpled the paper into a ball and shoved it back into his pocket.

'During the year that I lived in the Manse, almost thirty years ago now, Elen Morgan sat on the stairs with me at three o'clock in the morning more times than I can remember,' John began. His eyes scanned the large congregation. Gwil ap Dylan, his boss from the Merseyside Welsh Chaplaincy days, sat amongst a group of grey clergymen. John remembered that Elen had served for a number of years on the Home Mission Board so Gwil was probably there in an official capacity. 'It was Elen who helped me to accept that *God finds us where we are*,' John said to Gwil. 'When the doctors were saying I was mentally ill and the church was proclaiming me a sinner —' He paused, wondering if he'd use the word *gay* or *homosexual*. Turning his head he saw Paul Wynne sitting towards the back and looking so much older than his years. 'After the doctors' electric shock treatments failed to 'cure' me of my sexual attraction to other men, and no amount of prayers seemed able to change my nature, Elen Morgan took a huge risk. Through her love and acceptance, she showed me that I was acceptable in God's sight. And yet, even today, in the first years of a new century, the church still chooses not to recognise homosexuals as worthy neighbours.'

He let the shuffling and muttering echo for a moment and then smiled at Beca. 'But I'm not here to make a political speech,' he said to her. 'And neither do I wish to be mawkish or sentimental. I want to applaud Elen Morgan's commitment to social justice, which was so deeply rooted in Scripture. Elen clearly understood how aspects of our culture and our institutions – the education services, the church, the health service – sought to demonise people like me.' He faltered when he recognised Dr Griff Edwards, his tutor from his teacher's training year. In that moment he wondered how things might have been different if he'd come-out to him. 'Because Elen Morgan was so down-to-earth, and knew that she couldn't change the world, she helped me to understand that my journey through life would be a constant fight to hold on to my integrity, and that my journey, therefore, had to be my home.'

He shifted his gaze from Griff Edwards to Klaus, who'd loosened his tie and was looking anxious.

From years of conversations between them, Klaus knew that the Gospel John had come to recognise through the Morgans, and gone on to study in Berkeley, made for difficult reading – and uncomfortable living.

'Elen and Rhys Morgan showed me kindness the like of which I had never before experienced,' John continued. 'And one day, when I very glibly said that there was no way I could ever repay their kindness, Elen said that "kindnesses were for passing on".'

Having mastered the art of silences, he paused and scanned the congregation. Then he moved a step closer to the coffin and placed his hand on the smooth edge of the lid.

'Through Elen Morgan I was able to reclaim the will to live after attempting suicide, but in choosing life I became angry with those who had persecuted me. That anger could have turned into a festering bitterness had she not introduced me to Waldo Williams, who wrote that forgiveness is "crawling through thorns to be at the side of an old foe." I get tired of crawling through thorns, believe me, but I still think it's a safer option than becoming bitter and twisted.' He looked again at Griff and Paul and Gwil, and then he looked at Beca and her sisters. 'Through Elen Morgan I was saved. I think some of you here today will realise that for me to say such a thing will sound odd. It's neither easy language nor a comfortable concept for my theological taste... it's all a bit too evangelical.'

Some of the liberals in the congregation laughed.

'I'm a better person for having known Elen. Had I not known her I wouldn't be standing here today.'

There were coughs and foot-shuffles, side-glances and mutterings. John's fingers gripped the edge of the coffin lid. The thudding of his heart inside his chest was so startling he wondered if it might burst.